The Intimate
and Other Stories

The Intimate Strangers

and Other Stories

F. Scott Fitzgerald

ALMA CLASSICS

ALMA CLASSICS LTD
Hogarth House
32–34 Paradise Road
Richmond
Surrey TW9 1SE
United Kingdom
www.almaclassics.com

This collection first published by Alma Classics Ltd in 2015

Extra Material © Richard Parker

Printed and bound by CPI Group (UK) Ltd, Croydon, CR0 4YY

ISBN: 978-1-84749-566-2

Contents

Other books by F. SCOTT FITZGERALD
published by Alma Classics

All the Sad Young Men

Babylon Revisited and Other Stories

Basil and Josephine

The Beautiful and Damned

Flappers and Philosophers

The Great Gatsby

The Last Tycoon

The Last of the Belles and Other Stories

The Love Boat and Other Stories

The Pat Hobby Stories

Tales of the Jazz Age

Tender Is the Night

This Side of Paradise

F. Scott Fitzgerald (1896–1940)

Edward Fitzgerald,
Fitzgerald's father

Mary McQuillan Fitzgerald,
Fitzgerald's mother

Ginevra King

Zelda Fitzgerald

The Fitzgeralds' house in Montgomery, Alabama

The Fitzgeralds' grave in Rockville, Maryland,
inscribed with the closing line from *The Great Gatsby*

The June 1935 issue of *McCall's*, which included
Fitzgerald's story 'The Intimate Strangers'

The Intimate Strangers
and Other Stories

Indecision

1

THIS ONE WAS DRESSED in a horizon-blue Swiss skiing suit with, however, the unmistakable touch of a Paris shears about it. Above it shone her snow-warm cheeks and her eyes that were less confident than brave. With his hat, Tommy McLane slapped snow from his dark, convict-like costume. He was already reflecting that he might have been out with Rosemary, dancing around Rosemary and the two "ickle durls" down at the other hotel, amid the gleam of patent Argentine hair, to the soothing whispers of 'I'm Getting Myself Ready for You'.* When he was with Emily he felt always a faint nostalgia for young Rosemary and for the sort of dance that seemed to go on inside and all around Rosemary and the two "ickle durls". He knew just how much happened there – not much; just a limited amount of things, just a pleasant lot of little things strung into hours, moving to little melodies hither and thither. But he missed it; it was new to him again after four years, and he missed it. Likewise when he was with Rosemary, making life fun with jokes for her, he thought of Emily, who was twenty-five and carried space around with her into which he could step and be alone with their two selves, mature and complicated and trusting, and almost in love.

Out the window, the snow on the pine trees was turning lilac in the first dusk; and because the world was round, or for some such reason, there was rosy light still on that big mountain, the Dent de Something. Bundled-up children were splattering back to their hotels for tea as if the outdoors were tired of them and wanted to change its dress in quiet dignity. Down in the valley there were already bright windows and misty glows from the houses and hotels of the town.

3

He left Emily at her hotel door. She had never seemed so attractive, so good, so tranquil a person, given a half-decent chance. He was annoyed that he was already thinking of Rosemary.

"We'll meet in the bar down there at 7.30," he said, "and don't dress."

Putting on his jacket and flat cap, Tommy stepped out into the storm. It was a welcome blizzard and he inhaled damp snowflakes that he could no longer see against the darkening sky. Three flying kids on a sledge startled him with a warning in some strange language, and he just managed to jump out of their path. He heard them yell at the next bend, and then, a little farther on, he heard sleigh bells coming up the hill in the dark. It was all very pleasant and famil-iar, yet it did not remind him of Minneapolis, where he was born, because the automobile had spoilt all that side of north-western life while he was still a baby. It was pleasant and familiar, because these last five days here among alien mountains held some of the happiest moments of his life.

He was twenty-seven; he was assistant manager and slated for manager of a New York bank in Paris, or else he would be offered the option of Chicago next spring at a larger salary. He had come up here to one of the gayest places in Switzerland with the idea that if he had nothing else to think of for ten days he might fall in love. He could afford to fall in love, but in Paris the people he saw all knew it, and he had instinctively become analytical and cagey. Here he felt free; the first night had seen at least a dozen girls and women, "any one of whom"; on the second night, there had still been half a dozen; the third night there were three, with one new addition – Emily Elliot from the other hotel. Now, on the day after Christmas, it had narrowed down to two – Emily and Rosemary Merriweather. He had actually written all this down on a blotter as if he were in his office in the Place Vendôme, added and subtracted them, listed points.

"Two really remarkable girls," he said to himself in a tone not unlike the clumping squeak of his big shoes on the snow. "Two absolutely good ones."

Emily Elliot was divorced and twenty-five. Rosemary was eighteen.

He saw her immediately as he went into his hotel – a blonde, ravishing, southern beauty like so many that had come before her and so many yet to be born. She was from "N'Awlins 'rigin'ly", but now from "Athens, Joja". He had first spoken to her on Christmas Eve, after an unavailing search for someone to introduce him, some means to pierce the wall of vacationing boys within which she seemed hermetically sealed. Sitting with another man, he stared at her across the room, admiring her with his eyes, frankly and tauntingly. Presently she spoke to her escort; they crossed the room and sat down at the table next to him, with Rosemary's back just one inch from him. She sent her young man for something; Tommy spoke. The next day, at the risk of both their lives, he took her down the big bob run.

Rosemary saw him now as he came in. She was revolving slowly through the last of the tea hour with a young Levantine whom he disliked. She wore white and her face lighted up white, like an angel under an arc lamp. "Where you been?" her big eyes said.

But Tommy was shrewd, and he merely nodded to her and to the two "ickle durls" who danced by, and found a seat in a far corner. He knew that a surfeit of admiration such as Rosemary's breeds an appreciation of indifference. And presently she came over to him, dragging her bridling partner by an interlaced little finger.

"Where you been?" she demanded.

"Tell that spic to go count his piastres and I'll talk turkey with you."

She bestowed upon the puzzled darkling a healing smile.

"You don't mind, honey, if I sit this out? See you later."

When he had departed, Tommy protested, "'Honey'! Do you call him 'honey'? Why don't you call him 'greasy'?"

She laughed sweetly.

"Where you been?"

"Skiing. But every time I go away, that doesn't mean you can go dance with a whole lot of gigolo numbers from Cairo. Why does he hold his hand parallel to the floor when he dances? Does he think he's stilling the waves? Does he think the floor's going to swing up and crack him?"

"He's a Greek, honey."

"That's no reason. And you better get that word 'honey' cleaned and pressed before you use it on me again." He felt very witty. "Let's go to my boudoir," he suggested.

He had a bedroom and bath and a tiny *salon*. Once inside the door of the latter, he shot the bolt and took her in his arms, but she drew away from him.

"You been up at that other hotel," she said.

"I had to invite a girl to dinner. Did you know you're having dinner with me tonight?... You're beautiful."

It was true. Her face, flushed with cold and then warmed again with the dance, was a riot of lovely, delicate pinks, like many carnations, rising in many shades from the white of her nose to the high spot of her cheeks. Her breathing was very young as she came close to him – young and eager and exciting. Her lips were faintly chapped, but soft in the corners.

After a moment she sat with him in a single chair. And just for a second words formed on his lips that it was hard not to utter. He knew she was in love with him and would probably marry him, but the old terror of being held rose in him. He would have to tell this girl so many things. He looked closely at her, holding her face under his, and if she had said one wise or witty thing he might have spoken, but she only looked up with a glaze of childish passion in her eyes and said: "What are you thinking, honey?"

The moment passed. She fell back smoothly into being only a part of the day's pleasure, the day's excitement. She was desirable here, but she was desirable downstairs too. The mountains were bewitching his determinations out of him.

Drawing her close to him, lightly he said: "So you like the spics, eh? I suppose the boys are all spics down in New Orleans?"

As she squeezed his face furiously between thumb and finger, his mind was already back with Emily at the other hotel a quarter of a mile away.

2

TOMMY'S DINNER WAS NOT to be at his hotel. After meeting in the bar they sledged down into the village to a large old-fashioned Swiss taproom, a thing of woodwork, clocks, steins, kegs and antlers. There were other parties like their own, bound together by the common plan of eating fondue – a peculiarly indigestible form of Welsh rabbit – and drinking spiced wine, and then hitching on the backs of sleighs to Doldorp several miles away, where there was a townspeople's ball.

His own party included Emily; her cousin, young Frank Forrester; young Count de Caros Moros, a friend of Rosemary's – she played ping-pong with him and harked to his guitar and to his tales of machine-gunning his discontented fellow countrymen in Andalusia – a Cambridge University hockey hero named Harry Whitby, and lastly the two "ickle durls" – Californians who were up from a Montreux school for the holidays and very anxious to be swept off their feet. Six Americans, two Europeans.

It was a good party. Some grey-haired men of the golden Nineties sang ancient glees at the piano, the fondue was fun, the wine was pert and heady, and smoke swirled out of the brown walls and toned the bright costumes into the room. They were all on a ship going somewhere, with the port just ahead; the faces of girls and young men bore the same innocent and unlined expectations of the great possibilities inherent in the situation and the night. The Latins became Americans easily, the English with more effort. Then it was over and one hundred five-pound boots stamped towards the sleighs that waited at the door.

For a moment Tommy lingered, engrossed in conversation with Emily, yet with sudden twinges of conscience about Rosemary. She had been on his left; he had last seen her listening to young Caros Moros perform upon his extremely portable guitar. Outside in the crisp moonlight he saw her tying her sledge to one of the sleighs ahead. The sleighs were moving off; he and Emily caught one, and at the crisp-cracking whips the horses pulled, breasting the dark air. Past them figures ran and scrambled, the younger people pushing one another off, landing in a cloud of soft snow, then panting after the horses, to fling themselves exhausted on a sledge, or else wail that they were being left behind. On either side the fields were tranquil; the space through which the cavalcade moved was high and limitless. After they were in the country there was less noise; perhaps ears were listening atavistically for wolves howling in the clumps of trees far across the snow.

At Doldorp he stood with Emily in the doorway, watching the others go in.

"Everybody's first husband with everybody's first wife," she remarked. "Who believes in marriage? I do. A plucky girl – takes the count of nine and comes up for more. But not for two years; I'm over here to do some straight thinking."

It occurred to Tommy that two years was a long time, but he knew that girls so frequently didn't mean what they said. He and Emily watched the entrance of Mr Cola; nicknamed Capone, with his harem, consisting of wife, daughters, wife's friend and three Siamese. Then they went inside.

The crowd was enormous – peasants, servants from the hotels, shop-keepers, guides, outlanders, cow herders, ski teachers and tourists. They all got seats where they could, and Tommy saw Rosemary with a crowd of young people across the room; she seemed a little tired and pale, sitting back with her lips apart and her eyes fixed and sleepy. When someone waltzed off with Emily, he went over and asked her to dance.

"I don't want to dance. I'm tired."

"Let's go sit where we can hear the yodelling."

"I can hear it here."

"What am I accused of?" he demanded.

"Nothing. I haven't even seen you."

Her current partner smiled at him ingratiatingly, but Tommy was growing annoyed:

"Didn't I explain that this dinner was for a girl who'd been particularly nice to me? I told you I'd have to devote a lot of the evening to her."

"Go on devote it, then. I'm leaving soon."

"Who with?"

"Capone has a sleigh."

"Yes, you're leaving with him. He'll take you for a ride; you'll be on the spot if you don't look out."

He felt a touch of uneasiness. The mystery she had lacked this afternoon was strong in her now. Before he should be so weak as to grant her another advantage, he turned and asked one of the "ickle durls" to dance.

The "ickle durl" bored him. She admired him; she was used to clasping her hands together in his wake and heaving audible sighs. When the music stopped he gave her an outrageous compliment to atone for his preoccupation and left her at her table. The night was ruined. He realized that it was Rosemary who moved him most deeply, and his eyes wandered to her across the room. He told himself that she was playing him jealously, but he hated the way she was fooling with young Caros Moros; and he liked it still less when he glanced over a little later and found that the two of them were gone.

He sprang up and dashed out of the door; there was the snow, lightly falling, there were the waiting sleighs, the horses patient in their frozen harness, and there was a small, excited crowd of Swiss gathered around Mr Cola's sleigh.

"*Salaud!*" he heard. "*Salaud français!*"*

It appeared that the French courier, long accepted as a member of the Cola *ménage*, had spent the afternoon tippling with his master; the courier had not survived. Cola had been compelled to assist him outdoors, where he promptly gave tongue to a series of insults directed at the Swiss. They were all Boches. Why hadn't they come in the war? A crowd gathered, and as it included several Swiss who were in the same state as the Frenchman, the matter was growing complicated; the women were uncomfortable, the Siamese were smiling diplomatically among themselves. One of the Swiss was on the runner of the sleigh, leaning over Mrs Cola and shaking his fist in the courier's face. Mr Cola stood up in the sleigh and addressed them in hoarse American as to "the big idea?"

"Dirty Frenchmen!" cried the Swiss. "Yes, and during your Revolution did you not cut the Swiss Guards down to the last man?"

"Get out of here!" shouted Cola. "Hey, coachman, drive right over 'em! You guys go easy there! Take your hands off the sleigh… Shut up, you!" – this to the courier, who was still muttering wildly. Cola looked at him as if he contemplated throwing him to the crowd. In a moment Tommy edged himself between the outraged Swiss patriot and the sleigh.

"Ne'mine what they say! Drive on!" cried Cola again. "We got to get these girls out of here!"

Conscious of Rosemary's eyes staring at him out of a bearskin robe, and of Caros Moros next to her, Tommy raised his voice:

"*Ce sont des dames américaines; il n'y a qu'un Français. Voyons! Qu'est-ce que vous voulez?*"*

But the massacre of the Swiss Guards was not to be disposed of so lightly.

Tommy had an inspiration. "But who tried to save the Swiss Guards? Answer me that!" he shouted. "An American – Benjamin Franklin! He almost saved them!"

His preposterous statement rang out strong and true upon the electric air. The protagonist of the martyrs was momentarily baffled.

"An American saved them!" Tommy cried. "Hurray for America and Switzerland!" And he added quickly, to the coachman, "Drive on now – and fast!"

The sleigh started with a lurch. Two men clung to it for a moment and then let go, and the conveyance slid free behind the swiftly trotting horses.

"*Vive l'Amérique! Vive la Suisse!*"* Tommy shouted.

"*Vive la Fra—*" began the courier, but Cola put his fur glove in the man's mouth. They drove rapidly for a few minutes.

"Drop me here," Tommy said. "I have to go back to the dance." He looked at Rosemary, but she would not meet his eye. She was a bundle of fur next to Caros Moros, and he saw the latter drop his arm around her till they were one mass of fur together. The sight was horrible; of all the people in the world she had become the most desirable, and he wanted every bit of her youth and freshness. He wanted to jerk Caros Moros to his feet and pull him from the sleigh. He saw how stupid it had been to play so long with her innocence and sincerity, until now she scarcely saw him any more, scarcely knew he was there.

As he swung himself off the sleigh, Rosemary and Caros Moros were singing softly:

> "…I wouldn't stoop
> To onion soup;
> With corn-beef hash I'm all
> through—"

and the Spaniard winked at Tommy as if to say, "We know how to handle this little girl, don't we?"

The courier struggled and then cried in a blurred voice: "Beeb wa Fwance."

"Keep your glove in his mouth," said Tommy savagely. "Choke him to death."

He walked off down the road, utterly miserable.

3

HIS FIRST INSTINCT NEXT MORNING was to phone her immediately; his second was to sulk proudly in his room, hoping against hope that his own phone would ring. After luncheon he went downstairs, where he was addressed by the objectionable Greek who had danced with her at tea yesterday afternoon – ages ago.

"Tell me; you like to play the ping-pong?"

"It depends who with," Tommy answered rudely. Immediately he was so sorry that he went downstairs with the man and batted the white puffballs for half an hour.

At four he skied over to Emily's hotel, resolving to drive the other and more vivid image from his mind. The lobby was filled with children in fancy dress, who had gathered there from many hotels for the children's Christmas ball.

Emily was a long time coming down, and when she did she was hurried and distracted.

"I'm so sorry. I've been costuming my children, and now I've got to get them launched into this orgy, because they're both very shy."

"Sit and get your breath a minute. We'll talk about love."

"Honestly, I can't, Tommy. I'll see you later." And she added quickly, "Can't you get your little southern girl? She seemed to worry you a lot last night."

After half an hour of diffident grand marches, Emily came back to him, but Tommy's patience was exhausted and he was on his feet to go. Even now she showed him that he was asking for time and attention out of turn, and, being unavailable, she had again grown as mysterious as Rosemary.

"It's been a hard day in lots of ways," she explained as she walked with him to the door. "Things I can't tell you about."

"Oh, yes?" People had so many affairs. You never knew how much space you actually occupied in their lives.

Outdoors he came across her young cousin, Frank Forrester, buckling on his skis. Pushing off together, they drifted slowly down a slushy hill.

"Let me tell you something," Frank burst out. "I'm never going to get married. I've seen too much of it. And if any girl asked my advice, I'd tell her to stay out." He was full of the idea: "There's my mother, for instance. She married a second husband, and what does he do but have her spied on and bribe her maids to open her mail? Then there's Emily. You know what happened to her; one night her husband came home and told her she was acting cold to him, but that he'd fix that up. So he built a bonfire under her bed, made up of shoes and things, and set fire to it. And if the leather hadn't smelt so terrible she'd have been burnt to death."

"That's just two marriages."

"Two!" said Frank resentfully. "Isn't that enough? Now we think Emily's husband is having her spied on. There's a man keeps watching us in the dining room."

As Tommy stemmed into the driveway of his hotel, he wondered if he was really attractive to women at all. Yesterday he had been sure of these two, holding them in the hollow of his hand. As he dressed for dinner he realized that he wanted them both. It was an outrage that he couldn't have them both. Wouldn't a girl rather have half of him than all of Harry Whitby, or a whole spic with a jar of pomade thrown in? Life was so badly arranged – better no women at all than only one woman.

He shouted, "Come in!" to a knock at his salon door and, leaning around the corner, his hand on his dress tie, found the two "ickle durls".

He started. Had they inherited him from Rosemary? Had he been theirs since the superior pair seemed to have relinquished their claims? Were they really presuming that he might escort them to the fancy-dress ball tonight?

Slipping on his coat, he went into his parlour. They were got up as Arlésienne peasant girls, with high black bonnets and starched aprons.

"We've come about Rosemary," they said directly. "We wanted to see if you won't do something about it. She's been in bed all day and she says she isn't coming to the party tonight. Couldn't you at least call her up?"

"Why should I call her up?"

"You know she's perfectly crazy about you, and last night was the most miserable she ever spent in her life. After she broke Caros Moros's guitar, we couldn't stop her crying."

A contented glow spread over Tommy. His instinct was to telephone at once, but, curiously enough, to telephone Emily, so that he could talk to her with his newborn confidence.

The "ickle durls" moved towards the door. "You will call her up," they urged him respectfully.

"Right now." He took them each in one arm, like a man in a musical comedy, and kissed the rouge on their cheeks. When they were gone, he telephoned Rosemary. Her "hello" was faint and frightened.

"Are you sorry you were so terrible to me last night, baby?" he demanded. "No real piccaninny would—"

"You were the terrible one."

13

"Are you coming to the party tonight?"

"Oh, I will if you'll act differently. But I'll be hours; I'm still in bed. I can't get down till after dinner."

With Rosemary safely locked up again in the tranquil cells of his mind, he rang up Emily.

"I'm sorry I was so short with you this afternoon," she said immediately.

"Are you in love with me?"

"Why, no; I don't think so."

"Aren't you a little bit in love with me?"

"I like you a lot."

"Dear Emily. What's this about being spied on?"

"Oh, there's a man here who walked into my room – maybe by accident. But he always watches us."

"I can't stand having you annoyed," he said. "Please call on me if anything definite happens. I'd be glad to come up and rub his face in the snow."

There was a pregnant telephone silence.

"I wish I was with you now," he said gently.

After a moment she whispered, "I do too."

He had nothing to complain of; the situation was readjusted; things were back where they had been twenty-four hours ago. Eating dinner alone, he felt that in reality both girls were beside him, one on either hand. The dining room was shimmering with unreality for the fancy-dress party, for tonight was the last big event of the Christmas season. Most of the younger people who gave it its real colour would start back to school tomorrow.

And Tommy felt that in the evening somewhere – but in whose company he couldn't say – there would come a moment; perhaps the moment. Probably very late, when the orchestra and what remained of the party – the youth and cream of it – would move into the bar, and Abdul, with oriental delight in obscurity, would manipulate the illumination in a sort of counterpoint whose other tone was the flashing moon from the ice rink, bouncing in the big windows. Tommy had danced with Rosemary in that light a few hours after their first meeting; he remembered the mysterious darkness, with the cigarette points turning green or silver when the lights shone red, the sense of snow outside and the occasional band of white falling across the dancers as a door was opened and shut. He remembered her in his arms and the plaint of the orchestra playing:

"That's why Mother made me
Promise to be true
and the other vague faces passing in the darkness.
She knew I'd meet someone
Exactly like you."

He thought now of Emily. They would have a very long, serious conversation, sitting in the hall. Then they would slip away and talk even more seriously, but this time with her very close to him. Anything might happen – anything.

But he was thinking of the two apart; and tonight they would both be here in full view of each other. There must be no more complications like last evening; he must dovetail the affairs with skill and thought.

Emerging from dinner, he strolled down the corridor, already filled with graces and grotesques, conventional clouds of columbines, clowns, peasants, pirates and ladies of Spain. He never wore costume himself and the sight of a man in motley made him sad, but some of the girls were lovelier than in life, and his heart jumped as he caught sight of a snow-white ballet dancer at the end of the corridor, and recognized Rosemary. But almost as he started towards her, another party emerged from the cloakroom, and in it was Emily.

He thought quickly. Neither one had seen him, and to greet one with the other a few yards away was to get off on the wrong foot, for he had invented opening remarks for each one – remarks which must be made alone. With great presence of mind, he dove for the men's washroom and stood there tensely.

Emerging in a few minutes, he hovered cautiously along the hall. Passing the lounge, he saw, in a side glance, that Caros Moros was with Rosemary and that she was glancing about impatiently. Emily looked up from her table, saw him and beckoned. Without moving a muscle of his face, Tommy stared above her and passed on. He decided to wait in the bar until the dancing actually started; it would be easier when the two were separated in the crowd. In the bar he was hailed gratefully by Mr Cola; Mr Cola was killing time there desperately, with his harem waiting outside.

"I'm having them all psychoanalysed," he said. "I got a guy down from Zurich, and he's doing one a day. I never saw such a gloomy bunch of women; always bellyaching wherever I take 'em. A man I knew told me he had his wife psychoanalysed, and she was easier to be with afterwards."

Tommy heard only vaguely. He had become aware that, as if they had planned it in collusion, Emily and Rosemary had sauntered simultaneously into the bar. Blind-eyed and breathless, he strode out and into the ballroom. One of the "ickle durls" danced by him and he seized her gratefully.

"Rosemary was looking for you," she told him, turning up the flattered face of seventeen.

Presently he felt silly dancing with her, but, perhaps because of her admirers' deference to his maturer years, three encores passed and no one cut in. He began to feel like a man pushing a baby carriage. He took a dislike to her colonial costume, the wig of which sent gusts of powder up his nose. She even smelt young – of very pure baby soap and peppermint candy. Like almost every act he had performed in the last two days, he was unable to realize why he had cut in on her at all.

He saw Rosemary dancing with Caros Moros, then with other partners, and then again with Caros Moros. He had now been a half-hour with the "ickle durl"; his gaiety was worn thin and his smile was becoming strained when at last he was cut in on. Feeling ruffled and wilted, he look around, to find that Rosemary and Caros Moros had disappeared.

With the discovery, he came to the abrupt decision that he would ask her to marry him.

He went searching, ploughing brusquely through crowds like a swimmer in surf. Just as, finally, he caught sight of the white-pointed cap and escaping yellow curls, he was accosted by Frank Forrester:

"Emily sent me to look for you. Her maid telephoned that somebody tried to get into her room, and we think it's the man who keeps watching her in the dining room."

Tommy stared at him vaguely, and Frank continued:

"Don't you think you and I ought to go up there now and rub his face in the snow?"

"Where?"

"To our hotel."

Tommy's eyes begged around him. There was nothing he wanted less.

"We'd like to find out one way or another." And then, as Tommy still hesitated: "You haven't lost your nerve, have you? About rubbing his face in the snow?"

Evasion was impossible. Tommy threw a last quick glance at Rosemary, who was moving with Caros Moros back towards the dancing floor.

At Emily's hotel the maid waited in the lower hall. It seemed that the bedroom door had opened slowly a little way; then closed again quickly. She had fled downstairs. Silently Tommy and Frank mounted the stairs and approached the room; they breathed quietly at the threshold and flung open the door. The room was empty.

"I think this was a great flight of the imagination," Tommy scolded. "We might as well go back…"

He broke off, as there were light footsteps in the corridor and a man walked coolly into the room.

"*Ach je!*"* he exclaimed sharply.

"Aha!" Frank stepped behind him and shut the door. "We got you."

The man looked from one to the other in alarm.

"I must be in the wrong room!" he exclaimed, and then, with an uncomfortable laugh: "I see! My room is just above this and I got the wrong floor again. In my last hotel I was on the third floor, so I got the habit—'

"Why do you always listen to every word we say at table?" demanded Frank.

"I like to look at you because you are such nice, handsome, wealthy American people. I've come to this hotel for years."

"We're wasting time," said Tommy impatiently. "Let's go to the manager."

The intruder was more than willing. He proved to be a coal dealer from Berlin, an old and valued client of the house. They apologized; there was no hard feeling; they must join him in a drink. It was ten minutes before they got away, and Tommy led a furious pace back towards the dance. He was chiefly furious at Emily. Why should people be spied upon? What sort of women were spied upon? He felt as if this were a plan of Emily's to keep him away from Rosemary, who with every instant was dancing farther and farther off with Caros Moros into a youthful Spanish dream. At the drive of the hotel Frank said goodnight.

"You're not going back to the dance?"

"It's finished; the ballroom's dark. Everybody's probably gone to Doldorp, because here it always closes early on Sunday night."

Tommy dashed up the drive to the hotel. In the gloomy half-light of the office a last couple were struggling into overshoes; the dance was over.

"For you, Mr McLane." The night concierge handed him a telegram. Tommy stared at it for a moment before he tore it open.

GENEVA SWITZERLAND 2/1/31
H.P. EASTBY ARRIVED TONIGHT FROM PARIS STOP ABSOLUTELY
ESSENTIAL YOU BE HERE FOR EARLY LUNCH MONDAY STOP
AFTERWARDS ACCOMPANYING HIM TO DIJON
SAGE.

For a moment he couldn't understand. When he had grasped the utterly unarguable dictum, he took the concierge by both arms.

"You know Miss Merriweather. Did she go to Doldorp?"

"I think she did."

"Get me a sleigh."

"Every sleigh in town has gone over there; some with ten people in them. These last people here couldn't get sleighs."

"Any price!" cried Tommy fiercely. "Think!"

He threw down five large silver wheels on the desk.

"There's the station sleigh, but the horses have got to be out at seven in the morning. If you went to the stables and asked Eric…"

Half an hour later the big, glassed-in carryall jingled out on the Doldorp road with a solitary passenger. After a mile, a first open sleigh dashed past them on its way home, and Tommy leant out and glared into the anonymous bundles of fur and called "Rosemary!" in a firm but unavailing voice. When they had gone another mile, sleighs began to pass in increasing numbers. Sometimes a taunting shout drifted back to him; sometimes his voice was drowned in a chorus of 'Jingle Bells' or 'Merrily We Roll Along'. It was hopeless; the sleighs were coming so fast now that he couldn't examine the occupants; and then there were no more sleighs and he sat upright in the great, hearse-like vehicle, rocking on towards a town that he knew no longer held what he was after. A last chorus rang in his ears:

"Goodnight, ladies,
Goodnight, ladies,
Goodnight, lay-de-es,
I'm going to leave you now."*

4

H E WAS AWAKE AT SEVEN with the *valet de chambre* shaking his shoulders. The sun was waving gold, green and white flags on the Wildstrubel* as he fumbled clumsily for his razor. The great fiasco of the night before drifted over him, and he could hear even the great blackbirds cawing, "You went away too far," on the white balcony outside.

Desperately he considered telephoning her, wondering if he could explain to a girl still plunged in drowsiness what he would have had trouble in explaining in person. But it was already time to go; he drove off in a crowded sleigh with other faces wan in the white morning.

They were passing the crisp pale-green rink where Wiener waltzes blared all day and the blazing colours of many schools flashed against pale-blue skies. Then there was the station full of frozen breath; he was in the first-class carriage of the train drawing away from the little valley, past pink pines and fresh, diamond-strewn snow.

Across from him women were weeping softly for temporarily lost children whom they had left up there for another term at school. And in a compartment farther up he suddenly glimpsed the two "ickle durls". He drew back; he couldn't stand that this morning. But he was not to escape so readily. As the train passed Caux, high on its solitary precipice, the "ickle durls" came along the corridor and spied him.

"Hey, there!" They exchanged glances. "We didn't think you were on the train."

"Do you know," began the older one – the one he had danced with last night – "what we'd like?"

It was something daring evidently, for they went off into spasms of suppressed giggles.

"What we'd like," the "ickle durl" continued, "is to ask you if… we wondered if you would send us a photo."

"Of what?" asked Tommy.

"Of yourself."

"She's asking for herself," declared the other "ickle durl" indignantly. "I wouldn't be so darn fresh."

"I haven't had a photo taken for years."

"Even an old one," pursued the "ickle durl" timidly.

"And listen," said the other one. "Won't you come up for just a minute and say goodbye to Rosemary? She's still crying her eyes out, and I think she'd like it if you even came up to say goodbye."

He jerked forward as if thrown by the train.

"Rosemary!"

"She cried all the way to Doldorp and all the way back, and then she broke Caros Moros's other guitar that he keeps in reserve; so he feels awful, being up there another month without any guitar."

But Tommy was gone. As the train began traversing back and forth towards Lake Geneva, the two "ickle durls" sat down resignedly in his compartment.

"So then…" he was saying at the moment. "No, don't move; I don't mind a bit. I like you like that. Use my handkerchief… Listen. If you've got to go to Paris, can't you possibly come by way of Geneva and Dijon?"

"Oh, I'd love to. I don't want to let you out of my sight – not now, anyhow."

At that moment – perhaps out of habit, perhaps because the two girls had become almost indissolubly wedded in his mind – he had a sharp, vivid impression of Emily. Wouldn't it be better for him to see them both together before coming to such an important decision?

"Will you marry me?" he cried desperately. "Are we engaged? Can't we put it in writing?"

With the sound of his own voice the other image faded from his mind for ever.

Between Three and Four

1

THIS HAPPENED NOWADAYS, with everyone somewhat discouraged. A lot of less fortunate spirits cracked when money troubles came to be added to all the nervous troubles accumulated in the prosperity – neurosis being a privilege of people with a lot of extra money. And some cracked merely because it was in the air, or because they were used to the great, golden figure of plenty standing behind them, as the idea of prudence and glory stands behind the French, and the idea of "the thing to do" used to stand behind the English. Almost everyone cracked a little.

Howard Butler had never believed in anything, including himself, except the system, and had not believed in that with the intensity of men who were its products or its prophets. He was a quiet, introverted man, not at all brave or resilient and, except in one regard, with no particular harm in him. He thought a lot without much apparatus for thinking, and in normal circumstances one would not expect him to fly very high or sink very low. Nevertheless, he had a vision, which is the matter of this story.

Howard Butler stood in his office on the ninth floor of a building in New York, deciding something. It was a branch and a showroom of B.B. Eddington's Sons, office furniture and supplies, of which he was a branch manager – a perfect office ceremoniously equipped throughout, though now a little empty because of the decreased personnel due to hard times. Miss Wiess had just telephoned the name of an unwelcome caller, and he was deciding whether he hadn't just as well see the person now; it was a question of sooner or later. Mrs Summer was to be shown in.

Mrs Summer did not need to be shown in, since she had worked there for eight years, up until six months ago. She was a handsome and vital

22

lady in her late forties, with golden-greyish hair, a stylish-stout figure with a reminiscent touch of the Gibson Girl* bend to it, and fine young eyes of bright blue. To Howard Butler she was still as vivid a figure as when, as Sarah Belknap, she had declined to marry him nearly thirty years ago – with the essential difference that he hated her.

She came into his private office with an alert way she had and, in a clear, compelling voice that always affected him, said, "Hello, Howard," as if, without especially liking him, she didn't object to him at all. This time there was just a touch of strain in her manner.

"Hello, Sarah."

"Well," she breathed, "it's very strange to be back here. Tell me you've got a place for me."

He pursed his lips and shook his head. "Things don't pick up."

"H'm." She nodded and blinked several times.

"Cancellations, bad debts – we've closed two branches and there've been more pay cuts since you left. I've had to take one."

"Oh, I wouldn't expect the salary I used to get. I realize how things are. But, literally, I can't find anything. I thought, perhaps, there might be an opening, say, as office manager or head stenographer, with full responsibility. I'd be very glad of fifty dollars a week."

"We're not paying anything like that."

"Or forty-five. Or even forty. I had a chance at twenty-five when I first left here, and, like an idiot, I let it go. It seemed absurd after what I'd been getting; I couldn't keep Jack at Princeton on that. Of course, he's partly earning his way, but even in the colleges the competition is pretty fierce now – so many boys need money. Anyhow, last week I went back and tried to get the job at twenty-five, and they just laughed at me." Mrs Summer smiled grimly, but with full control over herself; yet she could only hold the smile a minute and she talked on to conceal its disappearance: "I've been eating at the soup kitchens to save what little I've got left. When I think that a woman of my capacity... That's not conceit, Howard; you know I've got capacity. Mr Eddington always thought so. I never quite understood—"

"It's tough, Sarah," he said quickly. He looked at her shoes – they were still good shoes – on top anyhow. She had always been well turned out.

"If I had left earlier, if I'd been let out before the worst times came, I could have placed myself; but when I started hunting, everyone had got panicky."

"We had to let Muller go too."

"Oh, you did," she said, with interest; the news restored her a measure of self-respect.

"A week ago."

Six months before, the choice had been between Mr Muller and Mrs Summer, and Sarah Summer knew – and Howard Butler knew that she knew – that he had made a ticklish decision. He had satisfied an old personal grudge by keeping Muller, who was a young man, clearly less competent and less useful to the firm than Mrs Summer, and who received the same salary.

Now they stared at each other; she trying to fix on him, to pin him down, to budge him; he trying to avoid her, and succeeding, but only by retreating into recently hollowed-out cavities in his soul, but safe cavities, from which he could even regard her plight with a certain satisfaction. Yet he was afraid of what he had done; he was trying to be hard, but in her actual presence the sophistries he had evolved did not help him.

"Howard, you've got to give me a job," she broke out. "Anything – thirty dollars, twenty-five dollars. I'm desperate. I haven't thirty dollars left. I've got to get Jack through this year – his junior year. He wants to be a doctor. He thinks he can hold out till June on his own, but someone drove him down to New York on Washington's Birthday, and he saw the way I was living. I tried to lie to him, but he guessed, and now he says he's going to quit and get a job. Howard, I'd rather be dead than stand in his way. I've been thinking of nothing else for a week. I'd be better dead. After all, I've had my life – and a lot of happiness."

For an instant Butler wavered. It could be done, but the phrase "a lot of happiness" hardened him, and he told himself how her presence in the office now would be a continual reproach.

Thirty years ago, on the porch of a gabled house in Rochester, he had sat in misery while John Summer and Sarah Belknap had told him moonily about their happiness. "I wanted you to be the first to know, Howard," Sarah had said. Butler had blundered into it that evening, bringing flowers and a new offer of his heart; then he was suddenly made aware that things were changed, that he wasn't very alive for either of them. Later, something she had said was quoted or misquoted to him – that if John Summer had not come along, she'd have been condemned to marry Howard Butler.

Years later he had walked into the office one morning to find her his subordinate. This time there was something menacing and repellent in his wooing, and she had put a stop to it immediately, definitely and finally. Then, for eight years, Butler had suffered her presence in the office, drying out in the sunshine of her vitality, growing bitter in the shadow of her indifference; aware that, despite her widowhood, her life was more complete than his.

"I can't do it," he said, as if regretfully. "Things are stripped to the bone here. There's no one you could displace. Miss Wiess has been here twelve years."

"I wonder if it would do any good to talk to Mr Eddington."

"He's not in New York, and it wouldn't do any good."

She was beaten, but she went on evenly: "Is there any likelihood of a change, in the next month, say?"

Butler shrugged his shoulders. "How does anybody know when business will pick up? I'll keep you in mind if anything turns up." Then he added, in a surge of weakness: "Come back in a week or so, some afternoon between three and four."

Mrs Summer got up; she looked older than when she had come into the office.

"I'll come back then." She stood twisting her gloves, and her eyes seemed to stare out into more space than the office enclosed. "If you haven't anything for me then, I'll probably just – quit permanently."

She walked quickly to the window, and he half-rose from his chair.

"Nine floors is a nice height," she remarked. "You could think things out one more time on the way down."

"Oh, don't talk that way. You'll get a break any day now."

"Businesswoman Leaps Nine Floors to Death," said Mrs Summer, her eyes still fixed out the window. She sighed in a long, frightened breath, and turned towards the door. "Goodbye, Howard. If you think things over, you'll see I was right in not even trying to love you. I'll be back some day next week, between three and four."

He thought of offering her five dollars, but that would break down something inside him, so he let her go like that.

2

H E SAW HER THROUGH the transparent place where the frosting was rubbed from the glass of his door. She was thinner than she had been last week, and obviously nervous, starting at anyone coming in or going out. Her foot was turned sideways under the chair and he saw where an oval hole was stopped with a piece of white cardboard. When her name was telephoned, he said, "Wait," letting himself be annoyed that she had come slightly before three; but the real cause of his anger lay in the fact that he wasn't up to seeing her again. To postpone his realization of the decision made in his subconscious, he dictated several letters and held a telephone conversation with the head office. When he had finished, he found it was five minutes to four; he hadn't meant to detain her an hour. He phoned Miss Wiess that he had no news for Mrs Summer and couldn't see her.

Through the glass he watched her take the news. It seemed to him that she swayed as she got up and stood blinking at Miss Wiess.

"I hope she's gone for good," Butler said to himself. "I can't be responsible for everybody out of work in this city. I'd go crazy."

Later he came downstairs into a belt of low, stifling city heat; twice on his way home he stopped at soda fountains for cold drinks. In his apartment he locked the door, as he so often did lately, as if he were raising a barrier against all the anxiety outside. He moved about, putting away some laundry, opening bills, brushing his coat and hanging it up – for he was very neat – and singing to himself:

"I can't give you anything but love, baby,
That's the only thing I've plenty of, baby…"*

He was tired of the song, but he continually caught himself humming it. Or else he talked to himself, like many men who live alone.

"Now, that's two coloured shirts and two white ones. I'll wear this one out first, because it's almost done. Almost done… Seven, eight, and two in the wash – ten…"

Six o'clock. All the offices were out now; people hurrying out of elevators, swarming down the stairs. But the picture came to Butler tonight with a curious addition; he seemed to see someone climbing up the stairs too, passing the throng, climbing very slowly and resting momentarily on the landings.

"Oh, what nonsense!" he thought impatiently. "She'd never do it. She was just trying to get my goat."

But he kept on climbing up flights of stairs with her, the rhythm of the climbing as regular and persistent as the beat of fever. He grabbed his hat suddenly and went out to get dinner.

There was a storm coming; the sultry dust rose in swirls along the street. The people on the street seemed a long way removed from him in time and space. It seemed to him that they were all sad, all walking with their eyes fixed on the ground, save for a few who were walking and talking in pairs. These latter seemed absurd, with their obliviousness of the fact that they were making a show of themselves with those who were walking as it was fitting – silent and alone.

But he was glad that the restaurant where he went was full. Sometimes, when he read the newspapers a lot, he felt that he was almost the only man left with enough money to get along with;

and it frightened him, because he knew pretty well that he was not much of a man and they might find it out and take his position away from him. Since he was not all right with himself in his private life, he had fallen helplessly into the clutches of the neurosis that gripped the nation, trying to lose sight of his own insufficiencies in the universal depression.

"Don't you like your dinner?" the waitress asked.

"Yes, sure." He began to eat self-consciously.

"It's the heat. I just seen by the papers another woman threw herself out of a ninth-storey window this afternoon."

Butler's fork dropped to the floor.

"Imagine a woman doing that," she went on, as she stooped for the fork. "If I ever wanted to do that, I'd go drown myself."

"What did you say?"

"I say I'd go drown myself. I can't swim anyhow. But I said if—"

"No, before that – about a woman."

"About a woman that threw herself out of a ninth-storey window. I'll get the paper."

He tried to stop her; he couldn't look at the paper. With trembling fingers he laid a dollar on the table and hurried out of the restaurant.

It couldn't possibly be her, because he had seen her at four, and it was now only twenty after seven. Three hours. A news-stand drifted up to him, piled with late editions. Forming the sound of "agh" in his throat, he hurried past, hurried on, into exile.

He had better look. It couldn't be Sarah.

But he knew it was Sarah. BUSINESSWOMAN, DISPIRITED, LEAPS NINE FLOORS TO DEATH. He passed another news-stand and, turning into Fifth Avenue, walked north. The rain began in large drops that sent up whiffs of dust, and Butler, looking at the crawling sidewalk, suddenly stopped, unable to go forward or to retrace his steps.

"I'll have to get a paper," he muttered. "Otherwise I won't sleep."

He walked to Madison Avenue and found a news-stand; his hand felt over the stacked papers and picked up one of each; he did not look at them, but folded them under his arm. He heard the rain falling on them in crisp pats, and then more softly, as if it was shredding them away. When he reached his door, he suddenly flung the soggy bundle down a basement entrance and hurried inside. Better wait till morning.

He undressed excitedly, as if he hadn't a minute to lose. "It's probably not her," he kept repeating aloud. "And if it is, what did I have to do with it? I can't be responsible for everybody out of work in this city." With the help of this phrase and a hot double gin, he fell into a broken sleep.

He awoke at five, after a dream which left him shaken with its reality. In the dream he was talking to Sarah Belknap again. She lay in a hammock on a porch, young once more, and with a childish wistfulness. But she knew what was going to happen to her presently – she was going to be thrown from a high place and be broken and dead. Butler wanted to help her – tears were running out of his eyes and he was wringing his hands – but there was nothing he could do now; it was too late. She did not say that it was all his fault, but her eyes, grieving silently and helplessly about what was going to happen, reproached him for not having prevented it.

The sound that had awakened him was the plop of his morning paper against the door. The resurgent dream, heartbreaking and ominous, sank back into the depths from which it came, leaving him empty; and now his consciousness began to fill up with all the miserable things that made their home there. Torn between the lost world of pity and the world of meanness where he lived, Butler sprang out of bed, opened the door and took up the paper. His eyes, blurred with sleep, ran across the columns:

BUSINESSWOMAN, DISPIRITED, LEAPS NINE FLOORS TO DEATH

For a moment he thought it was an illusion. The print massed solidly below the headline; the headline itself disappeared. He rubbed his eyes with one fist; then he counted the columns over, and found that two columns were touching that should have flanked the story – but no, there it was:

BUSINESSWOMAN, DISPIRITED, LEAPS NINE FLOORS TO DEATH

He heard the cleaning woman moving about in the hall and, going to the door, he flung it open.

"Mrs Thomas!"

A pale Negress with corded glasses looked up at him from her pail.

"Look at this, Mrs Thomas!" he cried. "My eyes are bad! I'm sick! I've got to know! Look!"

He held the paper before her; he felt his voice quivering like a muscle: "Now, you tell me. Does it say 'Businesswoman Leaps to Death'? Right there! Look, can't you?"

The Negress glanced at him curiously, bent her head obediently to the page.

"Indeed it does, Mr Butler."

"Yes?" He passed his hand across his eyes. "Now, below that. Does it say, 'Mrs John Summer'? Does it say, 'Mrs John Summer'? Look carefully now."

Again she glanced sharply at him before looking at the paper. "Indeed it does, Mr Butler. 'Mrs John Summer'." After a minute she added, "Man, you're sick."

Butler closed his door, got back into bed and lay staring at the ceiling. After a while he began repeating his formulas aloud:

"I mustn't get to thinking that I had anything to do with it, because I didn't. She'd been offered another job, but she thought she was too good for it. What would she have done for me if she'd been in my place?"

He considered telephoning the office that he was ill, but young George Eddington was expected back any day, and he did not dare. Miss Wiess had gone on her vacation yesterday, and there was a substitute to be broken in. The substitute had not known Mrs Summer, so there would be no discussion of what had happened.

It was a day of continuing heat, wasted unprolific heat that cradled the groans of the derrick and the roar of the electric riveters in the building going up across the street. In the heat every sound was given its full discordant value, and by early afternoon Butler was sick and dizzy. He had made up his mind to go home, and was walking restlessly about his office when the thing began to happen. He heard the clock outside his office ticking loud in the hot silence, heard the little, buzzing noise it made, passing the hour; and at the same moment he heard the sigh of pneumatic hinges, as the corridor door swung open and someone came into the outer office. Then there wasn't a sound.

For a moment he hoped that it was someone he would have to see; then he shivered and realized that he was afraid – though he did not know why – and walked towards his own door. Before reaching it, he stopped. The noise of the riveting machine started again, but it seemed farther away now. For an instant he had the impression that the clock in the next room had stopped too, but there it was again, marking rather long seconds against the silence.

Suddenly he did not want to know who had come into the next room; yet he was irresistibly impelled to find out. In one corner of his door was the transparent spot through which almost the whole outer office was visible, but now Butler discovered a minute scrape in the painted letter B of his name. Through it he could see the floor, and the dark little hall giving on the corridor where chairs for visitors were placed. Clamping his teeth together, he put his eye to this crack.

Tucked beneath the chair and criss-crossing the chair legs were a pair of woman's tan shoes. The sole of one shoe turned towards him, and he made out a grey oval in the centre. Breathlessly he moved until his eye was at the other hole. There was something sitting in the chair – rather, slumped in it, as if it had been put down there and had immediately crumpled. A dangling hand and what he could see of the face were of a diaphanous pallor, and the whole attitude was one of awful stillness. With a little choking noise, Butler sprang back from the door.

3

I T WAS SEVERAL MINUTES before he was able to move from the wall against which he had backed himself. It was as if there was a sort of bargain between himself and the thing outside that, by staying perfectly still, playing dead, he was safe. But there was not a sound, not a movement in the outer office, and after a while a surface rationality asserted itself. He told himself that this was all the result of strain; that the frightening part of it was not the actual phantom, but that his nerves should be in a state to conjure it up. But he drew little consolation from this; if the terror existed, it was immaterial whether it originated in another world or in the dark places of his own mind.

He began making a systematic effort to pull himself together. In the first place, the noises outside were continuing as before; his office, his own body, were tangible as ever, and people were passing in the street; Miss Rousseau would answer the pressure of a bell which was within reach of his hand. Secondly, there could, conceivably, be some natural explanation of the thing outside; he had not been able to see the whole face and he could not be absolutely sure that it was what he thought it was; any number of people had cardboard in their shoes these days. In the third place – and he astonished himself at the coolness with which he deliberated this – if the matter reached an intolerable point, one could always take one's own life, thus automatically destroying whatever horror had come into it.

It was this last thought that caused him to go to the window and look down at the people passing below. He stood there for a minute, never quite turning his back on the door, and watched the people passing and the workmen on the steel scaffolding over the way. His heart tried to go out to them, and he struggled desperately to assert the common humanity he shared with them, the joys and griefs they had together, but it was impossible. Fundamentally, he despised them and – that is to say, he could make no connection with them, while his connection with the thing in the next room was manifest and profound.

Suddenly Butler wrenched himself around, walked to the door and put his eye to the aperture. The figure had moved, had slumped farther sideways, and the blood rushed up, tingling, into his head as he saw that the face, now turned sightlessly towards him, was the face of Sarah Summer.

He found himself sitting at his desk, bent over it in a fit of uncontrollable laughter.

How long he had sat there he did not know, when suddenly he heard a noise, and recognized it, after a moment, as the swishing sigh of the hinges on the outer door. Looking at his watch, he saw that it was four o'clock.

He rang for Miss Rousseau and, when she came, asked: "Is anyone waiting to see me?"

"No, Mr Butler."

"Was there someone earlier?"

"No, sir."

"Are you sure?"

"I've been in the filing room, but the door was open; if anyone had come in I'd surely have heard them."

"All right. Thanks."

As she went out, he looked after her through the open door. The chair was now empty.

4

HE TOOK A STRONG BROMIDE that night and got himself some sleep, and his reasoning reassumed, with dawn, a certain supremacy. He went to the office, not because he felt up to it, but because he knew he would never be able to go again. He was glad he had gone, when Mr George Eddington came in late in the morning.

"Man, you look sick," Eddington said.

"It's only the heat."

"Better see a doctor."

"I will," said Butler, "but it's nothing."

"What's happened here the last two weeks?"

BUSINESSWOMAN, DISPIRITED, LEAPS NINE FLOORS TO DEATH

"Very little," he said aloud. "We've moved out of the Two Hundredth Street warehouse."

"Whose idea was that?"

"Your brother's."

"I'd rather you'd refer all such things to me for confirmation. We may have to move in again."

"I'm sorry."

"Where's Miss Wiess?"

"Her mother's sick; I gave her three days' vacation."

"And Mrs Summer's left... Oh, by the way, I want to speak to you about that later."

Butler's heart constricted suddenly. What did he mean? Had he seen the papers?

"I'm sorry Miss Wiess is gone," said Eddington. "I wanted to go over all this last month's business."

"I'll take the books home tonight," Butler offered conciliatingly. "I can be ready to go over them with you tomorrow."

"Please do."

Eddington left shortly. Butler found something in his tone disquieting – the shortness of a man trying to prepare one for even harsher eventualities. There was so much to worry about now, Butler thought; it hardly seemed worthwhile worrying about so many things. He sat at his desk in a sort of despairing apathy, realizing at lunchtime that he had done nothing all morning.

At 1.30, on his way back to the office, a chill wave of terror washed suddenly over him. He walked blindly as the remorseless sun led him along a path of flat black and hostile grey. The clamour of a fire engine plunging through the quivering air had the ominous portent of things in a nightmare. He found that someone had closed his windows, and

34

he flung them open to the sweltering machines across the street. Then, with an open ledger before him, he sat down to wait.

Half an hour passed. Butler heard Miss Rousseau's muffled typewriter in the outer office, and her voice making a connection on the phone. He heard the clock move over two o'clock with a rasping sound; almost immediately he looked at his watch and found it was 2.30. He wiped his forehead, finding how cold sweat can be. Minutes passed. Then he started bolt upright as he heard the outer door open and close slowly, with a sigh.

Simultaneously he felt something change in the day outside – as if it had turned away from him, foreshortening and receding like a view from a train. He got up with difficulty, walked to the door and peered through the transparent place into the outer office.

She was there; her form cut the shadow of the corner; he knew the line of her body under her dress. She was waiting to see if he could give her a job, so that she could keep herself and her son might not have to give up his ambitions.

"I'm afraid there's nothing. Come back next week. Between three and four."

"I'll come back."

With a struggle that seemed to draw his last reserve of strength up from his shoes, Butler got himself under control and picked up the phone. Now he would see – he would see.

"Miss Rousseau."

"Yes, Mr Butler."

"If there's anyone waiting to see me, please send them in."

"There's no one waiting to see you, Mr Butler. There's—"

Uttering a choked sound, he hung up the phone and walked to the door and flung it open.

It was no use; she was there, clearly discernible, distinct and vivid as in life. And as he looked, she rose slowly, her dark garments falling about her like cerements – arose and regarded him with a wan smile, as if, at last and too late, he was going to help her. He took a step backward.

Now she came towards him slowly, until he could see the lines in her face, the wisps of grey-gold hair under her hat.

With a broken cry, he sprang backward so that the door slammed. Simultaneously he knew, with a last fragment of himself, that there was something wrong in the very nature of the logic that had brought him to this point, but it was too late now. He ran across the office like a frightened cat, and with a sort of welcome apprehension of nothingness, stepped out into the dark air beyond his window. Even had he grasped the lost fact that he sought for – the fact that the cleaning woman who had read him the newspaper could neither read nor write – it was too late for it to affect him. He was already too much engrossed in death to connect it with anything or to think what bearing it might have on the situation.

5

MRS SUMMER DID NOT GO ON into Butler's office. She had not been waiting to see him, but was here in answer to a summons from Mr Eddington, and she was intercepted by Eddington himself, who took her aside, talking:

"I'm sorry about all this." He indicated Butler's office. "We're letting him go. We've only recently discovered that he fired you practically on his own whim. Why, the number of your ideas we're using… We never considered letting you go. Things have been so mixed up."

"I came to see you yesterday," Mrs Summer said. "I was all in and there was no one in the office at the moment. I must have fainted in the chair, because it was an hour later when I remembered anything, and then I was too tired to do anything except go home."

"We'll see about all this," Eddington said grimly. "We'll… It's one of those things…" He broke off. The office was suddenly full of confusion; there was a policeman and, behind him, many curious peering faces. "What's the matter?… Hello, there seems to be something wrong here. What is it, officer?"

A Change of Class

1

NOT TO IDENTIFY THE CITY too closely, it is in the east and not far from New York, and its importance as a financial centre is out of proportion to its small population. Three families, with their many ramifications and the two industries they all but control, are responsible for this; there is a Jadwin Street and a Jadwin Hotel, a Dunois Park and a Dunois Fountain, a Hertzog Hospital and a Hertzog Boulevard.

The Jadwins are the wealthiest; within miles of the city one cannot move out of their shadow. Only one of the many brothers and cousins is concerned with this story.

He wanted a haircut and, of course, went to Earl, in the barber shop of the Jadwin Hotel. A black porter sprang out of his lethargy, the barbers at work paid him the tribute of a secret stare, the proprietor's eyes made a quick pop at the sight of him. Only Earl, cutting a little boy's hair, kept his dignity. He tapped his shears against his comb and went over to Philip Jadwin.

"It'll be five minutes, Mr Jadwin," he said without obsequiousness. "If you don't want to wait here, I can telephone up to your office."

"That's all right, Earl; I'll wait."

Philip Jadwin sat with glazed eyes. He was thirty-one, stiffly handsome, industrious and somewhat shy. He was in love with a typist in his office, but afraid to do anything about it, and sometimes it made him miserable. Lately it was a little better; he had himself in hand, but as he receded from the girl her face reproached him. At twenty-one or forty he might have dashed away with her to Elkton, Maryland, but he was at a conventional age, very much surrounded by the most conservative branch of his family. It wouldn't do.

As he seated himself in Earl's chair, a swarthy man with long prehensile arms entered the barber shop, said, "Hello, Earl," flicked his eyes over Jadwin and went on towards the manicurist. When he had passed, Earl threw after him the smile that functions in the wake of notoriety.

"He gave me a half-bottle of rye today," said Earl. "It was open and he didn't like to carry it with him."

"Well, don't cut my ear off," said Jadwin.

"Don't you worry about that." Earl glanced towards the rear of the shop and frowned. "He gets a lot of manicures."

"That's a pretty manicurist."

Earl hesitated. "I'll tell you confidentially, Mr Jadwin, she's my wife – has been for a month – but being both in the same shop, we thought we wouldn't say anything as long as we're here. The boss might not like it."

Jadwin congratulated him: "You've got a mighty pretty wife."

"I don't like her manicuring bootleggers. This Berry, now, he's all right – he just gave me a half-bottle of rye, if that coon ain't drunk it up – but I tell you, I like nice people."

As Jadwin didn't answer, Earl realized he had gone beyond the volubility he permitted himself. He worked silently and well, with deft, tranquillizing hands. He was a dark-haired, good-looking young man of twenty-six, a fine barber, steady and with no bad habits save the horses, which he had given up when he married. But after the hot towel an idea which had been with him since Jadwin came in came to the surface with the final, stimulating flicker of the drink in his veins. He might be snubbed, he might even lose a customer, but this was the year 1926 and the market had already grasped the imagination of many classes. Also he had been prompted to this by many people, among them his wife.

"Hert-win preferred seems to be going up, Mr Jadwin," he ventured.

"Yes." Jadwin was thinking again of the girl in his office, or he wouldn't have broken a principle of his family by saying: "But watch it next week when…" He broke off.

"Going up more?" Earl's eyes lit excitedly, but his hands applying the bay rum were strong and steady.

"Naturally, I believe in it," said Jadwin with caution, "but only as an out-and-out buy."

"Of course," agreed Earl piously. "No face powder, that's right."

Going home in the streetcar that night, he told Violet about it: "We got two thousand dollars. With that I think I can get the new shop in the Cornwall Building, with three chairs. There's about twenty regular customers I'd be taking with me. What I could do, see, is buy this stock and then borrow money on it to buy the shop with. Or else I could take a chance on what he told me and buy it on margin. Let me tell you he ain't putting out much; he's vice-president of Hert-win. His old man is Cecil Jadwin, you know... What would you do?"

"It would be nice to make a lot," said Violet, "but we don't want to lose the money."

"That helps."

"Well, it would be nice to have a lot of money. But you decide."

He decided conservatively, content with his prospects, liking his work in the cheerful, gossipy shop, loving his wife and his new existence with her in a new little apartment. He decided conservatively, and then Hert-win moved up twenty points in as many hours. If he had played on margin, as had one of the barbers in whom he had confided the tip, he would have more than doubled his two thousand.

"Why don't you ask him for another tip?" suggested Violet.

"He wouldn't like it."

"It don't hurt him. I think you're crazy if you don't ask him again."

"I don't dare."

Nevertheless, he delayed the negotiations about the shop in the Cornwall Building.

One day about a week later, Philip Jadwin came into the shop in a wretched humour. The girl in his office had announced that she was quitting, and he knew it was the end of something, and how much he cared.

Earl, cutting his hair and shaving him, was conscious of a sinking sensation; he felt exactly as if he were going to ask Mr Jadwin for money. The shave was over, the hot towel – in a moment it would be too late.

"I wonder if Hert-win is going to make another quick rise," Earl said in a funny voice.

Then Jadwin flared out at him. Sitting up in the chair, he said, in a low, angry voice: "What do you take me for – a racetrack tipster? I don't come here to be annoyed. If you want to keep your customers…"

He got out of the chair and began putting on his collar. For Earl that was plenty. Against his own better tact and judgement, he had blundered, and now he grew red and his mouth quivered as he stood there with the apron in his hand.

Jadwin, tying his tie at the mirror, was suddenly sorry; he had snapped at three persons this morning, and now he realized that it must be his own fault. He liked Earl; for three years he had been his customer, and there was a sort of feeling between them; a physical sympathy in the moments when Earl's hands were passing over his face, in the fine razor respecting its sensibility, or the comb, which seemed proud in the last fillip with which it finished him. Earl's chair was a place to rest, a sanctuary, once he was hidden under an apron and a lather of soap, his eyes trustfully closed, his senses awake to the pleasant smells of lotions and soap. He always remembered Earl handsomely at Christmas. And he knew that Earl liked him and respected him.

"Look here," he said gruffly. "I'll tell you one thing, but don't go lose your shirt on it, because nothing's certain in this world. Look at the paper tomorrow; if the appellate-court decision in the Chester case is against the railroads, you can expect a lot of activity in all Hert-win interests." And he added carefully, "I think. Now don't ever ask me anything again."

And so Earl blundered into the golden age.

2

"SEE THAT FELLOW GOING OUT?" the barbers said to their customers three years later. "Used to work here, but quit last year to take care of all his money. Philip Jadwin gave him some tips… G'bye, Earl. Come in more often."

He came often. He liked the familiar cosmetic smell from the mani-cure corner, where the girls sat in white uniforms, freshly clean and faintly sweating lip rouge and cologne; he liked the gleaming nickel of the chairs, the sight of a case of keen razors, the joking abuse of the coloured porter that made the hours pass. Sometimes he just sat around and read a paper. But he was hurried tonight, going to a party, so he got into his car and drove home.

It was a nice house in a new development, not large or lavish, for Earl wasn't throwing away his money. In fact, he had worked in the barber shop two years after he needed to, taking ten-cent tips from men he could have bought out a dozen times over. He quit because Violet insisted on it. His trade didn't go with the coloured servant and the police dog, the big machine for outdoors and the many small noisy machines for the house. The Johnsons knew how to play bridge and they went quite often to New York. He was worth more than a hundred thousand dollars.

In his front yard he paused, thinking to himself that it was like a dream. That was as near as he could analyse his feelings; he was not even sure whether the dream was happy or unhappy – Violet was sure for both of them that it was happy.

She was dressing. She took very good care of herself; her nails were fever-coloured and she had a water wave or a marcel every day. She had been sedate as a manicurist, but she was very lively as a young wife; she had forgotten that their circumstances had ever been otherwise and regarded each step up as a return to the world in which she belonged, just as we often deceive ourselves into thinking that we appertain to the milieu of our most distinguished friend.

"I heard something funny today—" Earl said.

But Violet interrupted sharply: "You better start putting on your tuxedo. It's half-past six."

They were short and inattentive with each other, because the world in which they moved was new and distracting. They were always rather pathetically ashamed of each other in public, though Earl still boasted of his wife's chic and she of his ability to make money. From the day when they moved into the new house, Violet adopted the manner of one following a code, a social rite, plain to herself but impossible for Earl to understand. She herself failed to understand that from their position in mid-air they were constrained merely to observe myopically and from a distance, and then try to imitate. Their friends were in the same position. They all tried to bolster up one another's lack of individuality by saying that so-and-so had a great sense of humour, or that so-and-so had a real knack of wearing clothes, but they were all made sterile and devitalized by their new environments, paying the price exacted for a passage into the middle class.

"But I heard something funny," insisted Earl, undressing, "about Howard Shalder. I heard downtown that he was a bootlegger; that he was Berry's boss."

"Did you?" she said indifferently.

"Well, what do you think about it?"

"I knew about it. Lots of nice people are bootleggers now – society people even."

"Well, I don't see why we should be friends with a bootlegger."

"But he isn't like a bootlegger," she said. "They have a beautiful home, and they're more refined than most of the people we know."

"Well, look here, Violet. Would you go to the home of that Ed that used to sell us corn when we lived on—"

Indignantly she turned around from the mirror: "You don't think Mr Shalder peddles bottles at back doors, do you?"

"If he's a bootlegger we oughtn't to go round with them," Earl continued stubbornly. "Nice people won't have anything to do with us."

"You said your own self what a lovely girl she was. She never even takes a drink. You were the one that made friends with them."

"Well, anyhow, I'm not going to the home of a bootlegger."

"You certainly are tonight."

"I suppose we got to tonight," he said unwillingly, "but I don't like to see you sitting next to him and holding hands – even in kidding. His wife didn't like it either."

"Oh, sign off!" cried Violet impatiently. "Can't we ever go out without your trying to spoil it? If you don't like the ones we know, why don't you get to know some others? Why don't you invite some of the Jadwins and the Hertzogs to dinner, if you're so particular?"

"We ought to be able to have friends without their being boot—"

"If you say that again, I'll scream."

As they went down their walk half an hour later, they could hear the radio playing 'The Breakaway'* in Shalder's house. It was a fine machine, but to Earl it did not sound like the promise of a particularly good time, since if he turned on his radio he could have the same music. There were three fine cars in front of the house; one had just driven up, and they recognized a couple they had met there before – an Italian-American, Lieutenant Spirelli, and his wife. Lieutenant Spirelli wore an officer's uniform. Howard Shalder, a big, tough young man with a twice-a-day beard and a hearty voice, stood hospitably on his front steps. Like all people who have lived by rendering personal service, Earl had a sharp sense of the relative importance of people; because he was a really kind man, this didn't show itself in snobbishness. Nevertheless, as they crossed the street the sight of the broken-English Italian in his inappropriate uniform depressed him, and he felt a renewed doubt as to whether he had risen in the world. In the barber shop both Shalder and Spirelli would have been part of the day's work; meeting them this way seemed to imply that they were on the same level, that this was the way he was. He didn't like it. He felt he was in Mr Jadwin's class – not Mr Jadwin's equal, but a part of the structure to which Mr Jadwin belonged.

He crossed the street a little behind Violet. The sun was still yellow, but the tranquillity of evening was already in the air, with the cries of birds and children softened and individualized. Not the most bored captive of society had any more sense of being in a cage than had Earl as he walked into that house to have fun.

That was, a little later in the evening, the exact mood of Mr Philip Jadwin, but he was escaping instead of entering. The dinner dance at the country club had affected him as singularly banal; it was an exceptionally wet, prenuptial affair, and he was on the wagon, so a moment arrived when he could stand it no longer. His very leaving was fraught with nuisances – he was lapelled by a bore who told him of a maudlin personal grief; he was cornered by a woman who insisted on walking down the drive with him to talk about investments, in spite of the cloying fact that couples in every second parked car were in various stages of intimacy. Alone at last, he drove into the main white road and breathed in the fine June night.

He was rather bored with life, interested in business, but feeling somewhat pointless lately in making more money for himself, already so rich. Apparently the boom was going on for ever and things could take care of themselves; he wished he had devoted more attention to his personal desires. Three years ago he should have married that girl in his office who had made him tremble whenever she came near. He had been afraid. Now three of the relatives of whom he had been afraid were dead and a cousin of his had since married his stenographer and had not been very strongly persecuted, and she was making him a fine wife too.

This very morning Jadwin had discovered that the girl he had wanted and had been too cautious to take was now married and had a baby. He encountered her on the street; she was shy, she seemed disinclined to give him either her new name or her address. He did not know if he still loved her, but she seemed real to him, or at least someone from a time when everything seemed more real. The carefully brought-up children of wealthy Easterners grow old early; at thirty-four Philip Jadwin wasn't sure he had any emotions at all.

But he had enough sentiment to make him presently stop under the bright moonlight, look at an address in a notebook and turn his car in a new direction. He wanted to see where she lived, he wanted to eavesdrop on her; perhaps, if the lights were on, stare in on some happy domestic scene. Again, if her surroundings were squalid, he might give her husband a lift. A great girl; there was something about her that always moved him – only once in a lifetime perhaps...

He drove into a new street laid out with pleasant red-brick houses: it seemed to Jadwin that he had owned this land or the adjoining parcel himself a few years back. He drove slowly along between the lighted houses, peering for the number. It was a little after ten.

No. 42, 44, 46 – there. He slowed down further, looking at a brightly lit house which poured radio music out into the night. He drove a little past it and cut off his motor; then he could hear festive voices inside, and in a window he saw a man's black back against a yellow mushroom lamp. No poverty there: the house looked comfortable, the lawn well kept, and it was a pleasant neighbourhood. Jadwin was glad.

He got out of his car and sauntered cautiously along the sidewalk towards the house, stopping in the shadow of the hedge as the front door opened, gleamed, slammed and left a man standing on the steps. He was in a dinner coat and hatless. He came down the walk, and as Jadwin resumed his saunter they came face to face. At once they recognized each other.

"Why, hello, Mr Jadwin."

"Hello, there, Earl."

"Well, well, well," Earl was a little tight and he took a long breath as if it was medicine. "They're having a party in there, but I quit."

"Isn't that where the Shalders live?"

"Sure. Big bootlegger."

Jadwin started. "Bootlegger?"

"Sure, but if he thinks he can…" He broke off and resumed with dignity: "I live over the way. The house with the col… columnade." Then he remembered that Mr Jadwin had started him towards the acquisition of that house, and the fact sobered him further: "Maybe you remember—" he began, but Jadwin interrupted:

"Are you sure Shalder's a bootlegger?"

"Dead sure. Admits it himself."

"What does… how does his wife like it?"

"She didn't know till they were married. She told me that tonight after she had a cocktail – I made her take a cocktail because she was upset, because Shalder and my…" Again he changed the subject suddenly:

45

"Would you care to come over to my house and smoke a cigar and have a drink?"

"Why, not tonight, thanks. I must get along."

"I don't know whether you remember the tip on the market you gave me three years ago, Mr Jadwin. That was the start of all this." He waved his hand towards the house and brought it around as if to include the other house and his wife too.

A wave of distaste passed over Jadwin. He remembered the incident, and if this was the result, he regretted it. He was a simple man with simple tastes; his love for Irene had been founded upon them in reaction against the complicated surfaces of the girls he knew. It shocked him to find her in this atmosphere which, at best, was only a shoddy imitation of the other. He winced as bursts of shrill laughter volleyed out into the night.

"And believe me, I'm very grateful to you, Mr Jadwin," continued Earl. "I always said that if we ever had a son—"

"How are things going with you?" Jadwin asked hastily.

"Oh, going great. I've been making a lot of money."

"What are you doing?"

"Just watching the board," said Earl apologetically. "As a matter of fact, I'd like to get a nice position. I had to quit the barber business; it didn't seem to go with all the jack I made. But I've always been sort of sorry. There's Doctor Jordan, for instance. He tells me he's got over three hundred thousand dollars on paper and he still keeps on making five-dollar visits. Then there's a porter in the First National—"

They both turned around suddenly; a woman carrying a small bag was coming down the gravel path from the rear of the house. Where it met the sidewalk she stood for a moment in the moonlight, looking at the house; then, with a curious, despairing gesture of her shoulders, she set off quickly along the sidewalk. Before either Jadwin or Earl could move, the front door opened and a large man in a dinner coat dashed out and after her. When he caught up to her they heard fragments of conversation; excited and persuasive on his part, quiet and scornful on hers:

"You're acting crazy, I tell you!"

"I'm only going to my sister's. I'm glad I took the baby there."

"I tell you I didn't—"

"You can't kiss a woman before my eyes in my own house and have your friends go to sleep on my bed."

"Now, look here, Irene!"

After a moment she gave up, shrugged her shoulders contemptuously and dropped her bag. He picked it up, and together they went up the gravel path by which she had come out.

"That was her. That was Mrs Shalder," said Earl.

"I recognized her."

"She's a fine young woman too. That Shalder – somebody ought to do something to him. I'd like to go in there now and get my wife."

"Why don't you?" asked Jadwin.

Earl sighed. "What's the use? There'd just be a quarrel and they'd all make it up tomorrow. I've been to a lot of parties like this since I moved out here, Mr Jadwin. They all make it up tomorrow."

And now the house gave forth another guest. It was Violet, who marked her exit by some shrill statement to people inside before she slammed the door. It was as if the others, entering through the kitchen, had forced her out in front. Coming down the walk, she saw Earl.

"Well, I never want to see that bunch again," she began angrily.

"Sh!" Earl warned her. "Look, Vi; I want you to meet Mr Jadwin. You've heard me speak of him. This is my wife, Violet, Mr Jadwin."

Violet's manner changed. Her hand leapt at her hair, her lips parted in an accommodating smile.

"Why, how do you do, Mr Jadwin? It's a pleasure indeed. I hope you'll excuse my looks; I've been..." She broke off discreetly. "Earl, why can't you ask Mr Jadwin over to our home for a drink?"

"Oh, you're very kind, but—"

"That's our home across the way. I don't suppose it looks so very much to you."

"It looks very nice."

"Yes…" said Violet, combing her mind for topics. "I saw in the papers that your sister is getting married. I know a woman who knows her very well – a Mrs Lemmon. Do you know her?"

"I'm afraid I—"

"She's very nice. She has a nice home on Penn Street." Again she smoothed her hair. "My, I must look a sight – and I had a wave this afternoon."

"I've got to be going along," said Jadwin.

"You sure you don't want a drink?" asked Earl.

"No, another time."

"Well, goodnight then," said Violet. "Any time you're passing by and want a drink, we'd be very happy if you just dropped in informally."

They went across the street together, and he saw that the encounter with him had temporarily driven the unpleasant evening from their minds. Earl walked alertly and Violet kept patting at various parts of her person. Neither of them looked around, as if that wasn't fair. The party in the Shalders' house was still going on, but there was a light now in a bedroom upstairs, and as Jadwin started his car he stared at it for a moment.

"It's all awfully mixed up," he said.

3

NOWHERE IN AMERICA was the drop in the market felt more acutely than in that city. Since it was the headquarters of the Hert-win industries, and since everyone had the sense of being somehow on the inside, the plunging had been enormous. In the dark autumn it seemed that every person in town was more or less involved.

Earl Johnson took the blow on his chin. Two thirds of his money melted away in the first slumps while he looked on helplessly, grasping at every counsel in the newspapers, every wild rumour in the crowd. He felt that there was one man who might have been able to help him; if he had been still a barber and shaving Mr Philip Jadwin, he might have asked, "What had I better do now?" and got the right answer. Once he even called at his office, but Mr Jadwin was busy. He didn't go back.

When he met a barber from the Jadwin Hotel shop, he could not help noticing the grin back of the sympathetic words; it was human to regard his short-lived soar as comic. But he didn't really understand what had happened until several months later, when his possessions began to peel away. The automobile went, the mortgaged house went, though they continued to live there on a rental, pending its resale. Violet suggested selling her pearl necklace, but when he consented she became so bitter that he told her not to.

These few things were literally all they had – old washing machines, radios, electric refrigerators were a drug on the market. As 1930 wobbled its way downhill, Earl saw that they had salvaged nothing – not the love with which, under happy auspices, they had started life, no happy memories, only a few transient exhilarations; no new knowledge or capability – not a thing – simply a space where three years had been. In the spring of 1930 he went back to work. He had his old chair, and it was exciting when his old customers came in one by one.

"What? Earl! Well, this is like old times."

Some of them didn't know of his prosperity, and of those who did, some were delicately silent, others made only a humorously sympathetic reference to it, no one was unpleasant. Within a month, personal appointments took up half his time, as in the old days – people popping in the door and saying, "In half an hour, Earl?" He was again the most popular barber, the best workman in the city. His fingers grew supple and soft, the rhythm of the shop entered into him, and something told him that he was now a barber for life. He didn't mind; the least pleasant parts of his life were hangovers from his prosperity.

For one thing, there was Mr Jadwin. Once his most faithful customer, he had come into the shop the first day of Earl's return, startled at the sight of him and gone to another barber. Earl's chair had been empty. The other barber was almost apologetic about it afterwards. "He's your customer," he told Earl. "He's just got used to coming to the rest of us while you were gone, and he don't want to let us down right away." But Jadwin never came to Earl; in fact, he obviously avoided him, and Earl felt it deeply and didn't understand.

But his worst trouble was at home; home had become a nightmare. Violet was unable to forgive him for having caused the collapse in Wall Street, after having fooled her with the boom. She even made herself believe that she had married him when he was rich and that he had dragged her down from a higher station. She saw that life would never bounce him very high again and she was ready to get out.

Earl woke up one April morning, aware, with the consciousness that floats the last edge of sleep, that she had been up and at the window for perhaps ten minutes, perhaps a half-hour.

"What is it, Vi?" he asked. "What are you looking for?"

She started and turned around. "Nothing. I was just standing here."

He went downstairs for the newspaper. When he returned she was again at the window in the attitude of watching, and she threw a last glance towards it before she went down to get breakfast. He joined her ten minutes later.

"One thing's settled," he said. "I was going to sell the Warren Files common for what I could get, but this morning it ain't even in the list of stocks at all. What do you know about that?"

"I suppose it's just as good as the rest of your investments?"

"I haven't got any more investments. Here's what I'm going to do: I'm going to take what cash I got left, which is just about enough, and buy the concession for the new barber shop in the Hertzog Building. And I'm going to do it now."

"You've got some cash?" Violet demanded. "How much?"

"There's two thousand in the savings bank. I didn't tell you because I thought we ought to have something to fall back on."

"And yet you sell the car!" Violet said. "You let me do the housework and talk about selling my jewellery!"

"Keep your shirt on, Vi. How long do you think two thousand would last, living the way we were? You better be glad we got it now, because if I have this barber shop, then it's mine, and nobody can lose me my job, no matter what happens."

He broke off. She had left the breakfast table and gone to the front window.

"What's the matter out there? You'd think there was a street parade."

"I was just wondering about the postman."

"He'll be another hour," said Earl. "Anyhow, about a month ago I took an option on this shop for two hundred dollars. I've been waiting to see if the market was ever going to change."

"How much did you say was in the bank?" she asked suddenly.

"About two thousand dollars."

When he had gone, Violet left the dishes on the table and went out on the porch, where she sat down and fixed her eyes on the Shalder house across the way. The postman passed, but she scarcely saw him. After half an hour Irene Shalder emerged and hurried towards the streetcar. Still Violet waited.

At half-past ten a taxi drew up in front of the Shalder house and a few minutes later Shalder came out carrying a pair of suitcases. This was her signal. She hurried across the street and caught him as he was getting into the cab.

"I got a new idea," she said.

"Yes, but I got to go, Violet. I got to catch a train."

"Never mind. I got a new idea. Something for both of us."

"I told you we could settle that later – when I get things straightened out. I'll write you next week; I swear I will."

"But this is something for right now. It's real cash; we could get it today."

Shalder hesitated. "If you mean that necklace of yours, it wouldn't much more than get us to the coast."

"This is two thousand dollars cash I'm talking about."

Shalder spoke to the taxi man and went across the street with her. They sat down in the parlour.

"If I get this two thousand," said Violet, "will you take me with you?"

"Where'll you get it?"

"I can get it. But you answer me first."

"I don't know," he said hesitantly. "Like I told you, that Philadelphia mob gave me twenty-four hours to get out of town. Do you think I'd go otherwise, just when I'm short of money? Irene went out looking for her old job this morning."

"Does she know you're going?"

"She thinks I'm going to Chicago. I told her I'd send for her and the kid when I get started."

Violet wet her lips. "Well, how about it? Two thousand dollars would give you a chance to look around – something to get started with."

"Where you can get it?"

"It's in a bank, and it's as much mine as it is Earl's, because it's in a joint account. But you better think quick, because he wants to put it into a barber shop. Next he'd want me to go back to manicuring. I tell you I can't stand this life much longer."

Shalder walked up and down, considering. "All right. Make me out a cheque," he said. "And go pack your grips."

At that moment Irene Shalder was talking to Philip Jadwin in his office in the Hertzog Building.

"Of course you can have your position back," he said. "We've missed you. Sit down a minute and tell me what you've been doing."

She sat down, and as she talked he watched her. There was a faint mask of unhappiness and fright on her face, but underneath it he felt the quiet charm that had always moved him. She spoke frankly of all that she had hoarded up inside her in two years.

"And when he sends for you?" he asked when she had finished.

"He won't send for me."

"How do you know?"

"I just know. He… well, I don't think he's going alone. There's a woman he likes. He doesn't think I know, but I couldn't help knowing.

Oh, it's all just terrible. Anyhow, if he sends for anybody, it'll be for this woman. I think he'd take her with him now if he had the money."

Philip Jadwin wanted to put his arm around her and whisper, "Now you've got a friend. All this trouble is over." But he only said: "Maybe it's better for him to go. Where's your baby?"

"She's been at my sister's since Monday; I was afraid to keep her in the house. You see, Howard has been threatened by some people he used to do business with and I didn't know what they might do. That's why he's leaving town."

"I see."

Several hours later Jadwin's secretary brought in a note:

Dear Mr Jadwin: As you probably know, I took an option on the new barber shop, depositing two hundred with Mr Edsall. Well, I have decided to take it up and I understand Mr Edsall is out of town, and I would like to close the deal now, if you could see me.

Respectfully,
Earl Johnson

Jadwin had not known that Earl held the option, and the news was unwelcome. He felt guilty about Earl, and from feeling guilty about him it was only a step to disliking him. He had grown to think of him as the type of all the speculation for which big business was blamed, and having had a glimpse afterwards at the questionable paradise that Earl had bought with his money, he looked at the story and at its victim himself with distaste. Having avoided Earl in the other barber shop, he was now faced with having him in the building where he had his own offices.

"I'll see if I can talk him out of it," he thought.

When Earl came in he kept him standing. "Your note was rather a surprise to me," he began.

"I only just decided," said Earl humbly.

"I mean I'm surprised that you're going on your own again so quickly. I shouldn't think you'd plunge into another speculation just at this time."

"This isn't a speculation, Mr Jadwin. I understand the barber business. Always when the boss was gone I took charge; he'll tell you that himself."

"But any business requires a certain amount of financial experience, a certain ability to figure costs and profits. There've been a lot of failures in this town because of people starting something they couldn't handle. You'd better think it over carefully before you rush into this."

"I have thought it over carefully, Mr Jadwin. I was going to buy a shop three years ago, but I put the money into Hert-win when I got that tip from you."

"You remember I didn't want to give you the tip and I told you you'd probably lose your shirt."

"I never blamed you, Mr Jadwin – never. It was something I oughtn't to have meddled with. But the barber business is something I know."

"Why should you blame me?"

"I shouldn't. But when you avoided my chair I thought maybe you thought I did."

This was too close to home to be pleasant.

"Look here, Earl," said Jadwin hurriedly. "We've almost closed with another party about this barber shop. Would you consider giving up your option if we forfeit, say, two hundred dollars?"

Earl rubbed his chin. "I tell you, Mr Jadwin, I got just two thousand dollars and I don't know what to do with it. If I knew any other way of making it work for me – but nowadays it's dangerous for a man to speculate unless he's got inside information."

"It's dangerous for everybody always," remarked Jadwin impatiently. "Then, do I understand that you insist on going into this?"

"Unless you could suggest something else," said Earl hesitantly.

"Unless I give you another tip, eh?" Jadwin smiled in spite of himself. "Well, if that's the way it is… Have you got the money here?"

"It's in the savings bank. I can write you a cheque."

Jadwin rang for his secretary and gave her a scribbled note to telephone the bank and see if the money was actually on deposit. In a few minutes she sent word that it was.

"All right, Earl," said Jadwin. "It's your barber shop. I suppose in a few months you'll be sold out for laundry bills, but that's your affair."

The phone on his desk rang and his secretary switched him on to the teller at the savings bank:

"Mr Jadwin, just a few minutes after your secretary called, a party presented a cheque drawn on Earl Johnson's account."

"Well?"

"If we honour it, it leaves him a balance of only sixty-six dollars instead of two thousand and sixty-six. It's a joint account and this cheque is signed by Violet Johnson. The party wishing to cash it is Howard Shalder. It's made out to his order."

"Wait a minute," said Jadwin quickly, and he leant back in his chair to think. What Irene Shalder had said came back to him: "There's a woman he likes... he'd take her with him now if he had the money." Now evidently the woman had found the money.

"This is a damn serious thing," he thought. "If I tell them to cash that cheque, Earl probably loses his wife, and with my connivance." But in the back of his mind he knew that it would set Irene Shalder free.

Philip Jadwin came to a decision and leant forward to the receiver:

"All right, cash it." He rang off and turned to Earl. "Well, make out your cheque. For two thousand dollars."

He stood up, terribly aware of what he had done. He watched Earl bent over his chequebook, not knowing that the cheque would come back unhonoured and that the whole transaction was meaningless. And watching the fingers twisted clumsily about the fountain pen, he thought how deft those same fingers were with a razor, handling it so adroitly that there was no pull or scrape; of those fingers manipulating a hot towel that never scalded, spreading a final, smooth lotion...

"Earl," he said suddenly, "if somebody told you that your wife was running away with another man – that she was on her way to the station – what would you do?"

Earl looked at him steadily. "Mr Jadwin, I'd thank God," he said.

A minute later he handed the cheque to Jadwin and received a signed paper; the transaction was complete.

"I hope you'll patronize us sometime, Mr Jadwin."

"What? Oh, yes, Earl. Certainly I will."

"Thank you, Mr Jadwin. I'm going to do my best."

When he had gone, Jadwin looked at the cheque and tore it into small pieces. By this time Shalder and Earl's wife were probably at the station.

"I wonder what the devil I've done," he brooded.

4

SO THAT IS HOW EARL JOHNSON happens to have the barber shop in the Hertzog Building. It is a cheerful shop, bright and modern; probably the most prosperous shop in town, although a large number of the clients insist on Earl's personal attentions. Earl is constitutionally a happy and a sociable man; eventually he will marry again. He knows his staff and sticks to it, and that is not the least important or least creditable thing that can be said about him.

Once in a while he plays the horses on tips that he gets from the paper the shop subscribes to.

"All right, sir," he says, "in twenty minutes then. I'll wait for you, Mr Jadwin."

And, then, back at his chair: "That's Philip Jadwin. He's a nice fellow. I got to admit I like nice people."

The soul of a slave, says the Marxian. Anyhow that's the sort of soul that Earl has, and he's pretty happy with it. I like Earl.

Diagnosis

1

FOR A WHILE THE BIG LINER, so sure and proud in the open sea, was shoved ignominiously around by the tugs like a helpless old woman: her funnels gave a snort of relief as she slid into her pier at last. From the deck Sara Etherington saw Charlie standing waiting for her in New York, and something happened to her. The New York that she had watched with ever new pride and wonder shrank into him; he summed up its flashing, dynamic good looks, its tall man's quickstep, and all was as familiar as it had been four months before. Then, as she caught his attention, she saw that something was different and strange about him; but as she bounced into his arms at the foot of the gangplank she forgot it in the thrilling staccato joy of the meeting.

"Darling, darling—"

"Let me look—"

They stood under "E" for the customs inspection, and Sara noticed a funny new line between his fine eyes, and that, instead of handling things casually, he fussed and fretted with the customs agent as if it were a hopelessly tangled matter. "I'll have to hurry back to the office," he said several times.

The people from the boat, passing, darted a last glance at her, because she had been the prettiest girl on the passenger list. She was tall, with fresh, starry eyes that did whatever her mouth did – that really were amused or anxious or sad when her mouth was. Through the summer men had told her about it in Europe, but there was Charlie, Charlie ringing in her mind, and many times in those months she had dreams that he snatched her up on his charger and raced her away. He was one

57

of those men who had a charger; she always knew it was tethered out-side, chafing at its bit. But now, for once, she didn't hear it, though she listened for the distant snort and fidgeting of hoofs.

Later they were alone together, and with his arms around her, she demanded:

"Why are you so pale? Is my boy working too hard? Isn't everything all right, now I'm home? We'll have each other permanently so soon."

He jerked his head backward in an uncharacteristic, challenging gesture, as if to say: "All right, since you brought it up!" and remarked: "Do you read the papers? Do you realize how things are here?"

"You're not in trouble, are you?"

"Not yet – at least not immediately."

"Well, let's be glad of that. Just for now let's not…"

He shook his head, looking out somewhere she couldn't follow.

"You don't understand," he shot forth. "You've only just arrived; wait a few days. Everything's collapsed and nobody knows what to do about it." With a sudden effort he got himself under control: "I know this isn't the way to meet you, Sara. I'm sorry. Maybe I exaggerate, though I don't see how; but…" Again his eyes were fixed on some dark point ahead of him, and hastily Sara changed the subject:

"Did Ben make the Triangle or whatever it was at Princeton?* Oh, listen – I've got the most gorgeous Greek and Roman soldiers for Dicky – and Egyptians. I want to keep them myself. And a dressing gown from Tripler for Ben, and a secret for you."

This reminded him of something: "Those people on the pier seemed to have plenty of luxuries in their trunks. I was rather astonished."

"But aren't we supposed to buy things? Isn't that the trouble?"

"The trouble is…" he said, and again stopped himself.

He was so handsome and his face was so kind, and his voice, with southern gentlenesses still lingering in it! Never, in the year of their engagement, had Sara seen him show a worry or care. Four months ago she had left a successful young Wall Street man, self-made, sturdy and cynical, who had happened through the first market collapses with no enormous losses and with his confidence unimpaired. Tomorrow she must find out exactly what had made the difference.

Tomorrow was Sunday, and Charlie called for her and took her to his apartment, where he was father and mother to his two younger brothers. Ben was at college; Dicky, who was eleven, spread out the soldiers with the sober eyes and eager fingers of delight.

They were Roman legionaries with short, bright swords and helmets and shields shining with gilt, a conqueror in his chariot with six horses and an entourage of sparkling, plumed Roman knights, captured Gauls in chains, Greeks in buskins and tunics of Ionian blue, black Egyptians in flashing desert reds with images of Isis and Osiris, a catapult and, in person, Hannibal, Caesar, Rameses and Alexander.

Charlie stared at the splendid panoply.

"Things like that," he said absently – "I wonder if they'll make them much longer."

Setting up the soldiers, Sara didn't answer.

"It seems almost blasphemous," Charlie continued, and then to Dicky: "You'd better eat, drink and be merry. This is quite possibly the last nice present you'll ever have. You may be glad of an old bat and ball up some smashed alley."

With the look of alarm that sprang into Dicky's eyes, Sara realized that such remarks had been made to him before.

"That's preposterous," she said sharply. "I think it's awful to let children in on the Depression. They can't do anything about it; they can only be afraid. They don't understand that grown people don't mean everything they say."

"But I do mean it. Let them know the truth. If we hadn't lived in a golden dream so long, maybe we could face things better."

That afternoon Sara tried again as they drove quietly through Central Park.

"Tell me calmly what's happened to you," she asked him. "You know I love you, and maybe I could help. I can see how all this gloomy time is on your nerves, but there's something else, and telling me about it will do you good."

Charlie tightened his arm around her. "You're a sweet, brave person," he said. "But, Sara, I'll swear to you there's nothing else. I had an insurance examination just last month and they told me I was in fine shape. I was glad, because I have a horror of falling sick just now. Financially, I've been lucky. And I love you more than anything in the world."

"Then we'll be married next month?"

He looked at her hesitantly. "If you think it's wise, just at this time."

She laughed, a little sadly. "Everybody can't stop being in love until business picks up."

"It seems sort of a big step right now."

"Are you throwing me over?"

"That's absurd. I only said—"

Her sigh interrupted him. "Charlie, what is it? Last winter you helped run a bread line, but you got it out of your head when you came away from it. When did this constant worry begin?"

"About the time you left. A friend of mine shot himself, and then a brokerage house here in New York crashed, and then all those banks out in Ohio. Everybody talked of nothing else. You'd go to a party, and as some woman was handing you a cocktail, she'd say, 'Do you know such and such a stock is off four points?' I began to realize that every speciality of ours is beginning to be made in some part of the world cheaper than we can make it in America. Do you know what the Five Year Plan—"

"Shut up, Charlie! I won't listen! Heavens, suppose it's true! You and I are young. We needn't be afraid to start over. I can't stand you going to pieces like this" – she looked at him mercilessly – "lying on your back and kicking."

"I'm thinking about you and about Dicky. I'm getting a job for Ben this June. If he waits another year to graduate, there may be no more jobs left."

Then Sara realized she was talking to a sick man and that for the moment there was nothing more to say. She tried to gain his confidence by listening without argument. She suggested that he go away for a while, but he laughed at the suggestion.

"Why, Eddie Brune went away for three days, leaving word he wasn't to be disturbed. When he got back he found…"

Sara was sick at heart. For almost the first time in her life she didn't know what to do. She knew enough about modern psychology to guess that Charlie's mood might be an externalizing of some private trouble, but she knew also that Charlie thought that psychoanalysis was a refuge for the weak and the unstable.

As the days passed, she found that her tenderness could no longer reach him. She was frightened.

Then, at the week's end, he came to see her with sleepless and despairing eyes.

"You think I'm crazy," he broke out. "You may be right. Quite possibly. There are some times – especially in the morning when I've had a good sleep, or after a cocktail or two – when the troubles of the world seem to clear away and I feel like I used to about things. But those moments are getting rarer. One thing I know – Henry Cortelyou thinks I'm not so hot any more. He looks at me in a curious way and several times he's spoken shortly down at the office. I doubt if I'll be there much longer."

He talked coolly and logically. He wanted to release her from her promise to marry him. He had thought her return might help, but it hadn't. When he left the house their engagement was over, but her love for him was not over and her hope was not gone, and her actions had only begun.

2

THE NEXT MORNING SHE MADE an appointment to see Henry Cortelyou, the senior partner of the firm. Through him they had first met.

"Have you noticed anything strange about Charlie?" she asked.

"Yes. He's acting as if he's planning a nervous breakdown. People take things hard these days."

"I don't think it's that," Sara said slowly. She told about Dicky's soldiers, about Ben's leaving college and about the broken engagement. "People in actual want may be melancholy and suicidal just on account of the Depression, but that isn't Charlie's case. Just suppose a man had some secret trouble, some maladjustment with his surroundings. And then success picked him up and whirled him along for a couple of years so fast that he hadn't any time for normal anxieties. And then suddenly he was set down and told to walk – no more joy riding. Well, he'd find himself in a great silence and his private trouble would creep back, and perhaps he'd have forgotten how to deal with it. Naturally, he'd confuse it with the rough road he was travelling and blame every stone in the road rather than look at the truth. All this whining in limousines. Anyhow, I can't believe that Charlie is this way without reason."

"And what's the reason?"

"He'll have to find out himself," said Sara. "But I think the first thing you ought to do is to ask him to resign from the firm."

"That might be the last straw," objected Cortelyou. "As a matter of fact, his work goes well enough. Only he's rather depressing around the office lately, and we don't like the way he talks outside. It might make people think there was something the matter here."

"Then make him take a year's vacation without pay," said Sara. "He has plenty of money. He won't be surprised. And I think he needs to have all the things happen to him that he's afraid of and find out that they're not what's really the matter. I love him, Uncle Henry. I haven't given up at all."

"I'll take till tomorrow to think it over."

The following afternoon, when Charlie returned to his apartment, he found a letter from Sara. He was still so absorbed by his talk with Henry Cortelyou that he sat for a long time without opening it. The blow of his dismissal should have numbed him; actually he felt a certain relief. Now he would look for work and find out the worst; he would be part of that great army driven by the dark storm. As he mingled with it already in his mind, sharing its scant bread, he felt a satisfaction in the promise of submerging himself in it. Everything was gone – security, hope and love. He opened Sara's letter:

For the sake of the past, please do one last thing for me. Darling, I beg you to do this; I'm on my knees to you, trying to put into this letter the force with which I want you to do it. Do it blindly, unwillingly, because you loved me and for a little while we were happy together. I want you to see a man named Marston Raines, whose address I enclose. He is the wisest man I know, and not a psychoanalyst; his chief interest in life is old church music and he doesn't even like to use his gift for people. But to a whole lot of his friends he's been a sort of quiet god for years. I've told him about you and he said that maybe if you liked him he could help you. Darling, please.

Charlie dropped the letter.

"Quackery," he thought. "Sweeten the bitter pill by giving it a Greek name. Introvert, Extravert and Company. Good Lord, I'd rather be an ancient Israelite and think that a plague was the punishment of God than learn a lot of nice, soft new lies to tell to myself."

But when, at luncheon, he lost control and told little Dicky he had no job, and when afterwards he found Dicky crying in his room and talk-ing of selling his soldiers to keep from going to the poorhouse – then he saw himself momentarily from outside. He knew he couldn't go on like this, and he went back to Sara's letter.

It was late afternoon when he went to see Marston Raines. Raines lived in a high apartment on Madison Avenue, and as Charlie was admitted into a wide-vistaed room, the evening gem play of New York was already taking place outside the window. But as Charlie gazed at it, it seemed to him tawdry and theatrical, a great keeping-up of appearances after the reality was gone. Each new tower was something erected in defiance of obvious and imminent disaster; each beam of light a final despairing attempt to pretend that all was well.

"But it's not all right!" he exclaimed as Raines came into the room. "It looks all right for just a minute; after that it's simply an insult to people who see things as they are."

"But then, so is the Taj Mahal," Raines said, "and Notre-Dame de Paris and the Pantheon."

"But they had their time. For a while they represented a reality. These things are scarcely built; not a single generation saw them and passed away before we ceased to believe."

"In what?"

"In the future. In our destiny. In the idea, whatever it is."

"Have a cigarette… You'll stay to dinner, naturally."

"Why? Can you help me? Can you build up something that's gone? Certain organs reproduce themselves, like the liver, but what's gone out of me will never come back."

He looked closely at Raines, a man with soft, grey hair and the face of a fine old lady, dressed in a rumpled white flannel suit. His eyes were direct, but they only looked at Charlie occasionally, as if, when they did, they saw so much that it amounted to an intrusion. The background of the apartment was composed of the musical instruments of many lands and centuries, masses of musical books and folios and priceless old sheets and scores under glass. There was a bust of Mozart and one of Haydn.

"There's no use looking at things, because you don't like things," remarked Raines, in answer to his polite interest.

"No," said Charlie frankly, "I don't."

"You like only rhythms, with things marking the beats, and now your rhythm is broken."

"Everything's broken. The future's gone, love's gone, even the past seems a joke – it's gone too."

He was looking at the backgammon board spread before him.

"Do you mind playing one game with me? I always play at this hour," said Raines. "We'll be a long time here, so just let me keep my own direction, since you admit you haven't any. By the way, do you like me all right?"

"As well as I could like any stranger in my present condition."

"Good… You have some brothers, Sara says?"

"Three half-brothers."

"Really."

"My father had a son by his first marriage. I was his son by his second marriage, and there were two children by the third marriage – those are the two I'm bringing up."

"You're a southerner?"

"I came here from a small town in Alabama about ten years ago. When I'd more or less established myself I sent for my younger brothers, who had been with an aunt."

"You've done well here, haven't you?"

"I thought so, up until now."

"Your hand shakes; you rattle the piece against the board."

"Perhaps I'd better not play," said Charlie rigidly.

"I'll get you a little drink… You believe in something," he said, after a long time. "I don't know yet what it is. You're lucky to believe in something."

"I believe in nothing."

"Yes, you do. You believe in something that's crouching in this room very near you now – something that you tried to do without and couldn't do without. And now it's gradually taking form again and you're afraid."

Charlie sprang to his feet, his mouth quivering. "No!" he cried. "I'm… I'm…"

"Sit down," said Raines quietly. He looked at his watch. "We have all night; it's only eleven."

Charlie gave a quick glance around and sat down, covering his face for a minute with his hands.

3

TWO DAYS LATER CHARLIE CLAYHORNE got off the train at Montgomery, feeling strange as he felt himself enveloped by the familiar, unforgotten atmosphere of many Negroes and voices pleading calm and girls painted bright as savages to stand out against the tropical summer. The streets were busier than he remembered in those days when he considered Montgomery a metropolis. He wondered how severely they felt the Depression, and he was surprised when no beggars approached him in the street. Later, on the local train that bore him an hour farther south, he felt himself merging minute by minute with the hot countryside, the lush vegetation, the clay roads, the strange, sluggish, primeval rivers flowing softly under soft Indian names. Then Tuscarora; the broken-down station with the mules and horse rigs hitched in the yard. Nothing changed – the sign still hung crooked on the Yancy Hotel across the street.

Suddenly someone spoke to him, and then someone else – he had to struggle for their names. To his annoyance – for he wanted to be alone – they both followed him to the hotel and sat at his table while he had supper. He learnt that Pete, his elder brother, had a farm near here and often came to town. He learnt too that the Clayhorne place hadn't been rented for five years. Had he come to try to sell it? They had heard it was to be torn down, and at the news Charlie's heart gave a jump.

Mr Chevril, the Confederate veteran who had lived at the hotel for fifty years, limped over to join them.

"How are things down here?" Charlie asked. "I mean the cotton situation?"

He waited for their faces to change, as they did in New York when one asked about a man's business, but here was not that sudden dispirited expression of the mouth and eyes.

"Are there many people out of work and hungry?"

"Not so many that I see," one answered. "I heard tell of cases down country, and a lot of the niggers had a hard time last winter."

"It's terrible in New York," Charlie said defiantly, as if they were holding out on him.

"You see, we never had much of a boom down here, though they did lay the foundations of a cotton factory over at King's Hill; so I guess we don't feel the Depression so much. Never was much cash money in this town."

Old Mr Chevril spat tobacco juice. "I don't think you fellas know what hard times are," he said. "When we got back here from Appomattox Courthouse in Sixty-five, I had a mule from the horse artillery, and Jim Mason had one plough that Stoneman hadn't smashed, and we had a crop planted before we dared think how we'd eat next winter. And we did a sight less hollerin' than you see in these Yankee newspapers."

"You don't understand," said Charlie angrily. "When you have primitive conditions hardship is just a matter of degree, but when the whole elaborate economic structure…"

He broke off as he saw that they were not following him. He felt that he must get away and be alone. Their faces seemed insensitive, uncomprehending, not to be communicated with. He made an excuse to go to his room.

It was still daylight, the red heat had gathered for one last assault upon the town; he wanted to wait until dark. He looked from the window at a proud, white-pillared Acropolis that a hundred years ago had been the centre of a plantation and now housed a row of stores, at the old courthouse with its outside staircase and at the brash new courthouse being built in its front yard, and then at the youths with sideburns lounging outside the drug store. The curious juxtapositions made him feel the profound waves of change that had already washed this country – the desperate war that had rendered the plantation house obsolete, the industrialization that had spoilt the easygoing life centring around the old courthouse. And then the years yielding up eventually in this backwater those curious young products who were neither peasants, nor bourgeois nor scamps, but a little of all three, gathered there in front of the store. After the next wave of change, would there be pigeon cotes in Wall Street, and then what, and then what?

He pulled himself together sharply. It was growing darker. He waited until it was quite dark before he went out and sauntered by a circuitous route to the edge of town. Then he set off down a clay road, white-bright in the moonlight, towards the house where he had been born.

The road went through a tangled wood he knew well, and that had not changed, but the house, breaking out suddenly against the sky, startled him. It seemed smaller, but its silhouette was a face that he knew and that knew him. It was a white-columned manor house dating from the time when the Cherokee War had made living safe in these parts; a first attempt to bring ease and spaciousness to a land from which the frontier had only just been pushed away. Now it was an irreparable wreck, with rotting timbers exposed like bones. Feeling in his pocket for candles and matches, Charlie pushed open the drunken pretence of a door and went inside.

Through the must and dust he smelt a familiar odour, unidentifiable but nostalgic. There was some broken furniture about, split stuffing and rusty springs, stained mattresses and a one-wheeled baby carriage – things that no one would carry away.

Charlie set his candle down and listened to the silence. Then he went over to the mantelpiece; it had settled forward, away from the wall, leaving the crack where mantel and wall had touched. He tried gently, then more determinedly, to pull it farther out, but there was only a sound of plaster splitting; it yielded no more.

"That's all right," he breathed to himself. He took from his pocket a wire and straightened it, leaving a hook at the end; then poking it down through the crack at the extreme left, he fished. There was no bite. After a moment he put his eye sideways and flashed a pocket light inside the crack; it was empty.

Cold with fear, he sat down in a broken rocker. Almost immediately he got up and looked into the corresponding crack at the other end, and the blood rushed back into his hands and feet again. In a moment he had drawn out an envelope covered with dust and mould. He brushed off the square white envelope. He did not know what was inside it, and if he should destroy it no living person would ever know or even guess that it had existed. Moreover, he would not know himself and could believe what he liked.

But would that solve anything? The element of conscience was now so deeply tangled with the element of fear that there was no certainty of any relief in merely knowing that he would never be found out. If he opened it, though, there would presumably be further commitments, shameful and difficult; while if he destroyed it there would be something done and finished. He held the evidence in his hands as he had a certain afternoon ten years before.

He was twenty, then, and the head of the family. His older brother, Pete, was serving in prison upstate; his younger brothers were children; his father was senile, but only Charlie realized it; the old man was well preserved and still made a suave, masterly appearance on his daily trip to town.

Characteristically the father turned against Charlie. He informed him he was taking him out of his will and substituting the imprisoned Pete as arbiter of the younger children's destinies. And one day Charlie saw Julia and Sam, the servants, signing some document in his father's room.

One afternoon a few weeks later, he went into his father's room and found the old man dead in his chair. Charlie was alone. He took the key from the dead man's neck and opened the strongbox. There was the will he had made in his sane mind, and there beside it was a new envelope, marked "To be opened after my death". With the envelope under his coat Charlie went into the living room. Julia was in the hall and, calling her sharply, he pointed to his father's room. When she had gone in he slipped the letter into the crack of the mantelpiece and heard it fall lightly a foot below.

There was no complication; no one spoke of the envelope or of a later will. The fortune was less than had been expected – sixteen thousand dollars in money and property, to be divided among the three younger children. Charlie's share gave him his start in New York.

New York was very far away now, he thought; and he himself was far away from the conscientious boy who had worried about the letter for years. Rightly or wrongly, he had defrauded his elder brother. He held the letter in his hand and opened it slowly, like a man unwinding the last bandage from a wound. Even as he bent to read it, there was a sound outside as if someone had moved on the creaky porch.

"Who's there?" he called, shoving the letter into his pocket. No answer. Maybe a night-bound Negro, seeking shelter. Charlie leant forward and blew out the candle. Simultaneously there was a loud knocking at the front door.

Grasping the broken arm of a chair, Charlie took two steps towards the hall. As he reached it, the door opened and a figure blocked out the moonlight, paused and then took a step forward.

"Just a minute there!" Charlie cried. He threw his flashlight upon a mild little man in country clothes. The man stood still and remarked in a placid voice:

"That's Charlie, isn't it? Don't you know your brother?"

One by one, Pete's features revealed themselves.

"Come in," Charlie said. "I'll light the candle."

"I wondered why you put it out."

They sat with the flickering light between them. Pete's face was trivial and sad, with something broken in it, but it was not the map of degeneracy Charlie had somehow expected to see.

"I heard this evening you were in town," said Pete. "You weren't at the hotel, and so I reckoned you'd come out here to look the old place over."

"It looks like hell, doesn't it?"

"Sure does. My wife and I tried living here a year, but she was afraid it would come down on our heads, so we moved to Lowndes County."

"How are things going with you?" asked Charlie.

"Going all right." The little man spoke up suddenly and eagerly. "I've been fixing to write you for a long while."

Charlie's heart rose in his throat.

"Yeah, I been wanting to talk to you," Pete continued. "You know, Charlie, I'm good now. You know? I mean I'm good. I want to do right. After I got out of the pen up in Birmingham I came back here for a while and tried to farm this place." He paused and lowered his voice and he leant forward. "Charlie, did it ever strike you the old man left mighty little money for what we guessed he had?"

Charlie looked up. "Yes, it struck me at the time."

"Well, there was ten thousand dollars cash under the spring house." Pete stared at Charlie, licking his lips uncertainly. "Wait a minute. Don't say anything yet awhile. Well, after I found it I tried to figure like it was my share that I'd been done out of. I bought my farm in Lowndes

County. But I got full up with corn one night and told my wife and, shucks, you know, we don't like to go to prayer meeting with that thing on our conscience. She's got religion, and thinking of it about drives her nutty, and I don't feel too good about it myself."

"I can understand," Charlie said.

"I figure you might be willing to make an arrangement. I got a couple thousand left and I could put a little mortgage on the farm. If I paid you all – you and the boys – thirty-five hundred dollars, then I'd have my fourth of what daddy left."

"You can keep it all, Pete. I'll make it up to Ben and Dicky."

"Hold on! I wasn't asking—"

"I've had the luck. You wouldn't believe how much money I've made up there, and I guess I can keep on. I'll look out for Ben and Dicky."

Was it a fortnight ago he had told Ben he must leave college?

"Keep it," he repeated. "Daddy didn't mean that money for us, or he'd have mentioned it."

Pete laughed nervously. "Well, you sound to me like a right good fellow."

"I'm a louse," admitted Charlie. "But just like you, I want to get square and start over. So listen."

He reached his hand into his pocket, drew out the paper, and unfolded it; he shut his eyes and opened them, ready for whatever he should see.

The paper he had thought was a will was not a will; it was a letter addressed to himself. He read aloud:

"*To my good son Charlie: You thought I did not mean it – you thought I was crazy. I am drawing my will over again, changing one little thing. Part of my money is where it's none of your business, and I am going to my Maker taking that secret with me, so I am leaving out the part that tells where to find it. I have not got any loving sons, so it will go to whoever finds it. It wasn't so smart to quarrel with your old daddy after all.*"

"By golly!" Pete exclaimed. "Then you knew all the time that there was more money somewhere?"

"No," said Charlie slowly. "I hadn't had time to open this letter."

4

ONE MORNING A FORTNIGHT LATER, Sara telephoned to Marston Raines.

"Charlie Clayhorne is back in town," she said.

"Have you seen him?"

"He came to see me yesterday. He's been down in Alabama where he was born."

"Does he seem better?"

"I think so. That's what I telephoned you about. It's me now – something seems to have happened to me."

"Tell me about it."

"He came in yesterday afternoon and sat down and said, 'I'm all right now, Sara!' Nothing more than that, though I rather encouraged an explanation."

"That's good. It looks as if he's cleared it up."

"Then he told me he'd gone to work in a bond house – of course, after he left I called up Henry Cortelyou at once and asked Henry to give him a chance, and of course Henry was glad to. I didn't tell Charlie – anyhow, Charlie said he thought he saw his future clear before him again and he asked me whether I could ever again consider marrying him. Marston, I didn't know what to tell him. When he was so sick, I'd have married him to try and help, but now I seem to have exhausted myself about him. I love him – I'll always somehow love him, but I don't feel the impetus to do anything more. Seeing a man break down like that – I wonder if he won't always depend on me for his sense of direction – and I would want to depend on him for that."

"But he was sick," Marston interrupted. "And you must keep remembering that. Any doctor or nurse will tell you the strongest men are like drowning kittens when they're sick. It may make you cynical about men in general, but it needn't discourage you about Clayhorne."

Silence on the wire for a moment.

"I'll have to think it over."

"You're in a state of reaction. When love is intact, the merest pin prick – a touch of jealousy, for instance – will start it ticking again."

"Thank you," Sara said. "I'll have to think it over."

At five that evening she went over to Charlie's apartment. Dicky was in the living room, digging into a confusion of wrapping paper and string.

"Isn't Charlie funny?" he cried presently. "Last month he was talking about how extravagant those soldiers were you brought me from Europe, and now's he's sent me up a whole lot more – with Napoleon in it! And look at this one—"

"It's Joan of Arc."

"And knights charging and bow-and-arrow shooters! Look, this is an executioner, and here are a whole lot of other people. I don't know what they are."

"Isn't that wonderful?"

"Yes," said Dicky. "Ben's home, but Charlie isn't… Ben!"

When Charlie came in she saw his face in the hall a minute before he saw her, and she knew then with sudden illumination that she was looking at the face she had expected to see on the pier a month before. All of him was there again.

"A nice thing has happened, Sara," he told her. "Henry Cortelyou called up. He wants me back."

"Yes, I…" Sara stopped herself. That was something he needn't ever know. It was a compensation for his solitary trip into his own buried past where she could not follow. Everything was fine now.

Marston Raines was right – his sending the soldiers to Dicky was enough to start the clock ticking again, and Sara felt a sudden shiver of emotion. Everything was all right again now; she belonged to somebody. She grew happier and happier. Suddenly she was wildly happy and she couldn't keep it to herself.

Flight and Pursuit

1

IN 1918, A FEW DAYS BEFORE the Armistice, Caroline Martin, of Derby, in Virginia, eloped with a trivial young lieutenant from Ohio. They were married in a town over the Maryland border and she stayed there until George Corcoran got his discharge – then they went to his home in the North.

It was a desperate, reckless marriage. After she had left her aunt's house with Corcoran, the man who had broken her heart realized that he had broken his own too; he telephoned, but Caroline had gone, and all that he could do that night was to lie awake and remember her waiting in the front yard, with the sweetness draining down into her out of the magnolia trees, out of the dark world, and remember himself arriving in his best uniform, with boots shining and with his heart full of self-ishness that, from shame, turned into cruelty. Next day he learnt that she had eloped with Corcoran and, as he had deserved, he had lost her.

In Sidney Lahaye's overwhelming grief, the petty reasons for his act disgusted him – the alternative of a long trip around the world or of a bachelor apartment in New York with four Harvard friends; more positively the fear of being held, of being bound. The trip – they could have taken it together. The bachelor apartment – it had resolved into its bare, cold constituent parts in a single night. Being held? Why, that was all he wanted – to be close to that freshness, to be held in those young arms for ever.

He had been an egoist, brought up selfishly by a selfish mother; this was his first suffering. But like his small, wiry, handsome person, he was all knit of one piece and his reaction were not trivial. What he did he carried with him always, and he knew he had done a contemptible and stupid thing. He carried his grief around, and eventually it was good

74

for him. But inside of him, utterly unassimilable, indigestible, remained the memory of the girl.

Meanwhile, Caroline Corcoran, lately the belle of a Virginia town, was paying for the luxury of her desperation in a semi-slum of Dayton, Ohio.

2

SHE HAD BEEN THREE YEARS IN DAYTON and the situation had become intolerable. Brought up in a district where everyone was comparatively poor, where not two gowns out of fifty at country-club dances cost more than thirty dollars, lack of money had not been formidable in itself. This was very different. She came into a world not only of straining poverty but of a commonness and vulgarity that she had never touched before. It was in this regard that George Corcoran had deceived her. Somewhere he had acquired a faint patina of good breeding, and he had said or done nothing to prepare her for his mother, into whose two-room flat he introduced her. Aghast, Caroline realized that she had stepped down several floors. These people had no position of any kind; George knew no one; she was literally alone in a strange city. Mrs Corcoran disliked Caroline – disliked her good manners, her southern ways, the added burden of her presence. For all her airs, she had brought them nothing save, eventually, a baby. Meanwhile George got a job and they moved to more spacious quarters, but mother came too, for she owned her son, and Caroline's months went by in unimaginable dreariness. At first she was too ashamed and too poor to go home, but at the end of a year her aunt sent her money for a visit and she spent a month in Derby with her little son, proudly reticent, but unable to keep some of the truth from leaking out to her friends. Her friends had done well, or less well, but none of them had fared quite so ill as she.

But after three years, when Caroline's child became less dependent, and when the last of her affection for George had been frittered away, as his pleasant manners became debased with his own inadequacies, and when her bright, unused beauty still plagued her in the mirror, she knew that the break was coming. Not that she had specific hopes of happiness – for she accepted the idea that she had wrecked her life, and her capacity for dreaming had left her that November night three years before – but simply because conditions were intolerable. The break was heralded by a voice over the phone – a voice she remembered only as something that had done her terrible injury long ago.

"Hello," said the voice – a strong voice with strain in it. "Mrs George Corcoran?"

"Yes."

"Who was Caroline Martin?"

"Who is this?"

"This is someone you haven't seen for years. Sidney Lahaye."

After a moment she answered in a different tone: "Yes?"

"I've wanted to see you for a long time," the voice went on.

"I don't see why," said Caroline simply.

"I want to see you. I can't talk over the phone."

Mrs Corcoran, who was in the room, asked, "Who is it?" forming the words with her mouth. Caroline shook her head slightly.

"I don't see why you want to see me," she said, "and I don't think I want to see you." Her breath came quicker; the old wound opened up again, the injury that had changed her from a happy young girl in love into whatever vague entity in the scheme of things she was now.

"Please don't ring off," Sidney said. "I didn't call you without thinking it over carefully. I heard things weren't going well with you."

"That's not true." Caroline was very conscious now of Mrs Corcoran's craning neck. "Things are going well. And I can't see what possible right you have to intrude in my affairs."

"Wait, Caroline! You don't know what happened back in Derby after you left. I was frantic—"

"Oh, I don't care…" she cried. "Let me alone; do you hear?"

She hung up the receiver. She was outraged that this man, almost forgotten now save as an instrument of her disaster, should come back into her life!

"Who was it?" demanded Mrs Corcoran.

"Just a man – a man I loathe."

"Who?"

"Just an old friend."

Mrs Corcoran looked at her sharply. "It wasn't that man, was it?" she asked.

"What man?"

"The one you told Georgie about three years ago, when you were first married – it hurt his feelings. The man you were in love with that threw you over."

"Oh, no," said Caroline. "That is my affair."

She went to the bedroom that she shared with George. If Sidney should persist and come here, how terrible – to find her sordid in a mean street.

When George came in, Caroline heard the mumble of his mother's conversation behind the closed door; she was not surprised when he asked at dinner:

"I hear that an old friend called you up."

"Yes. Nobody you know."

"Who was it?"

"It was an old acquaintance, but he won't call again," she said.

"I'll bet he will," guessed Mrs Corcoran. "What was it you told him wasn't true?"

"That's my affair."

Mrs Corcoran glanced significantly at George, who said:

"It seems to me if a man calls up my wife and annoys her, I have a right to know about it."

"You won't, and that's that." She turned to his mother: "Why did you have to listen, anyhow?"

"I was there. You're my son's wife."

"You make trouble," said Caroline quietly, "you listen and watch me and make trouble. How about the woman who keeps calling up George – you do your best to hush that up."

"That's a lie!" George cried. "And you can't talk to my mother like that! If you don't think I'm sick of your putting on a lot of dog when I work all day and come home to find…"

As he went off into a weak, raging tirade, pouring out his own self-contempt upon her, Caroline's thoughts escaped to the fifty-dollar bill, a present from her grandmother hidden under the paper in a bureau drawer. Life had taken much out of her in three years; she did not know whether she had the audacity to run away – it was nice, though, to know the money was there.

Next day, in the spring sunlight, things seemed better – and she and George had a reconciliation. She was desperately adaptable, desperately sweet-natured, and for an hour she had forgotten all the trouble and felt the old emotion of mingled passion and pity for him. Eventually his mother would go; eventually he would change and improve; and meanwhile there was her son with her own kind, wise smile, turning over the pages of a linen book on the sunny carpet. As her soul sank into a helpless, feminine apathy, compounded of the next hour's duty, of a fear of further hurt or incalculable change, the phone rang sharply through the flat.

Again and again it rang, and she stood rigid with terror. Mrs Corcoran was gone to market, but it was not the old woman she feared. She feared the black cone hanging from the metal arm, shrilling and shrilling across the sunny room. It stopped for a minute, replaced by her heartbeats; then began again. In a panic she rushed into her room, threw little Dexter's best clothes and her only presentable dress and shoes into a suitcase and put the fifty-dollar bill in her purse. Then taking her son's hand, she hurried out of the door, pursued down the apartment stairs by the persistent cry of the telephone. The windows were open, and as she hailed a taxi and directed it to the station, she could still hear it clamouring out into the sunny morning.

3

TWO YEARS LATER, LOOKING a full two years younger, Caroline regarded herself in the mirror, in a dress that she had paid for. She was a stenographer, employed by an importing firm in New York; she and young Dexter lived on her salary and on the income of ten thousand dollars in bonds, a legacy from her aunt. If life had fallen short of what it had once promised, it was at least liveable again, less than misery. Rising to a sense of her big initial lie, George had given her freedom and the custody of her child. He was in kindergarten now, and safe until 5.30, when she would call for him and take him to the small flat that was at least her own. She had nothing warm near her, but she had New York, with its diversion for all purses, its curious yielding up of friends for the lonely, its quick metropolitan rhythm of love and birth and death that supplied dreams to the unimaginative, pageantry and drama to the drab.

But though life was possible, it was less than satisfactory. Her work was hard, she was physically fragile; she was much more tired at the day's end than the girls with whom she worked. She must consider a precarious future when her capital should be depleted by her son's education. Thinking of the Corcoran family, she had a horror of being dependent on her son; and she dreaded the day when she must push him from her. She found that her interest in men had gone. Her two experiences had done something to her; she saw them clearly and she saw them darkly, and that part of her life was sealed up, and it grew more and more faint, like a book she had read long ago. No more love.

Caroline saw this with detachment, and not without a certain, almost impersonal regret. In spite of the fact that sentiment was the legacy of a pretty girl, it was just one thing that was not for her. She surprised herself by saying in front of some other girls that she disliked men, but she knew it was the truth. It was an ugly phrase, but now, moving in an approximately four-square world, she detested the compromises and evasions of her marriage. "I hate men – I, Caroline, hate men. I want from them no more than courtesy and to be left alone. My life is incomplete, then, but so be it. For others it is complete, for me it is incomplete."

The day that she looked at her evening dress in the mirror, she was in a country house on Long Island – the home of Evelyn Murdock, the most spectacularly married of all her old Virginia friends. They had met in the street, and Caroline was there for the weekend, moving unfamiliarly through a luxury she had never imagined, intoxicated at finding that in her new evening dress she was as young and attractive as these other women, whose lives had followed more glamorous paths. Like New York, the rhythm of the weekend, with its birth, its planned gaieties and its announced end, followed the rhythm of life and was a substitute for it. The sentiment had gone from Caroline, but the patterns remained. The guests, dimly glimpsed on the veranda, were prospective admirers. The visit to the nursery was a promise of future children of her own; the descent to dinner was a promenade down a marriage aisle, and her gown was a wedding dress with an invisible train.

"The man you're sitting next to," Evelyn said, "is an old friend of yours. Sidney Lahaye – he was at Camp Rosecrans."

After a confused moment she found that it wasn't going to be difficult at all. In the moment she had met him – such a quick moment that she had no time to grow excited – she realized that he was gone for her. He was only a smallish, handsome man, with a flushed, dark skin, a smart little black moustache and very fine eyes. It was just as gone as gone. She tried to remember why he had once seemed the most desirable person in the world, but she could only remember that he had made love to her, that he had made her think of them as engaged, and then that he had acted badly and thrown her over – into George Corcoran's arms. Years later he had telephoned like a travelling salesman remembering a dalliance in a casual city. Caroline was entirely unmoved and at her ease as they sat down at table.

But Sidney Lahaye was not relinquishing her so easily.

"So I called you up that night in Derby," he said. "I called you for half an hour. Everything had changed for me in that ride out to camp."

"You had a beautiful remorse."

"It wasn't remorse; it was self-interest. I realized I was terribly in love with you. I stayed awake all night…"

Caroline listened indifferently. It didn't even explain things; nor did it tempt her to cry out on fate – it was just a fact.

He stayed near her, persistently. She knew no one else at the party; there was no niche in any special group for her. They talked on the veranda after dinner, and once she said coolly:

"Women are fragile that way. You do something to them at certain times and literally nothing can ever change what you've done."

"You mean that you definitely hate me."

She nodded. "As far as I feel actively about you at all."

"I suppose so. It's awful, isn't it?"

"No. I even have to think before I can really remember how I stood waiting for you in the garden that night, holding all my dreams and hopes in my arms like a lot of flowers – they were that to me, anyhow. I thought I was pretty sweet. I'd saved myself up for that – all ready to hand it all to you. And then you came up to me and kicked me." She laughed incredulously. "You behaved like an awful person. Even though I don't care any more, you'll always be an awful person to me. Even if you'd found me that night, I'm not at all sure that anything could have been done about it. Forgiveness is just a silly word in a matter like that."

Feeling her own voice growing excited and annoyed, she drew her cape around her and said in an ordinary voice:

"It's getting too cold to sit here."

"One more thing before you go," he said. "It wasn't typical of me. It was so little typical that in the last five years I've never spent an unoccupied moment without remembering it. Not only I haven't married, I've never even been faintly in love. I've measured up every girl I've met to you, Caroline – their faces, their voices, the tips of their elbows."

"I'm sorry I had such a devastating effect on you. It must have been a nuisance."

"I've kept track of you since I called you in Dayton; I knew that, sooner or later, we'd meet."

"I'm going to say goodnight."

But saying goodnight was easier than sleeping, and Caroline had only an hour's haunted doze behind her when she awoke at seven. Packing her bag, she made up a polite, abject letter to Evelyn Murdock, explaining why she was unexpectedly leaving on Sunday morning. It was difficult and she disliked Sidney Lahaye a little bit more intensely for that.

4

MONTHS LATER CAROLINE CAME UPON a streak of luck. A Mrs O'Connor, whom she met through Evelyn Murdock, offered her a post as private secretary and travelling companion. The duties were light, the travelling included an immediate trip abroad, and Caroline, who was thin and run down from work, jumped at the chance. With astonishing generosity the offer included her boy.

From the beginning Caroline was puzzled as to what had attracted Helen O'Connor to her. Her employer was a woman of thirty, dissipated in a discreet way, extremely worldly and, save for her curious kindness to Caroline, extremely selfish. But the salary was good and Caroline shared in every luxury and was invariably treated as an equal.

The next three years were so different from anything in her past that they seemed years borrowed from the life of someone else. The Europe in which Helen O'Connor moved was not one of tourists but of seasons. Its most enduring impression was a phantasmagoria of the names of places and people – of Biarritz, of Mme de Colmar, of Deauville, of the Comte de Berme, of Cannes, of the Derehiemers, of Paris and the Château de Madrid. They lived the life of casinos and hotels so assiduously reported in the Paris American papers – Helen O'Connor drank and sat up late, and after a while Caroline drank and sat up late. To be slim and pale was fashionable during those years, and deep in Caroline was something that had become directionless and purposeless, that no longer cared. There was no love; she sat next to many men at table, appreciated compliments, courtesies and small gallantries, but the moment something more was hinted, she froze very definitely. Even when she was stimulated with excitement and wine, she felt the growing hardness of her sheath like a breastplate. But in other ways she was increasingly restless.

At first it had been Helen O'Connor who urged her to go out; now it became Caroline herself for whom no potion was too strong or any evening too late. There began to be mild lectures from Helen.

"This is absurd. After all, there's such a thing as moderation."

"I suppose so, if you really want to live."

"But you want to live; you've got a lot to live for. If my skin was like yours, and my hair... Why don't you look at some of the men that look at you?"

"Life isn't good enough, that's all," said Caroline. "For a while I made the best of it, but I'm surer every day that it isn't good enough. People get through by keeping busy; the lucky ones are those with interesting work. I've been a good mother, but I'd certainly be an idiot putting in a sixteen-hour day mothering Dexter into being a sissy."

"Why don't you marry Lahaye? He has money and position and everything you could want."

There was a pause. "I've tried men. To hell with men."

Afterwards she wondered at Helen's solicitude, having long realized that the other woman cared nothing for her. They had not even mutual tastes; often they were openly antipathetic and didn't meet for days at a time. Caroline wondered why she was kept on, but she had grown more self-indulgent in these years and she was not inclined to quibble over the feathers that made soft her nest.

One night on Lake Maggiore things changed in a flash. The blurred world seen from a merry-go-round settled into place; the merry-go-round suddenly stopped.

They had gone to the hotel in Locarno because of Caroline. For months she had had a mild but persistent asthma and they had come there for rest before the gaieties of the fall season at Biarritz. They met friends, and with them Caroline wandered to the Kursaal to play mild *boule* at a maximum of two Swiss francs. Helen remained at the hotel.

Caroline was sitting in the bar. The orchestra was playing a *Wiener Walzer*, and suddenly she had the sensation that the chords were extending themselves, that each bar of three-four time was bending in the middle, dropping a little and thus drawing itself out, until the waltz itself, like a phonograph running down, became a torture. She put her fingers in her ears; then suddenly she coughed into her handkerchief.

She gasped.

The man with her asked: "What is it? Are you sick?"

She leant back against the bar, her handkerchief with the trickle of blood clasped concealingly in her hand. It seemed to her half an hour before she answered, "No, I'm all right," but evidently it was only a few seconds, for the man did not continue his solicitude.

"I must get out," Caroline thought. "What is it?" Once or twice before she had noticed tiny flecks of blood, but never anything like this. She felt another cough coming and, cold with fear and weakness, wondered if she could get to the washroom.

After a long while the trickle stopped and someone wound the orchestra up to normal time. Without a word she walked slowly from the room, holding herself delicately as glass. The hotel was not a block away; she set out along the lamplit street. After a minute she wanted to cough again, so she stopped and held her breath and leant against the wall. But this time it was no use; she raised her handkerchief to her mouth and lowered it after a minute, this time concealing it from her eyes. Then she walked on.

In the elevator another spell of weakness overcame her, but she managed to reach the door of her suite, where she collapsed on a little sofa in the antechamber. Had there been room in her heart for any emotion except terror, she would have been surprised at the sound of an excited dialogue in the salon, but at the moment the voices were part of a nightmare and only the shell of her ear registered what they said.

"I've been six months in Central Asia, or I'd have caught up with this before," a man's voice said, and Helen answered, "I've no sense of guilt whatsoever."

"I don't suppose you have. I'm just panning myself for having picked you out."

"May I ask who told you this tale, Sidney?"

"Two people. A man in New York had seen you in Monte Carlo and said for a year you'd been doing nothing but buying drinks for a bunch of cadgers and spongers. He wondered who was backing you. Then I saw Evelyn Murdock in Paris, and she said Caroline was dissipating night after night; she was thin as a rail and her face looked like death. That's what brought me down here."

"Now listen, Sidney. I'm not going to be bullied about this. Our arrangement was that I was to take Caroline abroad and give her a good time, because you were in love with her or felt guilty about her, or something. You employed me for that and you backed me. Well, I've done just what you wanted. You said you wanted to her meet lots of men."

"I said men."

"I've rounded up what I could. In the first place, she's absolutely indifferent, and when men find that out, they're liable to go away."

He sat down. "Can't you understand that I wanted to do her good, not harm? She's had a rotten time; she's spent most of her youth paying for something that was my fault, so I wanted to make it up the best way I could. I wanted her to have two years of pleasure; I wanted her to learn not to be afraid of men and to have some of the gaiety that I cheated her out of. With the result that you led her into two years of dissipation…" He broke off: "What was that?" he demanded.

Caroline had coughed again, irrepressibly. Her eyes were closed and she was breathing in little gasps as they came into the hall. Her hand opened and her handkerchief dropped to the floor.

In a moment she was lying on her own bed and Sidney was talking rapidly into the phone. In her dazed state the passion in his voice shook her like a vibration, and she whispered, "Please! Please!" in a thin voice. Helen loosened her dress and took off her slippers and stockings.

The doctor made a preliminary examination and then nodded formidably at Sidney. He said that by good fortune a famous Swiss specialist on tuberculosis was staying at the hotel; he would ask for an immediate consultation.

The specialist arrived in bedroom slippers. His examination was as thorough as possible with the instruments at hand. Then he talked to Sidney in the salon.

"So far as I can tell without an X-ray, there is a sudden and widespread destruction of tissue on one side – sometimes happens when the patient is run down in other ways. If the X-ray bears me out, I would recommend an immediate artificial pneumothorax. The only chance is to completely isolate the left lung."

"When could it be done?"

The doctor considered. "The nearest centre for this trouble is Montana Vermala, about three hours from here by automobile. If you start immediately and I telephone to a colleague there, the operation might be performed tomorrow morning."

In the big, springy car Sidney held her across his lap, surrounding with his arms the mass of pillows. Caroline hardly knew who held her, nor did her mind grasp what she had overheard. Life jostled you around so – really very tiring. She was so sick, and probably going to die, and that didn't matter, except that there was something she wanted to tell Dexter.

Sidney was conscious of a desperate joy in holding her, even though she hated him, even though he had brought her nothing but harm. She was his in these night hours, so fair and pale, dependent on his arms for protection from the jolts of the rough road, leaning on his strength at last, even though she was unaware of it; yielding him the responsibility he had once feared and ever since desired. He stood between her and disaster.

Past Domodossola, a dim, murkily lighted Italian town; past Brig, where a kindly Swiss official saw his burden and waved him by without demanding his passport; down the valley of the Rhône, where the growing stream was young and turbulent in the moonlight. Then Sierre, and the haven, the sanctuary in the mountains, two miles above, where the snow gleamed. The funicular waited: Caroline sighed a little as he lifted her from the car.

"It's very good of you to take all this trouble," she whispered formally.

5

F OR THREE WEEKS SHE LAY perfectly still on her back. She breathed and she saw flowers in her room. Eternally her temperature was taken. She was delirious after the operation and in her dreams she was again a girl in Virginia, waiting in the yard for her lover. Dress stay crisp for him – button stay put – bloom magnolia – air stay still and sweet. But the lover was neither Sidney Lahaye nor an abstraction of many men – it was herself, her vanished youth lingering in that garden, unsatisfied and unfulfilled; in her dream she waited there under the spell of eternal hope for the lover that would never come, and who now no longer mattered.

The operation was a success. After three weeks she sat up, in a month her fever had decreased and she took short walks for an hour every day. When this began, the Swiss doctor who had performed the operation talked to her seriously.

"There's something you ought to know about Montana Vermala; it applies to all such places. It's a well-known characteristic of tuberculosis that it tends to hurt the morale. Some of these people you'll see on the streets are back here for the third time, which is usually the last time. They've grown fond of the feverish stimulation of being sick; they come up here and live a life almost as gay as life in Paris – some of the champagne bills in this sanatorium are amazing. Of course, the air helps them, and we manage to exercise a certain salutary control over them, but that kind are never really cured, because in spite of their cheerfulness they don't want the normal world of responsibility. Given the choice, something in them would prefer to die. On the other hand, we know a lot more than we did twenty years ago, and every month we send away people of character completely cured. You've got that chance because your case is fundamentally easy; your right lung is utterly untouched. You can choose; you can run with the crowd and perhaps linger along three years, or you can leave in one year as well as ever."

Caroline's observation confirmed his remarks about the environment. The village itself was like a mining town – hasty, flimsy buildings dominated by the sinister bulk of four or five sanatoriums; chastely cheerful when the sun glittered on the snow, gloomy when the cold seeped through the gloomy pines. In contrast were the flushed, pretty girls in Paris clothes whom she passed on the street, and the well-turned-out men. It was hard to believe they were fighting such a desperate battle, and as the doctor had said, many of them were not. There was an air of secret ribaldry – it was considered funny to send miniature coffins to new arrivals, and there was a continual undercurrent of scandal. Weight, weight, weight; everyone talked of weight – how many pounds one had put on last month or lost the week before.

She was conscious of death around her too, but she felt her own strength returning day by day in the high, vibrant air, and she knew she was not going to die.

After a month came a stilted letter from Sidney. It said:

I stayed only until the immediate danger was past. I knew that, feeling as you do, you wouldn't want my face to be the first thing you saw.

So I've been down here in Sierre at the foot of the mountain, polishing up my Cambodge diary. If it's any consolation for you to have someone who cares about you within call, I'd like nothing better than to stay on here. I hold myself utterly responsible for what happened to you, and many times I've wished I had died before I came into your life.

Now there's only the present – to get you well.

About your son – once a month I plan to run up to his school in Fontainebleau and see him for a few days – I've seen him once now and we like each other. This summer I'll either arrange for him to go to a camp or take him through the Norwegian fjords with me, whichever plan seems advisable.

The letter depressed Caroline. She saw herself sinking into a bondage of gratitude to this man – as though she must thank an attacker for binding up her wounds. Her first act would be to earn the money to pay him back. It made her tired even to think of such things now, but it was always present in her subconscious, and when she forgot it she dreamt of it. She wrote:

Dear Sidney: It's absurd your staying there and I'd much rather you didn't. In fact, it makes me uncomfortable. I am, of course, enormously grateful for all you've done for me and for Dexter. If it isn't too much trouble, will you come up here before you go to Paris, as I have some things to send him?

Sincerely,

Caroline M. Corcoran

He came a fortnight later, full of a health and vitality that she found as annoying as the look of sadness that was sometimes in his eyes. He adored her and she had no use for his adoration. But her strongest sensation was one of fear – fear that since he had made her suffer so much, he might be able to make her suffer again.

"I'm doing you no good, so I'm going away," he said. "The doctors seem to think you'll be well by September. I'll come back and see for myself. After that I'll never bother you again."

If he expected to move her, he was disappointed.

"It may be some time before I can pay you back," she said.

"I got you into this."

"No, I got myself into it… Goodbye, and thank you for everything you've done."

Her voice might have been thanking him for bringing a box of candy. She was relieved at his departure. She wanted only to rest and be alone.

The winter passed. Towards the end she skied a little, and then spring came sliding up the mountain in wedges and spear points of green. Summer was sad, for two friends she had made there died within a week and she followed their coffins to the foreigners' graveyard in Sierre. She was safe now. Her affected lung had again expanded; it was scarred, but healed; she had no fever, her weight was normal and there was a bright mountain colour in her cheeks.

October was set as the month of her departure, and as autumn approached, her desire to see Dexter again was overwhelming. One day a wire came from Sidney in Tibet stating that he was starting for Switzerland.

Several mornings later the floor nurse looked in to toss her a copy of the *Paris Herald* and she ran her eyes listlessly down the columns. Then she sat up suddenly in bed.

AMERICAN FEARED LOST IN BLACK SEA
Sidney Lahaye, Millionaire Aviator, and Pilot Missing Four Days. Tehran, Persia, 5 October...

Caroline sprang out of bed, ran with the paper to the window, looked away from it, then looked at it again.

AMERICAN FEARED LOST IN BLACK SEA
Sidney Lahaye, Millionaire Aviator...

"The Black Sea," she repeated, as if that was the important part of the affair – "in the Black Sea."

She stood there in the middle of an enormous quiet. The pursuing feet that had thundered in her dream had stopped. There was a steady, singing silence.

"Oh-h-h!" she said.

AMERICAN FEARED LOST IN BLACK SEA
Sidney Lahaye, Millionaire Aviator, and Pilot Missing Four Days. Tehran, Persia, 5 October...

Caroline began to talk to herself in an excited voice.

"I must get dressed," she said. "I must get to the telegraph and see whether everything possible has been done. I must start for there." She moved around the room, getting into her clothes. "Oh-h-h!" she whispered. "Oh-h-h!" With one shoe on, she fell face downward across the bed. "Oh, Sidney – Sidney!" she cried, and then again, in terrible protest: "Oh-h-h!" She rang for the nurse. "First, I must eat and get some strength; then I must find out about trains."

She was so alive now that she could feel parts of herself uncurl, unroll. Her heart picked up steady and strong, as if to say, "I'll stick by you," and her nerves gave a sort of jerk as all the old fear melted out of her. Suddenly she was grown, her broken girlhood dropped away from her, and the startled nurse answering her ring was talking to someone she had never seen before.

"It's all so simple. He loved me and I loved him. That's all there is. I must get to the telephone. We must have a consul there somewhere."

For a fraction of a second she tried to hate Dexter because he was not Sidney's son, but she had no further reserve of hate. Living or dead, she was with her love now, held close in his arms. The moment that his footsteps stopped, that there was no more menace, he had overtaken her. Caroline saw that what she had been shielding was valueless – only the little girl in the garden, only the dead, burdensome past.

"Why I can stand anything," she said aloud – "anything – even losing him."

The doctor, alarmed by the nurse, came hurrying in.

"Now, Mrs Corcoran, you're to be quiet. No matter what news you've had, you... Look here, this may have some bearing on it, good or bad."

He handed her a telegram, but she could not open it, and she handed it back to him mutely. He tore the envelope and held the message before her:

PICKED UP BY COALER CITY OF CLYDE STOP ALL WELL...

The telegram blurred; the doctor too. A wave of panic swept over her as she felt the old armour clasp her metallically again. She waited a minute, another minute; the doctor sat down.

"Do you mind if I sit in your lap a minute?" she said. "I'm not contagious any more, am I?"

With her head against his shoulder, she drafted a telegram with his fountain pen on the back of the one she had just received. She wrote:

PLEASE DON'T TAKE ANOTHER AEROPLANE BACK HERE. WE'VE GOT EIGHT YEARS TO MAKE UP, SO WHAT DOES A DAY OR TWO MATTER? I LOVE YOU WITH ALL MY HEART AND SOUL.

The Rubber Cheque

1

WHEN VAL WAS TWENTY-ONE his mother told him of her fourth venture into marriage. "I thought I might as well have someone." She looked at him reproachfully. "My son seems to have very little time for me."

"All right," said Val with indifference, "if he doesn't get what's left of your money."

"He has some of his own. We're going to Europe and I'm going to leave you an allowance of twenty-five dollars a month in case you lose your position. Another thing..." She hesitated. "I've arranged that if you should... if anything should happen to you" – she smiled apologetically – "it won't, but if it should – the remains will be kept in cold storage until I return. I mean I haven't enough money to be able to rush home... You understand, I've tried to think of everything."

"I understand," Val laughed. "Of course, the picture of myself on ice is not very inspiring. But I'm glad you thought of everything." He considered for a moment. "I think that this time, if you don't mind, I'll keep my name – or rather your name – or rather the name I use now."

His social career had begun with that name – three years before it had emboldened him to go through a certain stone gate. There was just a minute when if his name had been Jones he wouldn't have gone, and yet his name was Jones; he had adopted the name Schuyler from his second stepfather.

The gate opened into a heaven-like lawn with driveways curling on it and a pet bear chained in the middle – and a great fantastic, self-indulgent house with towers, wings, gables and verandas, a conservatory, tennis courts, a circus ring for ponies and an empty pool. The gardener, grooming some proud, lucky roses, swung the bowl of his pipe towards him.

"The Mortmains are coming soon?" Val asked.

Val's voice was cultivated – literally, for he had cultivated it himself. The gardener couldn't decide whether he was a friend or an intruder.

"Coming Friday afternoon," he allowed.

"For all summer?"

"I dunno. Maybe a week; maybe three months. Never can tell with them."

"It was a shame to see this beautiful place closed last season," said Val.

He sauntered on calmly, sniffing the aristocratic dust that billowed from the open windows on the ground floor. Where there were not maids cleaning, he walked close and peered in.

"This is where I belong," he thought.

The sight of dogs by the stables dissuaded him from further progress; then, departing, he said goodbye so tenderly to the gardener that the man tipped his cap.

After his adopted name his next lucky break was to meet the Mortmains, riding out on the train from New York four days later. They were across the aisle, and he waited. Presently the opportunity came and, leaning towards them, he proffered with just the right smile of amusement:

"Excuse me, but the tennis court *is* weeded, but there's no water in the pool – or wasn't Monday."

They were startled – that was inevitable; one couldn't crash right in on people without tearing a little bit of diaphanous material, but Val stepped so fast that after a few minutes he was really inside.

"…simply happened to be going by and it looked so nice in there that I wandered in. Lovely place – charming place."

He was eighteen and tall, with blue eyes and sandy hair, and he made Mrs Mortmain wish that her own children had as good manners.

"Do you live in Beardsly?" she enquired.

"Quite near." Val gave no hint that they were "summer people" at the beach, differentiating them from the "estate people" farther back in the hills.

The face of young Ellen Mortmain regarded him with the contagious enthusiasm that later launched a famous cold cream. Her childish beauty was wistful and sad about being so rich and sixteen. Mrs Mortmain liked him too; so did Fräulein and the parrot and the twins. All of them liked him except Ellen's cousin, Mercia Templeton, who was shy and felt somehow cut out. By the time Mrs Mortmain had identified him as a nobody she had accepted him, at least on the summer scale. She even called on Val's mother, finding her "a nervous, pretentious little person". Mrs Mortmain knew that Ellen adored Val, but Val knew his place and she was grateful to him for it. So he kept the friendship of the family through the years that followed – the years of his real education.

With the Mortmains he met other young people till one autumn his name landed on the lists of young men eligible for large dances in New York. In consequence the "career" that he pursued in a brokerage office was simply an interlude between debutante parties at the Ritz and Plaza where he pulsated ecstatically in the stag lines; only occasionally reminding himself of *Percy and Ferdie*, *The Hallroom Boys** in the funny paper. That was all right; he more than paid his entrance fee with his cheerfulness and wit and good manners. What stamped him as an adventurer was that he just could not make any money.

He was trying as hard as he knew how to learn the brokerage business, but he was simply rotten at it. The least thing that happened around the office was more interesting than the stock board or the work on his desk. There was, for instance, Mr Percy Wrackham, the branch manager, who spent his time making lists of the Princeton football team, and of the second team and the third team; one busy morning he made a list of all the quarterbacks at Princeton for thirty years. He was utterly unable to concentrate. His drawer was always full of such lists. So Val, almost helpless against this bad influence, gradually gave up all hopes of concentrating and made lists of girls he had kissed and clubs he would like to belong to and prominent debutantes instead.

It was nice after closing hours to meet a crowd at the movies on 59th Street, which was quite the place to spend the afternoon. The young people sat in the balcony that was like a club, and said whatever came into their minds and kicked the backs of the seats for applause. By and by an usher came up and was tortured for a while – kept rushing into noisy corners, only to find them innocent and silent; but finally the management realized that since he had developed this dependable clientele it were well to let them have their way.

Val never made love to Ellen in the movies, but one day he told her about his mother's new marriage and the thoughtful disposal of the body. He had a very special fascination for her, though now she was a debutante with suitors who had many possessions and went about the business of courtship with dashing intensity. But Val never took advantage of the romantic contrast between his shining manners and his shiny suits.

"That's terrible!" she exclaimed. "Doesn't your mother love you?"

"In her way. But she hates me too, because she couldn't own me. I don't want to be owned."

"How would you like to come to Philadelphia with me this weekend?" she asked impulsively. "There's a dance for my cousin, Mercia Templeton." His heart leapt. Going to a Philadelphia function was something more than "among those present were Messrs Smith, Brown, Schuyler, Brown, Smith". And with Ellen Mortmain! It would be: "Yes. I came down with Ellen Mortmain", or, "Ellen Mortmain asked me to bring her down".

Driving to Philadelphia in a Mortmain limousine, his role took possession of him. He became suddenly a new figure, "Val Schuyler of New York". Beside him Ellen glowed away in the morning sunshine, white and dark and fresh and new, very sure of herself, yet somehow dependent on him.

His role widened; it included being in love with her, appearing as her devoted suitor, as a favourably considered suitor. And suddenly he really was in love with her.

"No one has ever been so beautiful," he broke out. "All season there's been talk about you; they say that no girl has come out for years who has been so authentically beautiful."

"Val! Aren't you divine? You make me feel marvellous!"

The compliments excited her, and she wondered if his humorous friendliness of several years concealed some deep way he felt about her underneath. When she told him that in a month she was going to London to be presented at court, he cried:

"What shall I do without you?"

"You'll get along. We haven't seen so much of each other lately."

"How can I help that? You're rich and I'm poor."

"That doesn't matter if two people really..." She stopped.

"But it does matter," he said. "Don't you think I have any pride?"

Pride was not among his virtues, yet he seemed very proud and lonely to Ellen as he said this. She put her hand on his arm.

"I'll be back."

"Yes, and probably engaged to the Prince of Wales."

"I don't want to go," Ellen said. "I was never so happy as that first summer. I used to go to sleep and wake up thinking of you. Always, whenever I see you, I think of that and it does something to me."

"And to me. But it all seems so hopeless."

The intimacy of the car, its four walls whisking them along towards a new adventure, had drawn them together. They had never talked this way before – and never would have in New York. Their hands clung together for a moment, their glances mingled and blurred into one intimate glance.

"I'll see you at seven," she whispered when she left him at his hotel.

He arrived early at the Templetons'. The less formal atmosphere of Philadelphia made him feel himself even more definitely as Val Schuyler of New York, and he made the circle of the room with the confidence of a grand duke. Save for his name and his fine appearance, the truth was lost back in the anonymity of a great city and, as the escort of Ellen Mortmain, he was almost a visiting celebrity. Ellen had not appeared, and he talked to a nervous girl projecting muscularly from ill-chosen clothes. With a kindliness that came natural to him, he tried to put her at her ease.

"I'm shy," he said. "I've never been in Philadelphia before."

"I'm shyer still, and I've lived here all my life."

"Why are you?"

"Nothing to hang on to. No bridle – nothing. I'd like to be able to carry a swagger stick; fans break when you get too nervous."

"Hang on to me."

"I'd just trip you. I wish this were over."

"Nonsense! You'll probably have a wonderful time."

"No, I won't, but maybe I'll be able to look as if I am."

"Well, I'm going to dance with you as often as I can find you," he promised.

"It's not that. Lots of men will dance with me, since it's my party."

Suddenly Val recognized the little girl of three years ago. "Oh, you're Mercia Templeton."

"You're that boy—"

"Of course."

Both of them tried to appear pleasantly surprised, but after a moment Mercia gave up.

"How we disliked each other," she sighed. "One of the bad memories of my youth. You always made me wriggle."

"I won't make you wriggle any more."

"Are you sure?" she said doubtfully. "You were very superficial then. You only cared about the surface. Of course I see now that you neglected me because my name wasn't Mortmain; but then I thought you'd made a personal choice between Ellen and myself."

Resentment stirred in Val; he hated the reproach of superficiality unless he made it humorously about himself. Actually he cared deeply about things, but the things he cared about were generally considered trivial. He was glad when Ellen Mortmain came into the room.

His eyes met hers, and then all through the evening he followed the shining angel in bluish white that she had become, finding her through intervening flowers at table, behind concealing black backs at the dance. Their mutual glance said: "You and I together among these strange people – we understand."

They danced together, so that other people stopped dancing to watch. Dancing was his great accomplishment and that night was a triumph. They floated together in such unity that other beaux were intimidated, muttering, "Yes, but she's crazy about this Schuyler she came down with."

Sometime in the early morning they were alone and her damp, powdery young body came up close to him in a crush of tired cloth, and he kissed her, trying not to think of the gap between them. But with her presence giving him strength he whispered:

"You'll be so gone."

"Perhaps I won't go. I don't want to go away from you, ever."

Was it conceivable that they could take that enormous chance? The idea was in both their minds, and in the mind of Mercia Templeton as she passed the door of the cloakroom and saw them there crushed against a background of other people's hats and wraps, clinging together. Val went to sleep with the possibility burning in his mind.

Ellen telephoned his hotel in the morning:

"Do you still feel – like we did?"

"Yes, but much more," he answered.

"I'm making Mercia have lunch down there at the hotel. I've got an idea. There may be a few others, but we can sit next to each other."

Eventually there were nine others, all from last night's party, and Val began to think about his mother when they began lunch at two o'clock. Her boat left at seven thirty. But sitting next to Ellen, he forgot for a while.

"I asked some questions," Ellen whispered, "without letting anyone guess. There's a place called Elkton just over the Maryland border, where there's a minister…"

He was intoxicated with his haughty masquerade.

"Why not?" he said concretely.

If Mercia Templeton wouldn't stare at him so cynically from farther down the table!

The waiter laid a cheque at his elbow. Val started; he had had no intention of giving the party, but no one spoke up; the men at the table were as young as himself and as used to being paid for. He carried the cheque into his lap and looked at it. It was for eighty dollars, and he had nine dollars and sixty-five cents. Once more he glanced about the table – once more he saw Mercia Templeton's eyes fixed suspiciously upon him.

"Bring me a blank cheque," he said.

"Yes, sir."

In a minute the waiter returned.

"Could you come to the manager's office?"

"Certainly."

Waiting for the manager, he looked at the clock. It was quarter of four; if he was to see his mother off he would have to leave within the hour. On the other hand, this was overwhelmingly the main chance.

"I find I'm a little short," he said in his easy voice. "I came down for a dance and I miscalculated. Can you take my cheque on" – he named his mother's bank – "for a hundred dollars?"

He had once before done this in an emergency. He hadn't an account at the bank, but his mother made it good.

"Have you any references here, Mr Schuyler?"

He hesitated.

"Certainly – the Charles M. Templetons."

The manager disappeared behind a partition and Val heard him take up a telephone receiver. After a moment the manager returned.

"It's all right, Mr Schuyler. We'll be glad to take your cheque for a hundred dollars."

He wrote out a wire to his mother, advising her, and returned to the table.

"Well?" Ellen said.

He felt a sudden indifference towards her.

"I'd better go back to the Templetons'," she whispered. "You hire a car from the hotel and call for me in an hour. I've got plenty of money."

His guests thanked him for his hospitality.

"It's nothing," he said lightly. "I think Philadelphia is charming."

"Goodbye, Mr Schuyler." Mercia Templeton's voice was cool and accusing.

"Goodbye," Ellen whispered. "In an hour."

As he went inside a telegram was handed him:

YOU HAVE NO RIGHT TO CASH SUCH A CHEQUE AND I AM
INSTRUCTING BANK TO RETURN IT. YOU MUST MAKE IT UP OUT
OF WHAT MONEY YOU HAVE AND IT WILL BE A LESSON TO YOU.
IF YOU CANNOT FIND TIME TO COME TO NEW YORK THIS WILL
SAY GOODBYE.

MOTHER

Hurrying to a booth Val called the Templeton house, but the car had
not yet returned. Never had he imagined such a situation. His only fear
had been that in cashing the cheque he would be irritating his mother,
but she had let him down; he was alone. He thought of reclaiming the
cheque from the office, but would they let him leave the hotel? There
was no alternative – he must catch his mother before she sailed.

He called Ellen again. Still she was not there and the clock ticked
towards five. In a panic he seized his grip and raced for Broad Street
Station.

Three hours later, as he ran up the interminable steps of the pier and
through the long sheds, he heard a deep siren from the river. The boat
was moving, slowly, but moving; there was no touch with shore. He saw
his mother on deck not fifty feet away from him.

"Mother! Mother!" he called.

Mrs Schuyler repressed a look of annoyance and nudged the man
beside her as if to say: "That tall handsome boy there – my son – how
hard it is to leave him!"

"Goodbye, Val. Be a good boy."

He could not bring himself to return immediately to Philadelphia.
Still stunned by his mother's desertion, it did not occur to him that the
most logical way to raise a hundred dollars was to raise a million. He
simply could not face Ellen Mortmain with the matter of the cheque
hanging over his head.

Raising money is a special gift; it is either easy or very difficult. To try it in a moment of panic tends to chill the blood of the prospective lender. The next day Val raised fifty dollars – twenty-five on his salary, fifteen on his second father's cufflinks and ten from a friend. Then, in despair, he waited. Early in the week came a stern letter from the hotel, and in the same mail another letter, which caused him even more acute pain:

Dear Sir: It appears there has been some trouble about a cheque which I recommended the hotel to cash for you while you were in this city.
I will be greatly obliged if you will arrange this matter at once, as it has given us some inconvenience.

Very truly yours,

V. Templeton
(Mrs Charles Martin Templeton)

For another day Val squirmed with despair. Then, when there seemed nothing to do but hand himself over to the authorities, came a letter from the bank saying that his mother had cabled them word to honour the cheque. Somewhere in mid-ocean she had decided that he had probably learnt his lesson.

Only then did he summon the courage to telephone Ellen Mortmain. She had departed for Hot Springs. He hoped she did not know about the cheque; he even preferred for her to believe that he had thrown her over. In his relief at being spared the more immediate agony, he hardly realized that he had lost her.

2

V AL WORE FULL EVENING DRESS to the great debutante balls and danced a stately, sweeping *Wiener Walzer* to the sad and hopeful minors of 'So Blue'.* He was an impressive figure; to imported servants who recognized his lordly manners the size of his tips did not matter. Sometimes he was able to forget that he really wasn't anybody at all.

At Miss Nancy Lamb's debutante dance he stood in the stag line like a very pillar of the social structure. He was only twenty-two, but for three years he had attended such functions and, viewing this newest bevy of girls, he felt rather as if he himself were bringing them out.

Cutting in on one of the newest and prettiest, he was struck by a curious expression that passed over her face. As they moved off together her body seemed to follow him with such reluctance that he asked:

"Is something the matter?"

"Oh, Val…" She hesitated in obvious embarrassment. "Would you mind not dancing with me any more tonight?"

He stopped in surprise.

"Why, what's the matter?"

She was on the verge of tears.

"Mother told me she didn't want me to."

As Val was about to demand an explanation he was cut in on. Shocked, he retreated to the stag line and recapitulated his relations with the girl. He had danced with her twice at every party, once he had sat beside her at supper; he had never phoned her or asked if he could call.

In five minutes another girl made him the same request.

"But what's the matter?" he demanded desperately.

"Oh, I don't know, Val. It's something you're supposed to have done."

Again he was cut in on before he could get definite information. His alarm grew. He could think of no basis upon which any girl's mother should resent his dancing with her daughter. He was invariably correct and dignified, he never drank too much, he had tried to make no enemies, he had been involved in no scandal. As he stood brooding and trying to conceal his wounds and his uncertainty, he saw Mercia Templeton on the floor.

Possibly she had brought up from Philadelphia the story of the cheque he had cashed at the hotel. He knew that she didn't like him, but it seemed incredible that she would initiate a cabal against him. With his jaw set he cut in on her.

"I'm surprised to see you in New York," he said coldly.

"I come occasionally."

"I'd like very much to speak to you. Can we sit out for a minute?"

"Why, I'm afraid not. My mother... What is it you want to say?"

His eyes lifted to the group of older women who sat on a balcony above the dancers. There, between the mothers of the two girls who had refused him, sat Mrs Charles Martin Templeton, of Philadelphia, the crisp "V. Templeton" of the note. He looked no farther.

The next hour was horrible. Half a dozen girls with whom he usually danced asked him with varying shades of regret not to dance with them any more. One girl admitted that she had been so instructed but intended to dance with him anyhow; and from her he learnt the truth – that he was a young man who foisted bad cheques upon trusting Philadelphians. No doubt his pocket was full of such paper, which he intended to dispose of to guileless debutantes.

With helpless rage he glared up at the calm dowagers in the balcony. Then, abruptly and without knowing exactly what he was going to say, he mounted the stairs.

At the moment Mrs Templeton was alone. She turned her lorgnette upon him, cautiously, as one uses a periscope. She did not recognize him, or she pretended not to.

"My name is Val Schuyler," he blurted out, his poise failing him. "About that cheque in Philadelphia; I don't think you understand – it was an accident. It was a bill for a luncheon for your guests. College boys do those things all the time. It doesn't seem fair to hold it against me – to tell New York people."

For another moment she stared at him.

"I don't know what you're talking about," she said coldly, and swung herself and her lorgnette back to the dancers.

"Oh, yes, you do." He stopped, his sense of form asserting itself. He turned and went downstairs and directly to the coat room.

A proud man would have attended no more dances, but new invitations seemed to promise that the matter was but an incident. In a sense this proved true; the Templetons returned to Philadelphia, and even the girls who had turned Val down retracted on the next occasion. Nevertheless, the business had an inconvenient way of cropping up. A party would pass off without any untoward happening; the very next night he would detect that embarrassed look in a new partner and prepare for "I'm very sorry but…" He invented defences – some witty, some bitter, but he found it increasingly insupportable to go around with the threat of a rebuff imminent every time he left the stag line.

With the waning season he stopped going out; the younger generation bored him, he said. No longer did Miss Moon or Miss Whaley at the office say with a certain concealed respect, "Well, I see in the papers you were in society last night." No longer did he leave the office with the sense that in the next few hours he would be gliding through a rich and scintillant world. No longer did the preview of himself in the mirror – with gloves, opera hat and stick – furnish him his mead of our common vanity. He was a man without a country – and for a crime as vain, casual and innocuous as his look at himself in the glass.

Into these gloomy days a ray of white light suddenly penetrated. It was a letter from Ellen.

Dearest Val: I shall be in America almost as soon as this reaches you. I'm going to stay only three days – can you imagine it? – and then coming back to England for Cowes Week.* I've tried to think of a way of seeing you and this is the best. The girl I'm sailing with, June Halbird, is having a weekend party at their Long Island house and says I can bring who I want. Will you come?

Don't imagine from this that there'll be any more sappiness like last winter. You certainly were wise in not letting us do an absurd thing that we would have regretted.

Much love,
Ellen

Val was thoughtful. This might lead to his social resuscitation, for Ellen Mortmain was just a little more famous than ever, thanks to her semi-public swaying between this titled Englishman and that.

He found it fun to be able to say again, "I'm going to the country for the weekend; some people named Halbird…" and to add, "You see, Ellen Mortmain is home," as if that explained everything. To top the effect he sighed, implying that the visit was a somewhat onerous duty, a form of *noblesse oblige*.

She met him at the station. Last year he had been older than she was; now she was as old as he. Her manner had changed; it was interlaced with Anglicisms – the terminal "What?" the double-edged "Quite", the depressing "Cheerio" that always suggested imminent peril. She wore her new swank as light but effective armour around the vulnerability of her money and beauty.

"Val! Do you know that this has turned out to be a kids' party – dear old Yale and all that? Elsa couldn't get anybody I wanted, except you."

"That's my good luck."

"I may have to slip away to another binge for an hour or so – if I can manage it… How are you?"

"Well – and hopeful."

"No money yet?" she commented with disapproval.

"Not a bean."

"Why don't you marry somebody?"

"I can't get over you."

She frowned. "Wouldn't it have been frightful if we'd torn off together? How we'd loathe each other by this time!"

At the Halbirds' he arranged his effects and came downstairs looking for Ellen. There were a group of young people by the swimming pool and he joined them; almost immediately he was conscious of a certain tension in the atmosphere. The conversation faded off whenever he entered it, giving him the impression of continually shaking hands with a glove from which the hand had been withdrawn. Even when Ellen appeared, the coolness persisted. He began to wish he had not come.

Dinner explained everything: Mercia Templeton turned up as one of the guests. If she was spreading the old poison of the cheque story, it was time for a reckoning. With Ellen's help he might lay the ghost at last. But before dessert, Ellen glanced at her watch and said to Mrs Halbird:

"I explained, didn't I, that I have only three days here or I wouldn't do this dashing-off business? I'll join you later in Southampton."

Dismayed, Val watched her abandoning him in the midst of enemies. After dinner he continued his struggle against the current, relieved when it was time to go to the dance.

"And Mr Schuyler," announced Mrs Halbird, "will ride with me."

For a moment he interpreted this as a mark of special consideration, but he was no sooner in the car than he was undeceived.

Mrs Halbird was a calm, hard, competent woman. Ellen Mortmain's unconventional departure had annoyed her and there was a rough nap on the velvet gloves with which she prepared to handle Val.

"You're not in college, Mr Schuyler?"

"No, I'm in the brokerage business."

"Where did you go to school?"

He named a small private school in New York.

"I see." The casualness of her tone was very thin. "I should think you'd feel that these boys and girls were a little young for you."

Val was twenty-three.

"Why, no," he said, hating her for the soft brutality that was coming.

"You're a New Yorker, Mr Schuyler?"

"Yes."

"Let's see. You are a relative of Mrs Martin Schuyler?"

"Why, I believe – distantly."

"What is your father's name?"

"He's dead. My mother is Mrs George Pepin now."

"I suppose it was through your mother that you met Ellen Mortmain. I suppose Mrs Mortmain and your mother were—"

"Why, no – not exactly."

"I see," said Mrs Halbird.

She changed her tone suddenly. Having brought him to his knees, she suddenly offered him gratuitous and condescending advice.

"Don't you agree with me that young people of the same ages should go together? Now, you're working, for example; you're beginning to take life seriously. These young people are just enjoying themselves. They can only be young once, you know." She laughed, pleased with her own tact. "I should think you'd find more satisfaction with people who are working in the world."

He didn't answer.

"I think most of the girls' mothers feel the same way," she said.

They had reached the club at Southampton, but still Val did not reply. She glanced at him quickly in the light as they got out of the car. She was not sure whether or not she had attained her purpose; nothing showed in his face.

Val saw now that after all these years he had reached exactly no position at all. The cheque had been seized upon to give him a questionable reputation that would match his questionable background.

He had been snubbed so often in the past few months that he had developed a protective shell to conceal his injuries. No one watching him go through his minimum of duty dances that night would have guessed the truth – not even the girls, who had been warned against him. Ellen Mortmain did not reappear; there was a rumour of a Frenchman she had met on shipboard. The house party returned to the Halbirds' at three.

Val could not sleep. He lapsed into a dozing dream in which many fashionable men and women sat at a heaped table and offered him champagne, but the glass was always withdrawn before it reached his lips. He sat bolt upright in bed, his throat parched with thirst. The bathroom offered only persistently lukewarm water, so he slipped on his dressing gown and went downstairs. "If anyone saw me," he thought bitterly, "they'd be sure I was after the silver."

Outside the door of the pantry he heard voices that made him stop suddenly and listen.

"Mother wouldn't have let me come if she'd known he'd be here," a girl was saying. "I'm not going to tell her."

"Ellen made the mess," Val heard June Halbird say. "She brought him and I think she had her nerve to pass him off on us."

"Oh, let's forget it," suggested a young man impatiently. "What is he – a criminal or something?"

"Ask Mercia – and cut me some more ham."

"Don't ask me!" said Mercia quickly. "I don't like him, but I don't know anything really bad about him. The cheque you were talking about was only a hundred dollars, not a thousand, like you said; and I've tried a dozen times to shut mother up about it, but last year it was part of her New York conversation. I never thought it was so terrible."

"Just a rubber cheque? Don't embarrass Bill here. He's left them all over New York."

Pushing open the door, Val went into the pantry, and a dozen faces gaped at him. The men looked uncomfortable; a girl tittered nervously and upset a glass of milk.

"I couldn't help overhearing," Val said. "I came down for some water."

Presence he always had – and a sense of the dramatic. Without looking to right or left he took two cubes from a tray, put them in a glass and filled it from the faucet. Then he turned and, with his eyes still lifted proudly above them, said goodnight and went towards the door, carrying his glass of water. One young man whom he had known slightly came forward, saying: "Look here, Val, I think you've had a rotten deal." But Val pushed through the door as if he hadn't heard.

Upstairs, he packed his bag. After a few minutes he heard footsteps and someone knocked, but he stood silent until the person was gone. After a long while he opened his door cautiously and saw that the house was dark and quiet; carrying his suitcase he went downstairs and let himself out.

He had hardly reached one outlet of the circular drive when a car drove in at the other and stopped at the front door. Val stepped quickly behind some sheltering bushes, guessing that it was Ellen at last. The car waited tenderly for a minute; then Val recognized her laugh as she got out. The roadster passed him as it drove out, with the glimpse of a small, satisfied moustache above a lighted cigarette.

Ten minutes later he reached the station and sat down on a bench to wait for the early-morning train.

3

PRINCETON HAD A BAD FOOTBALL SEASON, so one sour Monday, Mr Percy Wrackham asked Val to take himself off, together with the irritating sound of "Hot-cha-cha" which he frequently emitted. Val was somewhat proud of being fired; he had, so to speak, stuck it out to the end. That same month his mother died and he came into a little money.

The change that ensued was amazing; it was fundamental as well as ostensible. Penniless, he had played the young courtier; with twenty thousand in the bank he revived in himself the psychology of Ward McAllister. He abandoned the younger generation which had treated him so shabbily, and, using the connections he had made, blossomed out as a man of the world. His apprenticeship had been hard, but he had served it faithfully, and now he walked sure-footed through the danger-ous labyrinths of snobbery. People abruptly forgot everything about him except that they liked him and that he was usually around; so, as it frequently happens, he attained his position less through his positive virtues than through his ability to take it on the chin.

The little dinners he gave in his apartment were many and charming, and he was a diner-out in proportion. His drift was towards the sophisti-cated section of society, and he picked up some knowledge of the arts, which he blended gracefully with his social education.

Against his new background he was more than ever attractive to women; he could have married one of the fabulously wealthy Cupp twins, but for the moment he was engrossed in new gusto and he wanted to be footloose. Moreover, he went into partnership with a rising art dealer and for a year or so actually made some money.

Regard him on a spring morning in London in the year 1930. Tall, even stately, he treads down Pall Mall as if it were his personal pasture. He meets an American friend and shakes hands, and the friend notices how his shirtsleeve fits his wrist, and his coat sleeve encases his shirtsleeve like a sleeve valve; how his collar and tie are moulded plastically to his neck.

He has come over, he says, for Lady Reece's ball. However, the market is mining him day by day. He buys the newspaper thrust into his hand, and as his eye catches the headline his expression changes.

A cross-channel plane has fallen, killing a dozen prominent people.

"Lady Doncastle," he reads breathlessly, "Major Barks, Mrs Weeks-Tenliffe, Lady Kippery…" He crushes the paper down against his suit and wipes imaginary sweat from his forehead. "What a shock! I was with them all in Deauville a week ago. I might even have taken that plane."

He was bound for the Mortmains' house, a former ducal residence in Cavendish Square. Ellen was the real reason for his having come to London. Ellen, or else an attempt to recapture something in his past, had driven him to withdraw from his languishing art business and rush to Europe on almost the last of his legacy. This morning had come a message to call at their town house.

No sooner was he within it than he got an impression that something was wrong. It was not being opened nor was it being closed, but unaccountably there were people here and there through the corridors, and as he was led to Ellen's own apartment he passed individuals whose presence there would have been inconceivable even in the fantastic swarms of one season ago.

He found Ellen sitting on a trunk in an almost empty room.

"Val, come and get me out of hock," she cried. "Help me hold the trunk down so they won't take it away."

"What is it?" he demanded, startled.

"We're being sold out over our heads – that's what. I'm allowed my personal possessions – if I can keep them. But they've already carted off a box full of fancy-dress costumes; claimed it was professional equipment."

"But why?" he articulated.

"We're poor as hell, Val. Isn't that extraordinary? You've heard about the Mortmain fortune, haven't you? Well, there isn't any Mortmain fortune."

It was the most violent shock of his life; it was simply unimaginable. The bottom seemed to have dropped out of his world.

"It seems we've been in the red for years, but the market floated us. Now we haven't got a single, solitary, individual, particular, specific bean. I was going to ask you, if you're in the art business, would you mind going to the auction and bid in one Juan Gris* that I simply can't exist without?"

"You're poor?"

"Poor? Why, we'd have to find a fortune to pay our debts before we could claim to be that respectable. We're quadruple ruined, that's what we are."

Her voice was a little excited, but Val searched her face in vain for any reflection of his own experience of poverty.

No, that something that could never possibly happen to Ellen Mortmain. She had survived the passing of her wealth; the warm rich current of wellbeing still flowed from her. Still not quite loving her, or not quite being able to love, he said what he had crossed the ocean to say:

"I wish you'd marry me."

She looked at him in surprise.

"Why, that's very sweet. But after all…" She hesitated. "Who are you, Val? I mean, aren't you a sort of a questionable character? Didn't you cheat a lot of people out of a whole lot of money with a forged cheque or something?"

"Oh, that cheque!" he groaned. He told her the story at last, while she kicked her heels against the trunk and the June sun played on her through a stained-glass window.

"Is that the reason you won't marry me?" he demanded.

"I'm engaged to another man."

So she was merely stepping from the wreck of one fortune into the assurance of another.

"I'm marrying a very poor man and we don't know how we'll live. He's in the army and we're going to India."

He experienced a vague envy, a sentimental regret, but it faded out before a stronger sensation; all around her he could feel the vast Mortmain fortune melting down, seeping back into the matrix whence it had come, and taking with it a little of Val Schuyler.

"I hope you didn't leave anything downstairs," Ellen laughed. "They'll attach it if you did. A friend of ours left his golf clubs and some guns; now he's got to buy them back at the auction."

He abandoned her, perched on top of the trunk, and walked solemnly back to the hotel. On his way he bought another paper and turned to the financial page.

"Good Lord!" he exclaimed. "This is the end."

There was no use now in sending a telegram for funds: he was penniless, save for ten dollars and a steamer ticket to New York, and there was a fortnight's bill to pay at the hotel. With a groan he saw himself sinking back into the ranks of the impecunious – like the Mortmains. But with them it had taken four generations; in his case it had taken two years.

More immediate worries harassed him. There was a bill overdue at the hotel, and if he left they would certainly attach his luggage. His splendid French calf luggage. Val's stomach quivered. Then there were his dress things, his fine shirts, the shooting suit he had worn in Scotland, his delicate linen handkerchiefs, his bootmaker's shoes.

He lengthened his stride; it seemed as though already these possessions were being taken from him. Once in his room and reassured by the British stability of them, the ingenuity of the poor asserted itself. He began literally to wind himself up in his clothes. He undressed, put on two suits of underwear and over that four shirts and two suits of clothes, together with two white piqué vests. Every pocket he stuffed with ties, socks, studs, gold-backed brushes and a few toilet articles. Panting audibly, he struggled into an overcoat. His derby looked empty, so he filled it with collars and held them in place with some handkerchiefs. Then, rocking a little on his feet, he regarded himself in the mirror.

He might possibly manage it – if only a steady stream of perspiration had not started to flow from somewhere up high in the edifice and kept pouring streams of various temperatures down his body, until they were absorbed by the heavy blotting paper of three pairs of socks that crowded his shoes.

Moving cautiously, like Tweedledum before the battle, he traversed the hall and rang for the elevator. The boy looked at him curiously, but made no comment, though another passenger made a dry reference to Admiral Byrd. Through the lobby he moved, a gigantic figure of a man. Perhaps the clerks at the desk had a subconscious sense of something being wrong, but he was gone too quickly for them to do anything about it.

"Taxi, sir?" the doorman enquired, solicitous at Val's pale face.

Unable to answer, Val tried to shake his head, but this also proving impossible, he emitted a low, negative groan. The sun was attracted to his bulk as lightning is attracted to metal, as he staggered out towards a bus. Up on top, he thought; it would be cooler up on top.

His training as a hall-room boy stood him in good stead now; he fought his way up the winding stair as if it had been the social ladder. Then, drenched and suffocating, he sank down upon a bench, the bourgeois blood of many Mr Joneses pumping strong in his heart. Not for Val to sit upon a trunk and kick his heels and wait for the end; there was fight in him yet.

4

A YEAR LATER, MR CHARLES Martin Templeton, of Philadelphia, faced in his office a young man who had evidently obtained admittance by guile. The visitor admitted that he had no claim upon Mr Templeton's attention save that he had once been the latter's guest some six years before.

"It's the matter of that cheque," he said determinedly. "You must remember. I had a luncheon forced on me that should have been your luncheon party, because I was a poor young man. I gave a cheque that was really a pretty good cheque, only slow, but your wife went around ruining me just the same. To this day it meets me wherever I go, and I want compensation."

"Is this blackmail?" demanded Mr Templeton, his eyes growing hostile.

"No, I only want justice," said Val. "I couldn't make money during the boom. How do you expect me to make it during the Depression? Your wife did me a terrible injury. I appeal to your conscience to atone for it by giving me a position."

"I remember about the cheque," said Mr Templeton thoughtfully. "I know Mercia always considered that her mother went too far."

"She did, indeed," said Val. "There are thousands of people in New York who think to this day that I am a successful swindler."

"I have no cheques that need signing," said Mr Templeton thoughtfully, "but I can send you out to my farm."

Val Schuyler of New York on his knees in old overalls, planting cabbages and beans and stretching endless rows of strings and coaxing tender vines around them. As he toiled through the long farming day he softly recapitulated his amazing week at Newport in Twenty-nine, and the *Wiener Walzer* he had danced with the Hon. Elinor Guise on the night of Lord Clan-Carly's coming of age.

Now another Scottish voice buzzed in his ear:

"Ye work slow, Schuyler. Burrow down into the ground more."

"The idiot imagines I'm a fallen aristocrat," Val thought.

He sat back on his haunches, pulling the weeds in the truck garden. He had a sense of utter waste, of being used for something for which nothing in his past had equipped him. He did not understand why he was here, nor what forces had brought him here. Almost never in his life had he failed to play the rules of the game, yet society had abruptly said: "You have been charming, you have danced with our girls, you have made parties go, you have taken up the slack of dull

people. Now go out in the backyard and try it on the cabbages."
Society. He had leant upon its glacial bosom like a trusting child,
feeling a queer sort of delight in the diamonds that cut hard into
his cheek.

He had really asked little of it, accepting it at its own valuation,
since to do otherwise would have been to spoil his own romantic
conception of it. He had carried his essential boyishness of attitude
into a milieu somewhat less stable than gangdom and infinitely less
conscientious about taking care of its own. And they had set him
planting cabbages.

"I should have married Emily Parr," he thought, "or Esther Manly,
or Madeline Quarrels, or one of the Dale girls. I should have dug in –
entrenched myself."

But he knew in his sadness that the only way he could have got what
he really wanted was to have been born to it. His precious freedom –
not to be owned.

"I suppose I'll have to make the supreme sacrifice," he said.

He contemplated the supreme sacrifice and then he contemplated the
cabbages. There were tears of helplessness in his eyes. What a horrible
choice to make!

Mercia Templeton rode up along the road and sat on her horse watching him for a long time.

"So here you are at last," she said, "literally, if not figuratively, at my
feet."

Val continued working as if she were not there.

"Look at me!" she cried. "Don't you think I'm worth looking at now?
People say I've developed. Oh, Lord, won't you ever look at me?"

With a sigh, Val turned around from the row of cabbages.

"Is this a proposal of marriage?" he asked. "Are you going to make
me an honest man?"

"Nobody could do that, but at least you're looking at me. What do
you see?"

He stared appraisingly.

"Really rather handsome," he said. "A little inclined to take the bit in your teeth."

"Oh, Heavens, you're arrogant!" she cried, and spurred her horse down the road.

Val Schuyler turned sadly back to his cabbages. But he was sophisticated now; he had that, at least, from his expensive education. He knew that Mercia would be back.

On Schedule

1

I N SEPTEMBER, RENÉ'S OLD HOUSE seemed pretty fine to him, with its red maples and silver birches and the provident squirrels toiling overtime on the lawn. It was on the outskirts of a university town, a rambling frame structure that had been a residence in the Eighties, the county poorhouse in the Nineteen-hundreds, and now was a residence again. Few modern families would care to live there, amid the groans of moribund plumbing and without even the silvery "Hey!" of a telephone, but René, at first sight of its wide veranda, which opened out into a dilapidated park of five acres, loved it for reminding him of a lost spot of his childhood in Normandy. Watching the squirrels from his window reminded René that it was time to complete certain winter provisions of his own, and, laying aside his work, he took a large sheet of paper ruled into oblongs and ran over it once again. Then he went into the hall and called up the front staircase:

"Noël."

"Yes, Daddy."

"I wish to see you, *chérie*."

"Well, you told me to put away the soldiers."

"You can do that later. I want you to go over to the Slocums' and get Miss Becky Snyder, and then I wish to speak to you both together."

"Becky's here, Daddy; she's in the bathtub."

René started. "In the bath…"

The cracks and settlings of the house had created fabulous acoustics, and now another voice, not a child's, drifted down to him:

"The water runs so slow over at the Slocums', it takes all day to draw a bath. I didn't think you'd mind, René."

"Mind!" he exclaimed vaguely. As if the situation was not already delicate. "Mind!" If Becky took baths here she might just as well be living here, so far as any casual visitor would conclude. He imagined himself trying to explain to Mrs Dean-of-the-Faculty McIntosh the very complicated reasons why Becky Snyder was upstairs taking a bath.

At that, he might succeed – he would have blushed to attempt it in France.

His daughter, Noël, came downstairs. She was twelve, and very fair and exquisitely made, like his dead wife; and often in the past he had worried about that. Lately she had become as robust as any American child and his anxieties were concentrated upon her education, which, he had determined, was going to be as good as that of any French girl.

"Do you realize that your school starts tomorrow?"

"Yeah."

"What is that?"

"Yes, Daddy."

"I am going to be busier than I have ever been in my life."

"With all that water?"

"With all that water – think of all the baths Becky could take in it. And with the nice cute little power plant of my own the Foundation has built me. So, for you, Noël, I have prepared a schedule, and my secretary has made three copies – one for you, one for me and one for Becky. We shall make a pocket in the back of your arithmetic in which to keep your copy. You must always keep it there, for if you lose it, then our whole day is thrown out of joint."

Noël shifted restlessly in her chair.

"What I don't understand," she said, "is why I can't take just like the other girls? Why I have to do a lot of goofy—"

"Do not use that word!"

"Well, why I can't do like everybody else?"

"Then you don't want to continue the piano."

"Oh, yes, piano; but why do I have to take French out of school every day?"

René rose, pushing his fingers distractedly over his prematurely iron-grey hair – he was only thirty-four.

"What is the use of explaining things to you?" he cried. "Listen. You speak perfect French and you want to preserve it, don't you? And you can't study in your school what you already know more accurately than a sophomore in the college."

"Then why—"

"Because no child retains a language unless she continues it till fourteen. Your brain…" René tapped his own ferociously. "It cannot do it."

Noël laughed, but her father was serious.

"It is an advantage!" he cried. "It will help you – it will help you to be an actress at the Comédie Française. Do you understand?"

"I don't want to be an actress any more," confessed Noël. "I'd rather electrolize water for the Foundation like you, and have a little doll's power plant, and I can keep up my French talking to you in the evening. Becky could join in, because she wants to learn anyhow."

Her father nodded his head sadly.

"Very well, then; all right." He brushed the paper schedule aside; being careful, however, that it didn't go into the wastebasket. "But you cannot grow up useless in this house. I will give you a practical education instead. We will stop the school and you can study sewing, cooking, domestic economy. You can learn to help about the house." He sat down at his desk thoroughly disgusted, and made a gesture of waving her away, to be left alone with his disappointment.

Noël considered. Once this had been a rather alarming joke – when her marks were unsatisfactory, her father always promised to bring her up as a fine cook. But though she no longer believed him, his logic had the effect of sobering her. Her own case was simply that she hated running around to extra lessons in the middle of the morning; she wanted to be exactly like the other girls in school.

"All right, then," she said. Both of them stood up as Becky, still damp and pink from her bath, came into the room.

Becky was nineteen, a startling little beauty, with her head set upon her figure as though it had been made separately and then placed there with the utmost precision. Her body was sturdy, athletic; her head was a bright, happy composition of curves and shadows and vivid colour, with that final kinetic jolt, the element that is eventually sexual in effect, which made strangers stare at her. Who has not had the excitement of seeing an apparent beauty from afar; then, after a moment, seeing that same face grow mobile and watching the beauty disappear moment by moment, as if a lovely statue had begun to walk with the meagre joints of a paper doll? Becky's beauty was the opposite of that. The facial muscles pulled her expressions into lovely smiles and frowns, disdains, gratifications and encouragements; her beauty was articulated, and expressed vividly whatever it wanted to express.

Beyond that, she was an undeveloped girl, living for the moment on certain facets of René du Cary's mind. There was no relation between herself and Noël as yet except that of fellow pupils – though they suspected each other faintly as competitors for his affection.

"So now," René pursued, "let us get this exact, darlings. Here we have one car, no telephone and three lives. To drive the car we have you" – this to Becky – "and me, and usually Aquilla's brother. I will not even explain the schedule, but I assure you that it is perfect. I worked on it until one this morning."

They sat obediently while he studied it with pride for a moment.

"Now here is a typical day: on Tuesday, Aquilla's brother takes me to laboratory, dropping Noël at her school; when he returns to house, Becky takes car to tennis practice, calls for Noël and takes her to Mademoiselle Ségur's. Then she does shopping – and so forth."

"Suppose I have no shopping?" suggested Becky.

"Then you do 'and so forth'. If there is no 'and so forth', you drive car to laboratory and catch bus home – in that case, I bring Aquilla's brother – I mean Noël" – he stared at the schedule, screwing up his eyes – "I bring Noël from Mademoiselle's back to school and continue home. Then" – he hesitated – "and then…"

Noël rocked with amusement.

"It's like that riddle," she cried, "about the man who had to cross the river with the goose and the fox and the—"

"Wait one minute!" René's voice was full of exasperated flats. "There is one half-hour left out here, or else Aquilla's brother will have to lunch before it is cooked."

Becky, who had been listening with a helpful expression, became suddenly a woman of sagacity and force. The change, expressed in every line of her passionate face, startled René, and he listened to her with a mixture of awe, pride and disapproval.

"Why not let my tennis lessons go this fall?" she suggested. "After all, the most important things are your experiment and Noël's education. Tennis will be over in a month or two. It just complicates everything."

"Give up the tennis!" he said incredulously. "Idiotic child! Of course you'll continue. American women must be athletes. It is the custom of the country. All we need is complete cooperation."

Tennis was Becky's forte. She had been New Jersey scholastic champion at sixteen, thereby putting the small town of Bingham upon the map. René had followed the careers of his compatriots Lacoste and Lenglen,* and he was very particular about Becky's tennis. He knew that already there had been a trickle of talk in the community about himself and Becky – this young girl he had found somewhere or nowhere, and had recently deposited in the keeping of Mr and Mrs Slocum on the adjacent truck farm. Becky's tennis had a certain abstract value that would matter later. It was a background for Becky – or rather it was something that would stand between Becky and her lack of any background whatsoever. It had to go into the schedule, no matter how difficult it made things.

René had loved his wife, an American, and after she faded off agonizingly in Switzerland, three years had dragged by before the tragic finality of the fact ceased to present itself at the end of sleep as a black period that ended the day before it began. Curiously crediting the legend that every seven years the human body completely renews itself, she had put a provision in her last sick will that if he married within seven years of her death, the moderate income she bequeathed him should accrue in trust for Noël. What he did after the seven years would be, Edith considered, an act of someone she had never known. The provision had not bothered him. It was rather a convenience to know that marriage was out of the question, and many a trap set for him had gone unsprung during his years as a widower in the college town. The income made it possible for him to stay in research, under the aegis of one of those scientific foundations that gravitated to the university, instead of seeking a livelihood as a pedagogue in a foreign land. In his own line he was a man with that lucky touch. Last year, in cleaning up the junk of someone else's abandoned experiment, he had stumbled upon an entirely new technique in the activation of a catalyst for bringing about chemical reactions. He felt that after another year he would be able to provide for Noël far better than could his wife's shrunken trust fund.

So, for a thousand days he wore his grief down, and eventually he found that his daughter was growing up and that work really was the best thing with which to fill a life. He settled down, and existence became as foreshortened as the rhythm of the college itself.

"My relations with my daughter," he used to say in those days, "are becoming what you call the Electra complex. If man was an adaptable animal, I should develop a lap and a very comfortable bosom and become a real mother to her, but I cannot. So, how can I put a stop to this father-and-daughter complex we are developing between us?"

The problem solved itself in its own terms. René was in love with youth, and one day he saw Becky Snyder's beauty peering over the back of a cut-down flivver stalled on the Lincoln Highway. It was an old flivver, even for its old-flivverish function of bearing young love from nook to nook. Jokes climbed feebly upon its sides and a great "Bingham HS 1932" defaced – if one can call it that – the radiator. René du Cary, aloof as any university don spending an afternoon on his bicycle, would have passed it with a shrug of amusement if he had not suddenly perceived the cause of the flivver's motionless position in the road – a deeply intoxicated young man was draped across the wheel.

"Now, this is too bad," he thought, when, with his bicycle in the back seat, he was conducting the car towards its destination. He kept imagining Noël in a like situation. Only when they had returned the young man and his movable couch to the bosom of his family, and he sat with Becky and her deaf aunt on the farmhouse stoop, did he realize how authentically, radiantly beautiful she was and want to touch her hair and her shining face and the nape of her neck – the place where he kissed Noël goodnight.

She walked with him to the gate.

"You must not permit that young man to call on you," he said. "He's not good for you."

"Then what do I do?" She smiled. "Sit home?"

He raised his hands.

"Are there no more solid citizens in this village?"

Becky looked impatient, as if he ought to know there weren't.

"I was engaged to a nice fellow that died last year," she informed him, and then with pride: "He went to Hamilton. I was going to the spring dance with him. He got pneumonia."

"I'm sorry," said René.

"There're no boys around here. There was a man said he'd get me a job on the stage in New York, but I know that game. My friend here – a girl, I mean – she goes to town to get picked up by students. It's just hard luck for a girl to be born in a place like this. I mean, there's no future. I met some men through playing tennis, but I never saw them again."

He listened as the muddled concepts poured forth – the mingled phrases of debutante, waif and country girl. The whole thing confused him – the mixture of innocence, opportunism, ignorance. It made him feel very foreign and far off.

"I will collect some undergraduates," he surprised himself by promising. "They should appreciate living beauty, if they appreciate nothing else."

But that wasn't the way it worked out. The half-dozen seniors, the lady who came to pour tea on his porch, recognized, before half an hour had passed, that he was desperately in love with the girl, that he didn't know it, that he was miserable when two of the young men made engagements with her. Next time she came, there were no young men.

"I love you and I want you to marry me," he said.

"But I'm simply… I don't know what to say. I never thought—"

"Don't try to think. I will think for us both."

"And you'll teach me," she said pathetically. "I'll try so hard."

"We can't be married for seven more months because… My Heavens, you are beautiful!"

It was June then, and they got to know each other in a few long afternoons in the swing on the porch. She felt very safe with him – a little too safe.

That was the first time when the provision in Edith's will really bothered René. The seven specified years would not be over until December, and the interval would be difficult. To announce the engagement would be to submit Becky to a Regents Examination by the ladies of the university. Because he considered himself extravagantly lucky to have discovered such a prize, he hated the idea of leaving her to rusticate in Bingham. Other connoisseurs of beauty, other discerning foreigners, might find her stalled on the road with unworthy young men. Moreover, she needed an education in the social civilities and, much as the railroad kings of the pioneer West sent their waitress sweethearts to convents in order to prepare them for their high destinies, he considered sending Becky to France with a chaperone for the interval. But he could not afford it, and ended by installing her with the Slocums next door.

"This schedule," he said to her, "is the most important thing in our lives; you must not lose your copy."

"No, dearest."

"Your future husband wants a lot; he wants a beautiful wife and a well-brought-up child, and his work to be very good, and to live in the country. There is limited money. But with method," he said fiercely – "method for one, method for all – we can make it go."

"Of course we can."

After she had kissed him and clung to him and gone, he sat looking out at the squirrels still toiling in the twilight.

"How strange," he thought. "For the moment my role is that of *supérieure* in a convent. I can show my two little girls about how good work is, and about politeness. All the rest one either has or hasn't.

"The schedule is my protection; for now I will have no more time to think of details, and yet they must not be educated by the money-changers of Hollywood. They should grow up; there is too much of keeping people children for ever. The price is too high; the bill is always presented to someone in the end."

His glance fell on the table. Upon it, carefully folded, lay a familiar-looking paper – the typewritten oblongs showed through. And on the chair where Becky had sat, its twin rested. The schedules, forgotten and abandoned, remained beside their maker.

"*Mon Dieu!*" he cried, his fingers rising to his young grey hair. "*Quel commencement!** Noël!"

2

WITH A SORT OF QUIVERING HEAVE like the attempt of a team to move a heavy load, René's schedule got in motion. It was an uncertain motion – the third day Noël lost her schedule and went on a school botany tour, while Aquilla's brother – a coloured boy who had some time ago replaced a far-wandering houseman, but had never quite acquired a name of his own in the household – waited for her two hours in front of the school, so that Becky missed her tennis lesson and Mlle Ségur, inconvenienced, complained to René. This was on a day that René had passed in despair trying to invent a process for keeping the platinum electrodes nicely blurred in a thousand glass cells. When he came home he blew up and Noël, at his request, had her supper in bed.

Each day plunged him deeper into his two experiments. One was his attempt to develop the catalyst upon which he had stumbled; the second was based on the new knowledge that there are two kinds of water. Should his plan of decomposing electrolytically one hundred thousand gallons of water yield him the chance of studying the two sorts spectrographically, the results might be invaluable. The experiment was backed by a commercial firm as well as by the Foundation, but it was already running into tens of thousands of dollars – there was the small power plant built for his use, the thousand platinum electrodes, each in its glass jar, as well as the time consumed in the difficult and tedious installation of the apparatus.

Necessarily, the domestic part of the day receded in importance. It was nice to know that his girls were safe and well occupied, that there would be two faces waiting for him eagerly at home. But for the moment he could not divert any more energy to his family. Becky had tennis and a reading list she had asked him for. She wanted to be a fine wife to René; she knew that he was trying to rear some structure of solidity in which they could all dwell together, and she guessed that it was the strain of the present situation that made him often seem to put undue emphasis on minor matters. When he began to substitute moments of severe strictness with Noël for the time he would have liked to devote to her, especially to her lessons – which were coming back marked "careless" – Becky protested. Whereupon René insisted that his intensity of feeling about Noël's manners was an attempt to save her trouble, to conserve her real energies for real efforts and not let them be spent to restore the esteem of her fellows, lost in a moment of carelessness or vanity. "Either one learns politeness at home," René said, "or the world teaches it with a whip – and many young people in America are ruined in that process. How do I care whether Noël 'adores' me or not, as they say? I am not bringing her up to be my wife."

Still, and in spite of everything, the method was not working. His private life was beginning to interfere with it. If he had been able to spend another half an hour in the laboratory that day when he knew Becky was waiting discreetly a little way down the road, or even if he could have sent an overt message to her, saying that he was delayed thereby, then the tap would not have been left on and a quantity of new water would not have run into the water already separated according to its isotope, thus necessitating starting over. Work, love, his child – his demands did not seem to him exorbitant; he had had forethought and had made a schedule which anticipated all minor difficulties.

"Let us reconsider," he said, assembling his girls again. "Let us consider that we have a method, embodied in this schedule. A method is better and bigger than a man."

"Not always," said Becky.

"How do you mean, not always, little one?"

"Cars really do act up like ours did the other day, René. We can't stand before them and read them the schedule."

"No, my darling," he said excitedly. "It is to ourselves we read the schedule. We foresee – we have the motor examined, we have the tank filled."

"Well, we'll try to do better," said Becky. "Won't we, Noël? You and I – and the car."

"You are joking, but I am serious."

She came close to him.

"I'm not joking, darling. I love you with all my heart and I'm trying to do everything you say – even play tennis: though I'd rather run over and keep your house a little cleaner for you."

"My house?" he stared around vaguely. "Why, my house is very clean. Aquilla's sister comes in every other Friday."

He had cause to remember this one Sunday afternoon a week later, when he had a visit from his chief assistant, Charles Hume, and his wife. They were old friends, and he perceived immediately the light of old friends bent on friendship in their eyes. And how was little Noël? They had had Noël in their house for a week the previous summer.

René called upstairs for Noël, but got no answer.

"She is in the fields somewhere." He waved his hand vaguely. "All around, it is country."

"All very well while the days are long," said Dolores Hume. "But remember there are such things as kidnappings."

René shut his mind swiftly against a new anxiety.

"How are you, René?" Dolores asked. "Charles thinks you've been overdoing things."

"Now, dear," Charles protested. "I—"

"You be still. I've known René longer than you have. You two men fuss and fume over those jars all day and then René has his hands full with Noël all evening."

Did René's eyes deceive him, or did she look closely to see how he was taking this?

"Charles says this is an easy stage of things, so we wondered if we could help you by taking Noël while you went for a week's rest."

Annoyed, René answered abruptly: "I don't need a rest and I can't go away." This sounded rude; René was fond of his assistant. "Not that Charles couldn't carry on quite as well as I."

"It's really poor little Noël I'm thinking of as much as you. Any child needs personal attention."

His wrath rising, René merely nodded blandly.

"If you won't consider that," Dolores pursued, "I wonder you don't get a little coloured girl to keep an eye on Noël in the afternoon. She could help with the cleaning. I've noticed that Frenchmen may be more orderly than American men, but not a bit cleaner."

She drew her hand experimentally along the woodwork.

"Heavens!" she exclaimed, awed. Her hand was black, a particularly greasy, mouldy, creepy black, with age-old furniture oil in it and far-drifted grime.

"What a catastrophe!" cried René. Only last week he had refused to let Becky clean the house. "I beg a thousand pardons. Let me get you—"

"It serves me right," she admitted, "and don't you do anything about it. I know this house like my pocket."

When she had gone, Charles Hume said:

"I feel I ought to apologize to you for Dolores. She's a strange woman, René, and she has no damn business butting into your affairs like this!"

He stopped. His wife was suddenly in the room again, and the men had an instant sense of something gone awry. Her face was shocked and hurt, stricken, as if she had been let down in some peculiarly personal way.

"You might not have let me go upstairs," she said to René. "Your private affairs are your own, but if it was anybody but you, René, I'd think it was a rather bad joke."

For a moment René was bewildered. Then he half-understood, but before he could speak Dolores continued coldly:

"Of course I thought it was Noël in the tub, and I walked right in."

René was all gestures now; he took a long, slow, audible breath; raising his hands slowly to his eyes, he shook his head in time to a quick *tck*, *tck*, *tck*, *tck*. Then, laying his cards on the table with a sudden downward movement of his arms, he tried to explain. The girl was the niece of a neighbour – he knew, even in the midst of his evasive words, that it was no use. Dolores was just a year or so older than that war generation which took most things for granted. He knew that previous to her marriage she had been a little in love with him, and he saw the story going out into the world of the college town. He knew this even when she pretended to believe him at the last, and when Charles gave him a look of understanding and a tacit promise with his eyes that he'd shut her up, as they went out the door.

"I feel so terrible," mourned Becky. "It was the one day the water at the Slocums' wouldn't run at all, and I was so hot and sticky I thought I'd just jump in for two seconds. That woman's face when it came in the door! 'Oh, it's not Noël,' she said, and what could I say? From the way she stared at me, she ought to have seen."

It was November and the campus was riotous once a week with violets and chrysanthemums, hot dogs and football badges, and all the countryside was a red-and-yellow tunnel of leaves around the flow of many cars. Usually René went to the games, but not this year. Instead he attended upon the activities of the precious water that was not water, that was a heaven-like, mysterious fluid that might cure mental diseases in the Phacochoerus, or perhaps only grow hair on eggs – or else he played valet to his catalyst, wound in five thousand dollars' worth of platinum wire and gleaming dully at him every morning from its quartz prison.

He took Becky and Noël up there one day because it was unusually early. He was slightly disappointed, because Noël was absorbed in an inspection of her schedule while he explained the experiments. The tense, sunny room seemed romantic to Becky, with its odour of esoteric gases, the faint perfumes of future knowledge, the low electric sizz in the glass cells.

"Daddy, can I look at your schedule one minute?" Noël asked. "There's one dumb word that I never know what it means."

He handed it towards her vaguely, for a change in the calibre and quality of the sound in the room made him aware that something was happening. He knelt down beside the quartz vessel with a fountain pen in his hand.

He had changed the conditions of his experiment yesterday, and now he noted quickly:

Flow of 500 cc per minute, temperature 255° C. Changed gas mixture to 2 vol. oxygen and 1.56 vol. nitrogen. Slight reaction, about 1 per cent. Changing to 2 vol. o and 1.76 vol. N. Temperature 283° C. Platinum filament is now red-hot.

He worked quickly, noting the pressure gauge. Ten minutes passed; the filament glowed and faded, and René put down figure after figure. When he arose, with a rather faraway expression, he seemed almost surprised to see Becky and Noël still there.

"Well, now; that was luck," he said.

"We're going to be late to school," Becky told him, and then added apologetically: "What happened, René?"

"It is too long to explain."

"Of course you see, Daddy," said Noël reprovingly, "that we have to keep the schedule."

"Of course, of course. Go along." He kissed them each hungrily on the nape of the neck, watching them with pride and joy, yet putting them aside for a while as he walked around the laboratory with some of the unworldliness of an altar boy. The electrolysis also seemed to be going better. Both of his experiments, like a recalcitrant team, had suddenly decided to function, realizing the persistence they were up against.

He heard Charles Hume coming in, but he reserved his news about the catalyst while they concentrated upon the water. It was noon before he had occasion to turn to his notes – realized with a shock that he had no notes. The back of the schedule on which he had taken them was astonishingly, inexplicably blank; it was as if he had written in vanishing ink or under the spell of an illusion. Then he saw what had happened – he had made the notes on Noël's schedule and she had taken it to school. When Aquilla's brother arrived with a registered package, he dispatched him to the school with the schedule to make the exchange. The data he had observed seemed irreplaceable, the more so as – despite his hopeful "Look! Look! Come here, Charles, now, and look!" – the catalyst failed entirely to act up.

He wondered what was delaying Aquilla's brother and felt a touch of anxiety as he and Charles walked up to Main Street for lunch. Afterwards Charles left, to jack up a chemistry-supply firm in town.

"Don't worry too hard," he said. "Open the windows – the room's full of nitrogen chloride."

"Don't worry about that."

"Well…" Charles hesitated. "I didn't agree with Dolores's attitude the other day, but I think you're trying to do too much."

"Not at all," René protested. "Only, I am anxious to get possession of my notes again. It might be months, or never, before I would blunder on that same set of conditions again."

He was hardly alone before a small voice on the telephone developed as Noël calling up from school:

"Daddy?"

"Yes, baby."

"Can you understand French or English better on the phone?"

"What? I can understand anything."

"Well, it's about my schedule."

"I am quite aware of that. You took away my schedule. How do you explain that?"

Noël's voice was hesitant: "But I didn't, Daddy. You handed me your schedule with a whole lot of dumb things on the back."

"They are not dumb things!" he exclaimed. "They are very valuable things. That is why I sent Aquilla's brother to exchange the schedules. Has that been done?"

"I was gone to French when he came, so he went away – I guess on account of that day he was so dumb and waited. So I haven't got any schedule and I don't know whether Becky is coming for me after play hour or whether I'm to ride out with the Sheridans and walk home from there."

"You haven't got any schedule at all?" he demanded, his world breaking up around him.

"I don't know what became of it. Maybe I left it in the car."

"Maybe you left it in the car?"

"It wasn't mine."

He set down the receiver because he needed both hands now for the gesture he was under compulsion to make. He threw them up so high that it seemed as if they left his wrists and were caught again on their descent. Then he seized the phone again.

"…because school closes at four o'clock; and if I wait for Becky and she doesn't come, then I'll have to be locked out."

"Listen," said René. "Can you hear? Do you want me to speak in English or French?"

"Either one, Daddy."

"Well, listen to me: goodbye."

He hung up. Regretting for the first time the lack of a phone at home, he ran up to Main Street and found a taxi, which he urged, with his foot on an imaginary back-seat accelerator, in the direction of home.

The house was locked; the car was gone; the maid was gone; Becky was gone. Where she was gone he had no idea, and the Slocums could give him no information… The notes might be anywhere now, kicked carelessly into the street, crumpled and flung away.

"But Becky will recognize it as a schedule," he consoled himself. "She would not be so formidable as to throw away our schedule."

He was by no means sure that it was in the car. On a chance, he had the taxi drive him into the coloured district with the idea that he might get some sort of orientation from Aquilla's brother. René had never before searched for a coloured man in the Negro residential quarter of an American city. He had no idea at first of what he was attempting, but after half an hour the problem assumed respectable dimensions.

"Do you know" – so he would call to dark and puzzled men on the sidewalks – "where I can find the house of Aquilla's brother, or of Aquilla's sister – either one?"

"I don't even know who Aquilla is, boss."

René tried to think whether it was a first or a last name, and gave up as he realized that he never had known. As time passed, he had more and more a sense that he was pursuing a phantom; it began to shame him to ask the whereabouts of such ghostly, blatantly immaterial lodgings as the house of Aquilla's brother. When he had stated his mission a dozen times, sometimes varying it with hypocritical pleas as to the whereabouts of Aquilla's sister, he began to feel a little crazy.

It was colder. There was a threat of first winter snow in the air, and at the thought of his notes being kicked out into it, buried beneath it, René abandoned his quest and told the taxi man to drive home, in the hope that Becky had returned. But the house was deserted and cold. With the taxi throbbing outside, he threw coal into the furnace and then drove back into the centre of town. It seemed to him that if he stayed on Main Street he would sooner or later run into Becky and the car – there were not an unlimited number of places to pass an afternoon in a regimented community of seven thousand people. Becky had no friends here – it was the first time he had ever thought of that. Literally there was almost no place where she could be.

Aimless, feeling almost as intangible as Aquilla's brother, he wandered along, glancing into every drugstore and eating shop. Young people were always eating. He could not really enquire of anyone if they had seen her, for even Becky was only a shadow here, a person hidden and unknown, a someone to whom he had not yet given reality. Only two things were real – his schedule, for the lack of which he was utterly lost and helpless, and the notes written on its back.

It was colder, minute by minute; a blast of real winter, sweeping out of the walks beside College Hall, made him wonder suddenly if Becky was going to pick up Noël. What had Noël said about being locked out when the school was closed? Not in weather like this. With sudden concern and self-reproach, René took another taxi and drove to the school, but it was closed and dark inside.

"Then, perhaps, she is lost too," he thought. "Quite possibly she tried to walk herself home by herself and was kidnapped, or got a big chill, or was run over."

He considered quite seriously stopping at the police station, and only decided against it when he was unable to think what he could possibly report to them with any shred of dignity.

"…that a man of science, has managed, in one afternoon, in this one little town, to lose everything."

3

MEANWHILE, BECKY WAS THOROUGHLY enjoying herself. When Aquilla's brother returned with the car at noon, he handed over Noël's schedule with no comment save that he had not been able to give it to Noël because he could not find her. He was finished with European culture for the day, and was already crossing the Mediterranean in his mind while Becky tried to pump further information out of him.

A girl she had met through tennis had wangled the use of one of the club squash courts for the early hours of the afternoon. The squash was good; Becky soaked and sweated in the strange, rather awesome atmosphere of masculinity, and afterwards, feeling fine and cool, took out her own schedule to check up on her duties of the afternoon. The schedule said to call for Noël, and Becky set out with all her thoughts in proportion – the one about herself and tennis; the one about Noël, whom she had come to love and learn with the evenings when René was late at the laboratory; the one about René, in whom she recognized the curious secret of power. But when she arrived at the school and found Noël's pencilled note on the gatepost, an epidemic of revolt surged suddenly over her.

Dear Becky. Had Daddy's schedule and lost it and do not know if you are coming or not. Mrs Hume told me I could wait at her house, so please pick me up there if you get this?
                                                            Noël

If there was one person Becky had no intention of encountering, it was Mrs Dolores Hume. She knew this very fiercely and she didn't see how she should be expected to go to Mrs Hume's house. She had by no means been drawn to the lady who had inspected her so hostilely in the bathtub – to put it mildly, she was not particular about ever seeing her again.

Her resentment turned against René. Looked at in any light, her position was that of a person of whom he was ashamed. One side of her understood the complications of his position, but in her fine glow of health after exercise, it seemed outrageous that anyone should have the opportunity to think of her in a belittling way. Rene's theories were very well, but she would have been a hundred times happier had they announced the engagement long before, even though every curious cat in the community stared at her for a month or two. Becky felt as if she had been kept in the kitchen, and she was developing a sense of inferiority. This, in turn, made her think of the schedule as a sort of tyranny, and several times lately she had wondered how much of herself she was giving up in the complete subservience of every hour of every day to another's judgement.

"He can call for Noël," she decided. "I've done my best all through. If he's so wise, he ought not to put me in such a situation."

An hour later, René was still unable to think where he had put her at all. He had planned the days for her, but he had never really thought before about how she would fill them up. Returning to his laboratory in a state of profound gloom, he increased his pace as he came in sight of the building, cursed with a new anxiety. He had been absent more than three hours, with the barometer steadily falling and three windows open; he could not remember whether he or Charles was to have spoken to the janitor about continuing the heat over the weekend. His jars, the precious water in his jars… He ran up the icy stairs of the old building, afraid of what he was going to see.

One closed jar went with a cracking plop as he stood panting inside the door. One thousand of them glistened in tense rows through three long rooms, and he held his breath, waiting for them to go off together, almost hearing the crackling, despairing sound they would make. He saw that another one was broken, and then another in a far row. The room was like ice, with a blizzard seeping through eight corners of every window; there was ice formed on the faucet.

On tiptoe, lest even a faint movement precipitate the nine hundred and ninety-seven catastrophes, he retreated to the hall; then his heart beat again as he heard the dull, reassuring rumble of the janitor's shovel in the cellar.

"Fire it up as far as you can!" he called down, and then descended another flight so as to be sure he was understood. "Make it as hot a blaze as possible, even if it is all" – he could not think of the word for kindling – "even if it is all small wood."

He hurried back to the laboratory, entering again on tiptoe. As he entered, two jars beside a north window cracked, but his hand, brushing the radiator, felt just the beginning of a faint and tepid warmth. He took off his overcoat, and then his coat, and tucked them in across one window, dragged out an emergency electric heater, and then turned on every electric appliance in the room. From moment to moment, he stopped and listened ominously, but there were no more of the short, disastrous dying cries. By the time he had isolated the five broken jars and checked up on the amount of ice in the others, there was a definite pulse of heat coming off the radiators.

As he still fussed mechanically around the room, his hands shaking, he heard Noël's voice in a lower hall, and she came upstairs with Dolores Hume, both of them bundled to the ears against the cold.

"Here you are, René," Dolores said cheerfully. "We've phoned here three times and all over town. We wanted Noël to stay to dinner, but she keeps thinking you'd be worried. What is all this about a schedule? Are you all catching trains?"

"What is what?" he answered dazedly. "You realize, Dolores, what has happened here in this room?"

"It's got very cold."

"The water in our jars froze. We almost lost them all!"

He heard the furnace door close, and then the janitor coming upstairs. Furious at what seemed the indifference of the world, he repeated:

"We nearly lost them all!"

"Well, as long as you didn't…" Dolores fixed her eyes upon a vague spot far down the late battlefield of gleaming jars. "Since we're here, René, I want to say something to you – a thing that seems to me quite as important as your jars. There is something very beautiful about a widower being left alone with a little daughter to care for and to protect and to guide. It doesn't seem to me that anything so beautiful should be lightly destroyed."

For the second time that day, René started to throw his hands up in the air, but he had stretched his wrists a little the last time, and in his profound agitation he was not at all sure that he could catch them.

"There is no answer," he groaned. "Listen, Dolores; you must come to my laboratory often. There is something very beautiful in a platinum electrode."

"I am thinking only of Noël," said Dolores serenely.

At this point, the janitor, effectually concealed beneath a thick mask of coal dust, came into the room. It was Noël who first divined the fact that the janitor was Becky Snyder.

Under those thoroughly unmethodical circumstances, the engagement of René and Becky was announced to the world – the world as personified and represented by Dolores Hume. But for René even that event was overshadowed by his astonishment at learning that the first jar had burst at the moment Becky came into his laboratory; that she had remembered that water expanded as it froze and guessed at the danger; that she had been working for three quarters of an hour to start the furnace before he had arrived; and, finally, that she had taken care of the furnace for two years back in Bingham – "because there was nothing much else to do".

Dolores took it nicely, though she saw fit to remind Becky that she would be somewhat difficult to recognize if constantly observed under such extremely contrary conditions.

"I suppose it all has something to do with this schedule I hear so much about."

"I started the fire with the schedule," remarked Becky, and then amended herself when René jumped up with a suddenly agonized expression: "Not the one with the notes on it – that was behind the cushions of the car."

"It's too much for me," Dolores admitted. "I suppose you'll all end by sleeping here tonight – probably in the jars."

Noël bent double with laughter.

"Why don't we? Look on the schedule, Daddy, and see if that's the thing to do."

I Got Shoes

THE LOVELY THING HURRIED into the hotel, rising on the balls of her feet with each step, and bumped on her heels before the desk clerk with an expression of "Here I am!" All the clerks were beginning to know vaguely who she was – a passed debutante who had done much dancing in the big ballroom several years before and was now connected with the city's principal paper.

"Good morning," said the clerk.

"I have an appointment with" – the Lovely Thing paused, savouring the sweetness of her words – "with Miss Nell Margery."

"Oh." The clerk became more sprightly, but was not properly overwhelmed. "You're Miss..." He glanced at a card. "Miss Battles?"

Haughtily, she let the question pass.

"I was to announce you anyhow." And he added familiarly, "If you knew how many girls've tried to crash her suite in the last twenty-four hours! We don't even send the flowers up any more. Oh, hello, this is the desk." Johanna felt the change in his tone. "Miss Battles is downstairs." And she fumed a little. Of course this young man could not be expected to know that society in this city still held itself rather above the stage – even above the best young actress in America. Nevertheless, her attitude towards Miss Margery underwent a certain revision, and encountering her friend Teeny Fay near the elevator she stopped a moment; let the great Nell Margery take a turn at waiting.

"How late were you up last night?" asked Teeny.

"Till two. Then I had to go to the office. How did it come out?"

"Oh, I smoothed her down and somebody smoothed him down. I'll tell you about it if you'll come have a glass of beer – I'm dead on my feet." She groaned and then came alive suddenly. "Say, I just rode down in the elevator with Nell Margery's maid."

"I'm on my way—"

"She's French and she was warm and bothered. She was complaining to the housekeeper because Nell Margery hadn't gotten one of her trunks of shoes! *One* of her trunks of shoes! And I've got three pairs."

"I know," Johanna asserted eagerly. "I read that she was too stingy to throw away any shoes she ever had. There's a warehouse where she has dozens of trunks of shoes, all of them practically new." Johanna paused regretfully. "Still, I suppose they're mostly out of style now."

Suddenly, conscience-stricken, she said, "But she's waiting for me!" – and rushed for a departing elevator.

"What? Why is she?" Teeny cried after her.

"Newspaper!" The gates shut behind Johanna.

Meanwhile, sixteen floors above, Miss Margery was discussing her future with a handsome weather-worn man named Livingstone, just arrived from New York and also, in the tradition of his famous namesake, recently arrived from parts unknown. His course towards Miss Margery had indeed begun at a station marked only by a Mayan image in the Brazilian jungle, proceeded down an unnamed river into the Branco, thence down the Negro and the Amazon to the sea, and northward in a fruit boat, and southward in a train. But though he had come from strange places, it was upon a familiar quest.

"…so it just occurred to me you might have changed your mind," he was saying.

"I haven't," confessed Miss Margery. "When an actress marries a society man—"

"I object to that phrase."

"—well, whatever you are – they're both taking a chance for the sake of vanity. He wants to parade her celebrity through his world, and she wants to parade his background through hers. 'Vanity Fair, saith the prophet'* – or you know what I mean."

Her face was heart-shaped, an impression added to by honey-coloured, pointed-back hair that accentuated the two lovely rounds of her temples. Her eyes were large almonds, with the curve amended by classically pencilled eyebrows, so that the effect during one of her rare smiles was a rakish gleam. At these times it was a face so merry that it was impossible not to smile back into the white mirrors of her teeth – the whole area around her parted lips was a lovely little circle of delight. When she grew grave again she was once more a keyboard, all resonant and gleaming – a generation of theatregoers had formed the habit of concentrating their attention on this face as it reflected the slightest adventures and responses of Nell Margery's heart.

"But we've got more of a basis than that," Livingstone objected. "God knows, I'm only happy working."

"Yes?" she said sceptically.

"I work as hard as you do, young woman!"

"You mean you play as hard as I work."

He smouldered resentfully in the embers of this old quarrel.

"Because I can afford to do things that don't bring in money—"

It was at this point that Miss Johanna Battles was announced.

"I won't be long," Nell promised him. "She's the niece of a great friend of mine. She does some society stuff for the paper here and I promised to see her."

Livingstone nodded moodily and looked about for something to read; Nell opened the door and greeted Johanna in that voice so identical with her beauty that, as far as it chose to reach, her beauty seemed to flow into the intervening space, dominating it, occupying it corporeally by a process of infiltration.

"I'm always glad to talk to a niece of Miss Walters. I think the best thing is for us to go into my bedroom. We can talk better there."

Johanna followed her into the bedroom, took the proffered chair, and Nell sat on the bed.

"You look like your aunt. She told me you wanted to go on the stage."

"Oh, no," said Johanna modestly. "I was in a few Little Theatre plays last year, but now I'm a newspaper woman."

"You've given up the other idea?"

"Yes. I still do a little publicity for them – I suppose because I just like to hang around there." She laughed apologetically. "The lure of the stage – I was there till two o'clock last night."

"Have you got a good Little Theatre here?"

"I suppose so." Again Johanna laughed. "Off and on. Last night everybody went to pieces again."

Miss Margery stared.

"Went to pieces?"

"Did they! I'll say they did. For two hours. I'll bet you could hear it blocks away."

"You mean a girl got hysterical? I've seen that happen after a forty-eight-hour rehearsal – usually with the girls you'd never suspect of being nervous."

"Oh, this wasn't just girls," Johanna assured her. "This was a woman and two girls and a man. They had to get a doctor for the man. Once they were all yelling together."

Nell looked puzzled.

"I don't quite understand," she said. "Was this a drinking party?"

"No, no, this was a play." Johanna tried to think of some way to explain more clearly, but gave it up. "They just went to pieces, that's all. I don't think it showed much till the last act, but afterwards in the dressing rooms – zowie!"

Nell looked thoughtful for a moment and Johanna couldn't help wondering why she should be interested in such a thing. In any case she was here to get an interview; so she began:

"Tell me, Miss—" But she was interrupted.

"Why, I thought the Little Theatres – they'd..." Nell broke off. "Of course I can remember lots of cases of people going up in the air – in pictures—"

"Why, I thought it happened all the time. I've seen lots of movies where—"

"I mean really. Still, I have seen it happen. But all the people who 'went to pieces', as you call it, on duty – well, they're in sanatoriums, or hunting for jobs. I suppose that's unfair – but it certainly is one of the real differences between an amateur and a professional."

Johanna was restless. Miss Margery seemed inclined to continue indefinitely on this trivial subject, and she wished she had not mentioned it. Her own duty was to switch the interview back to the victim, and she was possessed with a sudden, daring idea:

"Miss Margery…" She hesitated. "Miss Margery – somebody once told me you went in for collecting shoes."

Nell suddenly sat up from the pillow against which she leant and bent slowly towards Johanna, her eyes like the cut face of jewels.

"Say-ee-ee!" she boomed resonantly, and then in a higher but equally formidable key, with a sudden new tang in the tone that Johanna's friends might have described as common. "Say-ee-ee! Who told you to ask me that? You go back and tell your paper I don't answer questions about my personal life."

Flustered, Johanna fumbled for an apology. Nell jumped up and was suddenly at the window, a glitter of leaves in a quick wind, a blonde glow of summer lightning. Even in her state of intimidation Johanna noticed that she seemed to bear with her, as she moved, a whole dream of women's future; bore it from the past into the present as if it were a precious mystery she held in the carriage of her neck and arms.

"This has happened before," she said shortly. "And did I tell them where to get off! Shoes! If anybody wants to save books or postage stamps or diamond bracelets they're not hounded about it. My shoes! If anybody ever again…"

Suddenly Nell was aware of Johanna's stricken face.

"Oh, well, I suppose they told you to ask me." It had simultaneously dawned on her that her little outbreak might make a troublesome story itself, especially since she had just expressed superior surprise at those who behaved badly on duty. She wasn't on duty, but Miss Walters's niece might not make the distinction. Nell sat down on the bed again and everything went out of her voice except the velvet power.

"What did they tell you? That I was very stingy and kept all my old shoes?"

"Well… well, yes… well… well, not exactly…" Johanna stammered.

"Suppose I tell you a little story. It has something to do with that difference between amateurs and professionals I spoke about."

Relieved, Johanna sat back in her chair and, with Miss Margery's encouragement, lit a cigarette.

I was a stage child, you know, carried on as a baby in arms, nursed between acts on one-night stands, and all that. Until I was seven, I thought all grown people's kisses smelt of grease paint. Father was not an actor, but he was everything else around the theatre at one time or another, as long as he lived, and then it was just mother and me. Mother played comedy parts – she did a few bits in New York, and a few seasons in stock, but mostly she toured the little towns with the third- and fourth-string companies they used to put out after a New York success. Plays like *Secret Service* and *The Easiest Way* and *The Witching Hour** – your generation doesn't remember them. She took what she could get – one summer we played *Old Kentucky** in most of the ranch towns of Wyoming and Montana.

We always managed to eat and dress, and when it looked as if we wouldn't I never worried, because I knew Mother would fix it all right. I had nice clothes. I have a photograph of myself in some very nice clothes I had – nice clean flounces and ruffles and lace on my drawers, and sashes pressed and all that – like any little girl. I had nice clothes.

One day when I was ten years old – I won't tell you exactly how long ago, but it was before the war – we landed in Richmond, Virginia, in the middle of the summer. It was hot there – not that I minded, but I remember because I remember how the sweat kept pouring down people's faces and wilting men's collars and wetting the rims of women's dresses all through the day. And I remember from something else that I'll come to in a minute.

I knew that things were not going well, though Mother tried to scold me around cheerfully as usual. I was worried, for about the first time in my life. Mother had a small part in a road company that had followed a heat wave and stopped paying salaries – that was a familiar story in those days – but enough money had come from New York to take the company back there. Mother was broke, and in debt to most of the company besides, and they were broke too. She didn't like the idea of getting into New York in July, in that condition, so when she heard that the stock company at the other Richmond theatre could use somebody of her type she thought of trying for the job. The train that was taking the company to New York wasn't leaving for a couple of hours, so Mother and I started across town. We walked – Mother had only twenty cents left and we needed that to eat with that night.

I had cardboard in the soles of my shoes; I'd had that before but, as I told you, Mother always kept me very well dressed. Always very well dressed. It was just for a day or so sometimes when things were hard. But everything was so mixed up that last day with packing the trunks that I forgot to cut out a new piece of cardboard. I was just like any other child that age – you know, careless and forgetful.

But when Mother took my hand on the street and said we had to hurry I began to be sorry I had been so careless. My old cardboard was worn through; the sidewalk was just a stove lid, and Mother was dragging me along in the way older people do in a hurry, in a kind of shuffle that isn't either a walk or a run. I remember passing some coloured boys barefoot and thinking that if I could take off my shoes and carry them I could run beside her and touch other parts of the feet sometimes. But I knew from the determined way Mother walked that there was no time for that.

The wooden stairs of that other theatre felt cool. I wanted to take off my shoes, but Mother pulled me into the manager's office with her, and I was afraid that the manager might see the shoes and think we needed the job too bad. He looked like a mean man.

"What can you do?" he asked Mother.

"Just about everything; character comedy, comic maids, blackface, heavies, old ladies, comic juveniles…"

He laughed unpleasantly.

"Yes, you can do juveniles."

"I've played Sis Hopkins* more than once."

"Not since a long time, I'll bet. And you're not too happy in the face for playing comics."

Mother grinned at him – I knew how worried she was from her breathing and I wondered if he noticed.

"Come back in an hour," he said finally. "I've got somebody I've got to see first. Be here in one hour, sharp." We found out later he didn't have the principal authority after all.

Mother thought quick. The train for New York left in half an hour, and if she didn't get this job – well, it was better for a trouper to be "resting" in New York than in Richmond.

"All right," she agreed.

As soon as we were outside we started off faster than before. "I've got to get to the station before that train goes and have them give me my ticket so I can redeem it."

I said: "Mother, my shoes are worn out," and she answered vaguely, "We'll take care of that tomorrow." So, naturally, I didn't say any more.

I don't remember the walk to the station – not even whether my feet hurt or not, because now I was all worried with her. But I do remember getting there and finding that the train had been gone half an hour; we thought we had been walking faster, but actually we were tired and walking slower.

As soon as Mother found that at least her trunk hadn't gone, we started back to the stock theatre. I hoped we would take a streetcar, but Mother didn't suggest it. I tried to walk on the side of my feet, but it was very difficult and I kept slipping and Mother just saved me from falling by jerking me sharply ahead. It was the part of each foot that stuck out – first the size of a half-dollar and then the size of a dollar – that made all the trouble. Finally I couldn't bear to touch the ground with it, and after that it was even harder for Mother. She got terribly tired and all at once decided we could waste a minute sitting on the steps of the Confederate Museum.

It didn't seem the time to say anything – we had gone so far it didn't seem worthwhile. It was no use taking off my shoes now – anyhow, I was afraid to see what had happened down there. I was afraid, too, that if it was something awful and Mother found out, she might look less cheerful in the face and we wouldn't get the job. I guess things had been as bad with her before, but this was the first time I'd been old enough to realize it.

The last part of the walk was not so far, but this time I couldn't feel the stairs of the theatre like I had before, except they seemed sticky. There was another much nicer man with the manager; he gave Mother the job and a few dollars to go on with, and when we got outside again she seemed more cheerful, but by this time I was frightened about myself. I had to tell her. I saw a line of blood spots on the landing that I'd left coming in, so I sat down on the first step of the stairs, and suddenly I saw the blood come out all around my feet until they were islands in the middle of it. I was terribly frightened now and wished I hadn't tried to be Mother's brave girl. But I hoped the people inside the office would not hear her when she cried so loud, "Oh, my baby, my baby!"

After that I remember the pillow in the ambulance, because it was the biggest one I ever saw in my life.

The telephone rang and Nell Margery called into the living room: "Answer it, will you, Warren?"

"It's a hospital," he announced after a moment.

"Oh, I want to answer. It's a girl from the cast... Oh, thanks... Yes, I do want to know about her... Well, that's perfectly fine... Tell her we're all so glad, and that I'll be out for a minute late in the afternoon."

She bobbed the receiver and called the hotel florist. Meanwhile Livingstone had been leaning with his hands on the door frame between the rooms.

"What's all this about shoes?" he demanded. "Can't I listen in on the finish?"

"Sounds as if you have been listening."

"You left the door half-open, and there wasn't much to read and I opened Mr Gideon* at some rather difficult pages."

Nell sat on the bed again and continued, speaking always to Johanna.

After the soles of my feet got well we had better times. But for me the one fine time was the day I put on a brand-new pair of white button shoes. I'd sit down and look at them, then I'd stand up and look at them, then I'd walk a little bit. I took care of those shoes, I'll tell you – I whitened them twice a day. But eventually they got scuffed about, and when I was going to walk on in a one-line bit in Albany next fall Mother got me a new pair.

"Give me the others," said she. "They're too small for you, and the doorman's daughter..."

Perhaps she saw the look in my face, because she stopped right there. I picked up the discarded shoes and hugged them as if they were something living, and began to cry and cry.

"All right, all right," Mother said. "Keep them then, stingy cat."

I didn't care what she called me. I hid them where she or anybody else couldn't find them, and when the next pair got used up I hid them too, and the next pair, and the pair after that. Two years later, when I was beginning to play juveniles, a pair got thrown out one day, and then I will admit... well, what you said: I "went to pieces".

You'll ask why do I want the old shoes, and I'll have to answer, "I don't know." Maybe it's just some terrible fear of ever being without shoes again; maybe it's some repressed stinginess coming out in me, like that article said. But I know I'd rather give away a ring from my finger than a pair of shoes.

When Nell stopped there was an odd silence; she looking at the other two defiantly; Livingstone looking at her as if things weren't so serious as all that; Johanna wondering how soon it would be wise to speak; she chanced it:

"May I make a little story out of that for the paper?"

"Oh, I'd much rather you wouldn't," Nell said quickly. "I'd much rather you wouldn't. I didn't tell it to you for that – I told it to you to illustrate something we were talking about. What was it? Oh, yes, about professionals – after that I was always a professional."

"I don't quite understand," confessed Johanna. "Isn't a professional just... just an amateur who's arrived?"

Nell shook her head helplessly.

"I can't exactly explain – it's something about discipline on duty. We stage children – why, when we were fifteen if a director said to one of us, 'You, third girl from the left, take a dive into the bass drum!' we'd have done it without question."

Johanna laughed but persisted:

"Lots of girls have succeeded on the stage without being brought up to it."

"Then they've made their struggle in sacrifices and heartburns of wriggling out of their backgrounds, and in being able to stand all sorts of hardships and tough contacts that they weren't fitted for or brought up for." Nell shook her head again and got up. "I haven't made it clear. I wish some clever man were here to explain it. I just thought perhaps you'd understand."

They moved into the other room. Nell did not sit down, and Johanna, still unsatisfied, yielded to the hint that her time was up. Suddenly, she had support from a new quarter.

"I'm not that clever man you speak of, but I don't follow you either, Nell," said Livingstone. "You seem to be saying that everybody's got to go through misery to accomplish anything. Why, I know lots of them that just take it in their stride."

"Not if you know their real stories," Nell was thinking, but she was tiring herself with argument and she said nothing.

"The most successful explorers I know – why, it's been nuts for them. Most of them were brought up with guns in their hands—"

Nell nodded, breaking him off.

"Goodbye, Miss Battles." She flashed the heavenly cataclysm of her smile at her. "Nothing about shoes, remember! It might reflect on Mother, and she always dressed me as well as any little girl could be dressed. And remember me to your aunt."

Warren took a step into the doorway after Johanna, as if to atone for Nell's sudden lassitude – her own way of resting – and said with an appreciative eye on Johanna's lovely face:

"I hope you get some sort of story."

When he shut the door after her Nell was already sitting and gazing.

"So I'm an amateur," Warren said drily. "Nellie, what you mean back of what you say is that if you make money out of your work you're a professional, and if you don't you're an amateur. If you open a good beer parlour you're a professional, but if you fool with fever, and rocks in rapids that look the wrong colour in the dusk, and men like monkeys and monkeys like men, you're an amateur."

Still Nell didn't answer – still resting. She had to go on in three hours.

"I admit I haven't made money, but I think I could if I had to."

"Try it," she whispered.

He wanted to choke her – he wanted to move some part of his body violently; but he was under a social contract to keep most of them still, so he worked with his tongue against the left side of his upper jaw. He said:

"For that crack I'll tell you something. We sold forty-five reels of animal and nature stuff to a movie morgue for a sum that paid for the trip and left a margin." He was freezing more and more, but each time he spoke his voice was gentler; yet she felt the recession: "Only you, Nellie, could irritate me to the extent of making such a statement – you and the peak of Everest and the mouth of the Orinoco if I'd given them three years of absolute unwavering devotion." He paused, taking Nell in. "In fact, I might as well admit they're years in the red." Again he looked at her, but still Nell did not stir. "In fact, coming down here was just a waste of time." He picked up his hat. "In fact, there are, after all, those society girls that chill your shoulder blades who may have standards quite as high as yours." He went to the door. "In fact…" He stood for a moment, utterly disgusted at her failure to be moved, and then stepped out and closed the door after him.

Nell looked up at the closed door as if she expected it to open again; she jumped at a knock, but it was her maid, and Nell ordered the car in an hour to go to the hospital. She was tired and confused and she knew that it would tell a little bit in her performance tonight. Never had she tried so hard to put her ideas into words; notions of Warren Livingstone and old shoes were mixed up in her mind.

She looked down at her shoes; the satin fabric had been somehow scuffed open in breaking the seal on that hidden thing of her childhood.

"I'll need a new pair of shoes, Jaccy. These are done."

"Yes, madam."

Jaccy's Savoyard eyes lowered for a moment to the shoes Madame wore, then lifted quickly; but Nell had seen. She stared at Jaccy's foot that was the same size as her own.

"Is that why he went away? Because he suddenly saw me as a mean woman with an illogical streak one yard wide?"

And suddenly it seemed to her as if all those dozens and dozens and hundreds and hundreds of shoes made a barrier between him and her, between her and life, and she wanted to push it over or break through it. She jumped up.

"Jaccy!" And the maid turned. "Do you know... did you ever notice... our feet" – she hesitated, fighting through waves of old emotions, running against the stumps of old habits – "our feet are exactly the same size."

"Why, yes, madam." Jaccy's eyes danced and flickered. "Madame, I have often noticed it."

"Well, I thought that it was such a coincidence – my shoes would fit you exactly."

She took off the scuffed shoe quickly and tossed it to Jaccy, who examined it with covetous admiration.

"So I thought..."

Nell paused, breathing hard, and Jaccy, perhaps guessing what was going on inside her mistress, tried to help her over a difficult fence. "In fact – one day I took the liberty of trying on one of Madam's used shoes before I added it to the others."

Nell stiffened – Jaccy had dared! Her own shoes – to try one on! The phone rang and Nell took off her other shoe and, carrying it in her hand, crossed to the phone in her stocking feet. As she picked up the receiver she tossed the second shoe; watching her mistress's face, Jaccy caught it and said with obvious disappointment:

"Shall I—"

"Of course, put them with the others." Nell's voice was cold as she picked up the phone; then suddenly her voice was all expectant and doubtful:

"Well, you didn't go far on this latest exploring trip."

"Far enough," said Warren. "Far enough to make a great discovery."

"What was that – that I'm just a sort of shopkeeper after all?"

She heard him laugh over the phone.

"No. It was that I'm condemned to go through life never looking at another woman, except as something unreal, something stuffed and mounted, seeing only you alive. Wherever you are, or whatever you do, I'll always be stalking you in my mind; half a dozen times in these three years I've really seen you around the edge of a copse, or as a kind of shadow darting away from a water hole. I'll always be one of those hunters you read about – you know – saw a vision once and just had to keep going after it – had no choice. Won't that make me a sort of professional in the end?"

An enforced pause while the line crackled with other dissonances or harmonies.

"Where did you make this discovery?"

"Beside the telephone desk in the lobby."

"Come up, Warren!"

Nell leant back slowly in her chair, not relaxing, but nerving herself.

"Jaccy!" she said, breathing it in, and then, taking it big, feeling her heart pumping it down to the ends of her fingernails, the soles of her feet.

"Madame?"

"If you like, you can have those shoes. We're not saving them any more."

The Family Bus

1

DICK WAS FOUR YEARS OLD when the auto arrived at the Hendersons' – it was a 1914 model, fresh from the factory – but his earliest memory of it was dated two years later. Lest younger readers of this chronicle hesitate to embark on an archaeological treatise – about a mummy with doors in the back, gasoline lamps, gears practically in another street and, invariably, a human torso underneath and a woman all veil and muff perched serene on top – it were best to begin with a description of the vehicle.

This was not that kind of car. It was of an expensive make, low-slung for that period, with electric lights and a self-starter – in appearance not unlike the machines of today. The fenders were higher, the running board longer, the tyres more willowy, and undoubtedly it did stick up higher in the air. If it could be stood today beside, say, one of the models of 1927 that are still among us, you would not immediately be able to define the difference. The older car would seem less of a unit – rather like several cars each on a slightly different level.

This was not apparent to young Dick on the day he became conscious of the car; its sole fault was that it didn't contain Jannekin Melon-Loper, but he was going to make it contain her if his voice held out.

"Why ca' I ha' Ja'kin?"

"Because we're going some place," his mother whispered; they were approaching the gardener's cottage, and Jan Melon-Loper, father of the coveted Jannekin, tipped his large straw from a grape arbour.

"Oh, waa-a-a!" Dick wailed. "Oh, waa-a-a! I want Ja'kin!"

Mrs Henderson was a little afraid of the family retainers; she had grown up in a simpler Michigan where the gardener was known either as "the janitor" or "the man who cuts the grass". The baronial splendour made possible by the rise of the furniture company sat uneasily upon her. She feared now that Jan had heard her son's request and would be offended.

"All right," she said, "all right. This one more time, Dick."

He beamed as he ran into the cottage calling for his love; he beamed as, presently, he led her forth by the hand and embarked her at his side. Jannekin, a lovely little Hollander of five, mouthed her thumb shyly for a minute and then found ease in one of those mysterious children's games which consist largely of the word "Look!" followed by long intervals of concentration. The auto carried them far on the fair day, but they gazed neither at the river, nor the hills, nor the residences, but only at each other.

It was always to be the last time with Jannekin, but it never quite was. Dick grew up to ten and played with boys, Jannekin went to public school and played with girls, but they were always like brother and sister to each other, and something more. He told her his most intimate secrets; they had a game they played sometimes where they stood cheek to cheek for a moment and breathed deeply; it was as near as she would come to letting him kiss her. Once she had seen her older sister kissing a man, and she thought it was "ookey".

So, for the blessed hour of childhood, they eliminated the space between the big house and the small one.

Jannekin never came to the Hendersons'. They met somewhere about the place. Favourite of all rendezvous was the garage.

"This is the way to do," Dick explained, sitting at the gears of the car – it was "the old car" now; the place of honour had since been occupied by a 1917 limousine and a 1920 landaulet – "Look, Janny; look, Jannekin, Howard showed me. I could drive it if they'd let me. Howard let me drive it once on his lap."

"Could I drive it?"

"Maybe," he conceded. "Look, I'll show you how."

"You could drive," she said. "I'd just go along and tell you which way to turn."

"Sure," he agreed, without realizing to what he was committing himself. "Sure, I—"

There was an interruption. Dick's big brother Ralph came into the garage, took a key from behind a door and expressed his desire for their displacement from the machine by pointing briskly at each of them in turn and then emphatically at the cement floor.

"You going riding?" Dick asked.

"Me? No, I'm going to lie under the tank and drink gasoline."

"Where are you going?" asked Dick, as they scrambled out.

"None of your business."

"I mean if you're going out the regular way, would you let us ride as far as Jannekin's house?"

"I can stand it."

He was not pleasant this summer, Dick's brother. He was home from sophomore year at college, and as the city seemed slow, he was making an almost single-handed attempt to speed it up. One of that unfortunate generation who had approached maturity amid the confusions and uncertainties of wartime, he was footloose and irresponsible even in his vices, and he wore the insigne of future disaster upon his sleeve.

The Henderson place was on the East Hills, looking down upon the river and the furniture factories that bordered it. The forty acres were supervised by the resourceful Jan, whose cottage stood in the position of a lodge at the main entrance, and there Ralph stopped the car and, to the children's surprise, got out with them. They lingered as he walked to the gate.

Tee-hoo! he whistled discreetly, but imperatively. *Tee-ee-hoo!*

A moment later, Kaethe Melon-Loper, the anxiety, if not yet the shame, of her parents, came around the corner from the kitchen, hatted and cloaked, and obviously trying to be an inconspicuous part of the twilight. She shared with Jannekin only the ruddy Dutch colour and the large China-blue eyes.

"Start right off," she whispered. "I'll explain."

But it was too late – the explanation issued from the cottage personified as Mrs Melon-Loper and Mrs Henderson making a round of the estate. Both mothers took in the situation simultaneously; for a second Mrs Henderson hesitated, her eyebrows fluttering; then she advanced determinedly towards the car.

"Why, Ralph!" she exclaimed. "Where are you going?"

Calmly, Ralph blew smoke at his mother.

"I got a date – and I'm dropping Kaethe at a date she's got."

"Why, Ralph!" There was nothing much to add to this remark, which she repeated in a distraught manner. That he was not speaking the truth was apparent in his affected casualness as well as in the shifty, intimidated eyes of the girl sitting beside him. But in the presence of Kaethe's mother, Mrs Henderson was handicapped.

"I particularly wanted you to be at home tonight," she said, and Mrs Melon-Loper, equally displeased, helped her with:

"Kaethe, you get yourself out of the auto this minute."

But the car broke into a sound more emphatic than either of their voices; with the cut-out open in a resounding *tp!-tp!-tp!*, it slid off down the lane, leaving the mothers standing, confused and alarmed, in the yard.

Of the two, Mrs Melon-Loper was more adequate to the awkward situation.

"It should not be," she pronounced, shaking her head. "Her father will her punish."

"It doesn't seem right at all," said Mrs Henderson, following her lead gratefully. "I will tell his father."

"It should not be."

Mrs Henderson sighed; catching sight of the two children, who loitered, fascinated, she managed to assert herself:

"Come home with me, Dick."

"It's only seven," he began to protest.

"Never mind," she said with dilatory firmness. "I need you for something… Goodnight, Mrs Melon-Loper."

A little way down the lane, Mrs Henderson released on Dick the authority she could no longer wield over her elder son.

"That's the end of that. You're never to play with that dirty little girl again."

"She isn't dirty. She isn't even as dirty as I am."

"You're not to waste your time with her. You ought to be ashamed of yourself."

She walked so fast that he had trouble keeping up.

"Why ought I be ashamed of myself? Look, Mamma, tell me. Why ought I be ashamed of myself?"

He sensed that Ralph had no business driving off into the twilight with Kaethe, but himself and Jannekin – that was another matter. There was great domestic commotion about the affair during the next few days; Mr Henderson raged at Ralph around the library and the latter sat at meals with a silent jeer on his face.

"Believe me, Kaethe would go bigger in New York than most of the stuff that turns out at the country club," he told his father.

"I've made inquiries, and she has a bad reputation with the people she goes with."

"That's OK with me," Ralph said. "I think a girl ought to know something about life."

"Is dissipation 'life'? Sometimes I think you've got a bad heart, Ralph. Sometimes I think none of the money I've spent on your outside got through to your insides. I think now I ought to have started you in the factory at seventeen."

Ralph yawned.

"A lot you know about anything except tables and chairs."

For a week, though – due largely to the firmness of Jan – there were no more night rides. Ralph spent his leisure sampling the maiden efforts of pioneer bootleggers, and Dick, accustomed to the disorganization that, during the Twenties, characterized so many newly rich families in the Midwest, when there was scarcely a clan without its wastrel or scamp, concerned himself with his own affairs. These included finding out as much about automobiles as Howard, the chauffeur, could find time to tell him, and searching for his Jannekin again across the barriers that had been raised between them. Often he saw her – the flash of a bright little dress far away across the lawn, an eager face on the cottage porch as he drove out with his mother – but the cordon was well drawn. Finally, the urge to hear her voice became so insistent that he decided upon the clandestine.

It was a late August day, with twilight early and the threat of a storm in the air. He shut himself noisily in his room for the benefit of his mother's secretary, part of whose duties consisted of keeping an eye on him in this emergency; then he tiptoed down a back stairs and went out through the kitchen. Circling the garage, he made his way towards the cottage following the low bed of a stream, a route often used in "cops and robbers". His intention was to get as close as possible and then signal Jannekin with a bird call they had practised, but starting through a high half-acre of hay, he stopped at the sound of voices twenty feet ahead.

"We'll take the old bus" – it was Ralph speaking. "We'll get married in Mushegon – that's where some people I know did."

"Then what?" Kaethe demanded.

"I've got a hundred dollars, I tell you. We could go to Detroit and wait for the family to come around."

"I guess they can't do anything after we're married."

"What could they do? They're so dumb they don't even know I flunked out of college in June – I sneaked the notice out of the mail. The old man's weak – that's his trouble. He'll kick, but he'll eat out of my hand."

"You didn't decide this because you had these drinks?"

"I tell you I've thought of it for weeks. You're the only girl I…"

Dick lost interest in finding Jannekin. Carefully he backed out of the path he had made through the hay and returned to the garage to consider. The thing was awful – though Dick's parents were very incompetent as parents in the post-war world that they failed to understand, the symbol of parental authority remained. Scenting evil and catastrophe as he never had in his life, Dick walked up and down in front of the garage in the beginning rain. A few minutes later, he ran for the house with his shirt soaked and his mind made up.

Snitching or not, he must tell his father. But as they went in to dinner, his mother said: "Father phoned he won't be home... Ralph, why don't you sit up? Don't you think it looks rather bad?"

She guessed faintly that Ralph had been drinking, but she hated facing anything directly.

"S'mustard for the soo-oop," Ralph suggested, winking at Dick; but Dick, possessed with a child's quiet horror, could not give back the required smile.

"If Father will only come," he thought. "If Father will only come."

During an interminable dinner, he went on considering.

Howard and the new car were in town awaiting his father; in the garage there was only the old bus, and straightway Dick remembered that the key was kept behind the garage door. After a fragmentary appearance in the library to say, "I'm going up and read in my room," he darted down the back stairs again, out through the kitchen and over the lawn, drenched with a steady, patient stream.

Not a second too soon – halfway to the garage he heard the front door close and, by the light of the *porte-cochère*, saw Ralph come down the steps. Racing ahead, Dick found and pocketed the key; but he ran smack into Ralph as he tried to escape from the garage, and was grabbed in the darkness.

"What you doing here?"

"Nothing."

"Go back the house."

Gratefully, Dick got a start, not towards the house, where he would be easily cornered, but in the direction of the tall hay. If he could keep the key until his father arrived home...

But he had gone barely fifty feet, slipping on the indistinguishable mud, when he heard Ralph's running footsteps behind him.

"Dick, you take 'at key? Hey!"

"No," he called back indiscreetly, continuing to run. "I never saw the key."

"You didn't? Then what were you..."

His fingers closed on Dick's shoulder, and Dick smelt raw liquor as they crashed across a bed of peonies.

"You give me—"

"I won't! You let me—"

"You will, by—"

"I won't – I won't! I haven't got it!"

Two minutes later, Ralph stood up with the key in his hand and surveyed the sobbing boy.

"What was the idea?" he panted. "I'm going to speak to Father about this."

Dick took him up quickly.

"All right!" he gasped. "Speak to him tonight!"

Ralph made an explosive sound that expressed at once his disgust and his private conviction that he had best get from home before his father arrived. Still sobbing on the ground, Dick heard the old car leave the garage and start up the lane. It could hardly have reached the sanctuary of a main street when the lights of another car split the wet darkness, and Dick raced to the house to see his father.

"…They're going to Muskegon and they're on their way now."

"It couldn't have been they knew you were there and said it to tease you?"

"No, no, no!" insisted Dick.

"Well, then, I'll take care of this myself… Turn around, Howard! Take the road to Muskegon, and go very fast." He scarcely noticed that Dick was in the car beside him until they were speeding through the traffic on Canal Street.

Out of the city, Howard had to pick his way more carefully along the wet highway; Mr Henderson made no attempt to urge him on, but threw cigarette after cigarette into the night and thought his thoughts. But on a downgrade when the single light of a motorcycle came into sight on the opposite upgrade, he said:

"Stop, Howard! This may be a cop."

The car stopped; owner and chauffeur waved wildly. The motorcycle passed them, pulled up fifty yards down the road and came back.

"Officer."

"What is it?" The voice was sharp and hurried.

"I'm T.R. Henderson. I'm following an open car with…"

The officer's face changed in the light of his own bright lamp.

"T.R.," he repeated, startled. "Say, I was going to telephone you – I used to work for you. Mr Henderson, there's been an accident."

He came up closer to the car, put his foot on the running board and took off his cap so that the rain beat on his vivid young face as it twisted itself into sympathy and consideration.

"Your son's car went off the road down here a little way – it turned over. My relief heard the horn keep blowing. Mr Henderson, you'll have to get ready for bad news."

"All right. Put on your cap."

"Your son was killed, Mr Henderson. The girl was not hurt."

"My son is killed? You mean, he's dead?"

"The car turned over twice, Mr Henderson…"

…The rain fell gently through the night, and all the next day it rained. Under the sombre skies, Dick grew up suddenly, never again to be irresponsibly childish, trying to make his mother see his own face between herself and the tragedy, voluntarily riding in to call for his father at the office and exhibiting new interest in the purposes of the mature world, as if to say, "Look, you've got me. It's all right. I'll be two sons. I'll be all the sons you ever would have wanted." At the funeral he walked apart with them as the very cement of their family solidarity against the scandal that accompanied the catastrophe.

Then the rain moved away from Michigan into another weather belt and the sun shone; boyhood reasserted itself, and a fortnight later, Dick was in the garage with Howard while the latter worked on the salvaged car.

"Why can't I look up inside, Howard? You told me I could."

"Get that canvas strip then. Can't send you up to the house with oil on your new clothes."

"Listen, Howard," said Dick, lying under the engine with the basketed light between them. "Is that all it did – broke the front axle? It rolled over twice and only did that?"

"Crawl out and get me the wrench on the table," ordered Howard.

"But why wasn't it hurt?" demanded Dick, returning to the cave. "Why?"

"Built solid," Howard said. "There's ten years' life in her yet; she's better than some of this year's jobs. Though I understand that your mother never wants to see it again – naturally enough."

A voice came down to them from the outside world:

"Dick!"

"It's just Jannekin. Excuse me, Howard; I'll be back and help." Dick crawled out and faced a little figure in Sunday clothes.

"Hello, Dick."

"What do you want?" he asked, abstractedly rather than rudely; then awakening from mechanical preoccupations: "Say, who got all dressed up?"

"I came to say goodbye—"

"What?"

"—to you."

"Where are you going?"

"We're going away. Father has the van all loaded now. We're going to live across the river and Papa's going to be in the furniture business."

"Going away?"

She nodded so far down that her chin touched her breast bone, and she sniffled once.

Dick had restlessly got into the car and was pulling at the dashboard instruments. Suddenly frightened, he flung open the door, saying, "Come here," and, as she obeyed, "Why are you going?"

"After the accident – your father and mine thought we better go away… Oh-h, Dick!"

She leant and put her cheek next to his, and gave a sigh that emptied her whole self for a moment. "Oh-h-h-h, Dick! Won't I ever see you?"

For the moment, his only obligation seemed to be to stop her grief.

"Oh, shut up! Stop it, Janny Jannekin. I'll come to see you every day. I will. Pretty soon I'll be able to drive this old bus—"

She wept on inconsolably.

"—and then I'll drive over and…" He hesitated, then made a great concession: "Look, you can drive too. I'll begin to show you now, Janny Jannekin. Look! This is the ignition."

"Yes – hp – oh!" she choked forth.

"Oh, stop it… Put your foot here. Now press."

She did so, and almost simultaneously a ferocious howl issued from the cavern beneath the car.

"I'm sorry, Howard!" shouted Dick, and then to Jannekin: "But I'll show you how to drive it as soon as they let me take it out myself."

Full in the garage door, the sun fell upon the faces they turned towards each other. Gratefully he saw the tears dry on her cheeks.

"Now I'll explain about the gears," he said.

2

DICK CHOSE TECHNICAL HIGH as the best alternative, when it became plain that he could not return to St Regis. Since Mr Henderson's death there was always less money for everything, and though Dick resented growing poorer in a world in which everyone else grew richer, he agreed with the trustees that there was not twenty-five hundred extra to send him East to America's most expensive school.

At Tech he thought he had managed to conceal his disappointment politely. But the high-school fraternity, Omega Psi, which, though scarcely knowing him, elected him because of the prestige of his family, became ashamed of their snobbishness and pretended to see in his manner the condescension of a nobleman accepting an election to a fraternal order.

Amid the adjustments of the autumn he did not at first discover that Jannekin Melon-Loper was a junior in Tech. The thick drift of six years was between them, for she had been right – the separation in the garage was permanent. Jannekin, too, had passed through mutations. Her father had prospered in industry; he was now manager in charge of production in the company that had absorbed the Henderson plant. Jannekin was at Tech for a groundwork that would enable her to go abroad and bring back Bourbon, Tudor and Habsburg eccentricities worthy of Michigan reproduction. Jan wanted no more shiftless daughters.

Edgar Bronson, prominent member of Omega Psi, hailed Dick one morning in a corridor. "Hey, rookie, we took you in because we thought you could play football."

"I'm going out for it when—"

"It doesn't do the fraternity any good when you play the East Hill snob."

"What is all this?" demanded Dick, turning on him. "Just because I told some fellows I'd meant to go East to college."

"East-East-East," Edgar accused. "Why don't you keep it to yourself? All of us happen to be headed to Michigan, and we happen to like it. You think you're different from anybody else." And he sang as a sort of taunt:

> "The boys all are back at Michigan,
> The cats are still black at Michigan,
> The Profs are still witty,
> Ha-a-ha!
> The girls are still pretty,
> Ha-a-ha—"

He broke off as a trio of girls came around the corridor and, approaching, caught up the song:

> "—and the old
> How do you do?
> How are you?
> Says who?
> Goes on-on-and on."

"Hey, Jannekin!" Edgar called.

"Don't block the sidewalk!" they cried, but Jannekin left the others and came back. Her face escaped the pronounced Dutchiness of her sister's, and the coarseness that sometimes goes with it – nevertheless, the bright little apples of her cheeks, the blue of the Zuiderzee in her eyes, the braided strands of golden corn on the wide forehead, testified to the purity of her origin. She was the school beauty who let down her locks for the arrival of princes in the dramatic-club shows – at least until the week before the performance, when, to the dismay of the coach, she yielded to the pressure of the times, abbreviated the locks and played the part in a straw wig.

She spoke over Edgar to Dick, "I heard you were here, Dick Henderson."

"Why" – he recovered himself in a moment – "why, Janny Jannekin."

She laughed.

"It's a long time since you last called me that – sitting in the car in the garage, do you remember?"

"Don't mind me," said Edgar ironically. "Go right on. Did what?"

A wisp of the old emotion blew through Dick, and he concealed it by saying:

"We still have that car. It's still working, but I'm the only person left who can do anything with it when it doesn't."

"What year is it?" demanded Edgar, trying to creep into the conversation that had grown too exclusive to please him.

"Nineteen fourteen," Dick answered briefly, and then to Jannekin, with a modesty he did not feel about the car, "We keep it because we couldn't sell it." He hesitated. "Want to go riding some night?"

"Sure I do. I'd love it."

"All right, we will."

Her companions demanded her vociferously down the corridor; when she retreated, Edgar eyed Dick with new interest, but also new hostility.

"One more thing: if you don't want to get the whole fraternity down on you, don't start rushing Jannekin Melon-Loper. Couple of the brothers – I mean she's very popular and there's been plenty fights about her. One guy danced the last number with her at the June dance, and the boy that took her beat him up. Hear that?"

"I hear," answered Dick coldly.

But the result was a resolve that he put into effect during his date with her a week later – he asked her to the Harvest Picnic. Jannekin accepted. Hesitantly, not at all sure she liked this overproud boy out of the past, absorbed in his dual dream of himself and of machinery.

"Why do you want to take me? Because once we were…" She stopped.

"Oh, no," he assured her. "It's just that I like to take the prettiest. I thought we could go in this old bus. I can always get it."

His tone irritated Jannekin.

"I had a sort of engagement to go with two other boys – both of them have new cars." Then, feeling she had gone too far, she added: "But I like this one better."

In the interval he worked over the old bus, touching the worn places of its bright cream colour with paint, waxing it, polishing the metal and the glass, and tinkering with the engine until the cut-out was calculated to cause acute neurasthenia to such citizenry as dwelt between the city and Reed's Lake. When he called for Jannekin to escort her to the place of assembly, he was prouder of the car than of anything – until he saw whom he was taking to the dance. In deepest rose, a blush upon the evening air, Jannekin bounced rhythmically down the walk, belying the care she had put into her toilet for the night. With his handkerchief he gave a flick to the seat where she was to deposit her spotlessness.

"Good Lord! When I look at you – why, sometimes your face used to be as dirty as mine. Not ever quite – I remember defending you once. Mother said…" He broke off, but she added:

"I know. I was just the gardener's child to her. But why bring that up on an evening like this?"

"I'm sorry. I never thought of you as anything but my Janny Jannekin," he said emotionally.

She was unappeased, and in any case, it was too early for such a note; at the Sedgewicks' house she went from group to group of girls, admiring and being admired, and leaving Dick to stand somewhat conspicuously alone.

Not for long, though. Two youths towards whom he had developed a marked indifference engaged him in conversation about the football team, conversation punctuated by what seemed to him pointless laughter.

"You looked good at half today, Dick" – a snicker. "Mr Hart was talking about you afterwards. Everybody thinks that Johnson ought to resign and let you be captain."

"Oh, come on," he said, as good-humouredly as possible. "I'm not kidding myself about being good. I know he just needs my weight."

"No, honest," said one of the boys, with mock gravity. "Here at Tech we always like to have at least three of the backfield from the East Hills. It gives a sort of tone to the team when we play Clifton." Whereupon both boys snorted again with laughter.

Dick sighed and shook his head wearily.

"Go on, be as funny as you want to. You think I'm high-hat. All right, go on thinking it until you find out. I can wait."

For a moment, his frankness disconcerted them, but only for a moment:

"And the coach thinks maybe he could use that nifty racer of yours for end runs."

Bored by the childishness of the baiting, he searched for Jannekin in the crowd that now filled the living room and was beginning to drift out to the cars. He saw her flashing rose against a window, but before he could reach her, Edgar Bronson stopped him with serious hands on his shoulders:

"I've got something I particularly want to say to you."

"All right, say it."

"Not here; it's very private. Upstairs in Earl's bedroom."

Mystified, and glancing doubtfully over his shoulder to see if this could be a plot to steal Jannekin away, he followed Edgar upstairs; he refused the cigarette that training did not permit.

"Look here, Dick. Some of us feel that perhaps we've misjudged you. Perhaps you're not such a bad guy, but your early associations with a bunch of butlers and all that stuff soft of… sort of warped you."

"We never had any butlers," said Dick impatiently.

"Well, footmen then, or whatever you call them. It warped you, see?"

Under any conditions it is difficult to conceive of oneself as warped, save before the concave and convex mirrors of an amusement park; under the present circumstances, with Jannekin waiting below, it was preposterous and, with an expression of disgust, Dick started to rise, but Edgar persuaded him back in his chair.

"Wait a minute. There's only one thing wrong with you, and we, some of the fellows, feel that it can all be fixed up. You wait here and I'll get the ones I mean, and we'll settle it in a minute."

He hurried out, closing the door behind him, and Dick, still impatient, but welcoming any crisis that promised to resolve his unpopularity, wandered about the room inspecting the books, school pictures and pennants of Earl Sedgewick's private life.

Two minutes passed – three minutes. Exploding into action, he strode out of the door and down the stairs. The house was strangely silent and, with quick foreboding, he took the last stairs six at a time. The sitting room was unpopulated, the crowd was gone, but there was Jannekin, a faithful but somewhat sulky figure, waiting by the door.

"Did you have a good sleep?" she asked demurely. "Is this a picnic or a funeral?"

"It was some cuckoo joke. Some day I'll pull something on those guys that'll be really funny. Anyhow, I know a short cut and we'll beat them to the lake and give them the laugh." They went out. On the veranda, he stopped abruptly; his car – his beautiful car – was not where he had left it.

"My gosh! They've taken it! They took my car! What a dirty trick!" He turned incredulously to Jannekin. "And they knew you were with me too! Honestly, I don't understand these guys at all."

Neither did Jannekin. She had known them to behave cruelly or savagely; she had never known them to visit such a stupid joke on a popular girl. She, too, stared incredulously up and down the street.

"Look, Dick! Is that it down there – beyond the third lamp-post?"

He looked eagerly.

"It certainly is. But why…"

169

As they ran towards it, the reason became increasingly clear – startlingly clear. At first it seemed only that the car was somehow different against the late sunset; then the difference took form as varicoloured blotches, screaming and emphatic, declaratory and exclamatory, decorating the cream-coloured hulk from stem to stern, until the car seemed to have become as articulate and vociferous as a phonograph.

With dawning horror, he read the legends that, one by one, swam into his vision:

PARDON MY SILK HAT
WHAT AM I DOING IN THIS HICK TOWN?
ONLY FOUR CYLINDERS, BUT EACH ONE WITH A FAMILY TREE
STRAIGHT GAS FROM THE EAST HILLS
MARNE TAXI – MODEL 1914
WHY BALLOON TYRES WITH A BALLOON HEAD?

And perhaps the cruellest cut of all:

YOU DON'T NEED A MUFFLER WITH A CULTIVATED VOICE

Wild with rage, Dick pulled out his handkerchief and dabbed at one of the slogans, making a wide blur through which the sentence still showed. Three or four of them must have worked on the mural; it was amazing, even admirable, that it had been accomplished in the quarter-hour they had passed in the house. Again he started furiously at it with the already green blob of his handkerchief. Then he spied the convenient barrel of tar with the help of which they had finished the job after the paint gave out, and he abandoned all hope.

"There's no use, Dick," Jannekin agreed. "It was a mean trick, but you can't do anything about it now. You'll just ruin your clothes and make it all splotchy and give them the satisfaction of thinking you've been working on it. Let's just get in and go." And she added with magnanimity, "I don't mind."

"Go in this?" he demanded incredulously. "Why, I'd sooner…"

He stopped. Two years ago he would have phoned the chauffeur or rented another car, but now dollars were scarce in his family; all he could muster had gone into cosmetics for the machine.

"We can't go," he said emphatically. "Maybe I can find you a ride out and you can come back with someone else."

"Nonsense!" Jannekin protested. "Of course, we'll go. They're not going to spoil our evening with such a stupid stunt!"

"I won't go," he repeated firmly.

"You will so." She reverted unconsciously to the tone of six years before. "By the time we get there, it'll be almost too dark to read the… to see the things they painted. And we don't have to take streets where there're many people."

He hesitated, rebelling with her at being triumphed over so easily.

"Of course, we could go on the side streets," he admitted grudgingly.

"Of course, Dick." She touched his arm. "Now don't help me in; I don't want to get in the paint."

"When we're there," Dick told himself grimly, "I'll ask Mr Edgar Bronson aside for a little talk. And I'll do some painting myself – all in bright red."

She sensed his fury as they drove along dusty roads with few street lights, but great roller-coaster bumps at the crossings.

"Cheer up, Dick!" She moved closer. "Don't let this spoil the evening. Let's talk about something else. Why, we hardly know each other. Listen, I'll tell you about me; I'll talk to you as frankly as we used to talk. We're almost rich, Dick. Mother wants to move to a bigger house, but Father's very cautious, and he thinks it would look pushing. But anyhow we know he's got more than we know he's got – if you know what I mean."

"That's good." He matched her frankness. "Well, we've got even less money than people know we have, if you know what I mean. I've got as much chance of getting East to Boston Tech as this car has to get into the automobile show." A little bitterly, he added: "So they needn't have wasted all that sarcasm."

"Oh, forget it. Tell me what you are going to do."

"I'm not going to college at all; I'm going to Detroit, where my uncle can get me a place in a factory. I like fooling around cars. As a matter of fact…" In the light of recent happenings, he hesitated before he boasted, but it came with an irrepressible rush: "Over at Hoker's garage they phone me whenever they get a job that sticks them – like some new foreign car passing through. In fact…"

Again he hesitated, but Jannekin said, "Go on."

"…in fact, I've got a lot of little gadgets at home, and some of them may be worth patenting after I get up to Detroit. And then maybe I'll think of some others."

"I'll bet you will, Dick," she agreed. "You could always mend anything. Remember how you started that old music box that Father brought from the old country? You… you shook it or something."

He laughed, forgetting his temper.

"That was a brilliant hunch – young Edison in the making. However, it won't work with cars, because they usually shake themselves."

But when the picnic grounds came into sight, at first faintly glowing with many Japanese lanterns upon the twilight, then alive with bright dresses, a hard mood descended upon him. He saw a knot of boys gather at his approach and, looking straight ahead, he drove past the crowd that milled about the laden tables and to the parking place beyond. Voices followed them:

"Who'd have thought it?"

"Must be some eastern custom."

"Say, that's some jazzy little tank now."

As he swung the car savagely into an empty space, Jannekin's hand fell on his taut arm.

"What are you going to do, Dick?"

"Why, nothing," he answered innocently.

"You're not going to make a scene about this. Wait! Don't get out yet. Remember, you're with me."

"I'll remember that. Nothing'll happen around you."

"Dick, do you know who did this?"

"I know Edgar Bronson had something to do with it. And two others I'm pretty sure of, and—"

"Listen… Please don't get out, Dick." It was the soft voice of pleading childhood. "Listen, Dick. You could beat any of those three boys, couldn't you?"

"Beat them!" he repeated scornfully. "I could mop up the lake with them. I could ruin any two of them together, and they know it. I'm just wondering what part of the grounds they're hiding in – or maybe they're keeping their girls with them for protection."

He laughed with his chin up, and in the sound there was a wild foretaste of battle and triumph that frightened her and thrilled her.

"Then what would be the satisfaction, Dick?" she begged. "You know already you could beat them, and they know it, and everybody knows it. Now, if it was Capone Johnson…" This was an unfortunate suggestion; she stopped herself too late, as lines appeared between Dick's eyes.

"Maybe it was Capone Johnson. Well, I'll just show him he's not so big that he can—"

"But you know it wasn't him," she wailed. "You know he's the kindest boy in school and wouldn't hurt anybody's feelings. I heard him say the other day he like you specially."

"I thought he did," he said, mollified.

"Now we're going to get out and take our baskets and walk over as if nothing had happened."

He was silent.

"Come on, Dick; do it for Janny. You've done so many things for Janny."

Had she put it the other way – that she had done so many things for him – he would not have yielded, but the remark made it seem inevitable that he should do one more.

"All right." He laughed helplessly, but his laugh changed to an intake of breath as, suddenly, her young body pressed against him, all that rose colour crushing up to his heart, and he saw her face and eyes swimming under him where the wheel had been a minute before.

A minute later, perhaps even two, even three minutes later, she was saying:

"Let me get out by myself. Remember the paint." And then: "I don't care if I am mussed. At least none of them can say they've seen me so mussed before."

Hand in hand, with that oddly inimitable, not-to-be-masked expression on both their faces, they walked towards the tables beside the lake.

3

B UT AFTER A FEW MONTHS during which Dick laced up Jannekin's skating boots or kissed her lips in the many weathers of the long Michigan winter, they arrived at another parting.

Jannekin, borne up on the wings of the family fortune, was taken from Tech and sent to be fashionably educated in Europe.

There were forget-me-nots, but after a time there were fewer letters. Jannekin in Geneva, Jannekin in Paris, Jannekin in Munich; finally Jannekin at The Hague, being presented to the Queen of Holland – Miss Melon-Loper, the gardener's daughter, a splendid plant of the Netherlands that had taken root in the new world.

Meanwhile there was Dick in overalls, Dick with his face grease-black, Dick with his arm in a sling and part of a little finger gone. Now, after five years, there was Dick at twenty-three, assistant to the factory superintendent of one of the largest automobile plants in Detroit. Finally, there was Dick driving to his native city, partly on business and partly because word had reached him that Jannekin had once more set foot upon the shore of the republic. The news came through Edgar Bronson, who worked in a competing factory, but was more in touch with home than Dick. Dick wrote, and in return got a telegram inviting him to dine.

They were waiting for him on the porch of a big Dutch Colonial house – not old Jan, who had broken down under the weight of years and been put in a nursing home, but Mrs Melon-Loper, a stout patroon now, and proud of the family fortunes, and a scarcely recognizable

Jannekin, totally unlike the girl who had lost her voice cheering at the game with Clifton or led her basketball team in bloomers. She wasn't merely developed, she was a different person. Her beauty was as poised and secure as a flower on a strong stem; her voice was cool and sure, with no wayward instruments in it that played on his emotions. The blue eyes that pretended a polite joy at their reunion succeeded in conveying only the face value of the eyes themselves, even a warning that an intention of being amused lay behind them.

And the dinner was like too many other dinners; a young man and woman whose names Dick associated with the city's older families talked cards, golf, horses, country-club scandal; and it became evident to Dick that Jannekin herself preferred the conversation to remain on a thin, dehumanized level.

"After Detroit, we must sound provincial, Dick." He resented the irony. "But we happen to like it here, really. It's incredible, but we do. We have almost everything, but it's all in miniature. We even have a small version of a hunt club and a small version of the Depression – only we're a little afraid at the moment that the latter's going to eat up the former. Nevertheless, Mr Meredith here isn't any less of an MFH* because he has two pairs of boots compared to some Meadowbrook nabob with a dozen."

"Jannekin's subsidized by the chamber of commerce," Meredith said. "Personally, I think the place is a ditch, but she keeps arranging and rearranging things until we all think we're in Paris."

She was gone. Dick might have expected that. Once they had recaptured the past after a lapse of six years; it was too much to expect that it would happen again. There was nothing left of the Jannekin he had known, and he was not impressed with her as the ringmaster of the local aristocracy. It was even obvious that she was content to be top dog here because of a lingering sense of inferiority at having been born a servant's daughter.

Perhaps to another man her new qualities would have their value, but she was of no use to him any more. Before the end of the evening, he had dismissed her from his mind except as a former friend, viewed in enlightening perspective. But he went down the steps empty-hearted from the riddance of that face drifting between the dark and the windows.

Jannekin said, "Come over often, Dick."

With forced heartiness, Dick answered:

"I'm certainly going to!" And to himself he added, "But not to see you, my dear." He did not guess that she was thinking: "Why did I do this tonight? Whatever made me think he'd like it?"

On his way to the hotel, he stopped by the entrance to his old home. It was unoccupied and for sale. Even with part of the property converted into a real-estate development, there were few families in the city who could undertake its upkeep. Dick sighed, expressing he knew not what emotion.

Down at the hotel he could not sleep. He read a magazine for a while and then bent a long, fine piece of wire that he often carried with him into a shape that might some day be embodied in a spring. Once more he recapitulated to himself the impossibility of loving a girl for the third time, when she was not even the girl he had loved before; and he pictured himself with scorn as one of those faithful swains who live perennially in an old hope from sheer lack of imagination. He said aloud: "This thing is out of my mind for good." And it seemed to vanish obediently and he felt better; but he was not yet quite asleep at two o'clock when the phone pounded at his bedside. It was long distance from Detroit.

"Dick, I want to begin by telling you about McCaffray."

"Who is this speaking?"

"This is Bill Flint calling from the office. But first I want to ask you: were your father's initials T.R.?"

"What is this, anyhow?" Dick grumbled. "Are you having a party over there?"

"I told you I'm in my office in the drafting building and I've got a stack of files in front of me two yards high."

"This is a fine time of night—"

"Well, this is a damn important business."

"My father's initials? He didn't know an automobile from a velocipede."

"Shut up and I'll tell you the dope. Now, this McCaffray…"

Back in 1914, a pale little man named McCaffray had appeared in Detroit from nowhere, lingered a few weeks and then inconspicuously died. The little man had had a divine foresight about dual carburation fourteen years in advance of its time. The company experimentally installed his intake manifolds on the first six cars of a series, abandoned the idea, and let Mr McCaffray, with his unpatented scheme, wander off to a rival factory and thence on to his death. But within the last twenty-four hours it had become highly important to the company engineers to find out exactly what that intake manifold had looked like. One old mechanic remembered it hazily as having been "something like you want". Apparently no drawing of it was in existence. But though five of the six cars had been issued to company executives and long ago vanished, the sixth had gone out on a hurry order to a certain Mr T.R. Henderson.

"He was my father," Dick interrupted. "The car is here, laid up in a garage kept by an old chauffeur of ours. I'll have the intake manifold tomorrow."

The family bus again – he felt a rush of sentimentality about it. He'd never sell it; he'd put it in a special museum like the coaches at Versailles. Thinking of it warmly, affectionately, he drowsed off at last, and slept until eleven in the morning.

Two hours later, having accomplished the business that had brought him to the city, he drove to Howard's garage and found him filling a gas tank in front.

"Well, there, Dick!" Howard hurried over, wiping his hands on a ball of waste. "Say, we were talking about you. Hear they made you tsar of the auto industry."

"No, only mayor… Say, Howard, is the old car still running?"

"What car?"

"The old open bus."

"Sure. She never was any five-and-ten proposition."

"Well, I'm going to take her to Detroit." At Howard's expression, he stiffened with alarm. "She's here, isn't she?"

"Why, we sold that old car, Dick. Remember, you told me if I had an offer I could sell it for the storage."

"My God!"

"We got – let's see – we got twenty-two fifty, I think, because the rubber and the battery—"

"Who did you sell it to?"

Howard scratched his head, felt his chin, hitched his pants.

"I'll go ask my daughter how much we did get for it."

"But who bought it?" Dick was quivering with apprehension lest the company of Edgar Bronson, where Mr McCaffray once laboured, had snatched the thing from under his nose.

"Who?" he demanded fiercely.

"Jannekin Melon-Loper bought it."

"What?"

"Sure thing. She came down a month ago, and had to have that car. If you wait a second, I'll ask my daughter…"

But Dick was gone. Had he not been so excited he would have regarded the time and not rung the doorbell at the Melon-Lopers' before a luncheon party of women had risen from the table. As it was, Jannekin came out on the porch and made him sit down.

"I know you don't want to meet a lot of women, but I'm glad you came, Dick. I'm sorry about last night. I was showing off, I guess."

"Not at all."

"Yes, I was – and in such an idiotic way. Because at dinner it kept running through my head that once your mother had called me a dirty little girl."

He breathed in her sparkling frankness like a draught of fresh air and, as they laughed together, he liked her terrifically again.

"Jannekin, I want to see you soon; we have lots of the past to talk about, you and I. But this is a business call. Jannekin, I want to buy back that old car of ours."

"You knew I had it, then," she said guiltily. "I hated to think of it sitting there so... so aged and so neglected."

It was their old love she was talking about, and he knew it, but she hurried on:

"I hear about you sometimes – from Edgar Bronson. He's done very well, hasn't he? He came down last week and dropped in on me."

Dick frowned, with a resurgence of his old sense of superiority.

"Of all the boys who were at Tech, you two are most spoken of," went on Jannekin innocently.

"Well" – his voice held a touch of impatience – "I mustn't keep you from your luncheon."

"That doesn't matter. About the car – if you want it, you can have it, of course. I'll tell the chauffeur to run it around."

A minute later she reappeared, wearing an expression of distress.

"The chauffeur says it's gone. He hasn't seen it for weeks."

Dick turned cold inside.

"It's gone?"

"It must have been stolen. You see, I never bought it to use, but only—"

"This is extraordinary," he interrupted. "I really have to have that car. It's of the greatest importance."

At his change of tone, she hardened also:

"I'm sorry. I don't see what I can do about it."

"Can I look around in back myself? It might be behind the garage or somewhere."

"Certainly."

Scarcely aware of his own rudeness, Dick plunged down the steps and around the house. Wild suspicions surged through him – that Edgar Bronson had persuaded her to part with the car, and now Jannekin, ashamed, was lying to him. It was hard to imagine anyone stealing such an automobile; he searched every foot of the place as if it were

179

something that might be concealed behind a dog house. Then, baffled and raging, be retraced his steps and stopped suddenly within the range of a sentence that drifted out the kitchen window:

"She ask me, but I wan't goin' to tell her. The old man sell it to me last week with a old gun and fishing tackle, just 'fore they took him down to that institarium. He not givin' nothin' away. So I pay him eight dollar out of my wages and I sell the car to Uncle Ben Govan over to Canterbury for ten dollar. No, suh. Old man sold me that stuff fair and square, and I pay him for it. I just shet my mouth when Miss Jannekin ask me. I don't tell her nothin' *at* all."

Dick walked firmly in at the kitchen door. Observing the look in his eye, the chauffeur sprang to his feet, a cigarette dropping from his mouth. A few minutes later, Dick rounded the house again, sorry for his wild imaginings. Jannekin was on the veranda speeding a guest; impulsively, he walked up to her and declared:

"I'm going on an expedition, Janny Jannekin, and you're coming with me right away."

She laughed lightly: "These Motor Boys – he mistakes me for a spare part." But as he continued to regard her, she gave a startled sigh and the colour went up in her transparent cheeks.

"Well, very well. I don't suppose my guests will mind. After all, they've been telling me for months I ought to have a young man... Go in and break the news, Alice, will you? Say I'm kidnapped – try to get the ransom money together."

Pulled not so much by Dick's hand as by his exuberance, they flew to his car. On the way, across the river and up the hill to the darky settlement, they talked little, because they had so much to say. Yassuh, Uncle Ben Govan's house was that one down there. And in the designated hollow a dark, villainous antique came towards them, doffing, so as to speak, his corncob pipe. After Dick had explained his mission and assured him that they were not contesting his legal rights to the machine, he agreed to negotiate. "Yassuh, I got her roun' back. How much you want pay for her, boss?...

"Boss, she's yours." Carefully he requested and pocketed the money, and then led them round to where, resting beside a chicken coop, lay the familiar, cream-coloured body of the family bus – cushions, door handles, dashboard and all.

"But where's the chassis?" Dick exploded.

"Chassis?"

"The engine, the motor, the wheels!"

"Oh, that there part." The old man chuckled belittlingly. "That part I done soe a man. This here comfortable part with the cushions, it kept kind of easin' off the wheels when the man was takin' it away, so he lef' it here, and I thought I'd take these cushions and make me two beds for my grandchildren. You don't want to buy it?"

Firmly Dick retrieved ten of the twelve dollars, and after much recapitulation of local geography, he obtained the location of a garage and an approximation of its name.

"The thing sits quiet for five years," he complained as they raced back down the hill, "and then, at the age of about ninety, it begins to bounce around the country like a jumping bean!"

Finally they saw it. It stood in a row of relics back of the garage – a row which a mechanic was about to slaughter.

But one of them was not a junk to Dick and Jannekin as they rushed forward with reprieve in their eyes. There it was, stripped to its soul: four wheels, a motor, a floor board – and a soapbox.

"Take it away for twenty-five," agreed the proprietor, "as it stands. Say, you know, for a job nineteen years old, the thing runs dandy still."

"Of course, it does!" Dick boasted as they climbed on and set the motor racing. "I'm turning in my car on the trade."

"That's a joke!" called back the practical Jannekin as they drove away. "We'll be around for it."

They throbbed down Canal Street, erect and happy on the soapbox, stared at curiously by many eyes.

"Doesn't it run well?" he demanded.

"Beautifully, Dick." She had to sit very close to him on the box. "You'll have to teach me to drive, dear. Because there isn't any back part."

"We always sat in the front. Once I consoled you beside this wheel and then once you consoled me – do you remember?"

"Darling!"

"Where'll we go?"

"To heaven."

"By George, I think it'll make it!"

Proud as Lucifer, the flaming chariot swept on up the street.

No Flowers

1

"Now tell me again about the proms, Mother," begged Marjorie at twelve.

"But I've told you, over and over."

"But just tell me just once more, pulease, and then I'll go right to sleep."

"Well, let's see," her mother considered. "Well, I used to be invited to go to proms at certain colleges—"

"Yes, go on. Start at the beginning. Start about how they invited you and everything."

"Well, there was a boy I knew once, named Carter McLane—"

"Yes, go on, I like about that prom," enthused Marjorie, squirming closer to her mother.

"—and he seemed to think I was very nice, so he invited me to be his guest. So, of course, I was very excited—"

"What happened to him later?"

"But I've told you this so often. You know my stories as well as I do."

"I know, but I just like to hear you say the whole thing over."

"Why don't you close your eyes and go to sleep?"

But after her mother left, Marjorie lay awake half the night listening to orchestras playing in a great gymnasium bewitched into a paradise of flowers and banners; all night boy after boy cut in on her, until she could scarcely take a step before adjusting herself to a new rhythm – just like Hotsy Gamble, who was two years ahead of her in school and danced cheek-to-cheek and was Marjorie's current Ideal. All evening she drifted, a bright petal cluster among dark-trunked trees…

Six years later she went to her first prom, at the university where the women of her family had gone dancing for several generations. But she wore no orchids on the shoulder of her pale-blue organdie frock. This was because of Billy Johns's letter:

...don't expect me to send you any, and don't bring any. In these times (famous phrase) there are only a few guys can afford them, so the committee ruled them out altogether. Anyhow, you're flower enough for me – and for too many other people, damn it...

She heard also that there would only be one orchestra – not at all like her mother's stories of 1913, when Jim Europe and his bucks were enthroned at one end of the hall, and some Toscanini of tangos at the other. Lawdy, Lawdy! Next thing they'd be dancing to radio and it wouldn't be worthwhile going up there. What a break – to grow up into the middle of hard times, when all the luxury and revelry was subdued and everybody was economizing – economizing even on proms. Imagine!

"Probably there'll be champagne punch at the teas," said her mother innocently. "I do hope you won't touch any."

"Champagne punch!" Marjorie's scorn withered the plush in the chair car bearing them northward. "A girl will probably be lucky if she gets a glass of beer. Billy says they're giving the prom on a shoestring. Honestly, Mother, sometimes I think Father's right when he says that women your age don't know what's happening."

Her mother laughed; she let few things disturb her, and there were scarcely any more lines in her face than when, as Amanda Rawlins, she had ridden north on a similar pilgrimage.

"It may be more fun having it simpler," she said; but she added smugly, "Of course, in my day it was the event of a girl's year – except the year of her debut."

"More fun!" protested Marjorie. "Mother, try and realize you've had your fun, all that luxury and everything, but all we can do is watch it in the movies, and as often as not have to go Dutch treat to the movies."

"Well, Marjorie, we can still get off the train and go home."

Marjorie sighed.

"I'm not really complaining, Mother. I've been very lucky. But sometimes I wish boys didn't wear such old suits and have such old cars and worry about how much gasoline they can afford. Do you realize that one of the Chase twins is driving a taxi and John Corliss is a movie usher?"

"Well, then, at least *he* has new suits."

"Do you know what he'd planned to do? The diplomatic service."

"We haven't abolished the diplomatic service, have we?" her mother asked.

"No, but he failed his examinations, and they won't take them any more if they fail in their examinations. And let me tell you he's sore; he thinks there ought to be a revolution."

"I suppose he wants them to turn the examination list upside down." Marjorie sighed again.

"All that makes me boil is that you were young in a sort of golden age, and I've got to be young in a sort of tin age. I'm growing plain jealous."

But when the towers and spires of the university town swam into the range of the car windows, Marjorie warmed with excitement. This was *it*. The boys who milled around the station were not the legendary Chesterfields with Bond Street clothes and streamlined cars; nevertheless, the Gothic walls rose from the many acres of fine green grass with as much grace and aspiration as if this were a five-million-share day of the Twenties.

All afternoon there were teas, and then dinner at the club where her mother had come as a girl, and where they would lodge that night. Afterwards they went to a performance of the dramatic association and then to an informal dance; the prom took place tomorrow. Sometime during the evening Marjorie's mother repressed a yawn and faded off to bed. Others gave up, retired, but in the great hall of the club a half-dozen couples lingered while the hours began their slow growth towards dawn. Billy Johns beckoned to Marjorie, and she followed him through the dining room into a parlour beyond.

It was an old-fashioned chamber, Victorian and worn in contrast with the elaborateness of the rest of the club.

"This is called the Engagement Room," he said.

She looked around; there was an odd atmosphere about it, a nostalgia for another age.

"It was part of the old clubhouse on this site, and it meant a lot to some of the alumni members; so they had the architect build the new club building around it."

"The Engagement Room," she repeated.

As if at a signal, Billy took a step towards her. She kissed him quickly, stepping back from his arms.

"You're very handsome tonight," she said.

"Only tonight? Anyhow you can imagine why it's called the Engagement Room. It's haunted, you see. The old love affairs that first clicked here come back and click all over again."

"I can believe it."

"It's true." He hesitated. "I'm awfully glad to be in this room with you."

"Get me a glass of something cool," she said quickly. "Would you be a darling?"

He left the room obediently, and Marjorie, fatigued by the day, sank down in a big Victorian leather chair. Alternately she closed her eyes and pulled herself awake, thinking after a while, "Well, he certainly is taking his time about it." It was just at this moment that she realized that she was not alone in the room.

Across from her, sitting beside the gas fire that burned blue over imitation logs, were a young man and a girl. The man wore a wing collar and a blue bow tie; his coat buttoned high in an archaic fashion. The girl wore a gown voluminous of material, with huge puffed sleeves that were reminiscent of contemporary fashion, yet somehow different. Her hair, moulded close to her head in ringlets, served as a perch for a minute bonnet that, like the sleeves, suggested the present without being of it.

"I promised you my answer today, Phil. Are you ready?" She spoke lower and slower, "My dear, I'll be very proud and happy to announce our engagement in June."

There was an odd little silence; the girl continued:

"I would have said yes to you last month, because I knew then that I cared. But I'd promised Mother to take a while to think things over."

She broke off in surprise as the young man suddenly got up and paraded back and forth across the room – a look of misery, akin to fear, had come into his face. The girl looked at him in alarm and, as her profile caught the light, Marjorie recognized simultaneously her profile and her voice as the profile and voice of her mother's mother. Only now the voice was younger and more vibrant, the skin was of the texture that Italian painters of the decadence used for corner angels.

Phil sat down again, shading his eyes with his hand.

"I've got to tell you something... I don't know how."

Lucy's expression was drawn with apprehension; achieving an outward calm, she spoke in a clipped tone:

"Of course, Phil, if your ideas have changed, you must feel free to—"

"Nothing like that."

Somewhat relieved, Lucy said:

"Then won't you... won't you sit a little nearer while you tell me about it?"

Luther, the hall boy, stood at the door.

"Pardon, Mr Savage; Mr Payson would like to speak to you."

Phil nodded.

"All right, tell him I'll be there – very soon – presently. Tell him I'm almost ready."

"Phil!" Lucy demanded. "What is it?"

He blurted it out suddenly:

"I'm leaving college this afternoon, by request."

"You're expelled, Phil?"

"Something like that."

She went to him and put her arm over his shoulder. Watching them, Marjorie knew what was going to happen, because she had heard the story from her grandmother; yet, in the same breath, she was not sure, and she listened, tense with hope.

"Phil, what was it? Did you take too much champagne or something? It doesn't matter to me, Phil, because I love you. Do you think I'm such a lightweight that that could make a difference? Or did you fail some old examination?"

"No," and he added bitterly, "I passed an examination. I felt it was necessary to pass it – at any cost. And I did. It's not the faculty that's asked me to leave; the men waiting outside for me are two of my best friends. Did you ever happen to hear of a thing they've introduced here, the honour system?"

She had heard of it from her brother – a scarcely born tradition of this principality of youth: "I pledge my word of honour as a gentleman that during this examination I have neither given nor received aid."

"Why, Phil—"

"My degree depended on it, and I began thinking that if I flunked out, I'd never have the courage to tell you. Now I've got to tell you, because I happen to have been observed. My dear friends were kind enough to give me twenty-four hours, so that I could meet you and take you to the dance last night, but I'm sentenced to leave this locality for ever by six o'clock."

Lucy went slowly back to her own chair.

"You had to know," said Phil. "Sooner or later you'd have found out why I couldn't come here any more – to this place I've loved so much."

"Yes, I suppose I had to know," she agreed; after a pause, she added: "You didn't do it for me, Phil."

"In a way, I did."

"No, Phil. You did it for some part of you I'm not even acquainted with."

The boy came to the door again.

"Beg pardon, sir; Mr Payson says he must see you right now. He says to tell you it's quarter to six."

Phil nodded miserably.

"I'm coming." And then, harshly, to Lucy, "So what now?"

"That's all, isn't it?" she said in a dead voice. "We couldn't begin to build anything on a foundation of..." She looked at the floor.

"...of dishonour," he supplied. "I suppose not."

He came over and kissed her gently on her high white forehead. After he had gone out, she sat quiet, looking blindly towards the fire. Then suddenly she got up, tore the bouquet of lilies of the valley from her waist and flung it to the hearth.

"I could probably marry a cheat," she muttered, "but I couldn't marry a fool."

Coming into the room with the ice, Billy Johns said:

"So you've come to life again. I didn't like to murder sleep."

"I guess I was dozing," she explained.

"I guess so, either." He stooped beside the fireplace. "Look at the corsage; somebody's been bootlegging flowers against the rules."

2

MARJORIE'S MOTHER, having retired early, came downstairs at nine o'clock into the deserted lower floor of the club, with French windows open to a gentle, melancholy rain. At the foot of the stairs she turned and looked at herself in a pier glass, momentarily surprised that she knew instinctively where it was; but presently she was not surprised, remembering the day when she had first looked into the same glass. She examined her brown eyes, eyes more beautiful, less alert than her daughter's, examined the lovely shape of her face, her fine figure scarcely changed in twenty years.

She breakfasted in the panelled dining room with another chaperone. Amanda felt a certain impatience in being just another mother at a festival that she had several times come close to ruling. That was the year before she married, when she had been honoured by so many bids that she had placed several with less-sought-after girls in town.

After breakfast she began thinking about Marjorie; in the past few years she had realized that she was very far away from Marjorie; her own generation was pre-war, and so many things had happened since then. This

Billy Johns, for instance. Who was he? Just a boy who had visited in their city, who came from some vague part of the Midwest, and who, Marjorie informed her, was "stripped" – a reference not to nudist predilections but to his pocketbook. What were Marjorie's relations to him? And what next when a woman hadn't an idea how to guide and direct her own daughter?

She was smoking in what she remembered was called the Engagement Room; she remembered it very well indeed. She had once sat here trying helplessly to think for herself, as she had just now been trying to think for Marjorie.

It had been the more difficult to think for herself because of the intensity of the young man who was with her – not Carter McLane, who was taking her to the prom, but his room-mate. She had begun to wonder whether she was wasting time with Carter McLane. Most probably he didn't want to get married; he was too perfect. He had never so much as tried to commandeer a kiss; he went around "respecting" girls because he was afraid of life.

Sometimes she believed this.

In any case, the man beside her was different; he swept you off your feet. In many ways he wasn't up to Carter; he had no particular standards, he wasn't a hero in college, but he was "human" – and he made things so easy.

"Don't sit brooding," he begged. "We have such a short time alone together. That doesn't sound quite right, because Carter brought you, but such things have got to be decided right, because it's for ever. When two people are attracted to each other—"

"What makes you think that you attract me more than Carter does?"

"Of course I can't know that. The point is whether he's up to appreciating you."

"He respects me," she said drily.

"And do you like being respected?"

Someone began playing the piano in the music room across the court; two girls in evening dress ran down the corridor past the door. Howard came closer and whispered:

"Or would you rather be loved?"

"Oh, I'd rather be loved," she said – "I'd rather be loved."

But when he kissed her, she began thinking once more of Carter, with his gallant carriage, his wholehearted, reassuring smile. A melody was pouring in the open windows:

"To the Land of
The Never-never
Where we
Can love for ever…"

The tune said to Amanda that, despite the enchantment of the weekend, life was flowing by imperfect, unachieved. It was love for love's sake that she wanted. This time she didn't flinch when Howard kissed her.

"I've been waiting for this," he said. "Amanda, there's something I want you to do for me – only a little thing, but it means so much. I won't be seeing you tonight except on the dance floor, and I want to be knowing all the time that you feel like I do."

"What is it, Howard?" This was living, this was better, this was Now.

From a flower carton he took three orchids, the stems bound in silver, a corsage identical with the one she wore at the waist of her evening dress.

"I want you to wear these instead."

She had a moment of uncertainty; then, with Howard's voice, warm and persuasive at her ear, she unpinned Carter's corsage and replaced it with the other.

"Are you satisfied?"

"Almost."

She kissed him again. She felt excited and defiant. Once again the thin sweet notes of the piano surged in out of the spring dusk:

"A-pril rain – dripping hap-pily
Once a-gain – catch my love and me
Beneath our um-ber-ella cosy
The world will still be pink and rosy…"

Howard put the other orchids out of sight in a vase, and they strolled from the room, their hands pulling apart as they reached the lounge.

The evening was in full flower. The street of the clubs echoed to vehicles and voices; the gleaming shirt fronts and the dresses of many girls blended to one melodious pastel in the dusk. At the Musical Club's concert, Amanda had a slight reaction. Carter, leading the Glee Club, was very handsome up on the platform, and as forty masculine voices were signalled into sound at a nod of his head, she felt a sudden pride that he had asked her here. What a shame he was such a stick. Nevertheless, he was sufficiently impressed and engrossed to be annoyed when Howard's hand brushed hers purposely, and she would not meet his persistent eyes. When she was away from Carter she was free, since he had never spoken a word or a whisper of love, but in his presence it was somehow different.

With a contagious trembling, a universal palpitation that was the uncertainty of many girls at their first prom, and the concealed uneasiness of others, who feared that this would be their last, the young crowd poured out of the concert hall and down through the now starry night to the gymnasium, transformed with bunting and flowers. One of the orchestras was playing Hawaiian tunes as Amanda moved down the receiving line on Carter's arm. Her card, scrawled with the most prominent names in college, dangled from her glove. Formal deference was still paid to the old system, but long before midnight cards were lost or abandoned, and Amanda, whose young loveliness radiated here and there as she wished, swung from man to man in foxtrot or *maxixe*, conservative Boston or radical Ballin' the Jack, at the call of the alternating musics.

Carter McLane cut in on her once a dance, Howard more frequently. Swarming dozens followed her, the image of each man blotted out by the next. At the supper hour, the crowd swayed out into the trophy room to scatter along the wide stairs or to run for dusky pre-empted alcoves; it was in this pause that Amanda realized that she was not particularly happy.

She was glad to be alone and quiet with Carter. He was nicest when one was a little tired and in the clouds. Howard had hinted at joining them, but she discouraged the idea. As they found places in a far corner out of anyone's sight or earshot, she felt the atmosphere change suddenly and surprisingly. A light remark failed to reach Carter; instead of the protective, appreciative smile, he looked at her very seriously and as if he hadn't heard.

"Are you in the mood to listen to something important," he asked, "or are you still hearing the music?"

"What is it, Carter?"

"You," he said, and then, "I love that word. You."

"Doesn't it depend who you're with?"

"Yes."

Her heart had missed a beat and then begun to race. This was Carter, and he was different.

"Here is your hand," he said. "Here is the other hand. How wonderful – two hands."

She smiled, but suddenly she wanted to cry.

"Do you like questions?"

"Some questions."

"They've got to come at the right time, I think. I hope this is the right time, Amanda."

"Well, I don't know—"

"This is an old question. It's been hanging around me a year or so, but it never seemed the time to ask it. Did you ever read Ecclesiastes? 'There is a time to weep, and a time to laugh.'"

"No, I've never read it."

"Well, here's the question: I love you, Amanda."

"That's not a question."

"Isn't it? I thought it was. I thought it was a fine question. What would be a question?"

"Why, I suppose you'd just turn it about."

"Oh, I see. Do I love you? That doesn't sound right either. I never wanted to ask that question."

Her face came closer to him, and she whispered: "I'll just give you the answer without a question."

There was a silence in the corner for a minute and she felt the great difference between two embraces separated only by a few hours.

Presently he said: "I want you to do me a favour – unpin your corsage."

Amanda started; it was the second time that she had been asked this tonight. In a panic, she tried to think whether there was some observable difference in the two corsages, whether she and Howard had been watched in the Engagement Room. With uncertain fingers she obeyed.

"Thank you. I had them sent from New York this morning because the florist's here had been picked over."

As yet, she could detect no irony in his voice.

"Now unwrap the foil," he said.

She untied the ribbon and picked at the silver binding. Carter said nothing; he looked straight ahead with a faint smile, as if he expected her to speak.

"Now what?" she asked.

"Do you see what holds the stems together?"

"Why, nothing. I've taken off the foil."

Quickly he turned, took the orchids from her, staring at them; he picked up the ribbon and the silver paper and spread the latter flat. Then he glanced at the sofa and underneath it.

"Amanda, please stand up and spread out your dress."

She obeyed.

"My Lord, that's funny!" he exclaimed.

"What is it, Carter? I don't understand at all."

"Why, the stems were drawn through a ring under the foil – a diamond engagement ring that once belonged to my mother."

For a moment she stared at him in muted horror. Then she gasped and gave a frightened little cry; Carter, absorbed in his search, did not notice.

"Let me see," he mused anxiously. "I took off the foil and put the ring on the stems myself, after I left the florist's. The box was in my room in plain sight for ten minutes; then I gave it to Luther at the club, and told him to give it direct to you. Did he?"

"Why, yes," she said, regretting the admission immediately.

"And Luther – why, he's straight as a die." Carter brightened up with an effort: "But I wouldn't let the Koh-i-noor diamond ruin this evening. Presently I'll slip out and have a look around."

Miserably she played with her supper, while Carter told her the things she had waited long to hear – how he had started to speak several times, but had wanted to wait until after senior mid-years, when he could look ahead confidently to a start in the world.

And Amanda was thinking that when he left she must leave too; she must go back to the club, find the other orchids, possess the ring and account for the matter somehow – somehow.

A quarter of an hour later, with her cloak trying to conceal her face, she hurried towards the gymnasium door, and ran into Howard.

"Where are you going?" he demanded.

"Don't bother me, please, Howard. Let go my arm."

"Let me go with you."

"No!" She tore away and out the door, up a stone walk, a path, past buildings silver with starlight and late-burning yellow windows, over a highway and on to the street of the clubs.

In the great hall, a last sleepy misogynist lounged over a book; she passed him without speaking. In the Engagement Room she ran for the vase in which Howard had concealed the other corsage, grasping blindly with her hand; then she peered, she turned it upside down; the pin that had held the flowers to her waist fell out upon the table, nothing more. The jar was empty.

In despair she rang for the steward and sank down on a sofa fingering the pin. Luther appeared, knuckling weary eyes.

"No, madam, I haven't seen any orchages. Mr Carter McLane gave me a box this afternoon and I brought it direct to you. I had no other boxes to deliver, so it couldn't have been mixed up."

"I mean in this vase," she begged him.

There was a sound, and they both turned to see Carter standing just inside the door.

"What's all this?" he asked gravely.

Instinctively Amanda put the hand that held the pin behind her back.

"The young lady says there was an orchage in that jar," supplied Luther obligingly.

"All right, you might check up and see what servants might have been in here. That's all, Luther." As the steward withdrew, he demanded again of Amanda's frightened face, "What is all this?"

She was weeping a little in her throat.

"Oh, it was a silly mix-up." Her voice tried to be careless. "Somebody else sent me flowers, some crazy boy – from home – and I must have put them on by mistake."

Carter's face did not change.

"There's something more than that."

Just at this point, with their two pairs of eyes meeting and glinting each on each, Howard came into the room.

"Oh, I beg pardon." He looked at the vase on the sofa; then questioningly, but unprofitably, at Amanda; then, rather defiantly, at his room-mate. "I thought Amanda was alone. I followed her to see if I could help in any way."

Carter's eyes were equally inquisitive. He seemed to come to a conclusion, for suddenly he took from his pocket one of the little paper mats used to protect a dress from bouquet stains, and read aloud from the reverse side:

"'Dahlgrim & Son, Trenton'. Do you deal with that concern, Howard?"

Amanda could no longer keep her face from being aghast and despairing.

"You don't think he took the ring!" she cried.

"Of course not. He didn't even know about it." Carter's voice grew colder and colder word by word. "He took something much more valuable to me than that. I think I understand it all now."

Luther, the steward, returned from his quest.

"I'm pretty certain there's no orchages in the house, now, sir. All the under-stewards are gone home."

"All right, we'll find it. I might need it again some day."

He nodded to Amanda and went out quickly. In terror, she started after him.

"Carter," she cried, the tears streaming down her face. "Carter! Wait!" "Carter!"

Amanda Rawlins Clark, with little lines about her eyes, stood in the middle of the empty room. It was still raining outside, so that it was too dark to see if the jar still existed as part of the bric-a-brac in the room. Not that it mattered any more; McLane had been killed five years later on an army airfield in Texas. It was just that she would always remember a few minutes in a corner of the gymnasium, twenty years ago.

"And just think," she whispered to herself, "that was all I was ever going to have – those few minutes – and I didn't know it until they were over."

3

MARJORIE SLEPT LATE and appeared at luncheon in a vague and floaty state shared by the other night-blooming girls. The rain had stopped and fair weather loomed over baseball game and the prom. Billy Johns appeared and rescued her from the attentions of three young southerners who had not been asleep at all, and were urging her to fly in a plane with them to a dry state where they could "get a man's drink".

Her mother had decided not to stay for the prom, after all, so the hypothetical supervision of Marjorie was turned over to another chaperone. When Mrs Clark had embarked on the train, the young people looked very young indeed to her as they waved goodbye, standing against the sunshine; it made her sad to think how much they expected from life.

"It's now, right now," she wanted to cry out to them. "It's today, tonight; use it well."

Billy and Marjorie went to the game, where they were joined by a club mate known, for all his coal-black hair, as "Red" Grange, just as, a generation before, all Sloans were called "Tod" and all Doyles "Larry".

"More money than anybody in my class," Billy whispered, "yet he's the guy that put over the rule about no flowers. How's that for democratic?

He even gets patches sewed on all his new clothes; a lot of people do – the poverty racket." When the crowd poured lava-like from the stands, Billy and Marjorie strolled to the main street, and she waited for him outside Kurman's tailor shop for an abnormally long while. When he emerged at last, his cheery face was sobered with alarm.

"Whew!" he gasped.

"What's the matter?"

For a moment he hesitated, overwhelmed.

"Why, that lousy Kurman! Say, I've got to dig up something to wear; the dinner coat I had last night was only loaned for the evening. This Kurman's been making me one, but he won't come across except for cash."

"Well, can't you borrow it?"

"Who from? Everybody's hocked their watches to go to the prom." They strolled along, Billy lost in speculation.

"But can't you find some man who's going to wear his dinner coat and borrow his full dress? Or if he's going to wear his full dress, borrow his dinner coat," she added brilliantly.

"Too many people thought of that weeks ago," he said with regret. "I know one coat that was ripped in two, with one claimant pulling each tail."

What a time! What a state of things! No flowers, one band – the committee had almost decided on an undergraduate band – next they would dance to radio or assign a freshman to wind a phonograph. And now, of all absurdities, to find one's swain unable to release his evening clothes from the clutches of a tradesman. For a moment Marjorie was pervaded with melancholy; then she burst forth with helpless hilarity.

"It's so prepreposterous," she burbled. "It's like that boy in Seventeen who tried to buy a waiter's suit."

"I'll get me a uniform, all right," he said grimly.

She took his arm, liking him suddenly more than ever, the way he went about things. She knew his story – he had worked his way through with high credits, and managed to play on two minor athletic teams besides.

The minor problem of a costume – she had every confidence that he would take it in his stride.

It was after four. His first idea was to borrow, and they made a quick round of the campus possibilities, Marjorie waiting outside the entries while Billy went in, to reappear each time with the news that the man wasn't in or had only his own. Finally he gave this up and seemed to be considering some other plan that he did not reveal.

"I'm dropping you at the Dramat tea," he said. "Red or somebody'll take care of you. When I call for you I'll have a suit."

Marjorie was sure he would; she danced away the late afternoon without a doubt to disturb her pleasure. The initial resentment at having missed an age of exceeding swank faded out in the nostalgic harmonies as 'Smoke Got in Her Eyes', and she strolled along the 'Boulevard of Broken Dreams', or wiggled coolly through the 'Carioca'* with flushed and panting men. At 6.30 Billy arrived, his face relieved and lit with enthusiasm; after a single dance, he led her out.

"I had a hellish time. Good Lord, what hasn't happened since I left you here. But it came out all right."

"What happened?"

"Well, I was passing by the Students' Pressing Bureau and I looked in the window, and there was one last dress suit on a rack – probably forgotten. The door was locked, so I went in the window and wolfed the suit over to my room across the court to try it on. It was a bust; it would have made a nice suit of short pants for me. So I decided to take it back, and just as I was straddling the window, a proctor came along and I did some tall, quick arguing."

"But you got a suit?" she asked anxiously.

"Oh, I got one." He chuckled ferociously. "After that, my morale began to break down – or maybe it began to build up – survival of the fittest and all that. No pun intended."

"Where did you get it?"

"I went amoral, I tell you – that course in Nietzsche must be getting to me. I was walking along sort of morose, if you know what I mean, and

I was just about here, where we are now. And right about there was the delivery push wagon of the Students' Pressing with two or three dinner coats on it. I inspected them in an idle way, and what do you think – there was one just made to fit William Delaney Johns – perhaps not quite up to what the court tailor whips together for me but fair enough – fair enough. So imagine my surprise and indignation when I saw the tag pinned to it; it belonged to a particularly obnoxious freshman in my entry. I boiled. Why, in my father's time no freshman would have dared attend a prom. I thought of going to the senior council, the dean, the board of trustees—"

"But instead you took the suit."

"Well, yes," he admitted, "I took the suit. This is no time to shake the university to its foundations, but somebody had to protect that freshman from himself."

Marjorie was a little shocked, but she was amused too; it wasn't her affair.

Later, dressing at the club, she renewed in herself the anticipatory emotions of many generations, realizing that it was youth itself that was essential here; the casual trappings were shrinking in importance moment by moment. She might some day make her bow before royalty, but nothing would ever be quite such a test of her own unadorned magnetism as tonight.

She thought of Billy, feeling oh so friendly, almost loving him – or did she love him? If only he had the prospects of Red, what a background, this, for a courtship. Walking beside him, her gown of printed satin swishing close to his purloined dinner coat, she felt a tender satisfaction in his presence. She would be good to him tonight; she would make him feel that never, never, was she so happy; that through him she was realizing the fulfilment of a long, old dream.

"I want to stop by my room a minute," Billy said. "I didn't seem to have any studs, so I just buttoned my union-suit buttons through the dress-shirt buttonholes, and one of them didn't stand the strain. I've got to go up and stitch."

"Shall I come and do it for you?"

"Too dangerous. Wait here."

She sat on the dormitory steps. Just over her head was a lighted window, and after a minute a disconsolate voice floated out into the thickening dusk. It was a girl's voice, full of the kind of false cheer that veils a deep disappointment:

"We can go to the Glee Club concert anyhow. We can sit upstairs, like you said."

Then a man's voice, curdled with wretchedness:

"After you came all the way from Greenstream. I tell you I can find somebody to look after you. I'll make them. You're going to the prom."

"I'm going to stay with you. I'm not going to the prom without you."

"She's right, Stanley," said another woman's voice, Midwestern like the others. "Estelle wouldn't go without you. These other girls got a lot of boyfriends and Estelle would feel scared if she didn't have somebody to look after her. Never you mind. We can all walk down and hear the music, and that'll be nice, and I'm sure Estelle doesn't mind a bit."

"Mamma's right," said Estelle. "It wouldn't be nice to go without you."

Stanley sighed.

"If I could only get my hands on the guy who took my tuxedo. I'd knock his back teeth—"

"Don't let it fret you, Stan," urged Estelle. "We can maybe come down again."

Holding her breath, Marjorie mounted the steps of the dormitory. The door of the lighted room was ajar, and from the semi-darkness of the hall she looked in. A girl, very straw-haired, very young, dressed in an over-elaborate satin gown, sat on the arm of the chair occupied by the very miserable young man. The mother, rural and worn, looked on with helpless compassion.

"Don't take on so, Stan," the girl said, her lip quivering. "Honestly, I don't mind at all."

Quietly Marjorie ran up the stairs, looking for the room number to which she had addressed many letters. She went in to find Billy adjusting the secured button with satisfaction.

"Everything but a flower," he said smugly. "I agree it's all right not to send corsages to girls, but there's no rule against a girl sending a man a gardenia now and then."

"Billy," she said abruptly, "you can't wear that dinner coat to the prom."

"I can't, can't I? Why, I'm wearing it."

"There's a girl downstairs – she's that freshman's girl, and now they can't go to the prom. Oh, Billy, it means so much to her – so much more than it could ever mean to me. If you could see her, Billy. She's dressed all wrong and she must have been so proud of herself, and now she's just heartbroken."

"What? That freshman had the additional nerve to bring a girl?"

"It's no joke, Billy – not to them. This prom is probably the greatest thing that'll ever happen to her in her life."

"Well" – he sat down philosophically – "if the young punk's got a girl, I suppose that does change the face of the situation. Though he might have told me, before I went to all the trouble of stealing his suit."

Ten minutes later he returned the dinner coat to its owner, with the information that it had been delivered to his room by mistake. Watching again from the door, Marjorie saw the girl's face, and for a minute that was just as much fun as any prom.

Outside, Marjorie and Billy sighed together as they strolled over to the Glee Club concert.

"I guess Red takes you, the lucky goat," Billy mused. "And won't he be sorry, the wolf!"

"Oh, I'm not going without you," she exclaimed, her voice like Estelle's.

"Oh, yes, you are. You just don't know it."

After a long argument, Marjorie conceded that she might go in later for one dance.

Later they watched the couples entering the gymnasium and heard the first strains of 'Coffee in the Morning',* even danced to it for a moment on the grass; but a sort of melancholy stole over them both. On a mutual impulse they turned and began walking away from gaiety, away from Marjorie's first prom. The joke that they had good-humouredly built up around the situation had grown flat.

They reached the now deserted club and he followed her at a mourner's pace into the Engagement Room.

"This is a case of the strong being sacrificed to the weak," he complained – "of everybody being sacrificed. Think of the hundreds of young men on the very threshold – you know what a very threshold is – think of them seeking beauty and finding only the freshman's girl."

"Let's forget it," she said.

"All right," he agreed. "And do you know a better way than this?" He snapped out the lights overhead…

After a while he said: "Strange as it seems, as a matter of fact, I have a future, a real future. I might even ask you to share it with me if you were a little more grown up, if you'd been to a prom, for instance—"

"Oh, be quiet."

"—and absorbed some sophistication, and weren't just" – a brief interlude – "just mamma's girl."

He got up and lit them cigarettes.

"In fact, my mother has a brother with a Horatio Alger* complex, and he has said that if I got through college absolutely on my own, he'd do wonders for me. So, if he's alive in June, consider you have a suitor."

Marjorie had almost succeeded in forgetting the prom now; there was only this man with his proud poverty, his defiant gaiety. Just as she had always respected her grandmother of the gilded age as being less insulated from realities than her mother of the golden age, so she felt new communions of *noblesse oblige* in this tin age of struggle that her mother would not have understood. Marjorie had come to the university with no illusions; she left with none acquired. But she knew pretty certainly that she loved this man, and that some day she would marry him.

Mr Luther, the club manager, stood in the doorway of the room.

"Beg pardon, sir. Mr Grange came in and grew a little… drowsy on the lounge. I thought I might find someone to help me put him in bed before any ladies start coming in."

"Of course."

Suddenly the glow of one possessed by a hunch lighted up Billy's face.

"Of course!" he repeated jubilantly, and then, to Marjorie: "You wait here!"

Minutes later, on the stroke of midnight, Billy reappeared; he was clad in exquisite raiment, cut on Bond Street by a caterer to kings.

"If you loved me before," said Billy, "what do you think of me now?"

"I don't know," she answered doubtfully. "Has Red had patches sewed on the trousers of that too?"

He caught her close for a moment; then, with three good hours before them, they hurried out the door and over the campus towards the melody of 'Orchids in the Moonlight'.*

"No flowers," Marjorie panted.

But Billy could not entirely agree, and they stopped under an elm on President's Walk, so he could reassure himself that there was at least one.

New Types

1

S O IT WAS ALL TRUE THEN – these places, people, appurtenances, attitudes actually existed. Leslie Dixon had never really believed that they did, any more than one really believes in the North Pole or the country of the Pygmies. And since he had lived in China through weird and turbulent years he had had almost as much practice in believing as the Red Queen.*

There was, to begin with, a beach, seemingly the same beach that he had often regarded in the advertisements. It was a perfect beach, sand of Egypt, sky of Naples, blue of the Bahamas, sparkle of the Riviera – and all this not forty minutes from Times Square. Then there were these new, oddly shaped cars that slid along on tiptoe, glittering. They did not look a bit like cars to Leslie, they just looked like *something* – very much as German toys often look like the originals that went out of existence twenty years ago. These cars were the exact reverse of that; they looked as if they should not have come into existence for twenty years more. Likewise the bathing suits of the girl beside him and of the girls in front of him and the girls in front of them did not look like bathing suits, at least not in Dixon's idea of a bathing suit. They just looked like *something*. They made him want to laugh; they made him feel old and rather susceptible. He was thirty-four.

The girl beside him apparently had no idea of following up the introduction with anything approaching conversation. Only once had she surprised him with what was, for her, a perfect babble of talk.

"It's hot," she declared.

She was a rather tall girl. Her ash-blond hair seemed weatherproof save for a tiny curtain of a bang that was evidently permitted, even expected, to stir a little in a mild wind. She was ruddy brown and without visible make-up, yet with an unmistakable aura about her person of being carefully planned. Under minute scallops that were scarcely brows her eyes were clear and dark blue; even the irises were faintly blue and melted into the pupils' darkness. Her teeth were so white against the tan, her lips so red, that in combination with the blue of her eyes the effect was momentarily startling – as startling as if the lips had been green and the pupils white. She was undoubtedly up to all the specifications in the advertisements. About her back Leslie could scarcely guess, not wanting to stare; from the corner of his eye it seemed quite long, and he judged it was much like the backs in front of him.

"Do you want to go in the water?" he asked.

"Not yet," she answered.

After this impassioned argument there was an interruption. Two young men came up, seized the girl by the head and shoulders, twisted her, mangled her, were violently familiar with her, and then stretched themselves on the sand at her feet. During the bout the expression of her face did not change, nor the set of her hair; she only murmured, "Don't," in a purely formal way and turned to Dixon:

"Would you like to come to a dance my aunt is giving for me Wednesday?"

"Why, I'd like it very much, unless my cousin has made—"

"No. She's coming. My aunt is Mrs Emily Holliday and her house is The Eglantine on Holliday Hill. About nine o'clock."

"I think I know her – I think my mother knew her when we lived here."

The girl said without hesitation:

"That was a bad break for your mother. My aunt is the most obnoxious person. I try to stay out of the house as much as possible."

He was somewhat shocked and covered it with a question:

"Do you live with her?"

"I'm visiting her. However, she's so rich that I expect at any minute to be asked to pay board."

He laughed, but the subject had become embarrassing.

"Where do you live?"

"New York."

She said it in a way that has something final about it. New York!

"Where do you live?"

"I've lived a long time in the Far East, but now I think I'm home for good."

The two young men – they were of college age – turned and inspected him briefly during this conversation.

After their violent approach they had spoken no word, but now one of them said to the girl without looking at her:

"I hear Mrs Holliday feels the same way about you, Paula. Just a shallow, empty girl."

Paula's face was unmoved.

"I know. Inviting me here is the first thing she's done for any of the family in twenty years – when I saw that menagerie of animals she keeps I knew it was going to be the last."

Ellen Harris, Leslie's cousin, came up, dripping from the water. Here was a girl he understood, such a girl as had already been in circulation in 1922 when he left the States. The basis of Ellen's character was still "old-fashioned", something one could prophesy and rely on; she had eaten the salt of the flapper and turned responsive eyes towards the modern world, yet after marriage one was sure she would revert to type and become her mother, even her grandmother.

As if reminded by Ellen's arrival of the Sound's proximity, Paula and the two young men got up to go in, but Leslie lingered, lest Ellen think he had allied himself with them. He was aware dimly that Ellen found him attractive. His long residence in foreign part, his prominence in the family as an outstanding "success" gave her the feeling that he was valuable.

But Paula Jorgensen, the girl he had been sitting with, achieved no more than half the distance to the beach without being interrupted.

It was a small man, of very gross aspect, and he seemed to have no place in the picturesque surroundings. Evidently, though, he had power, for Paula, after his self-introduction, turned about patiently and led him back to her original camping ground.

Even if their curiosity had not been aroused, Leslie and Ellen would have had difficulty in not hearing the conversation that ensued:

"We all think" – the man uttered in one of those voices that, having achieved all nuances in their early stages, had no choice for emphasis but to talk louder and louder – "that if we pay you this—"

"Don't say 'if'," Paula interrupted. "You've got to pay me. I've got to have that money."

"Exactly! You got to. So have we. We're all embarked on the campaign. What we want is you got to be seen with your" – he glanced around, managing to sink his voice an octave in deference to Ellen and Dixon – "your swell friends, your society social friends, that's the point. We need first six flashlights to work on. One alone on, say, a staircase..." He paused again and kindly explained with enormous gestures what a staircase was – how it ran up and down. "Then we want groups, the sweller the nicer, some real classy people, you know, nothing cheap, you know, really the classy type. You know?"

Paula did not nod. It seemed to Leslie that she sighed faintly.

"All right," she said, "anything, but no more 'ifs'. I've got to have that money. Now go 'long."

"Thank you," said the man; then doubting the aptness of his phrase he amplified, "Thank you for your coinperation..."

As he stood doubting the validity of this coinage, Paula helped him. "Goodbye," she said.

He went, starting, by some curious combination of instincts, to raise his hat, then deciding against it, fading off in a highly bow-legged way, exigent even at a distance, down the beach.

Paula turned and smiled at them, without a trace in her eyes of having been bothered by the encounter.

Her expression seemed to say, "Well, that was that – we all have our troubles."

As she went down for her delayed swim, Ellen turned to Leslie.

"I wonder what Madame Holliday is going to think of that."

"Well, as a matter of fact, I have been thinking," he said, "something."

"Now tell me what you've been thinking about," Ellen said. "You have that brooding look."

"…about the advertisements; it seems they're all true. Everybody here had just the kind of teeth and hair and clothes and cigarettes and automobiles and expressions that the people have in the advertisements."

"Remember, this is a very swanky beach."

"Even allowing for that. The girl you introduced me to…"

He decided not to go on with this, but Ellen urged him.

"You mean Paula Jorgensen?"

"Yes. Why, she's the absolute type of all the girls in the ads – her face, the way she holds herself, what she says, or rather what she doesn't say."

Ellen had a readier explanation.

"As a matter of fact she has modelled for fashion magazines a great deal. But she *is* a very familiar type."

"I guessed as much."

"Oh, yes, the tall indifferent type. Paula could have lots of attention, but she doesn't seem very interested."

"What is she interested in?"

"Nothing, I guess."

But Leslie had decided differently – he had decided that Paula Jorgensen was interested in some form of perfection. It was perhaps a perfection that, in his unfamiliarity with the customs current in his country, he could not understand, a perfection of form, a purely plastic aim, as if towards a motionless movie, a speechless talkie.

"…her aunt invited her here apparently to abuse her," Ellen was saying. "Gave her a luncheon party and regaled half the table with the story of how Paula's father drank himself to death."

"Did Paula just take it?"

"She didn't say a word, didn't turn a hair; you'd have thought Mrs Holliday was talking about somebody in Africa… Hey! I almost forgot to tell you that you're invited to a dance *chez* there Wednesday, and you'll have a chance to make your own observations. This dance is all Paula's staying for – she never had any kind of a debut or anything like that." After a minute Ellen added: "Paula's an odd girl. She's very correct and all that, but she doesn't live with her family and she hasn't gone around much since she was seventeen. Just when everybody's forgotten her she seems to step out of a bandbox from somewhere."

Leslie met her again on the afternoon of that same day. This time she was in specification riding clothes and accompanied by two other young men, scarcely distinguishable from the two at the beach. They joined the group on the porch of the golf club and Leslie watched her as she accepted several introductions – not by a flicker of her face did she seem to see the people she met, or to be conscious of the group with which she stood, yet there was no touch of rudeness in her manner; it was rather an abnegation, the silence in company of a well-bred child.

Suddenly she saw Leslie Dixon and, leaving the others abruptly, came over to him. Thinking she might have something special to say, to ask, he waited for her to speak, but she merely took up a station beside him, caught his eye as if to report that she was there and then just stood, stood and waited.

Leslie decided that he too would just stand. They listened to the chatter that went on around them, they spoke to mutual acquaintances who passed. Once their glance met and they smiled just faintly.

After quite a long while she said:

"Well, I must go now."

And only then did he feel the need of some communication.

"How's your aunt?" he asked abruptly.

"She's awful," Paula reassured him. "By the way, don't forget the dance. Goodbye."

She turned away, but he called her back:

"Look, tell me one thing before you go. Just what are you waiting for?"

For a moment her eyes seemed startled. "Waiting?"

"Yes. I mean, what do you want to happen to you? What do you expect to happen to you? Listen to me! I think you're so particularly attractive that I've whooped up the nerve to ask you what you're preparing yourself for. Certainly it isn't for a man."

"A man?"

She spoke the word as if she had never heard it before.

"I mean you don't seem to…" Leslie was becoming embarrassed at his presumption. "I mean you treat yourself as if you were just something to display, fabrics or something. And you're a lot more than that, but what?" He was almost stammering, sorry now that he had spoken. Paula looked past him slowly.

"What do you want me to be?" she asked. "I could be anything they wanted me to be if I knew what it was." Then suddenly she looked him straight in the eye. "A lot of us don't know any more."

Acknowledging no one save with a faint set smile, she flicked her two escorts into motion with her crop and left the club.

2

H E DID NOT SEE HER ALONE AGAIN until the afternoon of her aunt's party, when they sat together in a rumble seat driving back from a boxing match in Greenwich.

"What would you say if I told you I was a little in love with you?" he said. He was quite sober and deliberate. A few little unattached sections of her sun-warm hair blew back and trickled against the lobe of the ear closest to him, as if to indicate that she was listening.

"I'd say the usual thing; that you hardly know me and I hardly know you."

"I'm thirty-four," he said gently. "I thought I might be able to dig up a few odds and ends out of the past and make a high ideal, and you could try and shoot at it."

She laughed, cheered, somehow, by his interest.

"I'm not equipped for an idealist. I saw my mother begin by believing in everything and end up with five children and just enough life insurance to pay for the funeral. Up to then I'd been the family orchid, then suddenly I was a telephone girl. Orchids can't turn into telephone girls and still be good idealists."

"Were you a good telephone girl?"

"Terrible. Tried the stage next, but so did a lot of other people. Then I got to be a model. I get along. I'm quite in demand as a matter of fact, but no one could ask me to believe again how kind the world is to everybody and all that. I take what I can get."

"The morality of a gold-digger."

"Without any gold," she murmured, "but plenty hard enough, or how could I stay on here with this awful woman who loathes me? If she's rotten to me at a luncheon party, do I let that spoil a nice, free meal?"

She swung her knees pressed together in his direction.

"Did I spring up and go through heroics and stomp out of the house on account of a few insults, just when she's giving me a big dance? Not I – I don't let myself get unhappy about the things that would make my mother unhappy. Tonight I have a new dress that an advertiser gave me because I worked overtime and sold a whole series for him; I'm going to be the centre of things for the first time in my life in a great, big, luxurious house; and I'm going to enjoy myself. If my aunt beats me with sticks when I go home, and accuses me of every crime in the dictionary, I'm still going to be gay tonight."

They dropped her at the house, a great-spreading wooden mansion of another era, overlooking the sea. A platoon of caterers had been working since morning, turning the extra-wide verandas into corridors of roses and festooning the two great rooms that, thrown open to each other, made the ballroom. Mrs Holliday was waiting when Paula entered; her little eyes darted around at the caterer's men setting up the long buffets.

"Where have you been?" she enquired, with a false patience. "Since this dance is largely for you, you might have been on hand to give what help you could."

"You told me to go away," Paula said. "You told me I was in the way."

"You were, but I didn't mean to go all afternoon. Who were you with?"

"Since you're interested, I was with the Dixon man."

"Since I'm interested? That's a nice way to address me! What Dixon man?"

"Leslie Dixon."

"Does he understand that you're only a visitor here?"

"He does if he understands English."

"Did you tell him you'd been acting as a model?"

"I told him everything necessary."

"I wouldn't reach too high if I were you – not with your heredity."

"I want to ask you a particular thing about tonight."

"What – about having the party on the lawn? I thought I went into that in detail with you. Older people feel heat and cold much more intensely – and just remember, everybody in my generation wasn't brought up in France."

"It wasn't about that, Aunt Emily. That's all settled. We couldn't have a platform put down at this hour if we had to. It was about…" She hesitated. "It means a great deal to me."

Her aunt interrupted her. "We don't seem to agree at all on what is important and what isn't important."

Paula shifted her foot around impatiently. "Aunt Emily—"

"Your own family have found you so difficult. I don't see why on earth I should ever have—"

"Aunt Emily, our time together is so short; now can't you really forget for a minute that you don't like me? Why, maybe… maybe I don't like you."

"What?" Mrs Holliday leant forward. Her face was suddenly strained and warped. "You don't like me? You mean that?"

For the moment, in the distortion of Mrs Holliday's face, Paula wondered if anybody liked anybody. It was a quintessence of hatred she saw in it, as if one wanted to bring hatred into the world as a commodity that could be played around with as harmlessly as one can play with affection. But having her axe to grind, Paula held her tongue. She was going to grind that axe, and a phrase from the recent diary of an explorer haunted her: that "many very different ends are achieved with blood in the ears". The first time she had read the phrase it had offended her, yet fundamentally she believed in "this man's world", and knew that men went through their own particular hells, and respected them, both for the fact itself and for their reticence about it. She recognized the difficulty of what she was trying to put over as one of the sordid businesses life can lay out for you.

But she was wise enough to put the first thing first and the third thing third – a harder alignment than one might think – and her first principle, her secret, called to her overwhelmingly so she knew that to carry out the idea of the advertising firm she would have to be photographed coming down the stairs, then again in the middle of the evening, and then, more especially, with certain prominent people whom she had chosen as being of her generation, people she could go on with in an exigency, people who could cooperate. However, she didn't feel this was the time to explain things to her aunt. There was no time to explain things to her. Mrs Holliday was one of those people to whom nothing could ever be explained.

"Aunt Emily, there may be strangers around."

Aunt Emily turned to her swiftly. "Men that my husband would not have received?"

The opportunities for comment on this left-handed remark sped by Paula's ear.

"I mean mechanical men, Aunt Emily. Photographers."

Still absorbed in the detail of seeing that the caterer's assistants would not abscond with the silver, Aunt Emily caught only the end of this.

"Well, we've had enough of that around today," she said, watching a man taking a dead bulb from a bank of lights. "Enough so-called mechanical men."

Paula gave up. She backed away.

She went upstairs. Presently Paula came down in a bathing suit for a quick dip in the Sound. Paula liked swimming alone; she had been alone so long that groups often tired her and embarrassed her; her easy reticent manner was a method of concealing this. It had been a long time since she had spoken out as frankly as she had to Leslie Dixon. His interest had surprised her.

After her swim she had a light supper in the breakfast room; her aunt did not come down.

Upstairs she took a quick tub, and then even more quickly she poured herself into her new dress, settling it with almost one motion, and then drew her lips in the mirror. Simultaneously a knock at the door brought a maid with a box of orchids from Leslie Dixon.

"And Mrs Holliday would like to see you, please," the maid added, "soon as possible."

Paula left the orchids in their box and went to her aunt's room. She came into the room absorbed in her own thoughts with "Yes, Aunt Emily" on her tongue, but she could not have told afterwards whether she had actually said it, for immediately she was aware of something unfamiliar and unexperienced about Mrs Holliday. She took a step forward, paused again, then ran towards her.

She was aware precisely at that moment that all her relations with Mrs Holliday were changed; her dislike, created automatically by Mrs Holliday's dislike for her, was vanished. She knew surely that the pale figure collapsed in the armchair was in a world without hatred, without human emotions. She went and listened for the heartbeat, hating the smell of the scent that her aunt used, inseparably associated for her with bullying and cruelty.

"Aunt Emily," she said, "wake up."

Downstairs, as if collaborating with her, the nascent orchestra drew unmotivated tears from the fiddles and piano wires. But the figure in the armchair did not move.

Paula dreaded to wait – she didn't believe it – she had a sharp reversion to a scene in her own childhood and heard repeating in her head:

"Brother made it up – it's a joke."

Then she arose from the armchair where she had taken refuge with the first shock; she approached the body and said in the most sincere outburst of tenderness she had felt in all their relations, "Aunt Emily!"

But still Aunt Emily did not move. A cigarette that Paula had brought in with her expired finally with the faintest of sounds, and, as if answering to a signal, Mrs Holliday's head fell sidewise.

Paula looked, then looked away; she looked sidewise, but in the sweep of her eyes around the room, from the cyclorama of the walls to the object for sympathy, found no help. Only a fat Victorian pincushion filled with an assorted variety of many-coloured-headed pins seemed to assure her that a well-brought-up girl would do the right thing.

"Aunt Emily," she said again.

"You..." she began, and stopped. She went over to her and, in a sort of rush, as if making up to her aunt for an early neglect, she said aloud:

"You... well, you hated me, didn't you? And you were the sister of my father. I guess you didn't mean to be so bad." She hesitated, breathing hard, half-sobbing, wondering how anybody could be so bad. "You didn't mean to be so bad, did you – did you?"

Her instinct was to shake her aunt impersonally, as if that would galvanize her into life.

"But," she thought, "you did even manage to be bad after you were dead."

Paula sat down again suddenly.

"I hate you," she said. "You're gone now and I'd like to respect you."

The air of a first tentative Wiener waltz climbed up the branches of the wisteria and choked the window. Once more Paula stood up, suffocated.

"All right, Aunt," she said, "you stay here – you be nice to me for once. Oh, I'm sure that you... that even you wouldn't mind, if you knew how important it was. You wouldn't, would you? You..."

Mrs Holliday's head drooped further.

"Aunt Emily," she said again, automatically.

"But this is so strange," she thought. "This is a cruel woman who might have helped us when we needed help and didn't choose to."

Then suddenly the image of the harassed publicity man who had asked for "coinperation" on the beach appeared to her with the awful "if" – the "if" that he had carried like the reminder of her secret – Paula stood up.

"Aunt Emily," she said, aloud, "you shouldn't have died. I suppose you did your best in your own way, but, but oh my, you shouldn't have died now because I needed tonight."

She was all tied up in her own problem now, and when she went to the grey figure in the chair and picked up the limp left arm to put it decently in the lap, the gesture was automatic. What did this mean to her?

Suddenly she realized the dance was cancelled, there was no dance. There was not only no dance, there was no opportunity. No dance, no chance. Nothing. In view of this new happening there would be none of the photographs specified, and no photographs automatically meant no money. Three hundred, that would do it, that was enough.

"You wouldn't know, you wouldn't care, where you are now."

She stood aloof, detached, questioningly, talking to her as one might talk to a baby.

She leant suddenly forward and rearranged her aunt's tie.

"There," she said.

She was thinking very fast now; she heard the orchestra change to a foxtrot downstairs.

"You wouldn't mind, would you?" she said. "If you knew, if you were the kind of person who cared about people. I mean you wouldn't mind since you're dead, doing something much kinder than you'd ever have done while you were alive?"

Paula had moved towards the door while she was saying this. Now she opened it, then shut it again and turned once more towards the figure in the armchair.

"It's just life against life, Aunt Emily. And you don't seem to have any, any more."

On an impulse, she ran across the room and kissed the still-cold brow. Then she went out, turned the key in the door, tried to think of any part of her apparel that would hold a key – nothing; she hesitantly explored the reliability of her bodice, and her sandals. No chance. She raised the corner of a rag rug and slipped the key under it and went down into the white thunderous boom of a flashlight pointed at the staircase.

3

LESLIE ASSUMED THAT IT WAS A VERSION of a ball that might have taken place twenty years earlier, but no, there were plenty of people who might have been present at either ball, but they were not the same people exteriorly or in their attitude.

Later he gazed as one of many half-puzzled spectators at the groupings of a dozen young people who posed in the middle of the dance floor. Among them he recognized the two young men from the beach, and again his mind slumped upon the helpless haunches of "I wonder what this is all about; it wasn't like this in my time".

In the glare of the flashlight she had seen Mr and Mrs Haggin, whom she knew her aunt had asked to stand in the receiving line; and with a dread that the dancing might start without her being there, she headed for them, perhaps heading for a solid rock, and with the qualification that it might be the rock upon which she would wreck herself.

"How do you do, Mrs Haggin? I'm Paula Jorgensen."

Suddenly she gave up and made a unit of her personality, and in the making of it realized that what had happened upstairs could not be fitted into the pattern of the evening downstairs. However, she was committed; she had nourished herself for a long time on the idea that courage was everything, so she could not afford to betray such a stand-by.

"…I believe you were to receive with my aunt. She's feeling the weather a little and she'd appreciate it if we'd just go on without her. She expects to be down later."

"I'm so sorry. Shan't I run up and see her first?"

"I think she's trying to sleep at the moment."

When the guests were told at the receiving line that Mrs Holliday was slightly indisposed, the hostess achieved a factitious popularity from the fact that she had sportingly commanded the dance to go on. There were, however, malicious individuals to wonder how she could have taken any other course. Presently the younger people forgot her, and with the great sweep of the 'Blue Danube',* the summer ball rocked into motion.

Early in the evening Paula saw Leslie waltzing with his cousin Ellen; later she found her eyes being swayed and pulled here and there and this and that way, and she finally settled with herself that they were being pulled towards him. When he cut in she was with him, almost before she knew it, in a niche of the obscure rose-scented darkness of the veranda.

Despite the fact that they were both by temperament on the romantic side, they had each, in different ways, been living a long time in the face of harsh reality. Irresistibly they picked out the material facts from a given situation. The one that interested him specifically at this time was the soft, swaying gowns that for a moment seemed to be the gowns of people that had waited for Jeb Stuart and the Gallant Pelham* to ride in out of the night; all the people there seemed to have for a moment that real quality which women have when they know that men are going towards death, and maybe will get there, and maybe not; and then that feeling centred in Paula. Not that Leslie belittled such efforts, such unexplored tragedies as might lie below the lacy furbelows swishing the dust from the age-old ballroom; but that all Leslie's thinking of the past, or future, had become embodied in the lovely figure of Paula as she shone out through a cloud of clinging, billowing white.

Thinking as she did about him, she was glad when a chance gave them the intermission together. But it was late and she didn't know whether she wanted to talk frankly to somebody or whether she could ever talk frankly any more, whether in the future everything had to be locked up inside for ever, locked into the feminine characteristic quality of patience, of standing and bearing what life had to offer. During the evening she had carried with her a special liking for this man.

She thought then suddenly of what was upstairs!

"Of all times," he was saying, "of all times not to make love to a girl – it's at her own dance."

"Debut," she interrupted. "Do you realize I'm having a debut at twenty-four? Look, I'd like to tell you…"

Someone swung her away from him and Leslie Dixon returned to his vantage point with the impression that there was a new fervour burning in her calm eyes. Wine of excitement – she had promised that she was going to enjoy herself.

With the evening singing on, the impression of her beauty deepening moment by moment, the dance itself gathering around her, dependent on her physical existence there, complete so long as she was on the floor, his desire to have some sort of share in her loveliness increased.

He took his cousin Ellen to supper. Afterwards he cut in on Paula as a number came to a close, and he was alone with her. The unrest, the peculiar abstraction remained in her eyes; she followed him out, not speaking when he suggested that they go into the garden.

She shivered.

"Cold," she said, "I'm cold and frightened. I've got to talk to somebody I can… can I trust you?" She looked at him searchingly. "I think maybe I can. Let's go somewhere we can be alone."

But in the seat of a dark car she changed her mind.

"No, not now – afterwards – after the dance." She sighed. "I said I was going to have a good time, and since I've gone this far…"

Then, for both of them, it was darkness on Long Island; then for a moment still sitting there close together they faded into the sweet darkness so deep that they were darker than the darkness, so that for a while they were darker than the black trees – then so dark that when she looked up at him saying, "Yes, I love you too," she could but look at the wild waves of the universe over his shoulder and say, "Yes, I guess I love you too."

Once more she crushed the puff of her shoulder flat against his shoulder.

"That was so nice," he said presently.

"If you knew how long it has been since I kissed anybody."

"But I told you I loved you."

"What a waste. But if it gives you any satisfaction, go on loving me—"

"Paula, now you can tell me what is bothering you."

"Let's go in. I want to have a whole lot of people telling me that I'm attractive."

She let herself be delivered into the dance and just before she was surrounded, beaten and made dim by an always increasing swarm of men, she heeded a signal from the stairs.

It was her aunt's maid trying to attract Paula's attention, yet afraid to wave at her; she compromised on a broken gesture that consisted of raising the hand as if for a knockout punch; and then she merely wiggled the second and third fingers. Paula obeyed the summons, steeling herself to what it might imply; but the maid only said: "Miss Paula, I think Mrs Holliday has locked herself in."

"Well, if she has, nothing can be done about it right at this minute."

"But she has never done that before."

"Please don't worry about that now; I'll go up in a minute and see."

Surprised at the casualness which she had mustered in dealing with the situation, Paula slid out again on one of the many arms available.

The violins hummed, the cello crooned, the kettledrum marched till after two; it was three before the last groups pried themselves away from the last of the champagne.

The publicity man was almost the last to go; Leslie Dixon was the last to say goodbye, and suggested himself he should do a little locking of French windows. She wondered momentarily if she had got much fun out of her debut; then once again she became conscious of the reality she must sooner or later face.

Leaving the lights burning she started upstairs, paying a passing deference to the fact that, while she had brought off the party, she had not finished well as an organizer: the caterer's men seemed to have left, and there seemed to be no servants on duty.

"It's over," she thought on the way. "Over. I have the money."

Reluctant to think further than that, Paula recognized there was no denying that Aunt Emily was very dead upstairs, but the forefront of her mind was really occupied by some necessity of explaining to Aunt Emily why she had done as she had.

There was, however, no more explaining to be done to Aunt Emily.

The upstairs maid came out of a patient doze on a big chair in the hall. As Paula started to search for the key with a kick of her heel under the rag rug, and found it was not there, she ran in a sudden hysteria past the maid and over to the edge of the balcony.

"Are you there, Leslie?" she called.

As if by a miracle he still was. He called up, mistaking her for the maid, "I'm trying to turn out these damn lights. Or do you want them to burn all morning?"

Paula could hear him fumbling with the unfamiliar fixtures. In a faint voice she called:

"It's me."

"Who?"

"It's... nobody."

In another panic she tore back past the maid, kicked aside the rag rug and finally found the key tangled in the rug itself.

She went in. Nothing was changed. The dead woman huddled in the chair. The room was close and Paula shoved up another window. Then she sat down on the side of the bed as she had before, and thought the same thing, but not in the same way.

It was done now; the outrage – if so it was – was perpetrated. She had the five hundred, she could afford the operation. But all the dislike that had previously lodged in her heart oppressed her now, as she stared at the object of it.

"Aunt Emily," she said aloud, "I wouldn't have done this for no reason. Please believe that, however unpleasant you..."

She paused. It wasn't right to talk to somebody who couldn't talk back, yet in a way she was helping Aunt Emily, explaining to some vague judge that Aunt Emily wouldn't have been the way she was if it were not for the forces that had produced her.

Suddenly, as if Aunt Emily was cognizant of what was taking place, her hand fell over the edge of the chair. At the same moment Paula saw that the door was opening and Leslie Dixon was on the threshold.

"I finally got the lights out," he said. "What is going on here? I've got to know."

"All right; come in then. You might as well know the whole story."

She had really been aware for some moments that he was the judge she had been waiting for.

She knew that he loved her – she had begun to love him, not with the love she associated with duty, with having to have five hundred dollars, but with the many lonely hours, long years of hours since she had been taken care of. She allowed for the chance that it might work out; she clutched at any straw and hoped it would turn out to be a girder.

So fixed had been Leslie's concentration on her and what harassed her, that only now did he become fully aware of the still figure in the chair. Then Paula saw his face preparing for an emergency.

In a minute he had grasped the situation, and rushed over to the figure slumped in the armchair, and took the pulse of the arm that had fallen down. Then he turned to Paula.

"She's dead," he said.

"Yes."

"Did you know she was dead?"

"She's been dead since nine o'clock tonight."

"And you knew she was dead all the time?"

"Yes, I knew she was dead."

"And so you went and had the party anyhow."

"Yes, I went and had the party anyhow."

He put his hands in his pockets; then he repeated, "You knew she was dead, and you went and had the party anyhow. How could you do that?"

"Yes, I knew she was dead – but we seem to have covered that."

He took a half-step away from her as though he were going to walk up and down the room; changing his mind he turned to her. "I swear I don't understand this."

Paula gave up; she began adapting the tempo of his walk, tapping her heels together.

"Don't complicate things any further!" she exploded. "Why did you come up here anyhow? I thought you'd gone home. I thought everybody had gone home."

As they both strained towards a solution, their eyes fell again upon the tangible presence of Mrs Holliday.

"Anyhow, that's the way it was," Paula said in an awed way.

"I can't believe it," Leslie said. "I can't believe that anybody could be so—"

"Neither can I," said Mrs Holliday.

For a moment each of them thought the other had spoken. They exchanged a sharp glance and gasped out a "What!" Then each seeing an embarrassed innocence in the other's face, they were compelled to bend their glances upon the fantastic fact that the word had come from one supposed to be communicating solely with angels.

"Well…"

"Well…"

Still they exchanged a last desperate glance, each hoping the other had spoken.

Leslie was the first to return to reality. He faced the voice and mustered up one helpless and strange word.

"Well."

"Well," said Mrs Holliday. She took up the arm that he had dealt with so reverently only a few minutes before, levelled it at him like a rifle and repeated:

"Well."

In the miasma of alarm the monosyllable was rapidly becoming sinister, but it was difficult to know what to substitute for it.

"But, Mrs Holliday, you don't really think…"

As Leslie heard his own voice he decided that this was not at all the remark with which this Lazarus should be greeted upon her resurrection, yet he could think of no other.

"Aunt Emily," Paula said, and stopped. She had said all she had to say to Aunt Emily some time before.

During this conversation Aunt Emily had been gradually taking control of the situation, at least in so far as she guessed that there was any situation. Her eyes fell upon Paula's evening dress, and associating it with something unpleasant she reached back into her own obscure depths to find some unpleasantness that would match it.

"The dance," she said hopefully.

Paula and Leslie fell eagerly on this tangible fact.

"The dance is over," Paula supplied.

"The dance is over. Have you gone crazy, Paula? Answer me at once. Who is this young man and what is he doing upstairs?"

Leslie took up the explanation.

"The dance is just over, Mrs Holliday. You didn't seem well, so Paula didn't want to wake you up."

"You mean I slept all through the dance?"

"It was impossible to wake you."

"What nonsense! What an outrage!"

It was awful, Paula agreed privately. But there was the five hundred. Nothing could destroy that. There was the five hundred.

"We were just about to phone your doctor," said Leslie.

"I was allowed to sleep through the dance!" Mrs Holliday sat there panting, so alive now that her vitality minimized their feeling for her.

"Where are the maids? Is there nobody I can count on? Where is Clothilde?"

Leslie went towards where he imagined the servants' quarters to be, and encountered Clothilde on the way.

"Here," he said and found five dollars. "Mrs Holliday locked herself in; she mustn't know that she did it. Any excitement tonight might…"

He said the rest with his shoulders and then hurried to a phone and called a doctor. That much accomplished he waited in the hall until Paula came out of her aunt's room, walking to the rhythm of Mrs Holliday's furious voice that followed her out the door.

"Well?" she asked.

The folds of her dress were tired but gracious. The orchids were still fresh upon her shoulder.

"Do you want to come over to my cousin's for the night? But maybe it'll make gossip."

"I'll be fine here."

"Your aunt'll have things figured out by tomorrow. At least she'll know there was something wrong."

"I'm going to leave before breakfast."

"Maybe that's wisest. Goodnight."

As he went down the stairs she saw him hesitate.

"Well," she said.

At the word he turned and looked back at her, and suddenly said "Well" again. The word seemed to have been used before between them; they faced each other, Paula from the top landing. Leslie trying to leave as politely as possible, to let her down easily, yet still with the intensity of feeling about her that had made him linger after the dance, made him be bold enough to push his way into the tragic trouble in which she was involved.

"So what?" he demanded.

"You don't know why I did what I did," she said. "I was fighting for life."

"Apparently, you can handle your own affairs better than I could handle them for you."

Paula put her left heel on the first step, then her right heel on the second step, and her elbow on the balcony railing, not in a casual way, but rather suggesting a compromise.

A physical response to her increasing nearness made Leslie say, "Well then, what? I can't swallow the idea of somebody looking for fun going as far as that."

Paula turned quickly and retraced her two steps up to the landing, throwing behind her: "You can't? Then goodnight."

"You're going to New York with me," he said.

"No; say goodbye now," Paula objected.

"Go and get your clothes."

"I'm not helpless. I'll get them in the morning."

"We're going now."

"Why?"

"Because we are. Go and get your stuff."

At this moment the doctor arrived and Paula in a lightning dash to her room was suddenly equipped.

4

WITH THE FALSE DAWN PUSHING UP the leaves over Long Island they borrowed the doctor's taxi and rode to the station. On the car seat, feeling the five-hundred-dollar cheque against her heart, safe now, the events of the evening assumed an unimportance. Even Leslie sitting across from her seemed remote and in the past, as compared to the problem of getting the money.

She felt gay. She felt light-headed. She had to express her rebirth of hope in words – now it took the form of teasing him.

"Would you like to know the truth – do men ever sometimes want to know the truth? Even in China?"

They were sliding into the station at the moment; it was a morning pulled ripe and cold, through the mouths of tunnels, breaking with them into New York.

"You told me about your idea of what was pleasure," he said in the taxi. "You said when you were fighting for your life there were no rules."

"I didn't say my life – I said fighting for life." Impatiently, suddenly she turned to him, "Would you like to actually contemplate the lowdown?"

She profited by his confusion: "Let me initiate you into the facts of one life—"

Leslie cut through her speech: "You… you have me down for a prig. I don't suppose there is anything much I can do about that—"

"Even if you wanted to," she amended.

"Even if I wanted to." He repeated her phrase slowly. "However, since we seem to keep up this argument I'll try to tell you what, what—"

"Don't bother to do all that," Paula suggested.

"Yes, I'll bother. The very fact that I do, or maybe did care about you deeply" – he paused and repeated "deeply" – "gives me a right to say what was in my mind, my heart."

"You seem to have a gift for words in China."

"Don't be mean."

"I'm not mean."

"Don't be. Try to think of me as an ignorant visitor to your shores. Let me just wonder. Let me wonder, for instance, why such… such a lovely person as you, that any man would like to know, admire or be near…" He hesitated. "All right then, why should a girl like that spend all her life preparing to go to some personal moving picture that never comes off? You can't always keep on being Narcissus looking into his pool.* You… you can't, you can't go on trying to get ready to fascinate some millionaire, or British nobleman."

"I did get myself a British nobleman. I was pretty precocious. I got him when I was seventeen."

"You mean you're married – no fooling?"

"Very much married."

"Recently?"

"A long time ago, when I was seventeen. My husband is an invalid." She smiled in a surprised way. "Isn't it preposterous? I'm a ladyship. I'm Lady Paula Tressiger, and I've never even been called it."

She leant forward and tapped the driver.

"Mind stopping at this drugstore for a moment?"

"Why?"

"To get some morphine."

"Why do you want to get morphine?" he demanded.

"'Cause till tonight I didn't have any money for a long time, but I've had the prescription in my bag for three weeks."

"I still don't know whether you're fooling…"

In the new-found confidence of the new morning she said: "Well, then you must be slow on the uptake."

She made her purchase hastily, and as she returned, said: "It's so close to my apartment. We might as well not have kept the taxi."

They drew up at a somewhat dingy brick front.

He followed her into a modest suite on the second floor, with a divan that he guessed became a bed on small provocation.

Then Paula opened the door of the other room. As if she was showing him a baby, she motioned him inside.

In the bed lay the thin figure of a man, a man so still that he scarcely seemed to be breathing.

The fact that he was carefully shaven made his extreme emaciation more apparent. Murmuring something in his ear, Paula ran her hand through the sparse hair. She adjusted the pillows and led Leslie back into the other room.

"He's been like that for seven years. Since a week after we were married. All right, ask me why I married him. All right, because home was hell. Eric came over to learn the banking business. He was all shot by the war, and shot with drink too, but I didn't know that then."

"He's paralysed?"

She nodded.

"We got married secretly – I was too young and mixed up about things, and ashamed and afraid to say anything. So I took care of him myself."

As if he had reproached her, Paula added hastily, "Oh, sometimes I had the very best medical attention for him, whenever I could afford it; once I kept him in a hospital for months."

"Yes, I see… I see."

"When I went to Aunt Emily's I had a woman who did every last thing. He doesn't need very much – he needs very little. Maybe I shouldn't have gone away and left him this time." Paula hesitated. "First you disliked me for what I did there, now you'll dislike me for going at all…

"…hate to tell you any more of the ways. But this money" – she touched her heart – "this is one of the most sordid. This money I got from the publicity agent, it'll give Eric his last chance, it's a pretty poor chance, one out of ninety-nine, but I tried to think the way *he'd* like to think. He'd rather take this chance than lie there for ever. Would you want to be like that for ever – lie on your back for seven years? Do you know how long seven years can be?"

God, it must have been so long, he thought, so long…

"Now he can have the operation, he can have…"

All he had misguessed, misjudged about her fell away, minute by minute.

"That's why you did that?"

"Did what?"

He could suddenly find no word or phrase for what she had done.

"I can't try to get in touch with the specialist tonight," she said abstractedly. "I'll call the hospital resident in the morning. But it is morning – I should have called long ago."

"If there is anything that I can do to help?"

Leslie realized that this was a false start.

But Paula was suddenly all full of life, and an upsurge of feeling made her cross the room, put her arms around him and kiss him on the lips.

"So, I did it, didn't I?" she said. "I did what I started out to do."

"Well, you seem to have. I'm amazed. I'm—"

"—so you go away," Paula advised him. "You forgive me, don't you?"

There was no answer to make. There was simply the feel of her cheek as he touched it that he knew he would carry with him for ever.

5

ERIC TRESSIGER, SECOND BARONET, was destined to be one more victim in his race's fight for life. In one moment they thought he was saved, in another he wavered, in a third he died.

At the end Leslie was waiting outside the operating room of the hospital. A nurse who knew him rushed out and said, "You're a relation of Mrs Tressiger – at least you're the only person that has called here regularly."

"Yes?"

"He died five minutes ago."

"I knew that," he said.

"His wife slapped right down against the floor. I never saw a girl do that before" – she was ripe with gossip – "except an anaesthetist who was taking care of—"

"Where is Mrs Tressiger now?"

By this time she was following Leslie along a corridor of the hospital. "No, she's not ill now, she…"

Paula was sitting in the waiting-room chair against an imitation of 1880 mosaic work. She looked well – she sat up straight, holding her purse. Leslie went to her so quickly that he brought up before her with a sort of slide upon the marble floor.

"My… Paula…" he began.

She looked up at him brightly, almost cheerfully.

"Now it's over," she said. "Now I'm going to be gay!"

"You mean that?"

"Yes, Leslie. Now it's done, now it's over."

He prepared to revise his opinions. Leslie had been face to face with the terrible floods in the Yangtze River in 1926, the delivering to solemn women of the bodies of brothers, fathers, sisters, children – seeing them taken up into death in the enveloping arms of their religion…

So with Paula now, facing her proud mask, he saw his country all over again. He felt simultaneously that awesome loneliness of that which had led them all here, and a pride in the fact that somehow they had done so many of the things they had promised to do in their hearts.

The ambition, of lonely farmers perhaps – but the cloth of a great race cannot be made out of the frayed lint of tired princes…

Instead of saying anything that he had meant to say, he said simply, "I understand."

"You do? Maybe I guess you do. Well then, that helps me to go home."

"What is home?" And he added: "Maybe I'm home."

"I guess you're home now," Paula admitted.

On their way out he said: "Isn't it nice to think of all the things we'll never have to talk over? We can start from scratch, like... like people do in advertisements."

Paula picked up his hand, touching her lips to his knuckles. They had no more to say to each other – only the little bang that did not agree with any weather blew a little in the wind of that sad and happy morning.

Her Last Case

1

WHEN MISS BETTE WEAVER got off the bus at Warrenburg, there was a storm in the sky, blowing east from the Blue Ridge. Washington had been stifling and, insulated by the artificially cooled bus, she was unprepared for the sharp drop in temperature; it was not what she expected from Virginia in July.

There was no car in sight to meet her and drops were already splattering the road, so she had time for only the briefest glance at the town before crossing to the drugstore for protection. It was an old town – an old church, an old courthouse, old frame or stone houses; over the main street hung the usual iron sign:

> Here a Squadron of Stuart's Cavalry
> Fought a Fierce Engagement with...

She read only that far – there had been such signs all along the road, and Bette's interest was as faint as that of most women in the record of old wars. But Virginia, the name itself, thrilled her – real Virginia, not just the swimming hotels of the shore. She thought of Marion Davies* in a hoop skirt dancing the lancers with handsome Confederate officers, and of books about gallant, fierce times and gracious houses and Negro "ha'nts". It was all a lovely blur – she was pretty sure that George Washington wasn't in the Civil War, and also that Château-Thierry* came a little later, but she was sure of little more.

Beyond that she felt suddenly strange and foreign and frightened; it was the arriving at a new lonely place with a storm in the air.

A large car slid into the courthouse circle, rounded it and drew up at the drugstore, and a Negro chauffeur got out.

Bette got her change from the hairpins she had bought and met him at the door.

"Miss Weaver?" He touched his hat and took her little satchel. "Sorry I'm late, but I got a flat outside of Warrenburg."

He shut the rear door on her and she felt safer in the big limousine, closed in against the thunder and the rain.

"Is it far?"

"Ten mile to the house."

He seemed a polite Negro, huge and protective, but with an asthmatic whispering voice. After a little way, she asked:

"How is Mr Dragonet?"

For a moment he didn't answer, he didn't move even the back of his shoulders as an indication that he had heard her, and Bette had the feeling of having been indiscreet. This was absurd, though, in view of the fact that she was here in the capacity of trained nurse, with due credentials from Baltimore authorizing her to take care of Mr Dragonet. Unmet, he was to her not a person but already a case. He was the last patient she would have – the last case for ever and ever.

The thought filled her with a certain sadness. Born and bred in a desolate little streak of wind and rain on the Pennsylvania border of Maryland, her days as probationer, "blue nurse", graduate nurse, had opened a new world to her. They had been happy years – she had had good cases; almost always nice men and women, who lived or died with respect and liking for her, because she was lovely to look at and considered a fine young nurse. She had taken every kind of case in her three graduate years – except infantile paralysis, which she avoided because she had three little nephews in Baltimore.

The Negro decided to speak, suddenly, as if after mature consideration.

"I don't say he is well, I don't say he ain't well. He don't seem to change to me, but they been lot of doctors round..."

As if he had spilt too much, he broke off suddenly, and Bette conceded he was right in saying nothing. Even Doctor Harrison in Baltimore had said very little; though she'd thought at the time it was because he was in a hurry.

It was a pity, he had said, that on her last case she should go so far away. Wouldn't she rather—

"No," Bette answered, "I'd rather do this. I've always taken potluck about cases and my name's at the head of the registry, so I'm going to take this one. I'm sort of suspicious about it."

"Well, I'm sort of relieved. Because this case needs somebody I know I can trust absolutely. You've had some psychiatry work… No, this isn't exactly a psychiatric case. It's hard to say just what it'll turn out to be."

"An old man?"

"Not old. Thirty-five, thirty-six. He was a patient of mine at Walter Reed military hospital just after the war. He got to believe in me, and that's why he wanted me to choose him a nurse from up here."

There were interruptions at this point, and Bette had practically to insist on further directives.

"Well, you ask what he's been taking as a sedative, and if it's a coal-tar product, give him that, in slow doses, and if it's paraldehyde, give him that, and if it's liquor, taper him off that. It's sleep he needs – sleep and food, and lots of both. Keep in touch with his doctor down there, and phone me if things get out of hand."

Doctor Harrison was known for a rather sly habit of making all subordinates – junior doctors, interns, nurses – figure out situations for themselves, and Bette suspected that there was going to be nothing more.

So – off then for the last time with the starched white uniforms, the sense of adventure, of being used for some purpose larger than herself, some need greater than her own. The last time – because in one month she would become housewife and handmaiden to young Dr Howard Carney, of the Mercy Hospital in New York.

The car turned off the road onto a clay pike.

"This is Dragonet land from now on," the chauffeur said. "Plenty bad road; had to fix it up in that dry spell, so it didn't set."

The house floated up suddenly through the twilight of the rain. It was all there – the stocky central box fronted by tall pillars, the graceful one-storey wings, the intimate gardens only half-seen from the front, the hint of other more secret verandas to face the long southern outdoors.

She waited, rather uncertain, rather awed, in the central hall, while he went for the housekeeper. From the hall she had an impression of great rooms on either side, massed with portraits and gilt-framed oil paintings – and books, books everywhere. There were certain houses where one simply jumped into uniform and took over from an anxious and confused family; there were others where the position of a trained nurse was uncertain. She must wait and see.

A worn Scotswoman came in and looked her over quickly.

"Whisper, take Miss Weaver's bag to the left wing... Perhaps you'd like some tea, Miss Weaver. Mr Ben has got to sleep for once, and I don't suppose you'll wake him up."

"Certainly not," Bette agreed. "I'll be—"

A voice, from somewhere on the dusky stairs that mounted out of the hall, startled and interrupted her:

"I was putting it over on you, Jean."

Mrs Keith snapped on a hall light against the dusk, and the owner of the voice became apparent. He was a handsome man with very dark, deep-set eyes; and Bette's first impression was that he was younger than she had expected. He was tall and well built, in a grey flowered dressing gown of Japanese silk; but it was his voice that caught and held her – it was the sort of voice that can "do anything with anybody", a voice that could beg, command, wheedle, storm or condemn. When he spoke, in no matter how low a tone, there seemed to be no other voice than his.

"Jean, you run along and leave Miss Weaver and me alone. Miss Weaver has a face that makes me sure she'll do me no harm... You like sick people, Miss Weaver, don't you? That's why you took up nursing."

Bette laughed, but rather uncertainly.

"Suppose I put on my uniform," she said. She would feel much better in her uniform, far more in armour, more able to cope with any situation. Not that she anticipated any. Doctor Harrison wasn't one to send her into a questionable environment, but Mr Ben Dragonet's facetious speech and the look of desperation in his eyes put her on guard. She was driven by a need to put on her uniform immediately. But:

"Not yet," Dragonet commanded. "I spent years of my life looking at nurses' uniforms, and I must say there's a certain monotony. Sit down and let me tell you my symptoms while you're still in personal plumage."

She was suddenly glad she had worn her best frock, but professional training made her obdurate, and formally she followed the beckoning finger of Mrs Keith towards the left wing.

"I won't be five minutes really. Remember, I've been travelling two hours."

He was still there when she returned, leaning against the balustrade in an attitude that changed to quick courtesy as he saw her.

"I didn't mean to be insistent. What I really wanted was not to be alone."

She sat down on a sofa in the hall.

"It's these damn nights," he went on. "I don't mind the days – it's between the first and second sleeps. I spend all day worrying about what I'll think in those hours."

"We'll fix that," she said confidently. "Don't you think I'd better talk to your doctor here right away and see what regime you're on?"

"I can tell you all that. Old Bliss lets me make my own regime. I was hoping you'd have a regime along. Haven't you got a nice regime in that black bag?"

"I must get in touch with your doctor here. Doctor Harrison expects it."

"All in good time. Have you got any clear idea what's the matter with me?"

"I know you've been generally run-down and have some old head wound that bothers you."

"And about ten other things. I seem to be something of a wreck, but it's only recently I can't seem to steer myself any more. One man had the effrontery to suggest that I go to a rest cure – as if it wasn't too damn restful here already. By the way, you better get the keys to the wine closet from Jean. This same man had the double effrontery to suggest that I drank too much, and I want to prove to you that has nothing to do with it. I'll want a nightcap this evening, because today I have nourished myself a little. But after tonight I won't want anything."

"All right."

"Now we'll go out on the big veranda and watch the rain for a while – that's one of my favourite stops in my nightly marches. I've found out more about my own house in these last three months than in all the rest of my life."

Bette felt that the time had come to assert her authority:

"Mr Dragonet, I think the first thing should be for you to get into bed and get some rest. Meanwhile I'll find out what they're giving you to eat, and just what medicines you've been taking. The more tired you get from talking and walking around, the harder it's going to be to relax."

"Miss Weaver, I didn't expect you till six o'clock. It's now half-past five. After six o'clock I'm your patient; until then – the veranda."

Reluctantly she preceded him – this was going to be more difficult than she had counted. There were times, professionally, when she had wished her person to have been less appealing.

He glanced at it quickly across the veranda – at a face whose every contour seemed to be formed to catch the full value of light or shadow, so that no angle could be turned far enough aside to obscure the delicate lines along the ridges of cheekbone, brow, chin and throat. A sculptor's, not a painter's face, but warmed and brought back into full life by the bright, healthy, warm blue eyes.

"You were wounded in the war?" she asked to get his attention off her. "Wounded? I was killed."

"But you got all well."

"Oh, yes. Up until six months ago I practised law in Winchester. Then things began to go haywire – other things that had nothing to do with

238

war – and now general deterioration has set in. But remember, up to six o'clock I'm your host, and I want to hear about you."

She took advantage of this to tell him that she was engaged to be married.

"It's always rather awful to hear of a girl who looks like you being engaged," he remarked. "Seems as if there's something unfair about it."

Her face rejected the personal quality of the compliment.

"…so this is my last case," she finished.

"It may be mine too," he said.

Oh, really, things were going too far. She couldn't imagine how she had been so unprofessional as to let it all get started in this direction. She rose quickly.

"Come now, Mr Dragonet, it's nearly six and we're going to get you to bed."

"Bed?" Obviously, the word revolted him, but he got up wearily. As they went towards the stairs he tried to stave off the eventuality: "But I ought to show you the sights of the house. It's quite a historic house. Do you see that window pane with the name scratched on it? Well, that was made by a diamond ring belonging to the Gallant Pelham – made on the morning of the day he was killed. You can see the year – 1864. You know who the Gallant Pelham was? He commanded Stuart's horse artillery at twenty-three. He was my hero when I was a boy."

The stairs were difficult for him, and once in his big bedroom he threw off the dressing gown wearily and flung himself on the huge bed. Bette looked around with the sense that he had filled the room, up to the dark moulding, with his own personal melancholy. She took his pulse and his temperature. Then she picked up a white-capped pin from the table beside the bed.

"Just what I need for my bonnet," she said lightly. "In fact, the regular pin. I bet you've had another nurse."

"I had a nurse from Winchester," he admitted, "but she was frightened; she went away."

"Well, I'm not frightened, but I'm very strict. Now you try and rest, and I'll get things started."

2

S HE SLEPT DEEP THROUGH the first part of the night, soothed by air softer than the air of the lush, over-rich Maryland nights. When she awoke with a start, she saw from her watch that it was three, and realized simultaneously that there was activity in the house. Slipping on her dressing gown, she opened the door that led through a library into the main hall, whence the voices were coming.

"Now be a good boy and go to bed," Jean, the housekeeper, was saying.

"I'd rather wander around, Jean. It's my form of exercise."

"You'll frighten the new nurse and she'll leave like the other one. Pretty soon you won't be able to get a nurse at all."

"Well, there's you to carry on."

"That isn't what you told me the other night."

"I told you that I'd asked Doctor Harrison to send me someone young and beautiful."

"Well, I don't think this one's going to spoil you. But now you mustn't frighten her. I know you mean no harm."

"Go and call her," he commanded.

"Now, Mr Ben—"

"I said, go and call her!"

Bette was already hurrying into her uniform. She left her room with Jean's "Pray God you can do something with him" ringing in her ear.

"Good evening, Miss Weaver," he said. "I came down to suggest an early-morning walk around the place. I notice that the false dawn has arrived and the more unsophisticated birds have been fooled into believing it." And as he saw her expressionless face, "Don't get afraid of me; these are just the perambulations of old stock – my father wandered and my grandfather wandered. He is the Confederate brigadier over your head. My grandfather used to wander around cursing Longstreet for not using his flanks at Gettysburg.* I used to wonder why he wandered, but now I'm not surprised. I've been weeping a lot over a long time, because they sent us up replacements, in 1918, that didn't know a trench mortar from a signal platoon. Can you believe that?"

"You've been drinking, Mr Dragonet," said Bette distinctly.

"I offered you the keys."

"I thought it would be better for you to keep them, but I'll take them now. In fact, I'll insist on keeping them as long as I'm in this house."

She knew, though, that in spite of having drunk something, he was not drunk. He was not the kind who would ever be drunk. Drink could not remedy whatever had happened to him.

"Old stock in old wars," he brooded. "And after that wandering." His eyes were full of tears. "What is it I've lost? Isn't there some woman somewhere that would know?"

"What do you mean?" she demanded.

"I thought you might know. After wars everything goes out of the men who fought them – everything except the war itself, but that goes on and on for ever. Don't you see this house is full of war? Grandmother made it a hospital, and sometimes the Virginia women got here to see their husbands, but the women from farther south usually came too late, she used to say."

He broke off and pointed: "There's the twins, my brothers – the two red-haired kids in the painting over the stairs. They're buried back in the family plot, but they may not even be the twins, because there was a mix-up at Montfaucon. Still – it may be the twins—"

"You must go to bed," she interrupted.

"But listen," he said in a strange, low voice. "I'll go, but first you must listen."

In the hall, dusky now with the real dawn, she felt an electric silence. And suddenly, as he said "Listen!" again and raised his finger, she felt the little hairs on her neck stand out from it, felt a tingling along her spine. In a split second it all happened. The great front door swung back slowly on its hinges and the hall was suddenly full of young faces and voices. Ben Dragonet sprang to his feet, his voice clear over the young voices, over the many voices:

"Can't you see it now? These were my people, bred to the sword, perished by the sword! Can't you hear?"

Even as she cried out frantically, clinging to the last shreds of reality, "You must go to *bed*! I'm going to give you more sedative!" she saw that the big front door was still open.

3

BETTE'S INTENTION AT SEVEN O'CLOCK that morning – when the sound of life in the kitchen relaxed her enough to read the magazine at which she had stared for three hours – was to leave by the first bus. But as it turned out, she did not leave. She bathed and then went upstairs and tiptoed into Ben Dragonet's room. Under the influence of the heavy sedatives, he was sleeping soundly; the lines of anxiety and nervous pain about his eyes and mouth had smoothed away and he seemed very young, with his neglected hair burrowed into the pillow. Sighing, she went down to her room, extravagantly donned her second clean uniform and waited for Doctor Bliss's visit.

He was an elderly man, with the air of having known all the Dragonets for ever, and he told her what she expected: the story of the breakdown of a very proud and stubborn man.

"People think a lot of Ben over in Winchester, and he's had chances to go in big firms in Baltimore and New York. But for one thing, he never got over the war. His two brothers were killed in the same aeroplane, pilot and observer; then he was wounded. Then, when he got well…"

The doctor hesitated, and Bette guessed, from a little trailing motion of his mouth, that he had changed his mind about making some other revelation.

"When did this start?" she asked.

"About Christmas. He walked out of his office one day without a word to his partners and just never did go back." He shrugged his shoulders. "He's got enough to live on, but it's too bad, because his law work *did* keep him from all this brooding. If I didn't have my work to do, I don't think I'd sleep nights either."

"But outside of that, is he absolutely sane?"

"Just as sane as any of us. The other nurse got uneasy about all that night prowling and walked out, but Ben wouldn't be rude to a burglar in his own house."

Bette decided suddenly and defiantly that she was going to stay – defiantly because she had begun to wonder how Dr Howard Carney up in New York would have approved her being on this case. He was a precise young man who knew what he wanted, and he had not wanted her to go on any more cases at all, as if he feared at the last moment she might become a casualty of her profession. But it was not so easy to sit around twiddling thumbs for two months. It eased her conscience to write him a letter while she waited for Ben Dragonet to wake up.

The sleep did him good. All day he was content to rest in bed, dozing from time to time, taking obedient medicine, eating what was prescribed, talking to her only a little, casually and impersonally. But once she caught his eye unexpectedly and found in it the hungry and despairing look of the night before, the look that said, mutely this time: "I thought perhaps there was a woman somewhere who could tell me…"

That night, with more sedatives, he slept through, though Bette lay awake anxiously between two and five, listening for his voice or his footstep downstairs.

Next day she said:

"I think you'd better dress and we can sit in the garden awhile."

"Good Lord!" he groaned, laughing. "Just as I'm getting my first rest in months, you order me out of bed."

"You'll have to tire yourself out a little in the daytime before you can sleep at night without sedatives."

"Well, you'll stay pretty close, won't you?"

"Of course."

He passed a tranquil day, still a little dazed and abstracted. For Bette it was a happy day with a cool, dry wind blowing the Virginia sunshine through the trees and along the eaves of the veranda. She had been in larger houses, but never one so rich in memories – every object she saw seemed to have a significance and a story. And at the same time a new picture of Ben Dragonet himself began to develop. He seemed gentle, uninterested in himself, adept in pleasing her and making her feel at home; and comparing that with the hysteria of the first night, she took his pulse carefully, wondering if it indicated any lesion of vitality.

But as the quiet days passed, she began to realize that this was his natural self, his natural attitude towards the world. Without any reference on his part to the condition in which Bette had found him, she gathered that he was beginning to see his way out and – from a chance remark – that he considered going back to work.

They came to know each other quite well. She told him about Howard and herself, and their plans, and he seemed interested.

Then she stopped telling him, because she perceived that it made him lonely. So they built up private jokes to take the place of personal discussions, and she was glad to see flashes of laughter sometimes in his dark eyes.

As the week waned he grew strong enough to protest at his invalid's regime; they took wider walks and splashed about one afternoon in the small swimming pool.

"Really, if you're getting well this quick, you don't need me any more."

"Ah, but I do though."

Next morning Bette, in borrowed jodhpurs, rode with him upon the pike.

She realized with a sort of surprise that he was no longer her patient – it was he who dominated the days. His fingers rearranged her reins this afternoon instead of her fingers taking his pulse, and with the change a sense of disloyalty to Howard lodged itself in her mind – or was it rather a sense that she should have felt disloyal? Howard was young and fresh and full of hope, like herself; this man was tired and worn and knew a thousand things she had never guessed at; yet the fact remained that he was no longer a patient to her. Divested momentarily of the shield of her uniform, she wondered that she had had the nerve to give him orders.

"…back in '62," he was saying, "Grandfather was wounded at Hanover Courthouse and the family had to go to him—"

"I thought we weren't going to talk about wars."

"This is just about the pike here. They started out at midnight with hoofs muffled and orders not to say a word. Children of ten take things literally; so, when mother's saddle girth, that had been put on badly, slipped and swung her right under the horse, she just hung there for ten minutes – upside down, afraid to open her mouth, until, luckily, somebody turned around and saw…"

Bette was half listening, half thinking that she had never been on a horse before except a plough horse at home, and how easy Ben Dragonet made it for her. And then, halfway home, she let herself say something she would not have said in uniform.

"You can be so nice," she said, and she heard Howard's voice in her ear protesting, and fought through it: "I never knew anyone who could be so nice."

Looking straight ahead, he remarked:

"That's because I'm in love with you." They walked their horses in silence – then he broke out suddenly: "Excuse me for saying that. I know your position has been hard enough here."

"I didn't mind your saying it," she answered steadily. "I took it as a great compliment."

"This insomnia," he continued, "gets a man in the habit of talking aloud to one's self, as if there was nobody there."

"What then?" she thought. "Oh, this is impossible. Am I falling in love with this man, this ruin of a man? Am I risking all that I ever thought was worthwhile?"

Yet, as she saw him from the corner of her eye, she had to resist actively a temptation to sway over towards him.

There were storm clouds in the west, and they went into a trot; there was a drizzle and thunder when they reached the straight driveway to the house. Bette saw Ben Dragonet's head go up, his eyes peer forward; he spurred his horse twenty feet ahead, pulled up, wheeled, dashed back and seized her bridle. In two minutes his face had changed – the repose of five days had vanished; the lines had creased back.

"Listen to me." His voice was strange and frightened. "There's some-one I have to see. It's very important. It may change things here; but you've got to stay on, whatever happens."

The two pair of startled hands on the reins made Bette's horse dance.

"You'd better go in alone," she said.

"Then you'd better get off and let me take the horse in." His eyes were full of a terrible appeal. "You won't leave me."

She shook her head, miserable with apprehension. Then she perched on a fence rail in the increasing rain as he rode towards the house with her horse in tow. Presently, over a bush, she could see two heads on the porch, one Ben Dragonet's, the other a woman's, saw them vanish into the square of the front door. Then she walked thoughtfully up to the house and entered through the separate door of her wing.

4

A LITTLE GIRL OF ABOUT NINE was in the room, a well-dressed little girl, apparently just walking around looking, a sad-eyed little girl of a lovely flushed darkness.

"Hel-lo," Bette said. "So I have a visitor."

"Yes," agreed the child calmly. "Jean told me this was the room I had when I was a little girl, and now I almost remember."

Bette caught her breath.

"You haven't been here for a long time?" she asked.

"Oh, no, not for a long time."

"And what's your name, dear?"

"I'm Amalie Eustace Bedford Dragonet," said the little girl automatically. "This is my father's house."

Bette went into the bathroom and started the water in the tub.

"And where do you live when you don't come here?" she asked, seeking time to collect her thoughts.

"Oh, we go to hotels. We like hotels," Amalie said without conviction, and added. "I had a pony when we lived here."

"Who do you go to hotels with?"

"Oh, my governess, or once in a while my mother."

"I see."

"Not father ever; father and mother have incability of temperence."

"Have *what*?"

"Incability of temperence. That's just a thing. So we go to hotels."

"Here!" Bette told herself sharply. "I'm coming down with nurses' curiosity. I can't let this child run along like this."

Aloud she said:

"Now, dear, I have to take my bath; I'm all wet, you see. Why don't you sit on a big veranda and see how many things you can remember in the garden?"

But when Amalie had departed, Bette stood silent a moment before she wrestled out of her jodhpurs. What did all this mean? Why hadn't she known that Ben Dragonet was married, or had been married? She felt exploited, exasperated – and then, to her sudden dismay, she realized that how she *really* felt was jealous.

Back in uniform, and feeling upset and confused, Bette went out into the library adjoining, and pulled a dusty volume of Pollard's *War Between the States** from the stacks and sat down to read.

Outside, the storm was crashing about now; from time to time the lights flickered low and the telephone gave out little tinkling protests that were less than rings.

Perhaps the very persistence of the thunder made Bette's hearing more acute in the intervals – or perhaps the position of her chair was in line with some strange acoustic of the house, for she began to be conscious of voices, voices not far away.

First there was a woman's laugh – a low laugh, but a real one with a sort of wild hilarity in it – then Dragonet's voice in a rush of indistinct words; and then, very clear and sonorous and audible in a lapse of the storm, the woman's voice saying:

247

"…since the day we took the big blind-looking gate together."

The voice was southern; Bette could even place it as Virginian. But it was not that which made her rise suddenly and pull a chair to the other side of the table; it was the quality of malice in it – of fierce, throaty feeling, as if the woman were letting the words slip up in calculated precision to her lips. Bette heard Ben Dragonet's voice once more in the excited tone of the night she had first come here; finally, then, she gave up the library entirely and went back into her bedroom.

She had hardly sat down when Jean was at the door.

"You have a long-distance call from Washington, Miss Weaver. Do you want to take it?"

"From Washington? But… of course I'll take it."

"You're not afraid of a shock in this storm?… No? Well, there's a phone in the library."

Bette went back into the library and picked up the receiver.

"Bette! This is Howard. I'm in Washington."

"What?"

"This is Howard, I tell you. Darling, what in Heaven's name are you doing down there in Virginia? From what Doctor Harrison says, I gather you're on some psychiatric case."

"Oh, no, it's not that at all. I thought you were in New York."

"My idea was to surprise you; then I found you were nursing at the South Pole. I want to see you."

"I wish you'd told me, Howard. I'm terribly sorry you got there and found me gone. I wanted to take one last case, Howard. I thought you'd…"

"Hello – hello!" Their connection was broken and resumed again: "It makes me uneasy…" Again a break. "…for a little while when you're off…"

The telephone went dead, with more little squeaks and murmurs. Bette bobbed the receiver without response; then gave up. She was somehow annoyed by his unannounced presence in Washington.

But she had no sooner returned to her room when Jean, evidently loitering outside, precipitated herself upon her, went almost to her knees, begging, imprecating.

"Oh, good Lord, Miss Weaver, that devil's here again! Can't you help him now? Is there nothing you can do to get rid of her?"

"I don't understand."

"Do you know what a witch is? Do you know what a devil is? Well, this is one. Do you know what appears when the earth opens and gives up things out of damnation? Well, this is one. Can't you do something? You know so much, almost like a doctor."

Vaguely terrified, Bette kept control of herself, shook the woman slightly and stood back from her.

"Now tell me what this is about!"

"His cousin, his wife that was. She's back again. She's there with him. She's breaking him all over again like she always did. I heard them laughing together – laughing awful, like they laughed when they were children and she first got hold of him. Listen! Can't you hear them laughing, as if they hated each other?"

"You'll have to tell me more clearly." Bette was fighting for breath, for time.

"It was she that did it; it wasn't the bullets in the war. I've seen it – I've seen her come and go. Six months past she came here, and six months he walked the floor in the night and turned for the liquor bottle."

"But they're divorced. The little girl said—"

"What's that to her, or to him. She owned him in her black heart when he was no higher than my shoulder, and she comes back to feed on his goodness, like a vampire feeding on his blood to live by."

"Why is she so bad for him?"

"All I know is what I've seen over and over," Jean insisted. "She's his poison, and I guess a man comes to like poison after he's had enough of it."

"But what can *I* do?"

A knock rattled the door at the end of a roll of thunder. It was the Negro butler, speaking in his tone of asthmatic kindness:

"Miss Weaver, ma'am, Mr Ben send you the message he goin' to have business to talk about at dinner. He says you take little Amalie for dinner here with you in the library."

"Of course."

Bette felt her tension decrease as she found that she was not to meet Ben's wife. When Amalie appeared presently, she was composed and controlled.

"So what did you do this afternoon?" she asked as they sat down at table. "Did you recognize things in the garden?"

Suddenly she perceived that Amalie's eyes were full of tears.

"Or was it raining too much to go out from the veranda?" she said cheerfully.

"Oh, I did," Amalie was sobbing suddenly. "I went out and only got a little wet, and then I came to another veranda, and I heard Mother tell Father she'd trade me for something."

"Nonsense!" Bette said. "You just thought you heard that."

"No I didn't. I heard her talk about the same thing to the man that's her friend now – before we left New York."

"Nonsense!" Bette repeated. "You heard some joke you didn't understand."

At the misery in Amalie's face, she felt her own eyes filling with angry tears, and she concentrated on distributing the supper.

"Take some beets anyhow. When I was your age, I used to think I heard people say things."

"She hates me!" the little girl interrupted vehemently. "I know. I wouldn't care if she traded me." Her face puckered up again. "But Father doesn't want me either."

"Now, Amalie!" Bette's voice was almost harsh to conceal her feelings. "If you don't stop this silly talk and eat your vegetables, I'm going to trade you. I'm going to trade you to a very silly cow who comes and moos outside my window whenever she mislays her calf."

Amalie's smile changed the course of her tears.

"Does she? Why does she mislay it?"

"Ask her. Just careless, I suppose."

Suddenly, even as Bette held out Amalie's plate, lightning flashed by the windows and they were in blackness.

"What is that?" came Amalie's voice, startled, across the dark room.

"Just the silly old storm."

"I don't think I'd like to live here."

"Don't you? I think it'd be wonderful to live here. There'll be candles in a moment. Don't you like candlelight?"

"I don't like the dark," insisted the little girl.

"What a silly idea to get in your head! Did some baby nurse put that idea in your head? Give me your hand while I get my flashlight."

Amalie clung close to her while Bette located it. The storm was directly over the house, but even now Bette could hear the woman's voice – it seemed to be coming nearer, coming into the hall.

"...of course I'm leaving. This is weather I like. You ought to know that... I know he can find the way back, and I know every inch of these roads, if he doesn't."

Then, as two candles wavered into the hall, came Ben Dragonet's voice, very cold and rigid:

"You're welcome to stay the night."

"Stay here!" The voice rose in scorn. "It would take a cyclone to keep me here – and you're hardly a cyclone, are you, Ben?"

The electric lights flashed on again for half a minute, and through the bedroom door Bette had a glimpse of a tall, handsome woman facing Dragonet in the hall. She was saying: "...so you won't take Amalie?"

"She'll be taken care of, but no child of yours can have a place in this house."

Quick as a flash, Bette shut her bedroom door and waited in anxiety lest Amalie had heard. Gratefully she listened to a small voice:

"What did Daddy say? I couldn't hear."

"He just said he'd be glad to look after you, dear."

A minute later a car crunched away on the wet drive; at almost the same moment the lights flashed on definitely – the storm was over.

"Now you're not scared, are you?" Bette asked Amalie.

"Not if the lights stay on."

"They will, now. So come out into the library and go on with your dinner. Here's Jean with two candles, just in case. Maybe she'll sit with you."

"Where are you going?" demanded Amalie doubtfully.

"I want to speak to your daddy for a minute."

She found him in the big reception room far across in the other wing. He was stretched wearily on a sofa, but he got up when she came in.

"I'm sorry about all that rumpus," he said. "I suppose you couldn't help hearing some of it. My wife's personality is sometimes too large for a private house."

"I was thinking of your daughter."

He dismissed the mention of his daughter impatiently.

"Oh, Amalie is… another matter. Amalie was always timid and anaemic. I tried to sit her on a horse when she was six, and she made a fuss and I somehow lost interest – her mother isn't afraid of anything that moves."

Bette's disgust rose:

"Your daughter is a sensitive little girl."

He shrugged his shoulders wearily and Bette continued, her temper mounting:

"I don't know anything about you and your wife, but you should have the intelligence and kindness to put yourself in the child's place."

She broke off as Jean came in, holding Amalie's hand.

"Miss Weaver, there's another phone call for you." She glanced nervously at Ben Dragonet. "I brought Amalie because she didn't want to be alone." Bette went to the phone. It was Dr Howard Carney.

"I'm in Warrenburg," he announced.

"What?"

"I told you I was coming, dear."

"In the storm I couldn't hear a word."

"I thought you said to come down. The idea was you were to slip away and see me for a minute."

She considered quickly, and said:

"You find some driver who knows the Dragonet place and come out here. This has been so strange and I'm so confused that I don't know what to do. Maybe seeing you will clear things up in my mind," she added doubtfully.

She returned to the reception room to find Ben Dragonet, Amalie and Jean sitting in three chairs, far apart, with the air of not having moved, smiled or spoken since she left. Oh, it was all so helpless. What could she do against all this dead weight of the past?

Suddenly Bette made up her mind and asked Jean to take Amalie out of the room. When they were gone, she said:

"Mr Dragonet, I've decided to go."

"You what?"

"It's too much for me. Your attitude towards Amalie decided me."

He frowned.

"I thought you liked me."

"I was beginning to. But this has put us back where we started. I've tried to stick it because I hated to quit on my last case, but... anyhow, I can't. My fiancé happens to be in the neighbourhood and he's coming up to take me away."

"But what'll I do?"

"Get another nurse – a nurse of more robust sensibilities."

There was nothing he could say except: "I'm very sorry. I'll make out your cheque." And he added slowly: "In exchange I'd be grateful for the key to the liquor closet."

Bette went into her room, changed her clothes and packed her bag. When Howard arrived, she embraced him quickly, and started into the reception room to say goodbye to Ben Dragonet, but he had heard the doorbell and he came out into the hall.

She introduced the men and examined them as they stood opposite each other; Howard, young, calm and efficient; Howard who stood for peace and healing; Ben Dragonet, dark and restive, who stood for pain and self-destruction and war. Oh, there was no question which she should choose.

"Won't you come in for a moment?" Dragonet asked; to her surprise, Howard accepted.

They talked impersonally and amicably, until, in a few minutes, the butler announced dinner.

"You've got to dine with me, doctor. Don't protest," Dragonet insisted. "You can't get anything fit to eat this side of Washington – and your fiancée has been too kind for me to let her starve."

Bette weakened, but Amalie came in and curtsied and stood uncertainly; looking at her, she hardened again.

Then Ben, catching her expression, somehow understanding it, capitulated, suddenly, gracefully and entirely.

"I have a little hostess here now," he said, resting his hand on Amalie's shoulder, "and I'm very glad, because I know she'll do the honours of the place very well… Amalie, will you be so kind as to take Doctor Carney's arm and lead the way in to dinner."

After dinner, when Bette had a moment with Howard, she gave him a censored version of the adventure; when he had heard he insisted on her staying on.

"…because I'll be very busy for a month, dear. I've got to go straight up to New York tonight. And since you did take the case, don't you think it'd be unprofessional to walk out on it?"

"I'll do what you think best."

He took her by the elbows.

"Little girl," he said, "I know I can trust you." Why had he come here, then? "I know that when you gave me your word, you gave it for ever. So I'm going away with every confidence that all your thoughts will be of me, as mine will be of you, while I'm struggling to bring us together."

"Oh, I know. I know how hard you work. And you know I love you."

"I know you do. I have every confidence – and that's why I think it's all right for you to stay on this case."

She thought a minute.

"All right, Howard."

He kissed her goodbye – for too long a time, it seemed to her. When Ben Dragonet reappeared, Doctor Carney shook hands and said:

"I'm sure that Miss Weaver will be very... very..."

Bette wished he would say no more, and he didn't. With a last fleeting pressure of her hand, he was gone, and she went to change back into her uniform.

When she returned to the reception room, her patient was sitting with Amalie on his knee.

"When can I have my pony?" she was saying.

"You have him now, only it won't be a pony – you're too big for a pony – it'll be a little horse. We have just the one for you. I'll show him to you in the morning."

He saw Bette and made a formal gesture of rising, arresting it before Amalie slid off his knee.

"You deserve congratulations, if that were a thing to tell a girl," he said. "He seems a mighty fine young man, that doctor of yours."

"Yes," she said absently, and then, with an effort, "He's a fine doctor. He's considered to have a big future."

"Well, frankly, I'm envious of him, but I don't believe you could have chosen better."

Amalie asked her:

"Are you going to marry him?"

"Why – yes, dear."

"And going away?" Her voice was concerned.

"Of course," Bette answered lightly. "But not before a week or so."

"I'm sorry," said Amalie soberly; then she broke out: "It's like hotels – whenever you get to like anybody, they go away."

"That's true," agreed Ben slowly. "Whenever you get to like anybody, they go away."

"I'll leave you two alone," Bette said quickly. "I have a letter to write."

"Oh, no, you won't. We want all of you we can get, don't we, Amalie?"

It was cool after the storm, so they sat in the big room for an hour.

"You look as if you're worrying," Ben said suddenly. "You've been worrying for five minutes."

"But I'm not worrying!" she exclaimed.

"Yes, you are," he insisted. "I knew all that row this afternoon would bother you."

"But I'm not worrying." She drew her face out of the lamplight.

She was worrying, though, in spite of the fact that Ben Dragonet had not yet guessed the reason. She was worrying how she could most kindly break the news to Howard that her last case was going to last for ever.

The Intimate Strangers

W AS SHE HAPPY? Her beach slippers felt strange on the piano pedals; the wind off the Sound blew in through the French windows, blew a curl over her eye, blew on her daringly bare knees over bright-blue socks. This was 1914.

"*The key is in the door*," she sang. "*The fire is laid to light, / But the sign upon my heart, it says 'To let'*."

Blow, breeze of the Sound, breeze of my youth, she thought, vamping chords to the undercurrent of the melody lingering in her mind. Here I can ask myself the things that I can never ask in France. I am twenty-one. My little girl is on the beach making moulds of the wet sand, my lost baby is asleep in a graveyard in Brittany; in twenty minutes my little boy will be fed for the last time from my own self. Then there will be an hour of sky and sea and old friends calling, "Why, *Sara*! Did you bring your ukelele, Sara? You have to come back sometimes, don't you, Sara? *Please* do the imitation of the old dancing master teaching the Turkey Trot."

Write the embassy in Washington, said a persistent undertone in the melody. Tell Eduard you're coming there to live like a good little wife until you sail. You're beginning to like your native land too much for one who married a Frenchman of her own free choice.

> I must ask you, Mr Agent, 'bout a problem of today
> And I hope that you can solve it all for me.
> I have advertised with smiles and sighs in every sort of way
> But there isn't any answer I can see...

Once again she felt the wind that ruffled the sheet music. She felt life crowding into her, into her childish, resourceful body with a child's legs and a child's restiveness, but disciplined in her case to a virtuosic economy of movement, so that whenever she wished (which was often) she could make people's eyes follow every little gesture she made; life crowding into her mind, wind-blown, newly winged every morning ("Eduard never knew what he married," sighed his relatives in their hideouts in the Faubourg, predicting disaster. "Some day he will give her too much liberty and she will flit just like that."); life crowded into her voice, a spiced voice with a lot of laughter, a little love, much quiet joy and an awful sympathy for people in it. "To Let" or not, her heart poured into her voice as it soared through the long light music room, finishing the song:

"The key is in the door, you'll find
The fire is laid to light
But the sign upon my heart…"

She stopped with a period, realizing that suddenly she was no longer alone on the piano bench. A very tall man with a body like the Leyendecker* poster of the halfback, and a face as mad with controlled exuberance as her own, had sat down beside her, and now he tinkled off the last notes in the treble with fingers too big for the keys.

"Who are you?" she said, though she guessed immediately.

"I'm the new tenant you mentioned," he answered. "I'm sending over my furniture this afternoon."

"You're Abby's beau. What's your name – Killem Dead or something?"

"Killian. Killian the silver-tongued. Are you the one that's Madame Sans-Gêne* or the Queen of France?"

"That must be me," she admitted.

They looked at each other, they stared, their mouths simultaneously fell just slightly ajar. Then they both laughed, bent almost double over the piano – and a moment later they were both playing 'To Let' in an extemporized arrangement for two parts, playing it loud in ragtime, singing it, alternating the melody and the second without a shadow of friction.

They stopped, they stared again; once more they laughed. His blue suit was dusty and there was mud and a little blood on his forehead. His teeth were very even and white; his eyes, sincere and straight as he tried to make them, as if he had been trying hard since early boyhood, were full of trouble for somebody. He had edged one of her feet off the treble pedal and she thought how funny her other bathing shoe looked beside this monumental base of dusty cordovan. Two yellow pigskin bags and a guitar case stood behind him.

"Abby's down at the beach with the others," she said.

"Oh, is she? Look, do you know this?…"

…Twenty minutes later, she jumped up suddenly.

"Heavens! I'm supposed to be feeding my son – the poor little… see you on a wave!"

She tore for the nursery. Margot greeted her tranquilly at the door.

"You needn't have hurried, Madame. I gave him his bottle and he took it like a glutton. The doctor said it did not matter, today or tomorrow."

"Oh."

But it did matter. Sara knelt beside the crib.

"Goodbye a little bit," she whispered. "Goodbye a little bit, small son. We shall meet."

Her breast felt heavy with more than milk.

…I can feed him tonight, she thought.

But no. To be sentimental over such a little milestone. In a sudden change of mood she thought:

I am only twenty-one – life's beginning all over. And in a rush of ecstasy she kissed Margot and tore downstairs towards the beach.

After the swimming, Sara and Killian each dressed quickly, Sara's comb trembling in her hair till she tried three times before achieving a part, till her voice answered Abby with the wrong answers, in the wrong tone or with meaningless exclamations that to her meant: "Hurry! Hurry!"

He was waiting on the piano bench. They sang 'Not That You Are Fair, Dear',* with his baritone following four notes and four words after her little contralto – that was the fad then. Their eyes danced and danced together. When Abby came in, Sara was on her feet clowning for him, and Abby was appalled, yet hypnotized by the pervasive delight they had created around themselves. As soon as they fully realized her presence – it took some minutes – they were very considerate to her. Abby accepted it in a sporting spirit – Sara had the privileged position of a lifelong ideal – and her own claim on Killian was only a fond hope. Anyhow Sara was happily married to the Marquis de la Guillet de la Guimpé, and would presently be going back with him to France.

Three days later the Marquis wrote to his wife from the French Embassy in Washington.

"...for two reasons I will be glad to leave, my dear little one; if the situation in Europe becomes more grave I want to be where I can join my regiment and not be tied to a desk in a neutral country."

...As he wrote this, Sara was giving a last fillip to her red-brown hair with a comb that slipped and wriggled again in her fingers...

"...second, and most important, because I don't want my little American to forget that she is of another country now, that this is only a pleasant excursion into the past – for her future lies ahead and in France."

...As he wrote this, Sara was not so much afraid of her heel taps on the silent stairs as of the sound of her heart, which anyone must hear since it was swollen to a throbbing drum.

"...twenty years seemed a long time to lie between us when we were married, but as you grow and develop it will seem less and less..."

...As he sealed the letter in Washington, the starlight of a Long Island veranda just revealed the dark band of an arm around the shadowy gossamer of Sara; there were two low voices like two people singing in chorus:

"Yes..."

"Oh, yes..."

"Anywhere, I don't care..."

"Nothing like this has ever happened, even faintly."

"I didn't know anything about this."

"I'd read about this, but I didn't think it was real."

"I never understood."

When they made their decision they were walking along the beach with their shoes full of sand and their hands clutched like children's hands.

…They were in a train bound for North Carolina. Killian had his guitar and Sara her ukelele. They had at least six concert hours a day from sheer exuberance, sheer desire to make a noise, to cry, "Here we are!" They were like a cavalry fleeing back from a raid, with an aroused enemy thundering behind them. Sometimes they laid aside the instruments and "did" the German band, Sara manipulating hands over mouth for a cornet, Killian growling for a deep tuba. They made friends immediately with conductors and brakemen and waiters, and when the door of their drawing room was open, the people in the car drifted up to the seats just outside. If they had tried they could have left no wider trail, but when they talked of such things they grew confused, incoherent with having so much to say to each other.

"…and then you left Harvard."

"Almost. I had this offer from the Red Sox and I wanted to take it. I wasn't getting any more education. Well, Father said to go ahead and be a fool any way I wanted, but Mother had a nervous breakdown. You can imagine how Mother is – my name's Cedric, you know. Sometime I'll show you my picture in curls and a skirt."

"Fauntleroy* period."

"Fauntleroy was a street urchin compared to me. But then I fooled them – I outgrew them. Anyhow, instead of going south with the Red Sox—"

"Shut the door."

He shut it.

When they were really alone they were no age at all – they were one indissoluble commingling of happiness and laughter. Only now did Sara realize the burden of these last four years of difficult adjustment, a burden carried gracefully and gaily because of the discipline of her training, a training in pride.

When they got out at Asheville and began to mount towards Saluda in a wretched bus, over the then wretched roads of slippery red clay, wires were already buzzing behind them. Mrs Caxton Bisby, eldest of Sara's sisters, summoned a council of war in New York, a famous detective agency began scanning the horizon, a reporter got himself a raise by an unscrupulous scoop, and it took a week before the Austrian ultimatum to Serbia pushed the story onto the second page. There were repercussions in the Faubourg Saint-Germain and the Hon. (and indefatigable) Mrs Burne-Dennison, another sister, wired from London to hold the fort, she was coming.

Meanwhile Killian had wangled a cabin, a wild broken shack above snow level, where they spent a hundred blessed hours making love and fires. Nothing was wrong, the pink light on the snow at five o'clock, the fallings-asleep, the awakenings with a name half-formed on the lips like a bugle rousing them.

On the other side there was only a torn calendar in the lean-to where the wood was, a calendar with a chromo of Madonna and Child. When she first saw it, stricken and aghast, Sara's face did not change – she simply stood very still – and *rained*. After that she didn't look towards the calendar when she went after wood.

They had no time for plans. They had no excuses, nothing to say. A week after they had left New York, Sara was back, sitting silent in highly charged drawing rooms, neither denying nor affirming. A question would be asked her, and she would answer "What?" in an abstracted way. Killian was God knew where.

A few days later she embarked with her husband and children for France. That is the first part of this story.

The war to Sara was a long saying of goodbyes – to officers whom she knew, to soldiers whom she tried to make into more than numbers on a hospital bed. Goodbyes to men still whole, at doorways or railroad stations, were often harder than goodbyes to the dying. Between men and women everything happened very quickly in those days, everything was snatched at, infinitesimal pieces of time had a value they had not possessed before...

...As when Sara turned the angle of a corridor in the Ritz and stopped momentarily outside an open door that was not her door. Stopped is not quite the right word – rather she hesitated, she balanced. After another step, though, she did stop, for a voice hailed her from the room.

"Where are you going in such a hurry?"

It came from the handsome man tying a civilian cravat meticulously before a mirror.

"Going along a hall."

"Well, look – don't. Come here a minute."

As already remarked, everything happened quickly in those days. In a moment Sara was sitting on the side of a chair in the room, with the door pulled to just enough for her to be unseen.

"How did you happen to look in at me?" the man demanded.

"I don't know. Men are attractive sometimes when they don't know it – you were *so* absorbed and puckered up over your tie."

"I wanted to have it right. I keep buying civilian ties with no chance to wear 'em. Back to the line tomorrow."

"I've got till tomorrow night."

"What are you?"

"A nurse – with the French."

He slipped on a white vest with obvious satisfaction in himself, and sat facing her. The shining, starlike eyes had met his in the mirror, the lithe figure with its air of teetering breezily on the edge of nothing, the mobile lips forming incisively every word they uttered were immediately attractive. His heart, stimulated by the nearing sea change of the morrow, went out to her.

"Why not have dinner with me tonight? I've got a date, but I'll call up and break it."

"Can't possibly," said Sara. 'What division are you with?"

"Twenty-sixth New England. Practically a Puritan – look, it'd be a lot of fun."

"Can't possibly."

"Then why did you look in at me?"

"I told you. Because of the way you were tying your tie." She laughed. "The first boy I ever fell in love with was a ship's bugler, because his trousers were so tight and smooth when he bent over to blow."

263

"Change your mind."

"No – I'm sorry."

In her room down the corridor, Sara shifted reflectively into an evening dress. She had no engagement for dinner, though there were many places she could have gone. Her own house in the Rue de Bac was closed; Eduard was with relatives at Grenoble, convalescing from a spinal wound which threatened a lifelong paralysis of his legs; it was from there that she had just come. The war was four years tired now, and as she walked with many millions through the long nightmare, there were times she had to be alone, away from the broken men who tore ceaselessly at her heart. Once she felt all the happiness of life in her fingertips – now she clung to little happenings of today or yesterday, gay ones or sad ones. If her heart should die, she would die.

A little later the American officer came up to her as she sat in the lobby.

"I knew you'd change your mind," he said. "I phoned and broke my other engagement. Come along – I've got a car."

"But I told you—"

"Don't be that way now – it's not like you."

"How do you know what I'm like?"

They drove over the dark "City of Light" and dined – then they went on to one of the few but popular nightclubs – this one, run by an enterprising American, moved to a new address every twenty-four hours to avoid the attention of the gendarmerie. They danced a lot and they knew many people in common, and, partly because talking to a man going back into the line was like talking to herself, Sara spoke of things she had not spoken of for years.

"No, I haven't been lonely in France," she said. "My mother was very wise, and she didn't bring us up to count on any happiness that we didn't help make ourselves."

"And you've never been in love with your husband?"

"No, I was never in love with my husband."

"Never in love at all?"

"Yes, I was in love once," she said, very low.

"When was that?"

"Four years ago. I only saw him for two weeks. I... understand that he's married now."

She did not add that ever since that two weeks she had heard Killian's voice singing around her, heard his guitar as an undertone to every melody, touched his hand before every fire. All through the war she had dressed his wounds, listened to his troubles, written letters for him, laid his hands straight for the last time and died with him, for he was all men – Killian the archangel, the silver-tongued.

...She got up early and went with the officer to the Gare du Nord. He was all changed now, in trench coat, haversack and shining revolver.

"You're very fine," he said tenderly. "This has been a very strange thing. I might have been more... well, more demonstrative last night, but—"

"No, no – it's much better this way."

Then the train went out towards the thunder and left a hollow of grey sky.

In the movies it is so simple to tell of time passing – the film fades out on a dressing station behind the Western Front, fades in on an opera ball in Paris with the punctured uniforms changed into tailcoats and the nurses' caps into tiaras. And why not? We only want to hear about the trenchant or glamorous moments in a life. After the war Sara went to balls in Paris and London, and the side of her that was an actress played butterfly for the dull, neophyte for the brilliant, great lady for the snob and – sometimes was most difficult of all – herself for a few.

Difficult, because it seemed to her that she had no particular self. She had a fine gay time with her children; she walked beside the wheelchair of the Marquis de la Guillet de la Guimpé for his last few years of life, but there was energy to spare that often sent her prying up mean streets or sitting for hours on the fence posts of quirky peasants; simple people said wise or droll things to her that were somehow a comfort. And she made the most of these things in the repeating. It was fun to be with Sara – even people who begrudged her the gaiety patronized her for an incorrigible *gamine*.

When the war had been over eight years and the Marquis had lain for twelve months in the tombs of his ancestors, Sara went again to a ball; she went alone, feeling flushed and excited, and very free – in the entrance she came to a stop, her eyes lighting up higher at the sight of a footman.

"Paul Pechard!" she exclaimed.

"Madame has not forgotten."

"Heavens, no! Were you wounded again? Did you marry Virginie?"

"I married, but not Virginie. I married an old friend of Madame's – Margot, who was *bonne* to her babies. She also works here in this house."

"Why, this is wonderful! Listen – I must go up and be polite for a moment – after that I'll go down by a back way and meet you and Margot in the pantry, and we can talk intimately. What?"

"Madame is too generous."

Up the stairs then on little golden slippers, looking years less than thirty-three, looking no age at all, down the receiving line speaking names out of the pages of Saint-Simon and Mme de Sévigné,* with everyone *so* glad to see her back in the world again – though, privately, a year seemed to many a very short mourning – then on quickly, shaking off men who tried to attach themselves to her, and down a narrow back staircase. Sara had felt that something would happen at this ball, which was why she had broken through her sister-in-law's disapproval at her going. And here was Paul Pechard and Margot, redolent of more intense days.

"Madame is more lovely than—"

"Stop it – I want to hear about you and Paul."

"I think we got married because we knew you, Madame."

It was probably true. So many things can happen in the shelter of some protective personality.

"Madame was wounded, we heard, and received a decoration."

"Just a splinter in the heel. I limp just a little when I walk – so I always run or dance."

"Madame always ran or danced. I can see Madame now, running to the nursery and dancing out of it."

"You dears – listen, I want to go up on that high balcony above the dance floor – do all the maids and everyone still watch the balls from there in this house? It always reminds me of when I was a child and used to look at dances in a nightgown through a crack in the door. It always seems so shiny when you watch like that."

They climbed to the shadowy gallery and gazed down at the ambulating jewels and shimmering dresses, dressed hair bright under the chandeliers, and all against the gleaming backdrop of the floor. From time to time a face turned up to laugh, or exchange a mute secret look, breaking the fabric of calculated perfection like round flowers among the straight lines of rooms; and over the kaleidoscope the music mingled with faint powder and floated up to the watchers in the sky.

Margot leant close to Sara.

"I saw an old friend of Madame's this morning," she said hesitantly. "I brought the oldest child back from England on the channel boat..."

In a wild second Sara knew what was coming.

"...I saw Mr Killian – the big handsome American."

Often we write to certain people that we "think of you all the time", and we lie, of course; but not entirely. For they are always with us, a few of them, so deep in us that they are part of us. Sometimes they are, indeed, the marrow of our bones, so if they die they live on in us. Sara had only to look into herself to find Killian.

...He knows I am free and he has come to find me, she thought. I must go home.

Even as she went down the stairs the strummings of a dozen years ago were louder than the music; they blended with the June wind in the chestnut trees. Her car was not ordered, so she hailed a taxi, pressed it to go faster.

"Has anyone phoned?"

"Yes, Madame – Mrs Selby and Madame de Villegris."

"No one else?"

"No, Madame."

It was eleven. He had been in Paris all day, but perhaps he was travelling with people. Or perhaps he was tired and wanted to sleep first and be at his best.

She looked at herself in the mirror more closely than ever before in her life. She was all gaudy and a little dishevelled with excitement, and she wished rather that he could see her now. But doubtless he would phone in the morning. Morning was his best time – he was an early-to-bed man. Nevertheless she switched a button so that the phone beside her bed would ring.

All morning she stayed in the house, faintly tired around her eyes from a restless night. After lunching she lay down with cold cream on her face, feigning sleep to avoid Noël, her sister-in-law, who wondered whether her early return from the ball did not indicate she had been snubbed for appearing in society so soon.

…Surely it was at teatime that he would call, the mellower, sweeter hour, and she took off the cold cream lest she face him with it, even on the phone. She listened with seven-league ears; she heard the teacups being gathered up in cafés on the Champs-Élysées, she heard the chatter of people pouring from the stores at five thirty, she heard the clink of tables being laid for dinner at the Ritz and Ciro's – then the clack of plates being piled and taken away. She heard black bells strike the hour, then taxis without horns – it was late. Sara tried to be very wise and logical; why should she have expected him – he might have been in Paris a dozen times since the war. At twelve she turned out her light.

At about three the phone woke her. A thick voice said in English:

"I'd like to speak to the lady of the house – the Marquise."

"Who is it?" mumbled Sara, and then, wide awake, "Is this… is…"

She heard a click as another receiver was taken up in the house.

"*Qui parle?*"*

"That's all right, Noël," said Sara quickly. "I think I know who it is." But the receiver did not fall into place again.

"Is this Sara?" said the man.

"Yes, Killian."

"Just got here. Sorry call you so late, but been business."

"Where are you?"

"Place in Montmartre – want to come over?"

…Yes, anywhere.

"No, of course not."

"I'll come see you then."

"It's too late." She hesitated. "Where are you staying?"

"Maurice."

Killian, the silver-tongued, fumbling with his words – and Sara hating drunkenness more than anything in her world. She hardly recognized her own voice as it said:

"Drink two cups of black coffee and I'll meet you in the lobby of the Maurice for an hour."

The receiver in Noël's room clicked just before her own.

Sara's mind had already sorted clothes for any time he might call. In the lower hall, Noël was waiting for her.

"Of course you're not going."

"Yes, Noël."

"You – my brother's widow – to meet a man in a public lobby at three in the morning."

"Now please—"

"—and I know very well who the man is."

Almost absent-mindedly Sara walked past her and out of the door. She found a cab at the corner of the Avenue de Bois and flew down through the city feeling higher and higher, with all the lost months coming back into the calendar with every square they passed…

He was handsome and straight as an athlete, immaculate and unrumpled in his dinner coat – he swayed on his feet.

"Haven't you got a suite?" she demanded. "Can't we go up there?"

He nodded. "Nice of you come."

"I'd have come a longer way than this, Killian."

Darkly and inconclusively he muttered: "Whenever there's been a moon – you know – moonlight."

…Two guitars leant against the sofa – Sara tuned one softly – Killian went to the window, put his head way out and breathed night air.

"'Tended look you up," he said, sitting in a chair beside the window. "Then got to know too many people on the boat. After that didn't feel fit to see you."

"It's all right. I understand. Don't talk about it. Come over here."

"After while."

The blown curtains fluttered around his head, obscuring it; she released a dry sob that she had held too long in her throat.

"What's the matter?"

"Nothing – except that you've been on a tear. You never used to do that, Killian – you used to be so vain of your beautiful self."

She felt something begin to slip away and in desperation picked up the guitar.

"Let's sing something together. We mustn't talk about dull things after all these years."

"But—"

"Sh-sh-sh!" Low in her throat she sang:

"Beside an eastbound boxcar
A dying hobo lay…"*

Then she said:

"Now you sing *me* something – yes, you can. I want you to – please, Killian."

He touched the strings unwillingly, and then gradually his mellow baritone rolled forth.

"—He had a million dollars and
he had a million dimes.
He knew because he counted them
a million times."*

While he sang Sara was thinking: is this adolescent the man whom I have loved so, that I love still? Now what? She made him sing again, as if to gain time, sing again and again until his fingers were dusting fainter and fainter chords and his voice was a sleepy murmur.

"But I can't," she exclaimed aloud suddenly.

He came to life startled.

"What?"

"Nothing."

Her exclamation was answer to the thought: can I kill the memory I have lived by so long? Ah, if he had never come!

"Are you free?" she asked him suddenly. "Did you come to ask me to marry you?"

"That was my idea. 'Course, you see me in rather bad light. Can't deny I've too much under my belt last week – and it isn't the first time."

"But, of course, that's over," she said hurriedly.

Yet how could she know? Each of them must have changed so, and she had to look at him from time to time to reassure herself even of his good looks. The dark mischief of his eyes gleamed back at her across the room. If it were only that, she sighed.

Yet she could not forget the girl who had known a wild delight in a mountain cabin...

Killian dozed, Sara moved around the room examining him impertinently from various corners, his Rodinesque feet, his clothes made of whole bolts of cloth, his great hand inert on the sounding board of the guitar. He complained faintly in his sleep and she woke him – automatically his voice rolled out of him again, deep and full, and the blunt fingers began to strum.

"Oh, Killian, Killian." She laughed in spite of herself, and sang with him:

"So merry you make me I'm
bent up double,
What is it in your make-up that
drives away trouble..."

…Dawn came through the windows very suddenly, and she remembered that it was the longest day in the year. As if impatient to begin it, the telephone jingled.

"The *beau-frère* and *belle-sœur** of Madame are below and wish to see Madame at once on a matter of the greatest—"

"I'll be down."

Gently she rocked Killian from a new slumber in his chair, and as his eyes opened unwillingly she laid her cheek alongside his, whispering in his ear.

"I'll be gone for half an hour, but I'll be back."

"That's all right," he murmured. "I'll play guitar."

The callers were in a small reception room, Noël and the Comte Paul, Eduard's brother. When she saw the agitation in their faces, decomposed by dawn, she knew that the scenes of twelve years ago were to be repeated.

"This is extraordinary—" Paul began, but Noël cut through him.

"To find you here, Sara! You, the widow of a hero, the mother of the son who bears his name, here in a *hotel* at this hour."

"You can't be very surprised," said Sara coldly. "You knew where to find me."

"Once when my brother was alive you dragged his name through the newspapers – now when he is in a hero's grave and cannot speak for himself, you intend to do it again."

"Eduard wanted me to be happy…"

She stopped – she was not happy, only miserable and confused. Weary with her two-day vigil, she wanted sleep most of all. But she did not dare sleep; she could not risk letting this thing slip out of her hand again.

"Would you like some coffee?" she suggested.

Noël refused, but Paul agreed vigorously and went to order it.

"Are you an old woman bewitched, wanting a pretty gigolo?" Noël cried. "Are there not hundreds of men of culture and distinction for you to know – you who have moved in the best society of Europe? Yes, even men to marry if you must, after a decent interval."

"You think that I'm going to marry Killian?"

Noël started.

"Well, aren't you? Isn't that your—"

Paul returned from the lobby.

"What concerns us chiefly is the children," he said. "Henri bears the senior title; he is the only marquis in France who walks with dukes, by the graciousness of the *Grand Monarque*."

"I know all that. I am proud of my son's name and I've tried to make him proud of it. But my part is almost done – they go to Brittany next week for the summer, and in the fall Miette will be fifteen and Henri thirteen and they'll go off to school."

"Then you've made up your mind to marry this... this species of six-day bicycle racer?" said Paul. "Oh, we've checked up on him from time to time – once he made himself a promoter of prizefights. Guh!"

"I've said nothing about marrying him."

She drank her coffee quickly – it was so confusing to try to think in their presence. Remembering many public scandals and misalliances, she wondered that each one had seemed so clean-cut in a sentence of gossip or a newspaper headline. Doubtless, behind every case, there were trapped and muddled people, weighing, buying a ticket to nowhere at an unknown price.

The porter brought her a cable – she read it and said to Noël:

"You cabled Martha Burne-Dennison in London."

"I did," said Noël defiantly. "And I cabled New York too, and at what a cost!"

The message said:

YOU CANNOT THROW YOURSELF AWAY ON A WILD MAN FROM NOWHERE THINK OF US AND YOUR CHILDREN I ARRIVE AT THE GARE ST LAZARE AT FIVE.

As she crumpled it, Sara wondered if the sun upstairs was in Killian's eyes, keeping him from sleep.

"You will come home now," they said. "We will rest; presently you will view your obligations in a different light."

…And it will be too late. In a panic she felt them close in on her. Ah, if Killian had come to her all whole and straight.

"My wrap is upstairs."

"We can send for it."

"No, I'm going myself."

Upstairs Killian cocked a drowsy eye at her.

"You were a long time."

She uttered a sort of groaning laugh.

"Are you under the impression you've been playing the guitar all this time?"

Suddenly he stood up, seemed to snap altogether. He stretched; his clothes fell into place; his eyes were clear as a child's and the colour was stealing back into his face. With this change came another. The faint silliness of last night faded out of his expression and all consideration, all comfort, all quintessence of eternal cheer and tireless energy came back into it. He looked at her as if for the first time, took a step – and then her dress crushed into his shirt bosom, and his stud, pressing her neck like a call button, set her heart scurrying and crying. And she knew.

"We've got to hurry," she gasped, breaking from him. "You start packing." She picked up the phone and, waiting for the connection, said in a choking little laugh, "We're running away again – they'll be after us – isn't it fun? We'll get married in Algiers – Abby's husband's consul-general. Oh, isn't it wonderful!

"Hello – is this Henriette? Henriette, pack me the blue travelling suit – shoes and everything – toilet articles – my personal jewels – and your own bag – be at the Gare de Lyon in an hour."

The shower was already roaring in Killian's bathroom. Then it stopped and he called out:

"I forgot I haven't any street suit or any baggage at all, except a couple of used dress shirts. Caught the night boat from Southampton and my things got stuck in the customs—"

"That's all right, Killian," she cried back. "We've got plenty – you and I – and two guitars."

Her beach slippers felt strange on the piano pedals – the wind off the Sound blew in through the lilac trees, blew on her bare brown shoulders, her brown, childish legs – this was 1928.

Blow, breeze of America, breeze of my youth, she thought. I am thirty-six; my daughter is almost grown and every morning she rides in the Bois de Boulogne; my son is here in America with me for the summer. Presently there will be an hour of sky and sea, with old friends calling, "*Please* do the imitation of the Frenchwoman teaching English, Sara!"

She swung around suddenly on the piano bench.

"You like the pretty picture?" she enquired of Abby.

"Picture of what?"

"Picture of Killian and Sara."

"Why not?"

"You might as well end your visit without any illusions," Sara said. "I haven't any idea where Killian has been these last four days – I didn't know he was going, where he went, when he'll be back – if ever. It's happened twice since we've been married. Anyhow, I've been doing a lot of thinking these last four days – I suppose all the thinking I've ever done in my life has been crowded into a few weeks – and it's just possible I'm not the right kind of wife for him. I've tried to run a civilized house, but he seems to get yearnings for the society of friendly policemen."

"Why, Sara—"

"Killian never grew up – that's all. Sometimes I try to make it funny – Mr and Mrs Jiggs."*

"But if my husband didn't go away sometimes—"

"It isn't just that, Abby. I thought that at last maybe I'd have the whole loaf I've never had. I've gone to fights with Killian and baseball games and six-day bicycle races, and broken my heart shooting lovely little

275

quail. I've admired his bottle-green hunting coat and played minstrel show with him at parties, but we just don't communicate. I'm getting very well acquainted with myself."

"You love Killian," Abby said.

"Yes, I love him – all I can find of him. Sometimes I say to myself that I'm expiating – there's a nice new word. Killian and I started wrong, so now I'm cast for Expiation. 'The former Marquise de la Guillet de la Guimpé was lovely in the role of Mrs Expiation.'" She stopped herself as if ashamed. "I've never talked about this before – the pride must be breaking down."

Killian came home just before dinner, looking exactly like the four days he'd been away. Sara had planned her act.

"Darling! I was sure you'd be home tonight." She went on drawing her lips in the mirror. "You go and shave and take a bath right away, because we're going to the opera. I've got your ticket."

Her voice was calm, but in the terrible relief of his return she drew three red moustaches on her upper lip.

He was himself again on the way back in the car, but only in the morning was the matter mentioned.

"You were pretty sweet about this," he said.

If he would only say more – what made him go? – if there was only something between them beyond the old electrical attraction. They lived lately in the growing silence, and intuition told her that this was one of those crucial quiet times when things are really settled. The battle was not joined; the message, if message there was, could still get through.

In the afternoon he went riding and Sara found herself missing him terribly. With the vague idea that they might talk more freely outside of walls – walls whose function is to keep people apart – she drove slowly along the country roads he frequented. After half an hour, she saw him far ahead of her – first a figure that might have been any man on any horse, and then at the next rise was Killian on his great roan mare. The fine figure against the sky fascinated her – she stopped her car until he passed from sight in another dip.

At the next hill he was still invisible, so she drove to a further viewpoint from which she could see for miles, but no Killian – he had turned off somewhere into the country.

Turning herself, she drove back slowly – after a quarter-mile she saw the mare grazing on the grassy hillside not far from the road. She left the car and walked up the hill. There in a grove of half a dozen trees she found him.

He lay on his side on the ground, cheek in his hand. Reluctant to surprise him in the solitude, Sara stood silent. After a few minutes he got to his feet, shook his head from side to side in a puzzled way, clapped his gloves together several times and turned about. As he moved she saw a gravestone, against which lay a bouquet of fresh flowers.

He came towards her, frowning a little.

"Why, Killian…"

He took her hand and they went down the hill together.

"That's Dorothy's grave," he said. "I bring flowers sometimes."

A vast silence stole over her. Killian had not mentioned his first wife half a dozen times since their marriage.

"Oh, I see."

"She used to like that little hill – I'm almost sure it was that hill – almost…" A touch of worry came into his voice. "…And we talked about building a house on it. So after she died I bought the piece of land."

The old limp from the war made Sara trip suddenly and he caught her by the waist, half-carrying her as they went on. Only when asphalt instead of the grass was underfoot did she say: "You cared for her a lot, Killian?"

He nodded, and she nodded as if in agreement.

"It was long ago," he said. "But she hated my wild times just as much as you do, and it seems to fortify me to come here."

His words fell unreal on Sara's ears – she had assumed always that his first marriage was a rebound, a substitute. Something broke from her heart that she regretted immediately:

"You forgot me right away."

He hesitated; then he said bluntly:

"I love you so much now that I can tell you this – that I wasn't really in love with you when we ran away together. I didn't realize at first how unhappy you were going to be afterwards."

She nodded, surprised at her own calmness.

"I'm beginning to understand some things," she said. "It explains about Paris."

"You mean the time during the war."

"The time I found you tying your tie in a mirror in the Ritz, and we acted it out that we were strangers who had picked each other up. I never quite understood why you didn't make love to me that evening. I supposed it was because my husband was wounded and you were helping me to the right thing." She paused thoughtfully. "And all the time you were being in love with your wife at home."

They stood by the car, their hands still clasped.

"She was lovely," Sara said, as if to herself. "Once I saw a picture of her in a magazine."

"I didn't see any advantage in bringing Dorothy's ghost in on our marriage," Killian said. "You thought that you and I had felt the same way all those years – and I let you think so. But I know now I was wrong – if you begin locking things up in a cupboard, you get so you never say half what's in your mind."

Here were her own words come back to her.

"What brought you to me after the war?" she persisted. And then added quickly, "Oh I don't care – you came for me and that was enough."

Her natural buoyancy tried to struggle back, beating against her pride. She had only made the mistake of believing that Killian's heart was a mirror of her own.

"I love you more than I did ten minutes ago," she said.

They hugged each other, cheek to cheek; their slim silhouette might have been that of young lovers vowed an hour before. Presently his attention left her as he exclaimed:

"Look at that darn mare!"

"It's all right – we can get her – jump in the car."

When they reached the mare Killian got out and caught it, and Sara drove on, turning at the next curve and waving back at him. But at the turn beyond that the road grew blurred for a moment and she stopped again, thinking of the green hill and the flowers.

"Sleep quiet, Dorothy," she whispered. "I'll take care of him."

Throughout a dinner party that night she was still thinking, trying to accept the fact that a part of Killian and a part of herself would always be strangers. She wondered if that were especially her fate, or if it were everyone's fate. From earliest childhood she remembered that she had always wanted someone for her own.

After coffee, they responded to a general demand, moved the piano bench to the middle of the floor, left only the firelight shining in the room. She sat beside Killian, making a special face of hers that was more like laughing than smiling, fingers pressed to a steeple over her heart, as he meticulously tuned his guitar, then at his nod they began. The Russian jibberish song came first – not knowing a word of the language, they had yet caught the tone and ring of it, until it was not burlesque but something uncanny that made every eye intent on their faces, every ear attune to the Muscovite despair they twisted into the end of each phrase. Following it, they did the always popular German Band, and the Spanish number and the spirituals, each time with a glance passing between them as they began another.

"You're not sad, are you?" he whispered once.

"No, you old rake," she jeered back at him cheerfully. "Hey! Hey! Scratch a marquise and find a pushover."

No one would ever let Killian and Sara stop, no one ever had enough, and as they sang on, their faces flushed with excitement and pleasure like children's faces, the conviction grew in Sara that they were communicating, that they were saying things to each other in every note, every bar of harmony. They were talking to each other as surely as if with words – closer than any two people in the room. And suddenly she was for ever reconciled – there would always be this that they had had from the beginning, music and laughter together, and it was enough – this, and the certainty that presently, when their guests were gone, she would be in his arms.

Note on the Texts

The text of 'Indecision' is based on the version published in the *Saturday Evening Post* (16th May 1931). The text of 'Between Three and Four' is based on the version published in the *Saturday Evening Post* (5th September 1931). The text of 'A Change of Class' is based on the version published in the *Saturday Evening Post* (26th September 1931). The text of 'Diagnosis' is based on the version published in the *Saturday Evening Post* (20th February 1932). The text of 'Flight and Pursuit' is based on the version published in the *Saturday Evening Post* (14th May 1932). The text of 'The Rubber Cheque' is based on the version published in the *Saturday Evening Post* (6th August 1932). The text of 'On Schedule' is based on the version published in the *Saturday Evening Post* (18th March 1933). The text of 'I Got Shoes' is based on the version published in the *Saturday Evening Post* (23rd September 1933). The text of 'The Family Bus' is based on the version published in the *Saturday Evening Post* (4th November 1933). The text of 'No Flowers' is based on the version published in the *Saturday Evening Post* (21st July 1934). The text of 'New Types' is based on the version published in the *Saturday Evening Post* (22nd September 1934). The text of 'Her Last Case' is based on the version published in the *Saturday Evening Post* (3rd November 1934). The text of 'The Intimate Strangers' is based on the version published in the *McCall's* (June 1935). The spelling and punctuation have been Anglicized, standardized, modernized and made consistent throughout.

Notes

p. 3, *I'm Getting Myself Ready for You*: A 1930 song by Cole Porter (1891–1964).

p. 9, *Salaud… Salaud français*: "Bastard! French bastard!" (French).

p. 10, *Ce sont des dames… vous voulez*: "They are American ladies; there's only one Frenchman. Well now! What do you want?" (French).

p. 10, *Vive l'Amérique… la Suisse*: "Long live America! Long live Switzerland" (French).

p. 17, *Ach je*: "Oh dear!" (German).

p. 19, *Goodnight, ladies… leave you now*: A song attributed to the American minstrel singer Edwin Pearce Christy (1815–62).

p. 19, *Wildstrubel*: A 3,244-metre-high mountain in Switzerland, on the border between the Bern and Valais cantons.

p. 23, *Gibson Girl*: The archetypal upper-class beautiful young woman, as found in the illustrations by Charles Dana Gibson (1867–1944).

p. 27, *I can't give you… I've plenty of, baby*: From the 1928 song by 'I Can't Give You Anything but Love, Baby' composed by Jimmy McHugh (1894–1969), with lyrics by Dorothy Fields (1905–74).

p. 43, *The Breakaway*: A reference to 'Breakaway', a 1929 song by Jack Hylton (1892–1965) and his orchestra.

p. 58, *Triangle or whatever it was at Princeton*: A reference to the Triangle Club, Princeton University's prestigious theatre group.

p. 95, *Percy and Ferdie, The Hallroom Boys*: Two popular comic strips by H.A. MacGill.

p. 102, *So Blue*: A 1927 song composed by Buddy DeSylva (1895–1950) and Ray Henderson (1896–1970), with lyrics by Lew Brown (1893–1958).

p. 105, *Cowes Week*: A major annual regatta held on the Solent in the south of England.

p. 112, *Juan Gris*: Juan Gris (1887–1927), a famous Spanish Cubist painter and sculptor.

p. 122, *Lacoste and Lenglen*: A reference to René Lacoste (1904–96) and Suzanne Lenglen (1899–1938), both highly successful French tennis players and sports celebrities of their day.

p. 126, *Mon Dieu… Quel commencement*: "My God!… What a start!" (French).

p. 141, *Vanity Fair, saith the prophet*: Presumably she means "Vanity of Vanities, saith the prophet" (Ecclesiastes 1:2).

p. 145, *Secret Service and The Easiest Way and The Witching Hour*: *Secret Service* is an 1895 play by William Gillette (1853–1937); *The Easiest Way* is a 1909 play by Eugene Walter (1874–1941); *The Witching Hour* is a 1907 play by Augustus Thomas (1857–1934)

p. 145, *Old Kentucky*: A reference to the 1893 play *In Old Kentucky* by Charles Dazey (1855–1938).

p. 147, *Sis Hopkins*: A fictional character created by the comic actress Rose Melville (1873–1946) for various plays and sketches in the 1890s, Sis Hopkins is an innocent girl from the countryside.

p. 149, *Mr Gideon*: A reference to the ubiquitous Bibles distributed by the evangelical Christian association Gideons International.

p. 175, *MFH*: Master of the Foxhounds, the title given to the person in charge of organizing the various sporting and administrative aspects of a fox hunt.

p. 199, *Smoke Got in Her Eyes… Carioca*: 'Smoke Gets in Your Eyes' is a 1933 song composed by Jerome Kern (1885–1945), with lyrics by Otto Harbach (1873–1963); 'Boulevard of Broken Dreams' is a 1933 song composed by Harry Warren (1893–1981), with lyrics by Al Dubin (1891–1945); 'Carioca' is a 1933 song composed by Vincent Youmans (1898–1946), with lyrics by Edward Eliscu (1902–98) and Gus Kahn (1886–1941).

p. 202, *Coffee in the Morning*: A 1934 song composed by Harry Warren (1893–1981), with lyrics by Al Dubin (1891–1945).

p. 203, *Horatio Alger*: Horatio Alger, Jr (1832–99) was the author of popular rags-to-riches novels aimed at young readers.

p. 204, *Orchids in the Moonlight*: A 1933 song composed by Vincent Youmans (1898–1946), with lyrics by Edward Eliscu (1902–98) and Gus Kahn (1886–1941).

p. 205, *as much practice in believing as the Red Queen*: A reference to Chapter 5 of Lewis Carroll's *Through the Looking Glass* (1871), in which the White Queen talks of how much she has practised believing in impossible things. Fitzgerald erroneously attributes this to another character in the novel, the Red Queen.

p. 219, *Blue Danube*: A famous 1866 waltz by Johann Strauss II (1825–99).

p. 219, *Jeb Stuart and the gallant Pelham*: Jeb Stuart (1833–64) was a prominent Confederate general in the Civil War; John Pelham (1838–63), nicknamed "the Gallant Pelham", was an officer under the command of Stuart who became famous for his bravery and adroitness on the battlefield.

p. 228, *Narcissus looking into the pool*: In Greek myth, Narcissus was a hunter who drowned after loving in love with a reflection of himself in a pool.

p. 233, *Marion Davies*: Marion Davies (1897–1961) was an American film star and prominent Hollywood socialite.

p. 233, *Château-Thierry*: A reference to the Battle of Château-Thierry of 18th June 1918, in which the American Expeditionary Forces contributed to an Allied win against the Germans.

p. 240, *Longstreet for not using his flanks at Gettysburg*: James Longstreet (1821–1904) was a prominent Confederate general in the American Civil War, who was criticized for his part in his side's defeat at the Battle of Gettysburg in 1863.

p. 247, *Pollard's War Between the States*: A reference to the multi-volume *Southern History of the War* (1862–64) by the pro-Confederate journalist Edward A. Pollard (1828–72).

p. 258, *Leyendecker*: J.C. Leyendecker (1874–1951), an American illustrator famous for his magazine covers and advertising posters.

p. 258, *Madame Sans-Gêne*: "Mrs Shameless" (French), the nickname of Marie-Thérèse Figueur (1774–1861), a famous French female soldier.

p. 259, *Not That You Are Fair, Dear*: A reference to the 1906 Broadway song 'Because You're You', composed by Victor Herbert (1859–1924), with lyrics by Henry Blossom (1866–1919).

p. 261, *Fauntleroy*: A reference to the protagonist of the novel *Little Lord Fauntleroy* (1886) by Frances Hodgson Burnett (1849–1924)

p. 266, *Saint-Simon and Mme de Sévigné*: A reference to the French diarist Duc de Saint-Simon (1675–1755) and Madame de Sévigné (1626–96), famous for her letter-writing.

p. 268, *Qui parle*: "Who's speaking?" (French).

p. 270, *Beside an eastbound... hobo lay*: Slightly modified lyrics from the American folk song 'A Little Stream of Whiskey'.

p. 270, *He had a million dollars... a million times*: Slightly modified lyrics from the vaudeville song 'Willie the Weeper'.

p. 272, *beau-frère... belle-sœur*: "Brother-in-law... sister-in-law" (French).

p. 275, *Mr and Mrs Jiggs*: A reference to Jiggs and his wife Maggie, the protagonists of the popular comic strip *Bringing up Father* by George McManus (1884–1954).

Extra Material

on

F. Scott Fitzgerald's

The Intimate Strangers
and
Other Stories

F. Scott Fitzgerald's Life

Francis Scott Key Fitzgerald was born on 24th September 1896 at 481 Laurel Avenue in St Paul, Minnesota. Fitzgerald, who would always be known as "Scott", was named after Francis Scott Key, the author of 'The Star-Spangled Banner' and his father's second cousin three times removed. His mother, Mary "Mollie" McQuillan, was born in 1860 in one of St Paul's wealthier streets, and would come into a modest inheritance at the death of her father in 1877. His father, Edward Fitzgerald, was born in 1853 near Rockville, Maryland. A wicker-furniture manufacturer at the time of Fitzgerald's birth, his business would collapse in 1898 and he would then take to the road as a wholesale grocery salesman for Procter & Gamble. This change of job necessitated various moves of home and the family initially shifted east to Buffalo, New York, in 1898, and then on to Syracuse, New York, in 1901. By 1903 they were back in Buffalo and in March 1908 they were in St Paul again after Edward lost his job at Procter & Gamble. The *déclassé* Fitzgeralds would initially live with the McQuillans and then moved into a series of rented houses, settling down at 599 Summit Avenue.

This itinerancy would disrupt Fitzgerald's early schooling, isolating him and making it difficult to make many friends at his various schools in Buffalo, Syracuse and St Paul. The first one at which Fitzgerald would settle for a prolonged period was the St Paul Academy, which he entered in September 1908. It was here that Fitzgerald would achieve his first appearance in print, 'The Mystery of the Raymond Mortgage', which appeared in the St Paul Academy school magazine *Now and Then* in October 1909. 'Reade, Substitute Right Half' and 'A Debt of Honor' would follow in the February and March 1910 numbers, and 'The Room with the Green Blinds' in the June 1911 number. His reading at this time was dominated by adventure stories and the other typical literary interests of a turn-of-the-century American teen, with the novels of G.A. Henty, Walter Scott's *Ivanhoe* and Jane Porter's *The Scottish Chiefs* among his favourites; their influence was apparent in the floridly melodramatic tone of his early pieces, though themes that would recur throughout Fitzgerald's mature fiction, such as the social difficulties of the outsider, would be introduced in these stories. An interest in the theatre also surfaced at this time, with Fitzgerald writing and taking the lead role in *The Girl from Lazy J*, a play that would be performed with a local amateur-dramatic group, the Elizabethan Drama Club, in August 1911. The group would also produce *The Captured Shadow* in 1912, *The Coward* in 1913 and *Assorted Spirits* in 1914.

At the end of the summer of 1911, Fitzgerald was once again uprooted (in response to poor academic achievements) and moved to the Newman School, a private Catholic school in Hackensack, New Jersey. He was singularly unpopular with the other boys, who considered him aloof and overbearing. This period as a social pariah at Newman was a defining time for Fitzgerald, one that would be echoed repeatedly in his fiction, most straightforwardly in the "Basil" stories, the most famous of which, 'The Freshest Boy', would appear in *The Saturday Evening Post* in July 1928 and is clearly autobiographical in its depiction of a boastful schoolboy's social exclusion.

Hackensack had, however, the advantage of proximity to New York City, and Fitzgerald began to get to know Manhattan, visiting a series of shows, including *The Quaker Girl* and *Little Boy Blue*. His first publication in Newman's school magazine, *The Newman News*, was 'Football', a poem written in an attempt to appease his peers following a traumatic incident on the football field that led to widespread accusation of cowardice, compounding the young writer's isolation. In his last year at Newman he would publish three stories in *The Newman News*.

Father Fay and the Catholic Influence

Also in that last academic year Fitzgerald would encounter the prominent Catholic priest Father Cyril Sigourney Webster Fay, a lasting and formative connection that would influence the author's character, oeuvre and career. Father Fay introduced Fitzgerald to such figures as Henry Adams and encouraged the young writer towards the aesthetic and moral understanding that underpins all of his work. In spite of the licence and debauchery for which Fitzgerald's life and work are often read, a strong moral sense informs all of his fiction – a sense that can be readily traced to Fay and the author's Catholic schooling at Newman. Fay would later appear in thinly disguised form as Amory Blaine's spiritual mentor, and man of the world, Monsignor Darcy, in *This Side of Paradise*.

Princeton

Fitzgerald's academic performance was little improved at Newman, and he would fail four courses in his two years there. In spite of this, in May 1913 Fitzgerald took the entrance exams for Princeton, the preferred destination for Catholic undergraduates in New Jersey. He would go up in September 1913, his fees paid for through a legacy left by his grandmother Louisa McQuillan, who had died in August.

At Princeton Fitzgerald would begin to work in earnest on the process of turning himself into an author: in his first year he met confrères and future collaborators John Peale Bishop and Edmund Wilson. During his freshman year Fitzgerald won a competition to write the book and lyrics for the 1914–15 Triangle Club (the Princeton dramatic society) production *Fie! Fie! Fi-Fi!* He would also co-author, with Wilson, the 1915–16 production, *The Evil Eye*, and the lyrics for *Safety First*, the 1916–17 offering. He also quickly began to contribute to the Princeton humour magazine *The Princeton Tiger*, while his reading tastes had moved on to the social concerns of George Bernard Shaw, Compton Mackenzie and H.G. Wells. His social progress at Princeton also seemed assured as Fitzgerald was approached by the Cottage Club (one of Princeton's exclusive eating clubs) and prominence in the Triangle Club seemed inevitable.

September 1914 and the beginning of Fitzgerald's sophomore year would mark the great calamity of his Princeton education, causing a trauma that Fitzgerald would approach variously in his writing (notably in *This Side of Paradise* and Gatsby's abortive "Oxford" career in *The Great Gatsby*). Poor academic performance meant that Fitzgerald was barred from extra-curricular activities; he was therefore unable to perform in *Fie! Fie! Fi-Fi!*, and took to the road with the production in an attendant capacity. Fitzgerald's progress at the Triangle and Cottage clubs stagnated (he made Secretary at Triangle nonetheless, but did not reach the heights he had imagined for himself), and his hopes of social dominance on campus were dashed.

The second half of the 1914–15 academic year saw a brief improvement and subsequent slipping of Fitzgerald's performance in classes, perhaps in response to a budding romance with Ginevra King, a sixteen-year-old socialite from Lake Forest, Illinois. Their courtship would continue until January 1917. King would become the model for a series of Fitzgerald's characters, including Judy Jones in the 1922 short story 'Winter Dreams', Isabelle Borgé in *This Side of Paradise* and, most famously, Daisy Buchanan in *The Great Gatsby*. In November 1915 Fitzgerald's academic career was once again held up when he was diagnosed with malaria (though it is likely that this was in fact the first appearance of the tuberculosis that would sporadically disrupt his health for the rest of his life) and left Princeton for the rest of the semester to recuperate. At the same time as all of this disruption, however, Fitzgerald was building a head of steam in terms of his literary production. Publications during this period included stories, reviews and poems for Princeton's *Nassau Literary Magazine*.

The USA entered the Great War in May 1917 and a week later Fitzgerald joined up, at least partly motivated by the fact that his

Ginevra King and Ill Health

Army Commission

uncompleted courses at Princeton would automatically receive credits as he signed up. Three weeks of intensive training and the infantry commission exam soon followed, though a commission itself did not immediately materialize. Through the summer he stayed in St Paul, undertaking important readings in William James, Henri Bergson and others, and in the autumn he returned to Princeton (though not to study) and took lodgings with John Biggs Jr, the editor of the *Tiger*. More contributions appeared in both the *Nassau Literary Magazine* and the *Tiger*, but the commission finally came and in November Fitzgerald was off to Fort Leavenworth, Kansas, where he was to report as a second lieutenant in the infantry. Convinced that he would die in the war, Fitzgerald began intense work on his first novel, *The Romantic Egoist*, the first draft of which would be finished while on leave from Kansas in February 1918. The publishing house Charles Scribner's Sons, despite offering an encouraging appreciation of the novel, rejected successive drafts in August and October 1918.

Zelda Sayre   As his military training progressed and the army readied Fitzgerald and his men for the fighting in Europe, he was relocated, first to Camp Gordon in Georgia, and then on to Camp Sheridan, near Montgomery, Alabama. There, at a dance at the Montgomery Country Club in July, he met Zelda Sayre, a beautiful eighteen-year-old socialite and daughter of a justice of the Alabama Supreme Court. An intense courtship began and Fitzgerald soon proposed marriage, though Zelda was nervous about marrying a man with so few apparent prospects.

As the armistice that ended the Great War was signed on 11th November 1918, Fitzgerald was waiting to embark for Europe, and had already been issued with his overseas uniform. The closeness by which he avoided action in the Great War stayed with Fitzgerald, and gave him another trope for his fiction, with many of his characters, Amory Blaine from *This Side of Paradise* and Jay Gatsby among them, attributed with abortive or ambiguous military careers. Father Fay, who had been involved, and had tried to involve Fitzgerald, in a series of mysterious intelligence operations during the war, died in January 1919, leaving Fitzgerald without a moral guide just as he entered the world free from the restrictions of Princeton and the army. Fay would be the dedicatee of *This Side of Paradise*.

Literary   Fitzgerald's first move after the war was to secure gainful
Endeavours employment at Barron Collier, an advertising agency, producing copy for trolley-car advertisements. At night he continued to work hard at his fiction, collecting 112 rejection slips over this period. Relief was close at hand, however, with *The Smart Set* printing a revised version of 'Babes in the Wood' (a short story that had previous appeared in *Nassau Literary Magazine* and

that would soon be cannibalized for *This Side of Paradise*) in their September 1919 issue. *The Smart Set*, edited by this time by H.L. Mencken and George Jean Nathan, who would both become firm supporters of Fitzgerald's talent, was a respected literary magazine, but not a high payer; Fitzgerald received $30 for this first appearance. Buoyed by this, and frustrated by his job, Fitzgerald elected to leave work and New York and return to his parents' house in St Paul, where he would make a concerted effort to finish his novel. As none of the early drafts of *The Romantic Egoist* survive, it is impossible to say with complete certainty how much of that project was preserved in the draft of *This Side of Paradise* that emerged at St Paul. It was, at any rate, more attractive to Scribner in its new form, and the editor Maxwell Perkins, who would come to act as both editor and personal banker for Fitzgerald, wrote on 16th September to say that the novel had been accepted. Soon after he would hire Harold Ober to act as his agent, an arrangement that would continue throughout the greatest years of Fitzgerald's output and that would benefit the author greatly, despite sometimes causing Ober a great deal of difficulty and anxiety. Though Fitzgerald would consider his novels the artistically important part of his work, it would be his short stories, administered by Ober, which would provide the bulk of his income. Throughout his career a regular supply of short stories appeared between his novels, a supply that became more essential and more difficult to maintain as the author grew older.

Newly confident after the acceptance of *This Side of Paradise*,   *Success* Fitzgerald set about revising a series of his previous stories, securing another four publications in *The Smart Set*, one in *Scribner's Magazine* and one in *The Saturday Evening Post*, an organ that would prove to be one of the author's most dependable sources of income for many years to come. By the end of 1919 Fitzgerald had made $879 from writing: not yet a living, but a start. His receipts would quickly increase. Thanks to Ober's skilful assistance *The Saturday Evening Post* had taken another six stories by February 1920, at $400 each. In March *This Side of Paradise* was published and proved to be a surprising success, selling 3,000 in its first three days and making instant celebrities of Fitzgerald and Zelda, who would marry the author on 3rd April, her earlier concerns about her suitor's solvency apparently eased by his sudden literary success. During the whirl of 1920, the couple's *annus mirabilis*, other miraculous portents of a future of plenty included the sale of a story, 'Head and Shoulders', to Metro Films for $2,500, the sale of four stories to *Metropolitan Magazine* for $900 each and the rapid appearance of *Flappers and Philosophers*, a volume of stories, published by Scribner in September. By the end of the year Fitzgerald, still in his mid-twenties, had moved into an apartment on New York's West 59th Street and was hard at work on his second novel.

Zelda discovered she was pregnant in February 1921, and in May the couple headed to Europe where they visited various heroes and attractions, including John Galsworthy. They returned in July to St Paul, where a daughter, Scottie, was born on 26th October. Fitzgerald was working consistently and well at this time, producing a prodigious amount of high-quality material. *The Beautiful and Damned*, his second novel, was soon ready and began to appear as a serialization in *Metropolitan Magazine* from September. Its publication in book form would have to wait until March 1922, at which point it received mixed reviews, though Scribner managed to sell 40,000 copies of it in its first year of publication. Once again it would be followed within a few months by a short-story collection, *Tales of the Jazz Age*, which contained such classics of twentieth-century American literature as 'May Day', 'The Diamond as Big as the Ritz' and 'The Curious Case of Benjamin Button'.

1923 saw continued successes and a first failure. Receipts were growing rapidly: the Hearst organization bought first option in Fitzgerald's stories for $1,500, he sold the film rights for *This Side of Paradise* for $10,000 and he began selling stories to *The Saturday Evening Post* for $1,250 each. *The Vegetable*, on the other hand, a play that he had been working on for some time, opened in Atlantic City and closed almost immediately following poor reviews, losing Fitzgerald money. By the end of the year his income had shot up to $28,759.78, but he had spent more than that on the play and fast living, and found himself in debt as a result.

The Fitzgeralds' high living was coming at an even higher price. In an attempt to finish his new project Fitzgerald set out for Europe with Zelda and landed up on the French Riviera, a situation that provided the author with the space and time to make some real progress on his novel. While there, however, Zelda met Édouard Jozan, a French pilot, and began a romantic entanglement that put a heavy strain on her marriage. This scenario has been read by some as influencing the final drafting of *The Great Gatsby*, notably Gatsby's disillusionment with Daisy. It would also provide one of the central threads of *Tender Is the Night*, while Gerald and Sara Murphy, two friends they made on the Riviera, would be models for that novel's central characters. Throughout 1924 their relations became more difficult, their volatility was expressed through increasingly erratic behaviour and by the end of the year Fitzgerald's drinking was developing into alcoholism.

Some progress was made on the novel, however, and a draft was sent to Scribner in October. A period of extensive and crucial revisions followed through January and February 1925, with the novel already at the galley-proof stage. After extensive negotiations with Max Perkins, the new novel also received its final title at about this time. Previous titles had included *Trimalchio* and *Trimalchio in West Egg*, both of which Scribner found too obscure for a mass readership, despite Fitzgerald's preference for them, while *Gold-Hatted Gatsby*, *On the Road to West Egg*, *The High-Bouncing Lover* and *Among Ash Heaps and Millionaires* were also suggestions. Shortly before the novel was due to be published, Fitzgerald telegrammed Scribner with the possible title *Under the Red, White and Blue*, but it was too late, and the work was published as *The Great Gatsby* on 10th April. The reception for the new work was impressive, and it quickly garnered some of Fitzgerald's most enthusiastic reviews, but its sales did not reach the best-seller levels the author and Scribner had hoped for.

Fitzgerald was keen to get on with his work and, rather misguidedly, set off to Paris with Zelda to begin his next novel. Paris at the heart of the Roaring Twenties was not a locale conducive to careful concentration, and little progress was made on the new project. There was much socializing, however, and Fitzgerald invested quite a lot of his time in cementing his reputation as one of the more prominent drunks of American letters. The couple's time was spent mostly with the American expatriate community, and among those he got to know there were Edith Wharton, Gertrude Stein, Robert McAlmon and Sylvia Beach of Shakespeare & Company. Perhaps the most significant relationship with another writer from this period was with Ernest Hemingway, with whom Fitzgerald spent much time (sparking jealousy in Zelda), and for whom he would become an important early supporter, helping to encourage Scribner to publish *The Torrents of Spring* and *The Sun Also Rises*, for which he also gave extensive editorial advice. The summer of 1925 was again spent on the Riviera, but this time with a rowdier crowd (which included John Dos Passos, Archibald MacLeish and Rudolph Valentino) and little progress was made on the new book. February 1926 saw publication of the inevitable follow-up short-story collection, this time *All the Sad Young Men*, of which the most significant pieces were 'The Rich Boy', 'Winter Dreams' and 'Absolution'. All three are closely associated with *The Great Gatsby*, and can be read as alternative routes into the Gatsby story.

Paris

With the new novel still effectively stalled, Fitzgerald decamped to Hollywood at the beginning of 1927, where he was engaged by United Artists to write a flapper comedy that was never produced in the end. These false starts were not, however, adversely affecting Fitzgerald's earnings, and 1927 would represent the highest annual earnings the author had achieved so far: $29,757.87, largely from

Hollywood

short-story sales. While in California Fitzgerald began a dalliance with Lois Moran, a seventeen-year-old aspiring actress – putting further strain on his relationship with Zelda. After the couple moved back east (to Delaware) Zelda began taking ballet lessons in an attempt to carve a niche for herself that might offer her a role beyond that of the wife of a famous author. She would also make various attempts to become an author in her own right. The lessons would continue under the tutelage of Lubov Egorova when the Fitzgeralds moved to Paris in the summer of 1928, with Zelda's obsessive commitment to dance practice worrying those around her and offering the signs of the mental illness that was soon to envelop her.

Looking for a steady income stream (in spite of very high earnings expenditure was still outstripping them), Fitzgerald set to work on the "Basil" stories in 1928, earning $31,500 for nine that appeared in *The Saturday Evening Post*, forcing novel-writing into the background. The next year his *Post* fee would rise to $4,000 a story. Throughout the next few years he would move between the USA and Europe, desperate to resuscitate that project, but make little inroads.

Zelda's Mental Illness

By 1930 Zelda's behaviour was becoming more and more erratic, and on 23rd April she was checked into the Malmaison clinic near Paris for rest and assistance with her mental problems. Deeply obsessed with her dancing lessons, and infatuated with Egorova, she discharged herself from the clinic on 11th May and attempted suicide a few days later. After this she was admitted to the care of Dr Oscar Forel in Switzerland, who diagnosed her as schizophrenic. Such care was expensive and placed a new financial strain on Fitzgerald, who responded by selling another series of stories to the *Post* and earning $32,000 for the year. The most significant story of this period was 'Babylon Revisited'. Zelda improved and moved back to Montgomery, Alabama, and the care of the Sayre family in September 1931. That autumn Fitzgerald would make another abortive attempt to break into Hollywood screenwriting.

At the beginning of 1932 Zelda suffered a relapse during a trip to Florida and was admitted to the Henry Phipps Psychiatric Clinic in Baltimore. While there she would finish work on a novel, *Save Me the Waltz*, that covered some of the same material her husband was using in his novel about the Riviera. Upon completion she sent the manuscript to Perkins at Scribner, without passing it to her husband, which caused much distress. Fitzgerald helped her to edit the book nonetheless, removing much of the material he intended to use, and Scribner accepted it and published it on 7th October. It received poor reviews and did not sell. Finally accepting that she had missed her chance to become a professional dancer, Zelda now poured her energies into painting. Fitzgerald would organize a show of these in New York in 1934, and a play, *Scandalabra*, that would be performed by the Junior Vagabonds, an amateur Baltimore drama group, in the spring of 1933.

His own health now beginning to fail, Fitzgerald returned to his own novel and rewrote extensively through 1933, finally submitting it in October. *Tender Is the Night* would appear in serialized form in *Scribner's Magazine* from January to April 1934 and would then be published, in amended form, on 12th April. It was generally received positively and sold well, though again not to the blockbusting extent that Fitzgerald had hoped for. This would be Fitzgerald's final completed novel. He was thirty-seven.

Final Novel

With the receipts for *Tender Is the Night* lower than had been hoped for and Zelda still erratic and requiring expensive medical supervision, Fitzgerald's finances were tight. From this point on he found it increasingly difficult to produce the kind of high-quality, extended pieces that could earn thousands of dollars in glossies like *The Saturday Evening Post*. From 1934 many of his stories were shorter and brought less money, while some of them were simply sub-standard. Of the outlets for this new kind of work, *Esquire* proved the most reliable, though it only paid $250 a piece, a large drop from his salad days at the *Post*.

Financial Problems and Artistic Decline

March 1935 saw the publication of *Taps at Reveille*, another collection of short stories from Scribner. It was a patchy collection, but included the important 'Babylon Revisited', while 'Crazy Sunday' saw his first sustained attempt at writing about Hollywood, a prediction of the tendency of much of his work to come. His next significant writing came, however, with three articles that appeared in the February, March and April 1936 numbers of *Esquire*: 'The Crack-up', 'Pasting It Together' and 'Handle with Care'. These essays were brutally confessional, and irritated many of those around Fitzgerald, who felt that he was airing his dirty laundry in public. His agent Harold Ober was concerned that by publicizing his own battles with depression and alcoholism he would give the high-paying glossies the impression that he was unreliable, making future magazine work harder to come by. The pieces have, however, come to be regarded as Fitzgerald's greatest non-fiction work and are an essential document in both the construction of his own legend and in the mythologizing of the Jazz Age.

Later in 1936, on the author's fortieth birthday in September, he gave an interview in *The New York Post* to Michael Mok. The article was a sensationalist hatchet job entitled 'Scott Fitzgerald, 40, Engulfed in Despair' and showed him as a

Suicide Attempt and Worsening Health

depressed dipsomaniac. The publication of the article wounded Fitzgerald further and he tried to take his own life through an overdose of morphine. After this his health continued to deteriorate and various spates in institutions followed, for influenza, for tuberculosis and, repeatedly, in attempts to treat his alcoholism.

His inability to rely on his own physical and literary powers meant a significant drop in his earning capabilities; by 1937 his debts exceeded $40,000, much of which was owed to his agent Ober and his editor Perkins, while Fitzgerald still had to pay Zelda's medical fees and support his daughter and himself. A solution to this desperate situation appeared in July: MGM would hire him as a screenwriter at $1,000 a week for six months. He went west, hired an apartment and set about his work. He contributed to various films, usually in collaboration with other writers, a system that irked him. Among these were *A Yank at Oxford* and various stillborn projects, including *Infidelity*, which was to have starred Joan Crawford, and an adaptation of 'Babylon Revisited'. He only received one screen credit from this time, for an adaptation of Erich Maria Remarque's novel *Three Comrades*, produced by Joseph Mankiewicz. His work on this picture led to a renewal of his contract, but no more credits followed.

Sheila Graham

While in Hollywood Fitzgerald met Sheila Graham, a twenty-eight-year-old English gossip columnist, with whom he began an affair. Graham, who initially attracted Fitzgerald because of her physical similarity to the youthful Zelda, became Fitzgerald's partner during the last years of his life, cohabiting with the author quite openly in Los Angeles. It seems unlikely that Zelda, still in medical care, ever knew about her. Graham had risen up from a rather murky background in England and Fitzgerald set about improving her with his "College of One", aiming to introduce her to his favoured writers and thinkers. She would be the model for Kathleen Moore in *The Last Tycoon*.

Among the film projects he worked on at this time were *Madame Curie* and *Gone with the Wind*, neither of which earned him a credit. The contract with MGM was terminated in 1939 and Fitzgerald became a freelance screenwriter. While engaged on the screenplay for *Winter Carnival* for United Artists, Fitzgerald went on a drinking spree at Dartmouth College, resulting in his getting fired. A final period of alcoholic excess followed, marring a trip to Cuba with Zelda in April and worsening his financial straits. At this time Ober finally pulled the plug and refused to lend Fitzgerald any more money, though he would continue to support Scottie, Fitzgerald's daughter, whom the Obers had effectively brought up. The writer, now his own agent, began working on a Hollywood novel based on the life of the famous Hollywood producer Irving Thalberg.

Hollywood would also be the theme of the last fiction Fitzgerald would see published; the Pat Hobby stories. These appeared in *Esquire* beginning in January 1940 and continued till after the author's death, ending in July 1941 and appearing in each monthly number between those dates.

In November 1940 Fitzgerald suffered a heart attack and *Death* was told to rest, which he did at Graham's apartment. On 21st December he had another heart attack and died, aged just forty-four. Permission was refused to bury him in St Mary's Church in Rockville, Maryland, where his father had been buried, because Fitzgerald was not a practising Catholic. Instead he was buried at Rockville Union Cemetery on 27th December 1940. In 1975 Scottie Fitzgerald would successfully petition to have her mother and father moved to the family plot at St Mary's.

Following Fitzgerald's death his old college friend Edmund Wilson would edit Fitzgerald's incomplete final novel, shaping his drafts and notes into *The Last Tycoon*, which was published in 1941 by Scribner. Wilson also collected Fitzgerald's confessional *Esquire* pieces and published them with a selection of related short stories and essays as *The Crack-up and Other Pieces and Stories* in 1945.

Zelda lived on until 1948, in and out of mental hospitals. After reading *The Last Tycoon* she began work on *Caesar's Things*, a novel that was not finished when the Highland hospital caught fire and she died, locked in her room in preparation for electro-shock therapy.

F. Scott Fitzgerald's Works

Fitzgerald's first novel, *This Side of Paradise*, set the tone for his *This Side of* later classic works. The novel was published in 1920 and was a *Paradise* remarkable success, impressing critics and readers alike. Amory Blaine, the directionless and guilelessly dissolute protagonist, is an artistically semi-engaged innocent, and perilously, though charmingly unconsciously, déclassé. His long drift towards destruction (and implicit reincarnation as Fitzgerald himself) sees Blaine's various arrogances challenged one by one as he moves from a well-heeled life in the Midwest through private school and middling social successes at Princeton towards a life of vague and unrewarding artistic involvement. Beneath Fitzgerald's precise observations of American high society in the late 1910s can be witnessed the creation of a wholly new American type, and Blaine would become a somewhat seedy role model for his generation. Fast-living and nihilist tendencies would become the character traits of Fitzgerald's set and the

Lost Generation more generally. Indeed, by the novel's end, it has become clear that Blaine's experiences of lost love, a hostile society and the deaths of his mother and friends have imparted important life lessons upon him. Blaine, having returned to a Princeton that he has outgrown and poised before an unknowable future, ends the novel with his Jazz Age *cogito*: "'I know myself,' he cried, 'but that is all.'"

Flappers and Philosophers

Fitzgerald's next publication would continue this disquisition on his era and peers: *Flappers and Philosophers* (1920) is a collection of short stories, including such famous pieces as 'Bernice Bobs Her Hair' and 'The Ice Palace'. The first of these tells the tale of Bernice, who visits her cousin Marjorie only to find herself rejected for being a stop on Marjorie's social activities. Realizing that she can't rid herself of Bernice, Marjorie decides to coach her to become a young femme fatale like herself – and Bernice is quickly a hit with the town boys. Too much of a hit though, and Marjorie takes her revenge by persuading Bernice that it would be to her social advantage to bob her hair. It turns out not to be and Bernice leaves the town embarrassed, but not before cutting off Marjorie's pigtails in her sleep and taking them with her to the station.

The Beautiful and Damned

The Beautiful and Damned (1922) would follow, another novel that featured a thinly disguised portrait of Fitzgerald in the figure of the main character, Anthony Patch. He was joined by a fictionalized version of Fitzgerald's new wife Zelda, whom the author married as *This Side of Paradise* went to press. The couple are here depicted on a rapidly downward course that both mirrored and predicted the Fitzgeralds' own trajectory. Patch is the heir apparent of his reforming grandfather's sizable fortune but lives a life of dissolution in the city, promising that he'll find gainful employment. He marries Gloria Gilbert, a great but turbulent beauty, and they gradually descend into alcoholism, wasting what little capital Anthony has on high living and escapades. When his grandfather walks in on a scene of debauchery, Anthony is disinherited and the Patches' decline quickens. When the grandfather dies, Anthony embarks on a legal case to reclaim the money from the good causes to which it has been donated and wins their case, although not before Anthony has lost his mind and Gloria her beauty.

Tales of the Jazz Age

Another volume of short stories, *Tales of the Jazz Age*, was published later in the same year, in accordance with Scribner's policy of quickly following successful novels with moneymaking collections of short stories. Throughout this period Fitzgerald was gaining for himself a reputation as America's premier short-story writer, producing fiction for a selection of high-profile "glossy" magazines and earning unparalleled fees for his efforts. The opportunities and the pressures of this commercial work, coupled with Fitzgerald's continued profligacy, led to a certain unevenness in his short fiction. This unevenness is clearly present in *Tales of the Jazz Age*, with some of Fitzgerald's very best work appearing beside some fairly average pieces. Among the great works were 'The Diamond as Big as the Ritz' and the novella 'May Day'. The first of these tells the story of the Washingtons, a family that live in seclusion in the wilds of Montana on top of a mountain made of solid diamond. The necessity of keeping the source of their wealth hidden from all makes the Washingtons' lives a singular mixture of great privilege and isolation; friends that visit the children are briefly treated to luxury beyond their imagining and are then executed to secure the secrecy of the Washington diamond. When young Percy's friend John T. Unger makes a visit during the summer vacation their unusual lifestyle and their diamond are lost for ever. The novella 'May Day' is very different in style and execution, but deals with some of the same issues, in particular the exigencies of American capitalism in the aftermath of the Great War. It offers a panorama of Manhattan's post-war social order as the anti-communist May Day Riots of 1919 unfold. A group of privileged Yale alumni enjoy the May Day ball and bicker about their love interests, while ex-soldiers drift around the edges of their world.

In spite of the apparent success that Fitzgerald was experiencing by this time, his next novel came with greater difficulty than his first four volumes. *The Great Gatsby* is the story of Jay Gatsby, born poor as James Gatz, an *arriviste* of mysterious origins who sets himself up in high style on Long Island's north shore only to find disappointment and his demise there. Like Fitzgerald, and some of his other characters, including Anthony Patch, Gatsby falls in love during the war, this time with Daisy Fay. Following Gatsby's departure, however, Daisy marries the greatly wealthy Tom Buchanan, which convinces Gatsby that he lost her only because of his penuriousness. Following this, Gatsby builds himself a fortune comparable to Buchanan's through mysterious and proscribed means and, five years after Daisy broke off their relations, uses his newfound wealth to throw a series of parties from an enormous house across the water from Buchanan's Long Island pile. His intention is to impress his near neighbour Daisy with the lavishness of his entertainments, but he miscalculates and the "old money" Buchanans stay away, not attracted by Gatsby's *parvenu* antics. Instead Gatsby approaches Nick Carraway, the novel's narrator (who took that role in one of the masterstrokes of the late stages of the novel's revision), Daisy's cousin and

The Great Gatsby

Gatsby's neighbour. Daisy is initially affected by Gatsby's devotion, to the extent that she agrees to leave Buchanan, but once Buchanan reveals Gatsby's criminal source of income she has second thoughts. Daisy, shocked by this revelation, accidentally kills Buchanan's mistress Myrtle in a hit-and-run accident with Gatsby in the car and returns to Buchanan, leaving Gatsby waiting for her answer. Buchanan then lets Myrtle's husband believe that Gatsby was driving the car and the husband shoots him, leaving him floating in the unused swimming pool of his great estate.

All the Sad Young Men   Of *All the Sad Young Men* (1926) the most well-known pieces are 'The Rich Boy', 'Winter Dreams' and 'Absolution'. All three have much in common with *The Great Gatsby*, in terms of the themes dealt with and the characters developed. 'The Rich Boy' centres on the rich young bachelor Anson Hunter, who has romantic dalliances with women, but never marries and grows increasingly lonely. 'Winter Dreams' tells the tale of Dexter Green and Judy Jones, similar characters to Jay Gatsby and Daisy Buchanan. Much like Gatsby, Green raises himself from nothing with the intention of winning Jones's affections. And, like Gatsby, he finds the past lost. 'Absolution' is a rejected false start on *The Great Gatsby* and deals with a young boy's difficulties around the confessional and an encounter with a deranged priest.

'Babylon Revisited' is probably the greatest and most read story of the apparently fallow period between *The Great Gatsby* and *Tender Is the Night*. It deals with Charlie Wales, an American businessman who enacts some of Fitzgerald's guilt for his apparent abandonment of his daughter Scottie and wife Zelda. Wales returns to a Paris unknown to him since he gave up drinking. There he fights his dead wife's family for custody of his daughter, only to find that friends from his past undo his careful efforts.

Basil and Josephine   Between April 1928 and April 1929, Fitzgerald published eight stories in the *Saturday Evening Post* centring on Basil Duke Lee, an adolescent coming of age in the Midwest, loosely based on the author's own teenage years. A ninth story, 'That Kind of Party', which fits chronologically at the beginning of the Basil cycle, was rejected by the *Saturday Evening Post* because of its description of children's kissing games, and was only published posthumously in 1951. These stories were much admired by both Fitzgerald's editor and agent, who encouraged him to compile them in a book with some additional stories. Fitzgerald did not act on this advice, but between April 1930 and August 1931 he published, again in the *Saturday Evening Post*, five stories focusing on the development of Josephine Perry, a kind of female counterpart to Basil Duke Lee. In 1934 Fitzgerald then considered collecting the Basil and Josephine stories in a single volume and adding a final one in which the two would meet and which would transform the whole into a kind of novel, but he shelved the idea, as he had doubts about the overall quality of the outcome and its possible reception. He was still favourable to having them packaged as a straightforward short-story collection, but this would only happen in 1973, when Scribner published *The Basil and Josephine Stories*.

The next, and last completed, novel came even harder, and it would not be until 1934 that *Tender Is the Night* would appear. This novel was met by mixed reviews and low, but not disastrous sales. It has remained controversial among readers of Fitzgerald and is hailed by some as his masterpiece and others as an aesthetic failure. The plotting is less finely wrought than the far leaner *The Great Gatsby*, and apparent chronological inconsistencies and longueurs have put off some readers. The unremitting detail of Dick Diver's descent, however, is unmatched in Fitzgerald's oeuvre.

Tender Is the Night

It begins with an impressive set-piece description of life on the Riviera during the summer of 1925. There Rosemary Hoyt, modelled on the real-life actress Lois Moran, meets Dick and Nicole Driver, and becomes infatuated with Dick. It is then revealed that Dick had been a successful psychiatrist and had met Nicole when she was his patient, being treated in the aftermath of being raped by her father. Now Dick is finding it difficult to maintain his research interests in the social whirl that Nicole's money has thrust him into. Dick is forced out of a Swiss clinic for his unreliability and incipient alcoholism. Later Dick consummates his relationship with Rosemary on a trip to Rome, and gets beaten by police after drunkenly involving himself in a fight. When the Divers return to the Riviera Dick drinks more and Nicole leaves him for Tommy Barban, a French-American mercenary soldier (based on Zelda's Riviera beau Édouard Jozan). Dick returns to America, where he becomes a provincial doctor and disappears.

The "Pat Hobby" stories are the most remarkable product of Fitzgerald's time in Hollywood to see publication during the author's lifetime. Seventeen stories appeared in all, in consecutive issues of *Esquire* through 1940 and 1941. Hobby is a squalid Hollywood hack fallen upon hard times and with the days of his great success, measured by on-screen credits, some years behind him. He is a generally unsympathetic character and most of the stories depict him in unflattering situations, saving his own skin at the expense of those around him. It speaks to the hardiness of Fitzgerald's talent that even at this late stage he was able to make a character as amoral as Hobby vivid and engaging on the page. The Hobby stories are all short, evidencing Fitzgerald's skill in his later career at compressing storylines that would previously have been extrapolated far further.

Pat Hobby Stories

The Last
Tycoon

Fitzgerald's final project was *The Last Tycoon*, a work which, in the partial and provisional version that was published after the author's death, has all the hallmarks of a quite remarkable work. The written portion of the novel, which it seems likely would have been rewritten extensively before publication (in accordance with Fitzgerald's previous practice), is a classic conjuring of the golden age of Hollywood through an ambiguous and suspenseful story of love and money. The notes that follow the completed portion of *The Last Tycoon* suggest that the story would have developed in a much more melodramatic direction, with Stahr embarking on transcontinental business trips, losing his edge, ordering a series of murders and dying in an aeroplane crash. If the rewrites around *Tender Is the Night* are anything to go by, it seems likely that Fitzgerald would have toned down Stahr's adventures before finishing the story: in the earlier novel stories of matricide and other violent moments had survived a number of early drafts, only to be cut before the book took its final form.

– Richard Parker

Select Bibliography

Biographies:
Bruccoli, Matthew J., *Some Sort of Epic Grandeur: The Life of F. Scott Fitzgerald*, 2nd edn. (Columbia, SC: University of South Carolina Press, 2002)
Mizener, Arthur, *The Far Side of Paradise: A Biography of F. Scott Fitzgerald*, (Boston, MS: Houghton Mifflin, 1951)
Turnbull, Andrew, *Scott Fitzgerald* (Harmondsworth: Penguin, 1970)

Additional Recommended Background Material:
Curnutt, Kirk, ed., *A Historical Guide to F. Scott Fitzgerald* (Oxford: Oxford University Press, 2004)
Prigozy, Ruth, ed., *The Cambridge Companion to F. Scott Fitzgerald* (Cambridge: Cambridge University Press, 2002)

ALMA CLASSICS

ALMA CLASSICS aims to publish mainstream and lesser-known European classics in an innovative and striking way, while employing the highest editorial and production standards. By way of a unique approach the range offers much more, both visually and textually, than readers have come to expect from contemporary classics publishing.

LATEST TITLES PUBLISHED BY ALMA CLASSICS

To order any of our titles and for up-to-date information about our current and forthcoming publications, please visit our website on:

www.almaclassics.com